KARDA

Adalta: Vol. I

By

Sherrill Nilson

Illustrations and cover by
Kurt Nilson

COPYRIGHTED MATERIAL

Karda: Adalta, Volume I Revised and Illustrated Edition

Copyright (©) 2018 by Sherrill Nilson

ISBN 13: 978-1-7322729-0-3

Second Edition

Cover art and illustrations copyright (©) Kurt Nilson

Published by Green Canoe, LLC 3701 S Harvard Ave #172

Tulsa, Oklahoma 74135

Printed in United States of America

Visit SherrillNilson.com, sherrill.nilson@gmail.com, @sherrill.nilson_author on Instagram, https://www.facebook.com/SLNilson/

❀ Created with Vellum

For my Family

With the collapse of Earth's systems, a flurry of Ark Ships left the planet

to establish colonies through the universe.

In the confusion, a handful of these ships were lost. The colony landing on Adalta was one of those.

Five hundred years later…

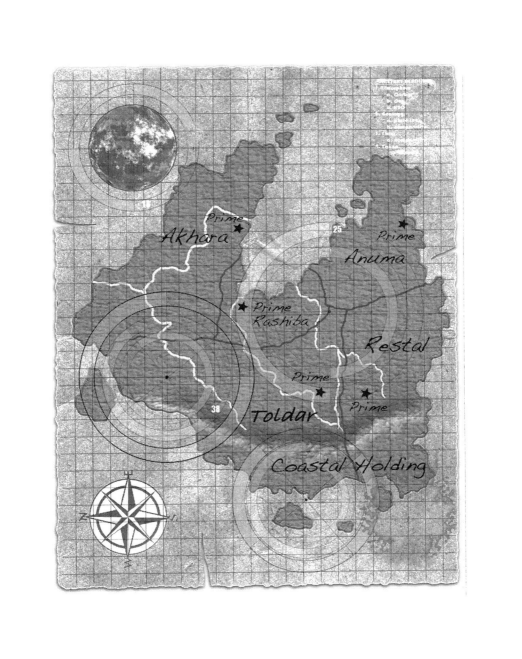

PROLOGUE

Tears stained the grubby cheeks of the small boy who passed through the kitchen. He hoped no one noticed him. He filched a sticky bun from a tray cooling at the end of the large table. A wooden spoon rapped his wrist, and he almost dropped the sweet.

"Ask next time, boy," said a gruff voice, and the cook laughed and shooed him on.

He flashed a practiced I'm-just-a-sweet-mischievous-boy grin back at her, but inside the worm of hatred and jealousy continued eating his soul. Even the cook had the talent he lacked. He didn't rub his wrist until he was out of her sight. She'd smacked the bruise his brother gave him at weapons practice.

His younger brother, who beat him at sword practice again. They were the same size though the boy was older by two years. His brother always beat him. To make it worse, Daryl felt so guilty when he did— like today—that he offered hints and advice about sword moves as if he were a mighty weaponsmaster. The boy always nodded and listened, his head tilted and his focus intense, smiles and gratitude hiding the burrowing worm of hatred, the centipede of rage. His was a small twelve-year-old body crammed to overflowing with jealousy.

Hate him. Hate him. Hate him. The words pounded in his head in time with the throb in his bruised wrist.

He made his way down the hall leading to the cellars. He bloodied a fingernail unfastening the rusty latch on the massive, iron-banded door and hauled it open, huffing with effort.

The boy jumped as high as he could, snagged a torch with the tips of his fingers and flipped it out of the holder. He snatched the brand from the floor before it snuffed out and passed into the dank corridor beyond, pulling the heavy door to behind him. His boots rang on the stone floor, and he made his way to the next room where a lone guard sat at a crude table half drunk, the remains of his meal pushed to one side.

The guard, Pol, leered at him with a look half lascivious, half fearful and licked his tongue across his thick bottom lip. The child knew Pol liked young boys, but he was the guardian's son—off limits. He pranced, slim hips swaying, across the guardroom to the metal door on the other side, his head tilted and his lips pursed in a provoca- tive smile. He cocked a hip and rolled a hand in a "come here" gesture. "Open it, Pol."

The guard's broad face flushed. Pol ducked his head, quirked a smile and lumbered over to open the door. The boy brushed against his arm and slipped through.

He climbed down worn stone steps to a narrow corridor lined on one side by small barred cells with sturdy iron locks. Wide-spaced torches threw dim light on the brick and stone walls. The cells held an air that both repulsed and called to him. A shadowy figure huddled in one, and a pale face looked up with desperation from another as he passed. It was scary. And titillating. He relished it.

Each time he came, he explored farther into the labyrinth of halls. He moved beyond the spaces that were still used and into the forbidden areas where little boys could get lost. Dust and spider webs covered everything except the center of the halls where no one but him had walked for years.

These underground passages enthralled him. The terror, fear, and pain-soaked stone and brick walls and floors spoke to him in a language his bones recognized. He breathed deep, sucking it in. He wanted to suck it into his body and hold it there.

Some of the rooms he passed were open. Some hid behind black iron doors as massive and formidable as the first. Most of them were locked, some only latched, though the latches were often rusted shut. He worked on them for weeks with a tool filched from the black-smith and managed to get several open. All he found was small, dank rooms with sweating stone walls, hard bunks, a few wisps of rotted straw, a hole in a corner with a faint reek of human waste.

But the last time he came he discovered a narrow door hidden in an uncanny there-yet-not-there twist of the walls at the end of a long hall- way. The spider webs were so thick he'd used the torch to burn his way through. Its walls were rough unbroken stone rather than the large blocks of the other passages.

He'd missed it at first. It flickered in and out of his sight. Someone had put a talent illusion on it that was decaying. It was so far back in the labyrinth of tunnels he carried chalk to mark his way so he wouldn't get lost. Arcane symbols were carved in the lintel and etched on the black wood door's intricate lock. He was determined to get it open. Last time the lock defeated him. He spent so much time on it that his torch sputtered and dimmed, and he'd run back before he found himself in complete darkness. This time he was better prepared. He carried a file, a small metal pry rod, a small hammer, and another torch. The child didn't care if the blacksmith's assistant he stole the tools from got beaten for losing them. He needed them.

Wedging his torch in a small hole in the wall that seemed fashioned for it, the boy touched the lock, jerking his fingers back from a faint tingle, but he persisted till his slender fingers swelled and bled, and the ancient lock finally clicked open. His hands stung, and his wrists ached. In spite of the cold in the corridor, salty sweat burned his eyes. There had been a spell on the lock.

The boy had no talent. He shouldn't have been able to force it open.

That intrigued him. Eager heat flushed his skin.

He moved the torch closer to better see the door. The strange mark- ings carved on the lintel hadn't been above any of the other doors. This

door was wood, smooth, dark, fine-grained. Just above the latch was a tiny mark, worn smooth. He traced it with his fingers to be sure it wasn't just a defect in the wood. Like the ones on the lock, it wasn't like any symbols or letters he had seen before.

He lifted the latch, smooth and black like the lock, coated with dust and cobwebs but not rusted at all. He felt the same slight sting of magic. It wasn't talent. That he knew. He could sense talent in others though he had none—the only person on Adalta born with no talent. His insides twisted and he swallowed against rage so old and familiar he might have been born with it.

He hesitated before he opened the door, the hand holding the torch shaking. Sudden warmth pulsed and spread low in his groin. There was power behind that door, and he ached for it. He pushed it open and stepped into a passage with smooth walls and ceiling that flowed and curved. Arcane symbols were carved in measured places along it. Small sharp rocks littered the floor.

He checked his torch—halfway burned—and picked up the extra one. The boy wasn't expected back until dinner. No one would miss him. No one ever missed him he thought, with a sourness he could taste, except The Good Brother. The Talented Brother. Familiar fury beat in his chest with the beat of his heart and pushed him on.

The boy stepped through the door feeling as though he stepped into a new life, a life with the power he had lacked since his birth. The long narrow hallway disappeared into the darkness beyond his torch light. Tripping in his eagerness, he walked through the twisting corridor that appeared endless, the only sounds his quick footsteps and his eager breath.

Finally, the passage ended. He stared in awe at an enormous space, at glittering walls and ceiling that disappeared in the darkness beyond the light of his torch. Scattered columns ran from ceiling to floor. But the cavernous space didn't make him feel small. A terrible power pressed against his body. He craved it, breathing it in through his open mouth, tasting it.

Tense, quivering with anticipation, he approached one of the pillars. Its surface was smooth and covered with vertical rows of symbols in narrow columns, calling to his anger, pulsing with faint light.

I can figure these symbols out. I know I can. They hold the secrets to the power I want. I know they do. I don't need to dance around waving a silly sword. There is power here. I'll be stronger than my brother. I know I will.

He traced the unfamiliar, angular symbols with trembling, lacerated fingers. He watched, fascinated, as dark blood seeped from his mangled fingers and was sucked into the carved symbols. A surge of heat knocked the boy to the stone floor, senseless.

When he came back to himself, an enormous figure stood above him, hazy and flickering in the torchlight. The child shook in fear and awe seeded with eager curiosity, even a glee that aroused pleasure deep and low in his belly.

"Who are you who comes to me?"

The resonant voice echoed through the chamber. It filled the boy's head until he thought it would burst. Black wings of pierced metal spread behind the towering figure with small, constant movements. The boy could see the pillar through the being that was both there and not there.

Its humanoid body was half mechanical and half flesh. The insect-like face with deep-set dark gold eyes was close enough to human to intensify his terror and anticipation. A silver medallion swung on a chain from one clawed hand, clutched by sharp-taloned digits with tiny gears for joints. The being stared at the boy for a long time. He didn't move. He couldn't move.

"You are but a child." Vipers of anger and frustration coiled in the cold words.

The being held the medallion out, and the boy reached for it. The being's fist closed it into his, and a delicious shudder shook the boy's body. Metal talons pricked his skin, leaving a weeping red weal across the back of his hand.

"I am the Itza Larrak. The last Larrak on this planet. It has taken me long and long and long to create you. You are my freedom and my revenge." The lipless mouth twisted. "The longer revenge ages, the sweeter it tastes. And mine has been aging for five hundred of this world's years."

The boy didn't move, didn't blink. His eyes burned. Sharp shocks danced in and over his body, through his muscles, up and down his bones.

The Itza Larrak's delicate, pierced metal wings opened and closed with melodic ringing. "I will teach you."

The Itza Larrak faded until it was gone, but the faint ringing still echoed, and the ominous sensation still lingered. The boy stood, frozen until the sound died away, but the menace remained—a promise. The medallion in his hand burned cold, frigid with latent power like that of the Itza Larrak and the strange-blood touched symbols on the pillars.

I will take it. The boy's thoughts soared. *I will take the power in these markings if it means years of bloody aching fingers to do it. The Itza Larrak will teach me, and I will learn.*

He pulled the chain over his head and tucked the medallion inside his shirt. It seared his thin chest with glacial cold and worked its way into his young soul with a familiarity he didn't notice.

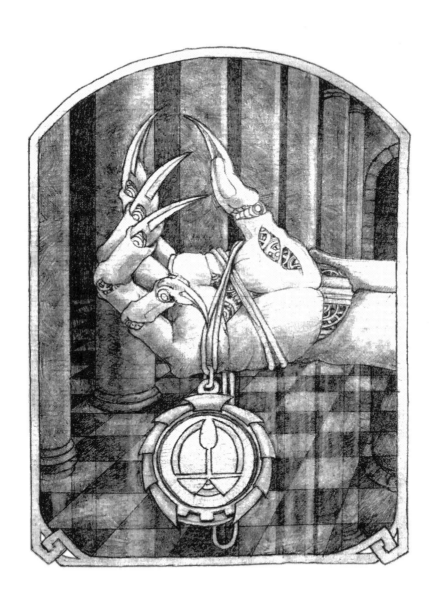

CHAPTER ONE

M arta Rowan sighed and rubbed her aching feet. The walk to
Rashiba Prime from the desolate barrens where the heli-
shuttle set her down was long—longer than she anticipated.
Distances always seemed shorter for eyes tracing planet surveys than
they were with feet on the ground in boots. Adalta's one continent
was immense.

Cold, wet wind from the barren rocky hills blew loose hair
across her face. Shelter under the small twisted evergreen next to the
rough road was welcome, and she leaned back against its furrowed
trunk.

Once again I start over. On a new planet, this time alone. It wasn't a new
thought. She'd just never felt so lonely before. *Maybe it's the desolation
here where nothing's been replanted.*

She shifted her butt off a small sharp rock and fished her water
bottle from her pack. Marta wondered if loneliness was why Father
never left her behind on the ship when he went on his missions after
her mother died—because an advance agent on a strange planet led
an isolated life, having to keep so much hidden.

Colonists on the diaspora planets were suspicious, even afraid of
those who'd elected to stay on the Ark ships and become traders

wandering the stars. Who would be suspicious of a father with a small girl? This was her second trip to a planet since he died and her first without a partner. Though her last partner hadn't been much better than being alone.

The late winter light shone warm in spite of the mist-laden air and the cooler climate under the enormous red sun. The rest was welcome. Whatever her doubts, it was good to be off the ship and on a new planet. She couldn't handle a job that trapped her aboard the immense consortium ship.

Father would have liked this barren, backward planet with its mix of Earth flora and fauna the colonists brought with them and the few native species that still survived. And its marvelous mix of the eighteenth Earth century and the modern, pre-collapse Earth civilizations. Bicycles and swords. Pre-collapse blue jeans and swirling spider-silk velvet cloaks that would have looked proper in Victorian England.

She tucked loose strands of hair behind her ears, lifted the auburn mass from her neck to cool it and finger-combed it into a thick knot on top of her head. She poked hair sticks through it, draped her short cape across her and settled back against the tree. Long legs stretched in front of her, she pointed and flexed her tired feet.

Too soon a spear of sunlight flared red against her eyelids and drove away the shade of the tree. Her head swirled out of sleep. Her eyes blinked at the glare of the sun now halfway from noon to the horizon in the west. Had she dozed that long? She stood and stretched. Her vertebrae made soft pops along her back. Parting the tough reeds that surrounded the stone-bottomed spring, she knelt to refill her water pouch.

Water swirled up around her hands. She froze, frowned. For a tiny bit of infinity she was surrounded by minnows that flashed silver in the light, moving with them as one. Then she was back, looking down as they scattered away from her hands.

She splashed her face with cold water to clear her head and drank her fill from cupped hands. This was the third time she'd gotten lost in something—something other. She forced her thoughts away from that and toward soaking her road-weary feet in the cold water.

The rumbling clatter of a wagon and an out-of-tune singing voice approached, and she pulled on her boots, grateful for the interruption. Maybe she could beg a ride.

Marta stepped behind the rough thicket on the other side of the spring. She shook the evergreen's fallen needles out of her long green wool split skirt, pulled down the sleeves of the matching waist-length jacket, and draped her cloak over her left arm. From the images sent to the ship by the spy bugs, her clothes were enough like the female patrol members that few of the travelers on the road through this empty countryside had bothered her. She figured the short sword at her belt helped.

A wagon appeared with a metal frame and wicker sides rolling on tall, rubber wheels and loaded with lumpy brown tow sacks. Marta recognized the silvery metal salvaged from the spaceship that brought the colonists. How had they been able to work that metal with their primitive forges? Space metal turned into a wagon pulled by a horse— this was the world she was assigned to in one image.

A small, wiry man wrapped in a voluminous cloak, his grey-flecked hair standing in an unruly crest handled the reins of the little brown mare that slowed as they neared the spring. Horse and driver had a similar look. The horse's mane grew out of a roach cut and stuck up like her handler's.

The man sang a final verse of a bawdy tavern song —out of tune and with feeling. She decided to chance it and stepped into view when he was still some distance away, one hand resting on her sword. He slowed the wagon and looked her over with alert and canny eyes. She detected the pungent presence of onions.

"So, girl. You have the look of one 'as walked for a bit."

She noted his country dialect and debated matching it. But it wouldn't be in character with her quasi-uniform, so she answered in common city speech. "I have." Marta took her hand off her sword hilt. "I see you have an empty place on the bench of your wagon— and maybe a place to stash my heavy pack?"

"By the look of that sticker you wear at your side, you have na worry 'bout traveling alone with a man, little bit that you are."

Marta figured she was a couple of inches taller than the wiry man and every bit as muscled. The well-worn staff in the holder beside him was of polished dark wood with iron-capped ends and a fine staff for a farmer or trader.

A smile lit his lined face with humor, making it almost handsome. "Well, as the lad what was to come with me on this journey met with some trouble in the shape of a girl's...um...heart, and this road being too well traveled by those who might be tempted to see if I carry some- thin' more'n onions, you'd be welcome. If you be handy with that piece of metal and don't just carry it for look."

"I do well enough." Marta slung her pack in the back wondering how bad her things would smell of onion when they parted. She blessed the sub-cortical language lessons. She'd passed her first test. "My name is Marta."

"I be Bren."

The little brown mare kept a steady pace. Cold drizzle moved in from the north making their afternoon wet and releasing the sharp smell of earth drinking rain. Vegetation was sparse—wiry bushes fit for nothing but holding the soil. And goats. Except for areas around springs, the colonists' re-seeding of the barren planet hadn't gotten this far. Wide-spaced pockets of growth sprouted from wind-blown seeds. How difficult survival must have been for those colonists on a world this barren. And they were immediately immersed in a war against other aliens who tried to take Adalta for their own. A war that hadn't ended until it rendered the continent all but empty of life.

Bren entertained her with stories of his village—he had a wicked sense of humor—and some of his bawdy songs. Marta joined in on the choruses. He knew a lot of those songs and a plethora of old legends and tales. His stories of terrible battles of the colonists and the Karda against an enemy called Itza Larrak were new to Marta. Most weren't in the background data she'd studied. She collected a trove of cultural information from him she would record in her Cue, her communicator, later.

"It was a terrible struggle those first years. Can you imagine?

The First Three Thousand were scatterin' seed as fast as they could, gettin' the animals out of stasis and the embryo banks, fightin' the terrible mutations caused by the circle."

The dry facts she'd studied for this mission gained color as she listened to his stories, imprinting them in her memory.

The wagon slowed, and Bren poked an elbow into her ribs. Marta caught herself on the side of the seat before she tumbled off and embarrassed herself. "Look there," he said, pointing up through a break in the clouds. "Karda."

Joy swelled in her chest, and she forgot to breathe. Two enormous flying figures were high in the sky, wings outstretched as they circled up a thermal. Sun glinted from bronze and gold wingtips. Their forelegs were tucked under, hind ones stretched behind. Manes and tails streamed.

"Oh, by the Lady Adalta," Bren breathed. "Did you ever see anythin' more beautiful?"

She watched the creatures rise ever higher into the sky, spread their wings wide in a glide, and disappear into the clouds. And something inside her shifted. Her whole body prickled with the need to see them again. To get close to them. She grabbed the side of the wagon to anchor herself. The few images the spy bugs had sent couldn't compare. *I can't believe I might fly on one of those beautiful beings. They are magical. What if I'm rejected for the training program? What if my cover story has too many holes?*

Well-trained as she was at blending in on a new planet, the possibility of getting recalled or caught was too real. On this, her first mission alone she would not, could not, fail. A cold, hard knot formed in her stomach. Getting expelled was not the only danger. She was going to have to guard against commitment that went too deep. That might be worse than not being accepted. The beautiful horse-bodied, hawk-headed Karda filled her mind. A sharp, involuntary shiver shot up her spine. How could she not become attached to them? But Adalta wasn't her home. She couldn't stay here forever.

The next day, their way changed from the barren hills of sparse grass and short, gnarled trees to forest of tall hardwood and conifers

—transplanted Earth species adapted to Adalta's red sun. In the slightly lighter gravity on Adalta, the trees grew to extraordinary heights. Sprawling limbs extended for impossible distances. Branches of conifers more than seventy feet long arched low, forming shadowed caves of shelter.

The needles and leaves of the evergreens were dark, dark green in the pale light of the red sun. Tiny emerging leaves and buds shimmered in a green haze in the crowns of the deciduous oaks and hickories and chestnuts—so tall that three horsemen could ride stacked one on top of the other and not get toppled by a stray branch. So much larger than images from Earth in the ship's files, yet still familiar.

Faint rustles came from the mat of leaves littering the floor beneath the trees. A small, red-furred animal, large triangular ears erect, stood on its haunches and watched her as the wagon passed, catching and holding her gaze. Feathery awareness touched her mind, a tiny tickle of consciousness.

Her eyes went wide. She could feel hunger and a strange, unafraid curiosity. The creature flicked a stubby tail and scurried into the under- brush. She knew its young were hungry. But how?

Animals in the wild just don't look you in the eye. They're shy and hide when they sense you coming. And how could I know it feels its young's hunger? Pain flared behind her right eye and settled there, throbbing.

Afternoon faded into evening. More and more feelings that didn't belong to her intruded into her consciousness—tendrils of curiosity, sensations of hunger, the hyper-awareness of small animals scuttling over the floor of the dense forest. The larger, patient awareness of two hunting predators drew her away from herself into the complex world of the forest.

Her stomach was empty in empathy. Her head ached. She rubbed an ache in her knee, then jerked her hand to her side when she saw Bren rubbing at his. It wasn't her knee that was hurting. She kneaded frown lines between her eyes. Just as she thought her head would burst, the cacophony of feelings began to fade.

"You feeling poorly, Marta?"

Bren's voice echoed with concern. It jerked her out of the eerie hyper-awareness. "Just a headache. I'll be ready for tea and soup tonight."

"Travelin' thus makes for some long days. It's my sittin' place what aches. We'll stop soon. There's a good spring ahead."

She hunched her shoulders against the light drizzle. Cold dread ached in her bones. She'd come out of stasis faster than normal, and the attendants had warned her about going planet-side too soon. *Is this strange hypersensitivity a lingering after effect? Will this compromise my ability to do my job?* She shook her head to clear it.

The well-sprung wagon swayed as it topped a low hill, and Marta looked, appalled, through the wide spaces between the tall tree trunks at a desolate valley filled by an enormous dark circle. The road curved around it well away from its edge instead of heading the more direct way across.

The surface was bare and pockmarked. Scattered trees grew with twisted black limbs and trunks. Air wavered above the ground in a heat-like haze despite the cold. Erratic dust devils wandered as if the drizzling rain couldn't reach them, though no wind stirred the dry leaves and branches of the trees along the road. Pieces of dull black metal littered the surface like bones. She stared open-mouthed. A scratchy prickling washed her skin.

Marta shifted on the padded seat and rubbed her arms. She felt violated—as if something unclean reached for her. She wanted a bath. A circle of young trees and saplings formed even rows around the edges of the desolation. Even winter-bare, their health made a vivid contrast to the deformed vegetation inside.

Her mind flashed on views of the planet from the ship. She realized the forest they traveled through was a huge bowl, enormous spreading trees at the outside growing shorter and spaced closer until only saplings surrounded the desolation at its center.

She tugged at the small gold ring in her ear, hesitant to ask, but she had to know. "What happened here?" she asked Bren. "It must have been something terrible." The troubling ever-present consciousness from the animals around her was absent from the circle. A greasy feeling of ugly wrongness hovered there.

He stared at her with genuine surprise. "You mean the Circle of

Disorder?"

Apparently, this was not something unusual on Adalta, and she should know about whatever this disorder was. She cursed the inadequate, haphazard briefing that overlooked this aberration. She missed her father, or even Galen Morel, her partner on the last planet. She shook her head again. She couldn't look away from the place.

"You've never seen a Circle of Disorder?" Bren's expression was puzzled.

"What happened here?" she repeated. "Are there more places like this?"

He didn't answer for a moment, then shrugged. "Circles of Disorder. How is it you do na know? Young ones are always warned."

Unsure what to say, she gambled on a semblance of the truth. "My... my father never told me. I don't remember ever seeing one."

"Dangerous thing, that, for a father na to tell a child. They've always been. It na be safe for anyone where power is distorted so. Some few's been cleared of the danger. That's why the Guardians plant the special bred trees and grasses. Over the years they cleanse the soil and order the power so's it'll meld back. I don't know how you ha' na heard on 'em, or seen 'em. When our ancestors came to Adalta, there were many, many more. Circles hundreds of kilometers across until the trees grew over them. Some still are. This is a small one. The Guardians can never stop the planting so long as the slightest circle left by the Larrak remains."

She held her mouth tight, ignoring his sideways look at her, and nodded. That was the problem with relying on the early scouts' information. They tended to stay in the settled Primes, their data limited to what they could discover there. The spy bugs roamed further, but they couldn't have sensed what she had—the pervasive evil that hovered as if it waited, beckoned. She continued to watch through the trees until they crossed the ridge. And wondered. What kind of power? And what or who are the Larrak?

15

The next morning was cold and wet. Marta and Bren rode wrapped against a freezing drizzle in blankets and cloaks, Bren's waterproof ground cloth stretched over them both. He stopped in the middle of a description of the western coastlands. He clucked at the mare, and the wagon sped up a little. They were leaving a broad meadow and approached another thick wood, the earthy smell of the damp forest humus reaching them on the light breeze.

"We be traveling through this wood for the rest of the day. Here is where I would'a sorely missed that big, brawny lad, Jeryl, the knothead, were you not wi' me. Stay awake, lass. And keep your sword close in that pretty scabbard. You'll not want to lose it here. There be'nt many folk in this wood, but they be dangerous." He clucked at the mare again, and they moved on at a brisk pace.

Marta let the tarp and blanket fall and adjusted her sword belt. They traveled at the faster clip for an hour. Then she sensed something to the right of the track ahead of them. Someone, not something. Two someones and they felt off, wrong, dangerous. She shook her head. *I'm going crazy, that's for sure. How can I feel someone there, when I don't see anyone?*

The sun's rays were still behind the trees to the east, the wooded trail dark beneath the trees. There was too much silence: no birdsong, no small animals rustling in the leaves. Though she tried to block it, the unease of the many small awarenesses surrounded them. And the two large, ugly human consciousnesses. Bren tensed, shook the reins and clucked to the horse to hurry her.

A dirty, rough-dressed man stepped from behind a large oak, a lip- twisted sneer on his face, and grabbed the mare's bridle, jerking her to a stop. A tall, wide-shouldered youth swaggered out behind him, a heavy knife almost as long as Marta's sword in one hand.

She saw Bren's eyes flick around looking for others. She sensed — she knew—there was no one else.

"Look here, boy. Visitors," the older man said. His smiling mouth gave Marta a too good look at too many bad teeth. He also wore a pair of knives as long as Marta's short sword strapped to his thighs. "I wonder what they brung for the toll."

"There be no toll on this road." Bren's voice came low and lazy, almost friendly.

Marta's tension eased. Bren might be well able to take care of himself.

"Now how else are we to feed our young 'uns," said the man. "A sack or three of yon onions and what coin you have will see you on your way. And if you have no coin, well, the girl can pay. We be a long time away from home."

The young man behind him leered at Marta, showing a few brown teeth. She felt sick. Adrenaline surged. Her body tensed, and she shrugged the tarp from her shoulders.

"Pa, I think they'll not have enough coin. She's pretty."

"A sack of onions I can spare, but there's naught else we'll give you." Bren stood to move to the back of the wagon, steadying himself with a hand on the stout black staff in the holder behind the seat.

"Oh, look, Pa. The lass wears a pretty little sword. Here, I'll take that and a taste o' you, too." He reached to drag her out of the wagon.

Marta let him pull her and rolled off. She used the momentum to gain her feet, careful not to spin away in the lighter gravity. Her sword was in her hand before she landed, her stance shoulder wide, one foot in front of the other, her body relaxed. Energy surged up her body from the earth to anchor her. It heightened her awareness of everything around her. The world slowed. A corner of her mind saw Bren leap down and face the older man, his ebony staff a blur.

The big youth looked her up and down. He grabbed his crotch and rocked it. "Ready for this big sword? Me thinks you'll enjoy it. Throw that little sticker down and just relax. I don' wanna hurt you." He leered. "You'll enjoy a little—" He said a word she didn't understand, but his intent was clear.

"Is that thing so little that you have to search for it in those dirty pants?" Marta smirked. "It doesn't seem big enough to do anything."

She kept her focus on the center of the younger man's body,

watching for movement. His face went dark with anger, and he lurched at her. The knife slashed wide, missing her.

Marta sidestepped, and he stumbled past. "Just leave us," she said, "and perhaps you'll live until someone less kind comes along." They were ignorant and inept, and they didn't scare her as much as the powerful pulse she felt from the ground around her. She bit her lip and told herself to concentrate. More good swordsmen got hurt by losing focus than by their opponent's skill with a sword. Stay in the moment. Watch for his mistakes. Then move fast and sure, no hesitation, no time for second thoughts. Hesitation and second thoughts meant certain pain, certain injury, certain death—or the "even worse" men like him always threatened when they faced a woman.

"Bitch." He charged again.

She stepped off the line and slashed his leading arm. Marta turned, sword en guarde, as he stumbled past, eyes wide. His arm spurted blood from the deep cut. Bone showed white through his slashed sleeve. His bloody fingers lost their grip. The knife dropped and sliced through the edge of his boot. He hit the ground on his backside. "Pa!" he yelled. But his pa was busy.

She heard Bren's staff whistle, and half turned to watch, one eye on the big youth.

Bren smacked the long knife out of the older man's hand. The staff whirled around and landed a loud, cracking blow on the bandit's head. The man fell. The fight had taken moments.

"What do you say, Marta, lass? Do you think we've paid our toll?" asked Bren.

"I think they are adequately recompensed," she answered with a grim smile.

"If recompensed means bloody, then I agree. We'll leave you then," he said to the pasty-faced boy trying to staunch the bleeding in his arm with his other hand. "And may you have as good 'a luck with your next toll collection. Though should it be another old man and a young lass, be more wary."

"Should we do something about his arm?" Marta nodded toward the youth.

"He'll not bleed to death. And if his pa recovers from the little bash on the head I gave him, he'll take care of it. Don't worry about them, lass. They're not worth it. We'll report 'em at the next village Guard Station. Akhara Quadrant is full of too many people like them. It could stand to lose a couple."

"If they're all as bad at fighting as these two, it probably will."

"Ye can't leave me here to bleed to death!" cried the young man.

"Oh, yes, lad. We can. I doubt you'll die from that little scratch. Though t'would leave the forest a safer place without you." Bren gathered up the three long knives and stowed them behind the wagon seat. He grinned and tossed two onions to the boy. "We don't want to be thieves. Here's payment for your knives." Then he walked to the head of the little mare which had stood, if not placid, at least steady, through it all. Bren rubbed the twitching ears and whispered to her for a moment.

Marta leaned against the trunk of a giant white oak that spread across the road. Her body tingled with unspent adrenaline that seeped away as though absorbed in a warm embrace from the tree. The feeling was comforting and strengthening. She blinked and whirled to look at the tree. She reached to put her hand on the trunk then hesitated and turned away, determined to ignore the feeling. Afraid her strange experience had not been imagination.

Bren and Marta climbed back into the wagon, pulled the tarp back over themselves, and drove without speaking for a time. "You fight well, lass," he said, breaking the silence.

"As do you, Bren. Though they weren't much challenge. May I see your staff?" He pulled it out of the holder behind him and handed it to her. It was unmarked despite the hit she'd heard his unfortunate opponent land on it with his heavy knife. "What's it made of?"

"Ironwood. Grows on a tiny holding tucked up against the mountains away to the south in a little corner of Akhara Quadrant."

"How did you come by it?" she asked, smoothing her hand down its black length.

His eyes crinkled. "I hav'na always been a onion farmer."

19

CHAPTER TWO

M id-morning the next day, Bren left Marta in a small market town, and she walked on toward Rashiba Prime. Traffic crowded the road—wagons, riders, walkers like her with packs and bulging sacks. This world was a mix of ancient and crude with elements salvaged from pre- collapse Earth, as were the other diaspora planets she'd worked on. But here, there was no high technology. A man pedaled past on a three-wheeled cycle, an enormous pack in the basket on the back. A family rode in an open horseless carriage with an ornate, brass-bound metal box behind the driver's seat, a thin wisp of steam rising from a small pipe in the box.

She didn't trust herself to talk to anyone. As the road grew busier, it was as if her vision were layered, and messages from everything and everyone around her echoed and bounced in her head. She had to step to the side of the narrow road and prop herself against a tree when a man and a woman in a buggy drove past. They sat silent and upright next to each other. His anger and her fear threatened to send Marta to her knees. And the bit in the mule's mouth pinched. It was too much.

Why are my empathic dampers not working? That's the first thing Father taught me about dealing with people so I didn't cry every time someone stubbed a toe. I've been using them for sixteen years. Since I was three. Why are they breaking down now? She managed to bolster the stone wall in her mind he'd taught her to use, with windows and shutters she could open and close. Bit by bit the confusion—and her vicious headache—subsided.

She stopped at the top of a rise in the road. Rashiba Prime filled the small valley below her and over the hill beyond. Sun glinted off hectares of greenhouses. A long row of warehouse pods from the colonists' ship, ceramic hulls shining as if new after hundreds of years, lined the long road across from the docks. What an immense under- taking these colonists started so many centuries before, yet so much remained to do to recover those spaces still all but devoid of life, ravaged in a half-legendary ancient conflict.

To the east, the bay sparkled brilliant blue-green under the rare cloudless sky. Distant shorelines dissolved into mist. A rambling red stone building with multiple towers and surrounded by high walls dominated the hill at the center of the town. The Prime Guardian's Keep with Adalta's university and the meeting rooms for the bi-annual Assembly of Guardians and Holders.

The country of Rashiba Quint was the first settlement established by the colonists. The other four were called quadrants, ruled by Guardians. There were an estimated forty-three thousand inhabitants in the quint, half in the capital, or prime, according to the data on her Cue. The whole of Adalta had little more than two and a half million people even five hundred years after the Ark ship arrived. The primary city of Rashiba was where the Adalta Assembly met in informal session yearly and formal every two years. The guardian of Rashiba was prime guardian of all Adalta and served as head of the Assembly.

Marta pushed through the underbrush on the verge of the road and made her way to a small clearing out of sight of the road. She fished in her pack for her Cue. It took several tries to connect and send the data she'd collected in the past few days. Her fingers trembled on its controls when she heard the brusque voice of the dispatcher. The minuscule device with its tiny vid feed was such a fragile thread of connection to the community so far above.

"I'll connect you to Director Morel."

Why connect me to him? Why is the Director of Planetary Findings interested in a routine check-in and data dump?

"Rowan." Kayne Morel's voice was hearty. It surprised her. "Glad to hear from you at last. Have you had difficulty getting through?" Despite the avuncular tone in his voice and the genial expression that flickered on her Cue, Morel did not do genial well. He was a cold, cold man.

She stared at the Cue, startled out of speech. Then: "Some. Your face is flickering. But this is my first try. I'm checking in before I get into Rashiba Prime and can't contact the ship for a while." His false-friend tone was so wrong. Or was it her inexperience and imagination? "Good. Good. Let me know as soon as possible when you settle. We chose an excellent cover for you. As I understand it, those Mi'hiru women fly all over Adalta on their creatures. You'll fit right in with your skill at handling alien creatures. Even your father was amazed at the connections you made with the ipsnoral on your last mission with him. In fact, I should dock your pay for the privilege of riding these creatures for your cover." His laugh was too loud and too long. She couldn't remember ever hearing him laugh like that, or laugh at all.

She and her father had worked for Kayne for years. His son, Galen, had been her partner on the last planet, and Kayne had never been this…pleasant. He was too effusive.

"We need to keep this short. We're experiencing difficulty with communication. All of the com sats are silent, and we have no visuals. We've lost them. I sent the ship's orbital schedule to your Cue. You'll have to coordinate reporting with that. We aren't able to stay in geosynchronous orbit and still be available to all of you agents down there."

His face flickered on the Cue, and a few moments of static clouded the screen. When it cleared, she said, "It may be a while. I have no idea what joining the Mi'hiru involves—if they screen my background too closely, it might get troublesome. Do you have more information for me?"

"Very little. For some reason, the spy bugs aren't working well. Several failed and disappeared. We can't figure out why. They send a sharp surge, then nothing. It takes the engineers hours to repair what they burn out here. I do have some preliminary reports from your fellow agents."

It didn't take long for Kayne to fill her in with what data he had. More names and a little additional information about the governing structure, most of which he'd already sent to her Cue. All he was interested in was a listing of Adalta's mineral resources.

"Please tell Cedar I'll start collecting plant samples for pickup as soon as possible. I'll—"

He interrupted her with a brusk, "Of course, of course. We need to work hard on changing their laws. Legislation is repressive and constricting about technology and weapons more advanced than swords and bows. These colonists are still adamant Luddites, even after half a millennium here." Kayne's words were sharp and quick. It seemed the biological/anthropological/ethnological studies she'd briefed for were secondary to legislative change for Kayne.

Changing laws? That's illegal. And why is he talking about changing laws when our cultural survey's barely begun? She swallowed the unease that clutched her gut. She couldn't antagonize him. He hadn't wanted her to take this assignment alone, and it would've been easier to accept his decision. But if she didn't try, next time would be more difficult. She'd gone to one of the other directors for help, and if she failed, she'd be consigned to the ship the rest of her life—life in a casket, a living death.

After a few more words, they ended the communication. Despite years of training and experience, she was nervous and uncertain. And uneasy about Kayne's words. Interfering in internal politics to the point of changing legislation skirted too close to Trade Alliance prohibitions for the giant trade ships that moved between the planets of the Diaspora. *He mentioned weapons. All trade ship consortiums are forbidden to trade in weapons, so why are the laws against them here a problem?*

Marta walked the main street toward the outskirts on the other side of the city, where the satellite map showed what she hoped was the Rashiba Guild House of the all-woman Mi'hiru—caretakers and trainers of the Karda. The cobbles under her feet were laid in tight, intricate patterns. The original colonists must have included some talented stonemasons. Since there'd been no trees for lumber for many years, all building was of stone and metal. Even now, wood was a luxury.

She shivered in the chill air and pulled out the rolled cloak lashed to her pack. It was late and getting cold, though it was closing in on spring, and the sun had been out much of the day. She'd thought she'd be happy stationed on a cool planet after the last scorching one. *Beware the changes you seek, Marta.*

Two and three-story houses of reddish-brown cut sandstone and brick with steep many-gabled roofs of baked clay tiles lined the street. Yellow light shone from arched windows and doors of the curb-level shops. Wide awnings protected walkers from the returned drizzle. Cooking odors filled the air, and people headed home in the early dusk. Shops closed and market stalls folded. Shopkeepers hurried their last customers out the door. She concentrated hard to keep the shutters in her mental wall closed and the flood of emotions out.

The crowd competed with horses, small steam carts, and bicycles for space on the narrow streets. Women in wool skirts to their boot tops, colorful shawls drawn up over their heads, and men in heavy jackets or cloaks long and short, some with wide rough trousers, some in Earth-style jeans, some in fitted pants tucked into high boots, swords at their waists.

The scene was an odd mixture of modern and ancient—swords instead of guns, bicycles, horse-drawn wagons, and those odd steam buggies instead of electric, hydrogen, or internal combustion vehicles. All the wagons, the carts, the bicycles were elegantly engineered and beautifully wrought. There was nothing crude or makeshift about them.

The restaurant window she passed, stomach growling, showed scattered tables covered with white cloths, laid with fine china and crystal that would be the envy of any hostess on the ship. *It will be interesting to see how much of Earth customs and concepts made it through the five hundred years since humans arrived here.*

She passed a tricycle cart with a small grill on the back that smelled of roast chicken and sausages, though the fire was cold and the last sausage sold right in front of her. Her stomach rumbled again. She asked the cart man for directions to the Mi'hiru Guild House.

His round face smiled. "Come to try for Mi'hiru training?" He waved a hand holding a long-handled fork. "Up this way past three streets, then to the right. Number fourteen on Sigall Street. Red rock wall. Iron and brass gate. Can't miss it. Good luck to you, Miss. Don't want to discourage you, but not many get favored. You haf'ta try, though, don't you?"

She passed a busy tavern. The tantalizing odor of roast meat and fresh bread escaped when a couple of men pushed through the door. Marta thought about stopping, but she didn't want to arrive at the guild house late. Civilized streets like these could turn feral with darkness.

Brass-banded double iron gates interrupted a long wall of the ubiquitous rough-cut red sandstone, the number 14 carved into the lintel above. She stood staring at them. There were other choices, other jobs, where she wouldn't fall under the scrutiny she was certain to find here. Women could be caravan guards or serve in the quint's guard. She could find work training horses, even if she had to start by cleaning stalls. There had to be many applicants to fly those incredible creatures.

Her fingers traced the small bronze bas-relief of a Karda and its rider in full flight. She put one hand on her chest below her throat, took a breath, swiped her other hand on her skirt and reached to pull on the knotted hemp rope hanging from a pulley. A bell clanged inside. When she finally heard hurried footsteps, the breath she didn't know she was holding whooshed out. One side of the gate opened, and a flushed young face surrounded by wild red curls appeared around its edge.

"Hello?" it asked.

"Hello, I'm Marta. I came to try for training as a Mi'hiru. May I come in?"

"Oh!" Acknowledgment flashed across the fresh face. "I'm the only one here right now. I'm not even supposed to be on gate duty yet, but there wasn't anyone else." She opened the gate and gave Marta a wild wits-end look. "We've had all kinds of emergencies today."

She chattered away as she led Marta across the slate-floored entry to the large dining hall. "I'm on gate duty because my mentor had errands to run today, and I was free. I'm studying to be a weaver." She looked back, and her tone turned tentative. "I'll show you the graduation piece I'm working on if you'd like to see it sometime."

"I'd like that." Marta hid her surprise. It appeared others besides Mi'hiru lived in the all-woman guild house. "I'd hoped to be here yesterday, but it took longer than I thought. I'm a little road weary. I'd appreciate a place to sit and get this pack off my shoulders."

"I guess that'll be all right. You can wait in the great room for Mother Cailyn. Here, let me take that." She grabbed Marta's pack.

The high-ceilinged, flagstone-floored room held dining tables and small groupings of comfortable chairs. Marta tried not to stare at a chimney-less, smoke-less stone stove at the center. A pile of glowing red coals radiated welcome warmth. The two talked a while —or one chattered and the other drooped. At last the young girl took pity on her and led her to the kitchen to introduce her to the cook for the day. Felice supplied a pastry-wrapped sausage, cheese, and a piece of warm cherry-apple tart with a hot mug of tea from the pot at the back of the black metal range. To Marta's relief, the talkative girl disappeared, citing duty. It was difficult to hold shields against all that eyes-wide innocence.

The guild mother walked in from the great room, shrugging off her long blue cloak, its neck and hem covered in geometric red embroidery, and caught Marta licking her fingers from the last of the tart. Cailyn was a tall, dark complexioned woman of middle age, greying black hair pulled up and wrapped tight in a bun. The planes of her hawk-nosed face were severe, uncompromising. She introduced herself, begged tart and tea from the cook, ushered Marta into a small study, and waved her to a chair. She moved to sit behind a table cluttered with papers and books bracketed by two thick candles inside tall glass chimneys.

"I understand you wish to apply for the Mi'hiru." She concentrated on her tea and tart, and asked, her tone casual, borderline disinterested, "Tell me about yourself. What made you decide to come here?"

Marta wanted this so bad she was forgetting to breathe. "I am from Dalpin in Akhara, a village high up in the Shimati hill country. My father was an independent trader working out of Akhara Prime. When he . . . when he got sick, we moved a few miles outside Dalpin. We settled up there because he loved the high hills, and it was seldom bothered by the constant fighting in the rest of the quadrant. The healers said he needed the dry air. After he died, the house felt too empty, but I didn't want to move to the village."

She paused and watched for Mother Cailyn's reaction to her next words. "They were suspicious of strangers. We were still newcomers even after five years. They didn't want me, and there wasn't any place for me there unless I married one of them."

Mother Cailyn's wry look was the first emotion Marta had noticed. The guild mother was hard to read, and Marta's senses were too raw to open the windows in her walls.

"It's not a very prosperous village. Besides I grew up on the road. With Father gone, the idea of settling in one place...well, it felt confining. And marrying one of the villagers...I...I couldn't."

The Mother nodded, and her face softened with her first hint of warmth.

"I loved to watch Karda flying over our valley. Sometimes they'd circle for hours—riding the thermals, Father said. I've always been a little in love with them, but I've never seen one up close except a glimpse of one at a tavern where I stayed two nights ago. Karda

Patrollers didn't come to Dalpin often, and we were never there when they did."

Marta looked down. *I've told cover stories like this for years. Why does this feel like an uncomfortable lie?*

"I notice you wear a sword. Most village girls don't," the guild mother said.

"Akhara Quadrant is not a peaceful place, and father wanted me to be able to defend myself if I needed to. We were on the road a lot. He made me practice my forms every day."

"He must have started teaching you when you were very young." Cailyn pushed her empty plate aside and took a sip of tea.

Even with her walls up, Marta felt the weariness in the guild mother as though Marta was just the latest in a long line of unsuccessful applicants to the Mi'hiru. She forced herself to keep her head up and ignore the tightness in her throat that made her want to say, "This is a mistake," and run from the room, the city, the planet.

"What makes you think you're suited for this work? Few are." Marta swallowed and leaned forward in her hard wooden chair, her hands so tight in her lap her fingers ached. "I'm good with animals of all kinds. No, better than good. I can get them to do things that no one else can. People often told me I should try for the training. That I'd be good enough. Karda are beautiful." She looked down, her voice dropped, and she said, "I feel...I feel like they call to me."

It wasn't a lie, and it was more than truth. Remembering the two Karda she and Bren had seen circling, a knot of desperate need grew in her belly. She pressed tight fists into it. She wanted this more than she had ever wanted anything. She wondered if she would ever find another breath.

The guild mother looked at her for a long time. Marta steeled herself into stillness.

"You realize that the choice of whether or not to favor you is not mine, nor any Mi'hiru's? It belongs to the Karda."

Marta looked at her, distressed. She hadn't expected this. "I don't understand. How do they choose who rides them? What do they do?" What if the Karda somehow knew she wasn't what she claimed and refused her?

The older woman grinned, her severe face brightened. "It never happens like it did in my namesake Cailyn's story, where a Karda lands in your village and selects you right out of your garden."

Marta was mystified. The problem with relying on Kayne's favorite tool, the spy bugs, was that they could watch and record, but they couldn't interact, and the information they gathered was sketchy. She had no idea what Cailyn was talking about. But Marta was an experienced fake.

"Let me show you to a room. You look like you need a bath and a good sleep. Breakfast will be in the dining hall beyond the great room at sun-up in the morning. Then we'll introduce you to the newest Karda to arrive. It may be you she came for. She's been waiting for someone for three tendays. We'll have to see. At least we can give you a comfortable place to stay the night."

Marta looked around and blinked, disoriented. The air rippled with light. She stood in a clearing surrounded by tall, dark trees. A rush of air pushed against her.

Landing with a flare of immense wings that blocked the sky was a strange, beautiful being, glowing translucent with the shimmery green of new leaves and the red gold of spring grass on the plains. The noisy wind of its back-winging whipped strands of hair across her face. It folded its wings tight to its horse body. Pale gold mane and tail gleamed. Marta stared, unmoving, in the cool green radiance that filled the clearing. The shining creature cantered to a stop in front of her, hawk head raised, the proud, curved beak formidable. Four slender legs ended in huge bird feet with long, wicked bronze talons. For an eternity, dark eyes the size of Marta's two fists held her until they bared her soul.

"It is well that you come, Marta Rowan."

The powerful voice rolled into her from the trees, the grasses, the very soil of the glen. The words reverberated with visions of desolation, destruction, and of hope. A fringe of wing feathers brushed her. Sizzling fire pulsed through bone and muscle. A terrible mélange of monstrous creatures and bloody swords, of an immense, uncanny cavern whirled in her mind until everything disappeared in a swirl of luminous, pearly fog. She turned, restless on the unfamiliar bed and fell away into sleep.

CHAPTER THREE

A shaky Marta followed Mother Cailyn down the spacious aisle of the mews to a roomy open stall. Her shoulders ached with tension. So much was riding on this. Her whole assignment. Success or failure. She was breathing so fast the cold air burned her sinuses. Cailyn stopped in front of a stall.

It was unlike any stall she'd ever seen on any world—half walls of smooth stone, flagstone floor, rare, gleaming, dark wood framing the opening. An enormous pile of clean golden straw lay in one corner partitioned off by another half wall of polished wood. Light from a row of clerestory windows at the back brightened the space. A long, bronze-colored flight feather lay against a side wall, reflecting fire in the light.

"This is Sidhari."

Marta couldn't move. Cailyn pushed her inside.

The enormous Karda was beautiful. No, she was beyond beautiful.

Her hawk head sat atop the long graceful neck of her horse body. A dark mane started just below the feathers of her crest, long and glossy. Her tail swept the ground. Sidhari's wings were lighter than the hair on her body—gold-tinted mahogany, with long, bronze-gold flight feathers.

Her sleek body shone. Her bay coat shaded to black from hocks and knees down. Four long, sharp, black talons tipped huge avian feet. Marta managed one step forward, and the Karda's mantled wings spread wall to wall. She raised her head. The large dark eyes in her predator's head looked her over, imperious, appraising her. Marta took another step. She took a deep breath, then another, and her shoulders loosened. This colossal creature with its fierce hooked beak should terrify her. But she didn't.

"Beautiful, isn't she?" The guild mother's words were a faint echo from far away.

Marta couldn't make her voice rise beyond a whisper. "She is beyond beautiful. She's magnificent. And huge. How can you ever control them?"

"You don't. She will be the one to tell you what to do." Cailyn paused, and her voice softened. "If she accepts you."

Cailyn continued, "This is Sidhari. She is by far the largest Karda any of us have ever seen aside from Altan Me'Gerron's Kibrath and Daryl Me'Vere's Abala." By the prefix Me, Marta knew these were men from the ruling class of Adalta. Their names were filed somewhere in her memory.

Cailyn held her hand out to the Karda. Sidhari bent down, and the guild mother scratched the top of her head, oblivious to the nearness of the huge curved beak. "If she accepts you, she will be yours to partner so long as you both agree. Often that means for life. She showed up from the wild a month ago. No one understands why, but that's how they come to us. She hasn't selected anyone yet. She refused to fly any of the Karda Patrol." Cailyn laughed, scratching harder. "Maybe this is the one you've been waiting for, my lady."

Marta wondered how tough those fine feathers must be to withstand that rough scratch.

"Come in and meet her. If she does select you, you'll need to spend some time getting acquainted. I'll be back later. I have work to do."

Marta's breath stopped again. It was hard to get her words out. "You're leaving me here with her? What do you mean if she selects me? What do I do?" All of a sudden she wasn't sure she wanted to be left alone with this huge creature, its fierce hooked beak, its piercing eyes.

Cailyn smiled and walked away, saying over her shoulder, "You'll be all right. More than all right if she chooses you." Then she turned back, her body still, her tone somber. "It's the way to become a Mi'hiru, Marta—the only way." She left.

Marta stepped, one slow foot at a time, toward Sidhari, looking up at the proud head, getting as close as she dared. The Karda's dark eyes caught hers. Sidhari held her entranced, examined her, exposed her to the core of her being. Marta sensed a rock-like solidity, an intelligence sharp and discerning, a quest for connection. Marta felt herself leaning toward it. Fear jolted her. Such deep connection was frightening, dangerous.

Her heart beating a timpani concerto in her chest, her hand reached to touch the soft, sleek hair of the long graceful neck, and she lost herself in the Karda's vast mind. Her consciousness spread wider and wider until she was the entire planet, her mind, her heart swirled beyond time and matter, until the scattered atoms of her being gathered with a soft susurrus of feathers sliding together, surrounding her, holding her. She was held, cherished, safe for the first time since her father died.

Her fingers curled, feeling the loose straw and the rough stones of the floor, feeling warmth against her cheek. She was sitting, resting against the warm shoulder of the Karda. Sidhari lay with her feet curled under her. Marta never wanted to move again. Light through the clerestory windows was dark with the deep rose of twilight. Marta started as she heard footsteps echo down the stone hallway of the mews.

"It looks like you've found a match, Sidhari." Cailyn leaned against the wide archway to Sidhari's stall. "You've been here all afternoon, Marta."

Marta stood, her legs shook. "Has it been that long? It felt like a few minutes." She managed to pull the words out of the fog in her head.

"The first time is always like that. You were lost, weren't you?"

"No." She rested her hand on Sidhari's shoulder, nearly the height of her own though Sidhari lay on the flagstones, her legs tucked under her body. Marta was still shaky. "I think I was found."

Sun glinted through the gold highlights of the mahogany hair flying around Marta's head and across her eyes. She'd been learning to fly on Sidhari for six tendays and still couldn't remember to braid her hair. It was loose from its bun again. She didn't care. Her legs tight against Sidhari's sides, the Karda's mane stinging her face, they stooped toward the ground. She watched it rush toward them, certain they would crash into the trees, then Sidhari swooped up in time, as she always did. Marta's stomach did a lurch, and they leveled out and rose toward the clouds again, spiraling up a thermal, letting the warm air carry them.

Reluctantly, she concentrated, as hard as she could, on the picture of the mews to Sidhari. That required a lot of innate empathy, which, she'd learned, was the primary prerequisite to being selected. What the others were, no one knew, but often empathy wasn't enough. With few exceptions, Karda only chose women as permanent partners. With no exceptions, only women could be Mi'hiru.

Tomorrow they would fly with a wing of the Rashiba Karda Patrol on their rounds. Mi'hiru were indispensable to other flyers who weren't able to communicate with the Karda they rode. When they projected a picture of where they were going into their Karda's minds, the other Karda in the wing got the message. Marta was terrified she wouldn't be able to do that. Some Mi'hiru acted as if they had actual conversations with their Karda. She didn't. Marta hoped it would feel like that to her, too, as their empathic connection matured.

Grabbing to catch her hair sticks before they tumbled to the ground, she swiped the hair back from her face and twisted it back up, working the sticks in place to hold it. The glide was long and glorious. They floated, Sidhari's wings spread wide, adjusting with small movements of wings and tail, suspended in endless space.

The slightest lean of Marta's body sent Sidhari wheeling on one wing in a stomach-churning turn or into a steep climb toward the clouds. Sometimes the Karda responded even before Marta signaled, as though she knew Marta's intention.

Green fields, pale with early growth outlined by rough stone walls, passed below them. They surrounded the small villages that dotted a forest that stretched as far as she could see. Here and there she saw trees crowned with green mist as tiny buds and leaves started their spring push.

All too soon she spotted the huge greenhouses and the square red stone towers of the citadel at Rashiba Prime that rambled over the hill at the center of the city. Tall arched windows with tiny panes glinted in the late morning light. Another Karda and rider glided in to land on the long runway meadow outside the mews. Sidhari began a slow spiral down, waited her turn, then touched down and loped down the field to the entrance to the mews.

Once inside, Marta unbuckled the myriad straps of the rigging, lifted the saddle to its rack in Sidhari's stall, and found the brushes in the tack cabinet on the wall. Currying Sidhari's coat, untangling her mane and long tail, checking her flight feathers, touching them with a little light oil—this was her second favorite thing.

She lifted each foot, checking the talons and the hard pads that covered the first section of each digit. When Sidhari landed, she fisted her feet, and only those horny pads hit the ground. They had to be checked carefully each time she groomed the Karda.

"How, by the lords of the great galaxies, do you Karda manage in the wild, or wherever you come from? Your tail is full of rats. That's what we get for such a wild flight today. I thought you were going to throw me out of that saddle more than once."

Sidhari looked back at her, amusement in her eyes. That's what made it so easy to talk to her. It was as though Sidhari understood every word Marta spoke. Even sometimes every thought she had.

"I wasn't ready to come in, but swords and lessons await. More on the quadrants of Restal and Toldar today, I think. That's where we're going Octday after next. Restal first for a month or so, then on to Toldar. I think they're planning on leaving me in Toldar for a lot longer. Mi'hiru are seldom assigned for longer than a few months in Restal for some reason I don't understand, but I guess we'll find out. I'm studying the maps hard so we don't get lost getting from here to there. That wouldn't make a very good impression."

A Mi'hiru's loyalty to the particular quadrant they were assigned to was only expected so long as they were attached there. They were moved from quadrant to quadrant in rotation—that removed the temptation to interfere in politics and allowed them to keep the independence essential to their relationship with the Karda. It also meant she could gather a broader base of information for the consortium.

Marta leaned into Sidhari's shoulder, breathing in her dry, spicy scent, brushing with long, firm strokes. Sidhari liked that and leaned back, eyes half closed, making contented clicking sounds with her vicious beak. When Marta finished, she decided she didn't smell bad enough of sweat and Karda to change for her workout in the arms salon.

She fished in her pack for the special small plastic packets of plant samples she'd gathered for Cedar today. Tomorrow she'd take them, with the others she'd accumulated, and land somewhere she could stash them for one of Cedar's tiny bio-system drones to collect and carry back to the ship.

Hiding them with the others in the straw close to the wall, she ignored her tiny flash of guilt when she told the Karda, "Don't let anyone find those, please." Sidhari looked at her as though she understood. "It wouldn't do for someone to find these bags on this world where plastic doesn't exist. Not this kind, anyway," she whispered to Sidhari, or herself.

The big arms salon was empty but for the two women, and silent but for the furious clacks of weighted wood practice swords. Without thought, Marta blocked a blow with her sword before she saw the slight move of Tayla's body, sensing it well before she should have. She slid to the side to avoid another strike and landed a blow on her instructor's ribs.

Tayla let out a loud "Oof" in spite of her thick, padded canvas vest. Marta stepped back and wiped sweat from her forehead, pushing back her damp hair. It had come loose from its knot again, and its heavy auburn length was in her way. She leaned down, head low, hands on her thighs, her opponent in the same position, both breathing hard.

She'd been in Rashiba Prime for seven tendays now. Her training period was nearly over, and the advantages she'd gotten from the lighter gravity were lessoning. She wouldn't be able to do more than hold her own against Tayla, the guild house armsmaster if she weren't sensing her moves in a way that was beyond her training.

"That was a good workout." Tayla panted and stretched her back, groaning. She was several inches taller than Marta, black-haired, arms ropy with muscle under smooth olive skin, her face marked by a faint white scar below her left eye. "I'm only telling you this because you're almost done with training, but you always surprise me. I've never had a trainee with such ability. Not only can you hold your own with me in sword work, but you put me on my back as often as not in hand-to- hand defense."

"Ha! Don't tell me that. Look at you. You look like you just strolled in, and I'm sopping. You're just trying to soften me up for next time." *And I don't know how I can anticipate your every stroke.* Marta grabbed a towel and mopped the back of her neck.

Tayla laughed. "I think you have stronger Air than I do. You're just that much faster."

Marta's hand stilled. *What does that mean? Air? What kind of answer am I expected to make to that comment? They speak of Air and Water and Earth as if they are something I'm supposed to know about. Or something I'm supposed to have.*

The two carried their quilted workout vests and weighted

39

wooden practice swords over to the pegs and chests lining the back wall of the salon. Marta grabbed another small towel from a hook and swiped at her face and arms. She fastened her long hair back into a tight knot with her hair sticks, which she'd found on the floor. Again. She knew she should cut it so her hair couldn't be grabbed in a fight, but it would have to be so short she didn't think she could bear it.

Without it, her face was too severe, her cheekbones too stark. She thought of it as the one thing about her that was beautiful. That and her long eyelashes. They made up for her strong—some called it stubborn—chin and the hump on her nose. She knew she'd never be thought of as a beauty—she refused to lose her hair.

"How did you learn so well?" Tayla asked. "I'd like to know who your teacher was. Maybe I could hire her."

Marta laughed. "Not a her. It was my father. I was his only son. He had no one else to teach, and I wasn't much for playing mommy with dollies. It was just the two of us. For most of my life, we traveled. He worked as a trader out of Akhara Prime. He wanted me to be able to protect myself." She nearly said, "This is one of the few planets where women are trained in weapons," and had to bite her lip. It was so hard being alone. She even missed Galen-of-the-frozen-face-and-I-work-hard-at-it.

Much of this story was true. She had learned from her father. He started when she was tiny and could barely hold up her little practice blade. The planets where they had lived and worked until he died were far from safe—primitive, feudal worlds as the post-diaspora planets often were. She was proficient with so many different weapons, from high to low-tech, she'd lost track.

"He figured that as a woman I would be fighting someone larger too often, so if I learned to defend myself against someone a lot bigger when I was little, I could only get better as I grew."

"The hand-to-hand fighting you do is very different. I'm learning a lot from you. Probably more than you've learned from me, to tell the truth." Tayla laughed and swiped at her face with a towel. "Leanna wants to go to a new place tonight. She says it's rowdy, and that's just what I want. Care to join us? It'll take me half an hour to get cleaned up. Why don't you meet us at the gate?"

Marta hesitated. She'd planned to study maps of the route from Rashiba to Restal tonight. And she was starting to get too close to Tayla. "Leanna always chooses the rowdy places. I think she just likes troublemakers." She heard her father's voice in her head. "Don't get attached, Marta. We won't be here long. Don't make leaving harder." *I hadn't realized how tempting it would be now that I'm by myself.*

Tayla added, her voice muffled through the towel, "And I'll ask Andra. She just lost a patient, and she needs to get out. She'll brood if we don't encourage her to get out and about. She's ready."

Marta gave in. "Sounds fun." The three of them were excellent sources of information about everything from fashion to the regulations of both Mounted and Karda Patrol to politics. And she'd been working hard. She'd earned a little fun with acquaintances she would probably not see often, if ever.

Sometimes she wished she'd agreed to have a partner, but she was determined to prove herself. If she started accepting partners, she'd end up always being second. That wasn't acceptable. It would be failure.

The four women walked two abreast down the narrow street. Short heavy burgundy cloaks trimmed in dark gold covered the three Mi'hiru's fitted jacket and split skirt uniforms. The fourth, Andra, wore a long cloak of light blue, the Healers' distinctive dark red geometric design embroidered around hood and hem. Street lanterns created spheres of light in the mist that fell, glistening off the stones of the street.

The tavern catered to members of Rashiba Guard, Mounted and Karda Patrols, and Mi'hiru. Leanna promised a fun crowd and good food. Noisy voices, clinking dishes and cutlery, the warm smells of roasting meat, and beeswax candles in gleaming brass and glass holders met them as they pushed inside out of the cold.

They wound through the crowded tavern, headed for a small table at the back near the smokeless stove with its glowing red stones, and laughed at the good-humored catcalls that came from the mostly male crowd.

"Watch it," Tayla said to one particularly persistent and slightly drunk youth. "I didn't get much of a workout today, and I feel the need to beat someone down tonight."

He laughed. "Please. Beat me down. Beat me down." He saluted them with a brimming mug.

Tayla ordered ale. Marta and Leanna decided on wine. Andra would be on duty later and passed. The serving girl set slices of bread dripping with toasted cheese, garlic, and tomato bits in the middle of the table, and they helped themselves.

Leanna took a sip of her wine and a bite of the bread. "Lots of garlic tonight. I'm afraid the garlic breath will fend off any suitors we might attract." She leaned forward as the chopped tomatoes tried to slide off the bread and spread themselves down the front of her blouse.

"I'm not so sure I want it to fend that last one off." Tayla laughed. "He's a cute one. Look at those arms—and those eyes." She rolled her own with a mock lascivious leer.

"Tayla! He's just a boy," Andra said, her eyes wide in teasing horror.

"Youth equals stamina, Andra. Youth equals stamina. Remember that advice always from your wise armsmaster. Plus they always go for older women. It's a challenge for them. And I like to meet that challenge." She put on a serious expression. "Anyway, you need to enjoy yourselves as much as you can tonight. Surana says there's a big storm coming. It's rain for several days, I'm afraid. You'll be practicing in it, bless your hearts. And the Karda hate it."

Surana was Tayla's Karda. Marta almost said, "You sound like Surana talks to you," but kept the words stuffed inside. Again she heard her father's voice. "Never make assumptions without hard data. Especially about behaviors you haven't seen before."

She felt a nudge of someone familiar at the shutters in the mental stone wall she had closed tight against the emotions in the tavern. Over her right shoulder, she saw Galen Morel behind a rather large man at the end of the bar on the back wall. He looked away, lifted his mug to his mouth, and turned his head.

Relief that their affair had ended on the last planet whooshed out of her. He was not, and never had been, what she wanted. Would she ever feel that special spark for anyone? She dropped her focus to her cup to cover a sudden rush of sadness and loss. She'd hoped for some- thing permanent, something deep and lasting with him. That wish had kept her eyes closed to who he was for a long time—so handsome he was beautiful, but closed, arrogant, remote.

Her first instinct was to turn away, not acknowledge him. He wasn't supposed to be in Rashiba, and he wasn't happy to see her. That feeling was strong enough to poke her shields hard. Maybe she should just ignore him. But why would he try to hide from her?

Finally, she just watched him, feeling sad, until she caught his attention. He'd never shown much expression, but she'd known him so long she could interpret the tiny changes he couldn't hide. She hoped he wasn't up to something he shouldn't be. It wouldn't be the first time —a good part of the reason they weren't together. He tipped his head toward the back hall, and she stood, excusing herself.

Her vision went black at the edges. She grabbed the back of her chair. She was suddenly not there in the crowded tavern—the loud noises faded. The intricate flagstone floor, the waxed bar with its brass rail, shelves of bottles glinting behind it, the plain polished tables and chairs disappeared.

For an endless moment, she watched in horror as Galen was wrapped in flame, screaming with pain and desperation. Then the noise of the tavern and its boisterous crowd flooded back, and her mental wall snapped into place. She drew a stuttering breath into her tight chest.

Shaken and disoriented, she watched him slip through the crowd toward the back of the tavern. He looked his usual self— nothing wrong. She was nauseous—cold sweat trickled from her temples and between her breasts. She looked around. No one had noticed anything. Her companions were still laughing with the

young man making cow eyes at Tayla. Marta stared down at the
worn stone floor, steadied herself on the back of her chair, and
followed Galen down the hall to a small back storeroom where they
wouldn't be disturbed.

"What are you doing here, Galen?" she asked, her voice shaking.
"Aren't you supposed to be in Anuma Quadrant?" She reached to
touch him. He flinched away, and she remembered. He never
tolerated even a casual touch he didn't initiate.

"What's the matter, Marta? You look upset—or sick."

"I…I'm fine. Just a hard workout this afternoon. You're
supposed to be way up in the northeast. Is something wrong? Did
your father send you to check on me?"

He looked down at her, and his brown eyes slid away from her
gaze. He ran his hand through his dark blond hair. "Uh, I'm on my
way to meet someone. Though it isn't any of your business, is it?"

"What are you so defensive about? I'm just concerned. I don't
want to be unprepared if something's changed. I'm to leave in less
than a tenday."

"Where are you going?"

"Your father wanted me to go to Restal and Toldar, and I've
managed to arrange it. First year Mi'hiru spend a few months in
each quadrant. I start with those two." A brief flash of something
she didn't recognize crossed his face. "I'm assigned to a brief time in
Restal, and then I go on to Toldar. Apparently those two countries, I
mean quad- rants, are the richest in resources on Adalta. And your
father says they both have young and handsome heirs."

"Using your sexy wiles now, are you? That's new."

"Not my idea. And I'm not happy about it. I've never seduced
anyone before. I don't even know how." Her mouth pursed in a
moue of distaste. "And to interfere in a planet's internal politics?
Why are we reduced to that? Gathering information about
government, culture, potential markets, resources for trade, that's all
we've ever done. All we're supposed to do. I don't know if I can do it
—or if I can make it work. It feels dirty."

"Let me think. Tall, elegant figure, auburn hair glinting with
gold, and long eyelashes around those blue, blue eyes." A flash of

humor flicked over his usual detached expression. "Oh, I think you can make it work. They'd be fools to resist. Take advantage, Marta. You might even have fun."

He leaned back against the wall. The tension in his shoulders made his movement awkward. Galen was never awkward. "Restal's in the foothills of the coastal range, isn't it? A barren place. Aside from the mines, it's all rocks, gullies, scrub trees, and goats. I don't envy you." Galen's eyes moved away, and he hesitated, expression softening.

He touched her arm. "I miss you, Marta." His eyes flicked away and back, and his face twisted into his usual ironic mask. "Especially since I found out about the consortium stock your father left you."

A grin broke a crack in his mask then he looked away. "I'm leaving early tomorrow. I'll be communicating with Father as soon as I'm outside the Prime. The ship's orbit should put it overhead then. I'll have to hurry to catch it. The disappearance of the satellites makes things difficult. I hope they've figured out what happened and can fix it. My Cue doesn't work half the time. I think I lose more data than I input." He shifted his feet and half turned to look back toward the crowded room. "Anything you want me to tell him?"

"No, Kayne briefed me before I left the ship, and I spoke to him just before I got to the Prime. I'll find a way to use my Cue if I need anything. Mine's working fine. Good luck, Galen. I doubt I'll see you before this tour ends." She reached out and touched his forearm. She thought of his burning figure and felt a need for contact. She tightened her hand. "Be careful."

He nodded and held her gaze. "You also, Marta." He walked back down the short hall, and Marta watched him wind his way through the crowd toward the door, her hand rubbing her chest. *What stock?*

CHAPTER FOUR

Marta unbuckled the leather straps of Sidhari's saddle rig. She lifted it onto the crude rack in the corner of the large open stall of the stable in the Talons Inn. *One day of flying through Restal leaves Sidhari and me as tired as six days of flying across Rashiba and the edge of Toldar.*

Sidhari had hunted for herself in the afternoon, but Marta asked the boy who lingered in the hall, watching her Karda with fascinated eyes, for tubers and seed-heavy hay, and she filled the large manger.

She picked up her heavy saddlebags. "Apparently one wild goat wasn't enough for you," she said as Sidhari attacked the food. "I'll see you in the morning. Looks like you're more tired than usual tonight. Rest well."

I talk to her as though she's a person, Marta thought as she walked across the guesthouse courtyard toward her dinner and a bed. *When it comes down to it, she's the only one I can trust. Sidhari doesn't know what I'm saying and can't answer back. What a sad way to live my life, connected to nothing and no one.*

No family, what few friends she'd made left behind, scattered on too many worlds. She curled her fingers, as if she could feel her father's hand around hers, anchoring her, then shook them out.

She'd made her decision. There was no reason to feel sad. She needed to concentrate on doing her job.

She pushed open the heavy wooden door and walked into a room full of villagers. Silent, expectant faces watched as she approached the lanky man at a plank bar in front of a shelf of bottles and a few stacked kegs of beer, ale, and probably cider. An array of initialed ceramic mugs hung from hooks on the wall.

"Good evening to you, Mi'hiru. We be honored to have you. M'name's Willem." He smiled broadly. "Tisn't often we have Karda landing here. I think everyone in the village dropped whatever they were doing to watch you come in. 'Twas a beautiful sight. Do you have all you'll need for your Karda?"

"Your son took care of us well. She'll be stuffed if she eats all he brought her. If you do half as well by me, I'll be satisfied."

"We've a fat roast hen'll be ready in a bit. Wife put it on the fire special for you soon's we saw you circlin' up there. There's a cherry apple tart with cream for your pleasure after."

"That's not necessary, but I will appreciate it. And if you have a bed to spare, I'll be more than happy." The smell of baking tarts and roast chicken rumbled her stomach and watered her mouth. Her tired muscles relaxed. It felt good to be welcomed so enthusiastically after days of no one to talk to who talked back.

Willem beamed and ushered her to the end of a long table nearest the hearth and put a mug of cider in front of her. "May our table provide you sustenance, may our land provide you work to suit your heart and hands, and may you find safety within our walls in your rest, Mi'hiru."

A row of expectant faces watched her as she sat. The woman next to her, a blush on her fresh young face, said hesitantly, "What's her name? Your Karda."

"Sidhari." *She asked Sidhari's name before she asked mine. That shows me who's important.*

"She was beautiful flying in. Her wings were all gold and glowing in the sunset." Her eyes shone with admiration and envy.

The flood-gates opened on a rush of questions. What was it like flying on a Karda? Did she get dizzy looking down? Wasn't Sidhari bigger than most Karda? Where was she going? Where was she from? Had she been a Mi'hiru long? How far could a Karda fly in a day? What did it take to be a Mi'hiru?

"Whoa, one question at a time." Marta laughed. "I'm headed for Restal Prime for my first assignment. I just finished my training in Rashiba Prime."

"Ha' you come about the Circles of Disorder?" This question came from a farmer seated with several others at a nearby table, his voice cutting through the others.

The room went silent. Curiosity lifted her inner eyebrow. Marta knew next to nothing about the strange circles barren of most life, surrounded by wide forests planted in rows.

She pulled at the gold ring in her ear. *How do I handle this? Drat the engineers who guide the spy bugs. Do they think nothing happens outside the big cities? The Primes?*

"No, but I noticed the circles seem to be larger as I get further into Restal. Much larger than in Rashiba or the edge of Toldar we flew over. I thought it was just that fewer trees grow here, so the circles are more visible." *No one ever wants to say much about the circles. I wish I knew more. I don't even know who it's safe to ask what questions. Those circles are alien—like they aren't even part of this planet.*

Feet shuffled, and eyes looked elsewhere. No one spoke until the old farmer said, anger lending strength to his voice, "Aye, the one outside our village be growin'. And killin' the trees around it. I ha' lost three goats to it. Found em bloody and slashed up terrible. Tell 'em in Restal Prime they got to do somethin' about that Adalta forsaken place afore it sucks all our talent in. There be no new trees planted for some years now. What comes from rule by strong talent 'stead of by those who know what's real." His last words were almost lost in his mutter.

Willem put a plate of short green beans, potatoes, and crisp-skinned chicken in front of Marta and refilled her mug of cider. "Pay no attention to Pargit, there. He's always the doomsayer.

48

Thinks it's his job. His goats probably wandered off and got eaten by a medgeran." He laughed uneasily and glared at the farmer.

Marta took a sip of cider, trying to ignore the exchange of glares. "Leave the Mi'hiru to her dinner now." He frowned at the crowd of villagers. "Mayhap she'll answer your questions and tell us some tales of the Karda after."

The rest went back to their beer and ale, though the table of older farmers continued to watch her. *They want to ask me more about these circles. I hope they don't. My ignorance might be suspicious.* Her hunger roared at the smell of the dinner in front of her, and she attacked the chicken as though it might run away. Adalta was the only world she'd been on where the food was this close to Earth-like, because the original life on the planet was almost decimated. They weren't close to finished rejuvenating and planting the enormous barrens, judging by what she'd seen from the ship and what they'd flown over since leaving Rashiba Prime.

When she finished, she excused herself, citing her long flight. She climbed the stairs behind Willem who carried her packs up to a small, neat room.

"I sent young Jon up to warm your room for you while you ate. It should last the night."

How? There's no fire in the room, not even a fireplace or stove. Yet it's warm. She sighed. *I'll have to leave that puzzle for when I'm not so tired.*

The room was scrupulously clean, a colorful quilt on the mattress atop an iron bed. Marta didn't care that the mattress looked lumpy. She'd fall into it on her face if Willem lingered at the door much longer. He scrubbed at his hair till it stood straight up, then fisted his big calloused hands at his sides.

"Pay no mind to Pargit. No need to be tellin' folks in Restal Prime about our problems. We do na' want to cause trouble."

Marta watched the countryside below her and Sidhari grow hilly and rough with washes and deep arroyos. Vegetation became more sparse, rocks more plentiful. This was another of the enormous

49

barren outlying areas not yet reseeded. What growth there was, other than spiky bushes and wiry grass, had blown in from other areas or planted around water sources and the strange circles.

She learned the land as they flew—its hills, villages, holdings—making a mental map. She'd be doing a lot of flying over this quadrant in the tendays to come. All she had was a few incomplete maps and a detailed picture of Restal Prime from the guild house library. She'd need more.

A hawk circled below them. She could feel its concentration on the ground and its sharp, hungry intent when it spied a snake sunning on a rock. She broke off her attention as it dove and snatched the snake, piercing its prey with sharp talons. Her makeshift wall slammed back up, cutting off the predatory glee of the hawk, the pain and distress of the snake.

The conflict—so immediate, so real—seared her mind. She'd let her mental wall drop, enjoying the serenity of Sidhari's flight. A headache spiked, a painful reminder to keep that wall up.

Sparse grass and meager clusters of trees below spread farther and farther apart. The countryside became gullied, barren, and desolate. They flew wide around three large Circles of Disorder with dead trees bordering their edges.

Sidhari tired faster the farther they flew into Restal. Her wing beats grew sluggish, too far apart, and they lost altitude. Worried, Marta started looking for a place with water to land and rest. Being on a planet that was mostly water meant she seldom had to look long for a spring or stream, though they seemed to be farther apart in this barren countryside.

She nudged Sidhari toward a small copse of trees to the right, but the Karda was already circling to land. Marta noticed a large group of men and horses in among the small trees, and Sidhari abruptly veered away. The men were heavily armed and not in uniform, so they weren't Restal Mounted Patrol.

She and Sidhari would find another place for their rest. This wasn't the first group she'd suspected of being raiders. There'd been another the day before. Two groups too many to suit her in the narrow slice of Restal they flew across. How many other bands like these roamed this quadrant?

By the time they found another place to land, Sidhari stumbled as her feet touched the ground. She cantered to a stop next to a fallen cottonwood, its weather-burnished trunk silver in the sun.

Marta jumped down. "I think I better take off the saddle and packs. This needs to be a longer rest than usual. We're both tired." Piling the gear against the trunk of the downed tree, she pulled dried meat from a bag meant for emergencies. She could see Sidhari was too tired to hunt.

"We'll stop early tonight whether we find a village or not, girl," she said as she put the meat down next to a muddy spring flowing sluggishly from under a small twisted evergreen, its banks full of tracks of birds and small animals. And one large one. She could smell the remains of that one's yesterday meal, but the odor was faint. Some- thing tickled the edge of her awareness through one of the windows in her mental wall. It made her mind itch.

Sidhari ate too slowly to suit Marta. She checked her over carefully as she learned in training, running hands down the slender legs, picking up each clawed foot, and inspecting the horny growths that formed a hoof-like surface when she curled her long digits for landing. Marta checked the long, cruel talons for cracks or splits. She nudged Sidhari to kneel and stretch out a wing. Feeling along the slender, hollow bones and long spring-steel muscles, she meticulously examined the flight feathers. Both wings were fine.

"We'll just eat our lunches and take a long nap. I'll make a hole in the mud of the spring. By the time we're ready to leave, there should be enough clear water for a long drink and to top up our water canvases in case we don't find another later."

By the time she finished her lunch and dug out the spring, Sidhari was dozing. Marta pulled a blanket out of a pack and wrapped it around herself, curling into the hollow left by the fallen tree, tall upstanding roots breaking the cold wind that blew endlessly across the barren hills, and bent the stiff grass low. She breathed in the clean, sharp, sinus-clearing smell of scattered aromatic bushes.

As soon as she settled on the bare ground of the hollow, the insistent tickle in her mind increased.

The anxiety of a small birbir scrounging for seeds under a shrub and the impatient hunger of her young intruded into Marta's awareness. Her eyes closed, and she knew there were fifteen antelope gathered over the hill to the east. She jerked up. She knew it. There was no uncertainty. She forced herself to lie back down without going to look.

Almost as tired as Sidhari, Marta tried to sleep. A covey of quail pecked through the short grass fifteen meters to her left out of sight across the spring. Their scattered emotions pinged like gravel tossed against the windows in her shields.

The itch in the back of her mind expanded into a dull headache. *I'm just tired. My imagination's working overtime. Lying on the ground isn't all that comfortable. I don't have that much empathy, and telepathy does not exist.*

Resisting the urge to look to confirm the quail were there, she fell asleep. The mental noises softened to a soothing song. One hand worked its way out of the blanket to rest in the grass, fingers digging into the red clay soil. She moved deeper into sound sleep, suffused with a feeling of deep comfort and a subtle hint of connection to something immense and enfolding.

Marta woke to sharp whistles. She opened her eyes, sat up slowly, and watched as the little covey of quail, blue topknots bobbing, came warily out of the grass to drink from the spring. She sensed the hunger and intense concentration of a fox carefully placing its feet, felt the brush of his body low to the ground. It moved closer.

How did she know that? She couldn't see it. The alarm of the quail hit her, and they exploded away in a thundering whirr of wings. The fox's frustration was intense, a sharp pain pulsing behind her eyes, making them water. She shut them tight. What was this? Why didn't it stop?

Marta looked up at the sky, rubbing her temples. The round glow of the huge red sun behind the clouds was far to the west. They'd slept the afternoon away. She ignored the frustration of the hungry fox slinking away and pushed up. Sidhari sat, legs tucked under her, head turned almost under one wing, watching her with those deep, dark eyes. *She senses my confusion.* Marta shook her head. Pain flashed. *I must be more tired than I realized. Maybe we better quit early and just stay here tonight.*

Sidhari continued to get more tired than usual the next day, her graceful ease of flight more labored. Ordinarily, she could glide for miles and miles between thermals, but she seemed to have to work harder. They had to add a long rest stop in the mornings. The closer they got to Restal Prime, the larger and more numerous the Circles of Disorder were.

The trees in the surrounding forests were mature—too many of those at the edges of the circles poked up like skeletons, stark white against the dark, barren ground encroaching on them. Sidhari stayed far away, circling wide, which added time to their journey.

They reached the top of a thermal and started a long glide, searching for another. Marta relaxed. The sensations that invaded her mind were less intense with altitude. Then, sudden disorienting loss and desolation flooded her. Dizzy, she grabbed the Karda's mane for balance.

Sidhari screamed. A spiral of Karda circled high in the distance.

Marta tried to turn Sidhari closer, but the Karda refused her signal and veered away. Dizzy, Marta grabbed the pommel handle for balance.

Fifteen Karda circled high, then descended and beat upward again. Their precise flight pattern formed a double helix aerial dance near the largest Circle of Disorder Marta had yet seen. She swallowed, her stomach queasy. Faint, deep, tolling cries rang through the air.

Even from as far away and as high as she and Sidhari soared, she could see the shape of a Karda sprawled at the edge of the circle. What could have killed it? Adaltans revered Karda. No one would have shot it. *Is it the circle? Is that why Sidhari always flies around so far from them?* The Karda's aerial dance was well away from the dead trees at the circle's edge.

Sidhari keened a long, deep bell-like tone. Marta felt her grief and desire to join the dance, but she flew on—so high Marta feared she'd pass out from the low oxygen. Then Sidhari slipped into a slow descent, leaving the Circle of Disorder, the dead Karda, and the aerial dancers behind. Cold wind dried the tears on Marta's cheeks.

Marta found a village to stay in each of the following nights of her journey to avoid sleeping on the ground again. In spite of that, she picked up more and more sensations of creatures. The closer they flew to the surface, the more intense the alien feelings.

In the guesthouses and inns where she stayed, she shut her walls tight, answered the same excited questions about the Karda, and found the same covert, fearful attitudes about the Circles of Disorder and the quadrant rulers.

The closer they got to Restal Prime, the more reticent the villagers became. And the more she noticed the poverty—smaller farms with fewer outbuildings, gaps in the stone fencing, roofs in disrepair visible even at the heights they flew.

There was little farming, mostly livestock, goats, unusual horned longhaired sheep, and not many cattle. Not much to tempt trade with the consortium, though wool from those sheep might be the source of the unusual tough fabric she'd found at market in Rashiba.

Pastureland was poor. At her last stop, the few villagers she'd seen were sullen. They had little to say to her, and there was no mention at all about the circles, though the ones she flew around were larger and the bands of skeletal trees wider. She saw no fresh plantings as there had been around the circles in Rashiba and the corner of Toldar they cut across.

They flew into the landing area near Restal Guild House late in the afternoon, several Karda flying to greet them as they got close. Sidhari landed smoothly, and they loped to the large mews. No one was there to meet her. From the empty stalls and saddle racks, she figured most of the Mi'hiru were out on patrol.

She found several unused stalls, so she picked one and forked clean straw into a corner for Sidhari to rest on. She found the stores of meat, tubers, and grains and helped herself, heaping the feed shelf full. Opening the brass tap over the water butt, she filled it brim full from the cistern on the roof. Fifteen minutes later she looked out and watched a Mi'hiru on a small light brown Karda with stark black wing stripes land and canter toward the mews. Nice landing. Three more Karda with riders in Karda Patrol uniforms followed the Mi'hiru.

The quiet mews filled with hungry Karda headed for their stalls and tired riders unsaddling, tossing packs toward the door, and raiding the feed room. A petite, mousy-haired Mi'hiru bounced off her Karda and waved toward Marta.

"I'll be with you soon as I get everyone settled," she called. Her delicate brown Karda practically danced to her stall, nudging her rider impatiently toward the food stores. "Stop pushing, Cystra. I'm moving as fast as I can."

Cystra nudged her again, and the Mi'hiru laughed. "Can I help?" Marta called back.

"That would be good, thanks. I need to check over the Karda as soon as these patrol guys get out of here. You can help with that. " She carried the food to her Karda's stall. "This is Cystra, by the way. Judging by the height of the head peering out over that stall, she must be half the size of your Karda."

"Sidhari," said Marta. "And she is unusually big."

"I'm Philipa. You must be Marta. We've been expecting you. I'm sorry there was no one here to meet you. I've been on patrol as you can probably tell. The others are either out on patrol themselves or didn't see you come in for some reason."

Marta started going over one of the patrol Karda. Two of the riders watched closely as they straightened and hung their tack. The third threw his saddle down in a tangle of straps and started to leave.

"Ulrik! Get back over here and pick up that saddle. And wait to see if your Karda checks out all right," one of the riders said. Tall, broad shoulders, sun-streaked brown hair tousled from the wind, the young man picked up his saddle and carried it to one of the saddle racks lined up against the wall opposite the stalls, arranging the long straps so they didn't get tangled.

"Readen wanted me to meet him as soon as we got in," Ulrik responded, his voice verging on sour.

"Mi'hiru are not stable hands. Your gear is your responsibility. And if you don't care about your Karda, you should. I don't care who's waiting." The man who spoke to Ulrik turned to Marta. "Sorry about that. His bad attitude doesn't extend to most of us. I'm Daryl, Patrol Commander." He extended his arm, his voice warm with welcome, his face solemn. He didn't look like he smiled often.

Marta grasped his arm. His grip was firm but polite. "Marta. New Mi'hiru. I'm glad to meet you." She stepped back from the Karda she had examined. "This is your Karda?"

"If he could ever belong to anyone, I guess he belongs to me. Or I belong to him. I'm his chosen, anyway. This is Abala."

The big sorrel Karda with bright copper head and wing tips looked over at Marta and ducked his head. He was as big as Sidhari.

He nodded his head as if to say hello and surprised her with his silent greeting. She smiled and nodded to him, not sure what to think about that.

"We're glad to have you. Our Mi'hiru are stretched pretty thin, as I'm sure Philipa will tell you. I'll just put my saddle up, take care of Abala, and get out of your way. I'm on patrol around Restal Prime this tenday, so I'm sure we'll meet again. Often. And I expect to see you soon at the keep for your welcome dinner."

"Oh? The keep?"

He grimaced. "You'd find out sooner or later. I'm unfortunate enough to be the heir. Much as I'd like to, I can't hide it. That's Eddard over there." The other patroller, hands full helping Philipa carry food to his Karda looked over and nodded.

Marta watched Daryl walk out of the mews. Brown, sun-striped hair pulled back in a tail down his broad back, he was certainly good looking. So this was one of the men Kayne wanted her to get close to. His honest, solemn face made the thought dirty. She wiped her hands on her skirt.

Marta and Philipa worked smoothly together after the three

patrollers left. One of the Karda had a bent flight feather. They straightened and pinned it carefully, imping the feather back into place.

"Ulrik is too hard on the Karda. It won't be long before they refuse to carry the man." Philipa's words interrupted Marta's thoughts.

"Does that happen often?" she asked, surprised.

"It seems to happen more here, starting at the very top. They won't carry the guardian's eldest son, Readen, at all. Never have, not even when he was a boy. Maybe because he was born without talent. I'd advise you not to bring that up where he can hear. Now, Daryl, the younger son you just met, they seem to love. Abala chose him, and I'm sure you know Karda seldom single out anyone but Mi'hiru and guardians. Daryl is one of the few I know about. Altan Me'Gerron from Toldar is another. But then, both of them are guardian heirs."

She wiggled her eyebrows and rolled her eyes suggestively. "If I had a chance to choose, I'd choose either one of them."

Marta forced a laugh. *Deciding who to choose isn't going to be a problem for me. I don't get to, not permanently. Not unless I find someone shipboard, and the chances of that are slim. I wouldn't want anyone who settled for that kind of life anyway.* She shrugged off the pang the thought gave her and moved to the other wing.

CHAPTER FIVE

The restaurant hummed with quiet conversation when the two Mi'hiru walked in. Marta strengthened her mental dampers. She didn't need the assault on her emotions that intruded even in small crowds. She was hungry, and Philipa said this place had exceptional food. Three men at a table in the far corner of the room were the focus of the energy in the room.

One, whose long brown hair and face resembled Daryl's, looked up as if expecting someone when they came in. Irritation flicked on his face, then disappeared in a laugh at one of his companions. Marta had seen him, Readen, the older of the guardian's two sons, in other taverns several times in the tendays she'd been in Restal, often with the same two Mounted Patrol guards and the center of activity, laughing, joking.

"Watch out for those two guards. The Karda refused to carry them when they applied to the Karda Patrol. They don't like Mi'hiru," Philipa murmured. "Readen's friendly enough and fun. He tolerates Mi'hiru, but that's about all. Karda won't accept him either. If the revolt against the so-called aristocracy of talent ever amounts to anything, he's probably the one who will lead it. He was born without any. Not even a hint. The only person in all our history to not have talent. And no one knows why."

There was that word again. Talent. Marta knew it meant something more here than the ability to play an instrument or write a poem. She was missing something critical about the people here, but she'd never noticed anything that resembled magic—except the Karda.

She and Philipa found a table across the room. Over the hand-written card with the menu, Marta watched the three men, curious about the older son who was not the heir. His features were close to his brother Daryl's, but where Daryl was solemn, watchful, Readen was outgoing and genial. He was expecting someone. His eyes flicked to the door every time it opened. Eyes that didn't reflect any geniality.

Philipa continued her tale of a Karda Patrol trainee. "He told me in a loud voice to order the Karda to fly close to the ground, so if he fell off, he wouldn't be hurt. He's the son of Me'Kammin, one of the wealthiest holders, and he's so round he'd roll if he fell. I don't think he's going to make the patrol. And I don't think he'll be disappointed. His father will be, but he won't. It's too much effort. Effort is not his thing."

Marta laughed, handed the card to the young server and ordered the lemon-rosemary chicken and orange potatoes Philipa suggested. They decided to split a bottle of house wine.

A cloaked man pushed through the door, hood pulled up to hide his face, looked around, spotted Readen, and moved to his table. Readen sent the two guardsmen to the bar with a laugh.

Something about the man's carriage struck Marta as familiar. He glanced around the room, pausing a fraction too long when his gaze crossed hers. She knew him. Galen Morel's eyes darted away from her. He sat with his back to her.

Was he trying to hide from her? Did he think she didn't recognize him? What was he doing in Restal? He was assigned to Anuma Prime, way up in the northeast. Too far for this to be a casual meeting, It must have taken him days if not tendays to get here. He didn't fly in. She'd know.

Galen said something, and Readen's head turned toward Marta. She looked away to listen to another of Philipa's stories of good looking men and conquest, a favorite topic of conversation with all Mi'hiru. Marta suddenly wished she weren't there, that Galen hadn't seen her.

The two men talked, voices low, for several minutes. Readen's hand slashed sideways as if insisting on something. Galen just kept shaking his cloaked head. Then Readen slammed his fist down on the table and pushed back in his chair. Galen got up to leave.

Marta wanted to forget her training and follow him out to ask what he was doing in Restal. He was a friend in the wrong place— maybe even in trouble—but Readen's attention sharpened on her, and she changed her mind. The I'm-a-friend-to-all look on his face flickered with something not so friendly.

Readen Me'Vere sat in the large leather chair in front of his fireplace, the cold hearth yawning before his unseeing eyes. He was furious. The new Mi'hiru recognized Morel, and her surprise was obvious. She'd almost gotten up to follow him out of the restaurant.

He pulled the medallion on the silver chain at his neck from beneath the tunic where it hid. The heavy silver was shaped in an ancient symbol no one else alive on Adalta would recognize. As always, sliding his fingers over it relaxed him, reminded him of the power he could create.

He had learned them, those arcane symbols from the hidden cavern beneath the keep. The lessons hard, painful, and terrifying, but over the years they brought him the power he craved. Readen might not have been born with the talent connection to Adalta that made Daryl the heir instead of him, but he could wrest power from the Circles of Disorder, and he could steal the flow of talent from those who had it. The Itza Larrak had taught him much. He was almost ready.

A light knock sounded at the door, and Galen Morel walked in without waiting for an invitation. His too-handsome face twisted with irritation. "Why did you call me back? I was safely on my way. It's a long journey without having to make part of it twice."

"She saw you, Galen. That Mi'hiru saw you in the restaurant last night where you so foolishly insisted we meet. How does she know you? Was she one of your dalliances in Rashiba Prime?" asked Readen, his tone low and menacing, nothing amiable left in it.

Galen sat slowly in the chair opposite Readen, unconcerned. "She's another agent. I know this is her area, but I thought I could avoid her. She might report seeing me, and there might be a note in the files no one will see. That's all. Father will take care of it. Nothing to be concerned about."

"She started to follow you out," Readen snapped.

Galen held up a hand, palm out with a "calm down" motion. "This deal is important to Father. Especially the heavy and rare minerals our ship sensors detected. Your ores in trade for the weapons and the equipment to mine the ores. Father is concerned if we don't do something, the Greater Council in Rashiba is sure to refuse us trade privileges because of your Luddite laws restricting technology."

He leaned back and crossed his legs. "So he is not going to let a report from a neophyte advance agent deter your goals. Our goals. We need you in charge in Restal. And beyond, if you manage it." He shoved a hand through his hair, pulling it away from his face and shaking it out. "We'll have to wait. Father can take care of her."

"Tell your father to recall her."

"He can't do that. There are no grounds. It's unnecessary, and further, she has support from outside his department." He twisted pursed lips to one side, looking over Readen's shoulder. "Perhaps I shouldn't have avoided her. I could have made up an excuse and bought her a glass of wine."

He shook his head, and his hair fell back to perfection. "Oh well, done is done. Father can head her off. But to be safe, put off the trials of the sample weapons I brought. I'll delay the delivery of the rest until she leaves Restal. As long as she doesn't see them, or any wounds they make, we'll be all right." He slapped his hands on the arms of the chair and stood.

"I'm not going to do that," Readen stated flatly. "The raids are all on the Toldar side of the border. She won't be going there. And my troops control the border, not Daryl with his Karda wings. Until I control Adalta, you won't get what you need here. If you won't take care of her, I will. I want those weapons."

And there was something about her that intrigued Readen. He sensed something unusual about her talent he might be able to use. Or perhaps it's the Itza Larrak that could use her.

"You'll get them, just have patience." Galen threw the words over his shoulder as he left.

Fury washed through Readen, and he fought for control until the door closed behind Galen, his hands in fists behind his back, his nails cut into his palms. Fury that someone not from this planet should have talent potential and not even know it, while he remained the only person on the entire planet without a trace. He'd seen, not for the first time, the talent potential in Galen, too.

More than a tenday went by before Marta had time off to fly out for a whole afternoon to give herself and Sidhari a much-needed taste of freedom. A palpable tension infused Restal Prime, even in the mews where it should be peaceful, and she welcomed the chance to get away. Unpartnered Karda seemed to avoid being here unless they were needed—it was still a mystery to her how they knew when they were—and it was lonely without their presence. She'd gotten used to it in Rashiba.

She washed up and changed her dirty work clothes for another warm divided skirt, a heavy jacket, and her long sheepskin vest, split front and back for riding. She ate the noon meal as fast as was polite and left for the mews, eager to spend alone time with Sidhari. And not so eager to make her report to the ship.

She and Sidhari soared up into flight, the sun warm on her shoulders.

She needed to report to Planetary Findings and leave her latest plant samples for pickup by the ship's biologist's tiny drones. She dug her Cue out of the bottom of her pack and tucked it in a pocket of her tunic. No bigger than the palm of her hand, an unexpected reluctance to use it made it hang heavy on her hip. Heavier than the sword she wore on the other hip.

Intricately worked to look like a small jewelry case with a mirror inside the fitted top, the Cue seemed innocuous—it even held a few bits of personal jewelry. She kept it muted and hidden, always, taking it out only when she was sure she was alone and could safely transmit the data she collected on culture, politics, and potential trade goods. When the consortium finally announced their presence, cultural missteps made in ignorance created problems.

They flew south and east for several hours, detouring around the edge of a large Circle of Disorder, so wide she couldn't see the other side, surrounded by stark skeletons of dead trees. Sidhari's distress beat at her, a physical assault that made Marta curl over the Karda's neck, hands stroking the smooth, shining hair, trying to comfort her, to sooth the quivering tension in her muscles. The dead trees along the innermost edges looked to be at least twenty years gone. Others looked stunted. No young trees appeared. It made Marta's skin feel greasy. Even as far from the circle as they flew, Sidhari's flight labored, her wings struggled for lift. Ordinarily, she could glide for kilometers on her enormous wings.

It frustrated Marta not to be able to ask questions about this strange anomaly without exposing ignorance and raising questions about her she couldn't answer. She'd already gotten a couple of odd looks from the other Mi'hiru. The sketchy information she had went no further than the fact that they were growing in Restal but not in the rest of the quadrants.

Yes, they were dangerous, but that didn't help her understand what they were. They were a critical part of the culture of Adalta that she was supposed to be collecting, and information about them was vital to fulfilling her mission. The sense that this was a major failure left a queasy feeling in her. Her first mission alone, and she was failing.

Sharp hunger pangs hit her stomach. Hunger not her own. Sidhari needed to hunt. More and more often, Marta picked up feelings, almost thoughts, from her Karda. They'd been on patrol with a wing of the Karda Patrol for the past tenday. They were seldom apart, and their rapport was developing, unlike anything Marta had ever known. Long conversations helped pass the time, and it surprised her every time she realized she was the only one doing the talking. They felt like real two- sided conversations.

The long flights without fresh meat were hard on Sidhari. Dried meat and grain wasn't enough. They circled high on a thermal, watching the ground below. Finally, she felt Sidhari spot something and saw a small herd of the antelope-like kurga below them. Their pale tan hides with vivid red stripes blended into the rough, red-dirt land- scape of mesas, gullies, and wide washes that dominated Restal outside the forests and the reclaimed fields surrounding the holds and villages.

Marta strung her bow and pulled an arrow from her quiver. She wasn't proficient at hunting from her Karda's back, but she'd try again. Sidhari dove for the ground, leveling out downwind of the herd, skimming the ground. Marta kept balance with the beats of Sidhari's wings and aimed. Timing her shot to both avoid the wings and hit her target—not an easy thing to do—she managed to wound one enough to slow it down. Sidhari's sharp talons grabbed the struggling kurga, broke its neck, and pulled back up into the air. Marta smiled and shook her bow above her head in triumph. This was the best she'd done ever.

"Well done, Sidhari. We're getting good at this. Finally. You aren't going to starve after all." The Karda gave a little swoop with her wings, and Marta felt something like a chuckle rumble in her chest. Even through the saddle rig.

She nudged Sidhari back toward the forest, searching for a meadow long enough for the Karda to land and take off again. One with plenty of grass, tubers, and the small cherry apples native to Adalta to round out Sidhari's meal. The ship would cross the sky just above the horizon today. She wouldn't have another chance to communicate for several tendays, and it had been at least that long since she'd reported last time.

Sidhari dropped the kurga and hit the ground at a canter,

slowed to a trot and stopped at the meadow's edge. Marta pulled loose the leg straps that held her to her saddle and Sidhari's back no matter what acrobatics they did in the air and slid down.

She pulled off the rig and curried the Karda with a brush from her pack. The thick grass of one of the few lush meadows in Restal nearly reached her thighs as she carried saddle and pack to the edge of the field. Sidhari tore into the kurga.

Marta found a small spring, put off taking out her Cue, and leaned against the smooth white trunk of a sycamore. Buds swelled along its silver branches, a few tiny leaves beginning to break through. Marta's dreamy thoughts were on nothing but the beautiful place and the warm sun.

"Hello, Tree," she said. And got an answer. Not words, but a clear, unmistakable answering surge of consciousness and sentience that knocked her off her feet. She dropped to the damp ground at the edge of the tiny stream, dizzy, her mind half capable of thought. Sidhari walked over and nudged her with her beak, settled down beside her and spread a wing over her.

Eventually, Marta shook herself out of her near trance, slipped out from under Sidhari's wing, and walked to the center of the clearing away from the sycamores.

What was that? What was happening to her? It was getting harder and harder to block these strange intruding sensations. First animals and birds, now a tree. And there's no one she could tell. Over and over her father and her trainers pounded it into her not to fall into a planet's superstitions or religious beliefs. To keep her distance and objectivity. This was too much. This was too much like believing in magical super-sentience. Kayne would never accept anything like this. This was beyond empathy. This was….

If she reported it, they'd assume she'd hallucinated. There would be days and days of testing. Who knew what they'd find, or do? Objectivity ruled—subjectivity was frowned on. She could be recalled, kept ship-side for this mission, maybe never allowed planet-side again. She'd never survive that. She kicked at a clump of grass and reinforced the wall in her head, picturing piles of bricks and buckets of mortar.

Angry and terrified, she fell to her knees, her head down, hands bracing her. She cried until she fell into exhausted sleep on the damp ground curled around her belly. When she finally woke, stiff and aching, she was sheltered against Sidhari's warmth, under one of her great wings, mentally centered again, and safe.

"Thank you, Sidhari," she whispered.

~You are all right. Your connection strengthens. Your mind is growing and growing hurts,~ whispered back, faint in her mind, just on the edges so she couldn't be sure it wasn't her own thought. That scared her again. Her senses were raw. It felt like an attack by some mystical...something.

And she was letting herself get too attached to Sidhari—to the extent of imagining she was talking back. Marta knew better. *Don't get attached. Don't get attached.* And she never had, however difficult it had been. Until now.

She shook herself out of those thoughts. The afternoon was passing, and she had her report to make, her job to do. She unpacked her samples of soils and plants, set the beacon for pickup, and searched the sky with the Cue to make her connection with the ship. Sidhari went back to digging for the tubers she loved. Marta sent her collected data and connected to dispatch. Kayne was not immediately available, and the officious communications officer refused to take her report or let her talk to anyone else.

"You are only to report to Director Morel," he repeated, twice, when she insisted. Finally, she heard Kayne's voice. His picture didn't come through. The Cue's screen was a storm of static.

"Rowan, it's about time you reported. Where have you been?" She couldn't decide whether it was irritation or concern in his voice. "If it weren't that the signal from your Cue has been steady, I'd have thought something happened to you."

"I'm in Restal, working. I told you it would take time to get here. I called in as soon as I could after I arrived. I've had trouble connecting. This is the third time I've tried."

"Not surprising, Marta. It's hectic up here. The engineers are worried. Things inexplicably stop working. Sometimes they fry circuits when they do. The satellites are gone, and the spy bugs are disappear- ing. Electro-magnetic disruptions move around over the planet, and few of our probes get through them.

"As the other agents report in, it's becoming apparent things don't look too well for us with the damn council and guardians of this planet. God save me from idealists. Their ruling philosophy has apparently not changed since they left Old Earth. They're determined not to fall into the mistakes they blame for Earth's collapse. Nineteenth century Old Earth Luddites through and through. Even the clothing is reminiscent of late nineteenth century. It seems it will go against every principle they have just to look at what we have to offer. Most agents report they'll be so appalled at the thought of even the simplest weapons they're likely to throw us out bodily if we try."

"Weapons?" said Marta. "Since when do we trade in weapons?" The Trade Alliance would be down on them with a vengeance.

He ignored her. "And, lords of the galaxies forbid they might look at anything that could make their miserable lives easier. They seem to revel in doing things in the most primitive ways possible and are smugly content with it. Technology's never progressed beyond the simplest steam mechanics, and even that works in some way none of you can discover."

"I take it you are not enamored of this beautiful planet." And their technology was not simple—she'd seen how their machines were beautifully designed and elegantly crafted. Just not electric or fossil fuel driven. Marta stifled her impatience. She could think of collectors, even some on their ship, who would be fascinated by some of what she'd seen and reported.

"Beauty does not make profits, Rowan. Trade and technology do. We can't make profits if we aren't even able to persuade them to look at what we have. To make things worse, some of the more sensitive items the scouts tested don't seem to work. Even the Cues work erratically. But enough of that, what have you learned of their culture and politics that can help in changing their minds? I wish we had the resources to force them to accept us."

"What?" she said. Surely he couldn't mean that. "What did you say?" It was a basic tenet of the trade federation that oversaw the consortium ships that no world could be forced to accept anything that their culture forbade.

"Don't be ridiculous, Rowan. You know I don't mean that. I'm frustrated. We need this trade badly. Particularly the neodymium, the samarium, and the lanthium our geo-probes found. The small amount of rare minerals we gathered from the scattered asteroid belts we mined on our way here isn't enough for trade when we move on, let alone our own needs."

There was a pause and Marta could hear him take a deep breath, trying to control his frustration. "We can't produce without those resources. And what can you find out about that mineral they use for fuel? The samples are unlike anything our geologists have ever seen. And we can't seem to make them burn. We know they burn. They heat every fireplace and stove down there. Have you been able to detect the ship from the planet? Our systems have been a little erratic. The engineers say our mirror shields are holding, but I'd rather trust someone on the ground."

Kayne talked so fast she knew he wasn't interested in her answers to his questions, but she said, "No, and I've made it a point to watch. Most of the time there's heavy cloud cover. No rumors about strange new moons in the sky either. I've sent data about the markets I visit when I accompany judiciars to the holdings and villages. The most interesting marketable good I've found is a fabric that's extremely strong, armor-like, and water repellant, from a hybrid or mutated sheep. There's some unbelievably fine porcelain from a small village not far from the Prime, made by one family for generations—translucent and incredibly strong, not just useful but also beautiful enough for collectors."

She went on, "As to the political hierarchy, Guardian Roland is an older man. Still healthy, but I've heard rumors he's beginning to fail in little ways. From what I've learned he's incredibly narcissistic, interested only in his pleasures, and is flagrantly misusing the resources of the quadrant. He holds court like one of the worst self-indulgent kings of pre-revolutionary France from Old-Earth history. There is a council, but he treats it as advisory, nothing else.

"It's the younger son, Daryl, who's his heir. I haven't discovered why it isn't the older one. Something about abilities they simply refer to as talent that Readen, the older son, doesn't have. Which is unheard of. I do hear occasional talk of a revolt against what they call the aristocracy of talent, but it seems to be just tavern talk. If it weren't that the holders and population like and trust Daryl, I wouldn't be surprised at an attempt by one of them to take control. But so far, they're satisfied to wait. He does what he can to mitigate his father's excesses."

Marta paced in small circles as she talked. "I haven't been presented to the guardian and his family yet. I'm finally invited to Restal Keep two days from now. It's a long overdue welcome, according to the Mi'hiru here, but that doesn't seem unusual for Restal. They don't hold Mi'hiru, or any women for that matter, with the same high regard as the rest of Adalta. Except for Daryl, the heir. He's Commander of the Karda Patrol, so I see him often in the mews. I sometimes accompany his wing of flyers on patrol, and I've begun to make friends with him."

But no matter what you say, I'm not going to whore myself for you. She pulled at her earring, hating the thought of what Kayne asked from her. A stray thought of her father jabbed her. She missed him. He would have been furious at even a hint of what Kayne wanted.

"I've crossed ways with the older son, Readen, a number of times as I've frequented taverns, the market, restaurants, listening to gossip and trying to better understand the cultural attitudes here. I've overheard him talking about better ways to accomplish the mining that brings in the most revenue. He owns a number of mines in the hills to the north where our sensors detected the heaviest mineral deposits, but from what I can deduce, their methods are primitive. I doubt he'd be resistant to anything that could help. Their methods are extremely labor intensive." She started to pull at the ring in her ear again but dropped her hand. Her ear was sore. It was a bad habit.

"Have you made progress in developing closer rapport with either of the sons? The reason we wanted you as me-hero, or whatever they're called, is because they're rumored to be more promiscuous. That should make getting close to them easier. Use your looks."

If you knew they were promiscuous, why did you choose them as my cover? I'm not. "Are you telling me to whore myself, Kayne?" She might as well make her distaste clear. She wasn't going to follow that order, whatever he said.

Her father would have ripped up the entire division of Planetary Findings if he'd even thought she'd be asked to do this. Kayne knew her degree of empathy made it impossible for her. No consortium agent had ever been asked to do that. He must be desperate. Why?

"Don't be ridiculous. You won't be taking money. The ridiculous concept that technology shouldn't be allowed to outstrip socio-cultural development is a significant obstacle to opening the planet to trade. We need to use whatever tools we can to influence them. You're being needlessly resistant. What progress are you making?"

"Though I think we're becoming friends, Daryl is careful not to fraternize too much with either his Karda patrollers or the Mi'hiru. He's serious about his duties as Commander."

"I have every confidence in you, Marta. I'm sure you'll find a way to influence him." His tone changed then, as he asked how she was coping with working alone. She could hear a note of caring in his voice. Kayne had been a good friend of her father's.

She relaxed a little and finished her report. Then she mentioned seeing his son, Galen. "I saw Galen here, Sir. Why is he in Restal? My territory. I saw him one evening in a restaurant, and he avoided me. It wasn't necessary. All the agents have stories in place to explain how we know each other. Did you send him to check on me? Have I done something to make you distrust me?"

Why do I suspect that? Do I feel guilty about something? A brief flash of her beautiful flight with Sidhari crossed her mind. *That has nothing to do with how I'm doing my mission. I am experienced enough at keeping my distance not to let my empathy get me too attached.* She swallowed the taste of guilt seeping into her thoughts.

After a short silence, he answered, his voice too casual. "Oh, no, Marta. He's in Anuma. Has been from the beginning. You were mistaken."

"He was here, Kayne. I saw him."

"I know it's difficult being down there on your own for the first time. You saw someone who reminded you of him. I know you were fond of Galen. You must miss him."

"He was hooded. But I know him. I'm certain it was him."

"It couldn't have been, Marta. He's in Anuma," he repeated, his voice soft with concern for her. But insistent.

She closed her eyes; heat built, pressing against her temples. She rubbed the back of her neck. She knew it had been Galen. And he hadn't been in Anuma since the beginning. She'd talked to him in Rashiba. *I won't think about that strange vision of him in flames.*

"Quit worrying about Galen and start concentrating on drawing the attention of one of the Me'Vere sons, preferably the heir, but if the other one shows interest, take advantage. That's your job, not Galen. I know it's hard for you, working alone, missing your father. But you can do it, Marta. I have faith in you."

Kayne terminated their connection. Marta switched the Cue off, not certain how she felt about their conversation. She stretched out in the soft grass under the warm sun, rare even in late spring.

Strengthening her mental walls against the intruding consciousness that was so much stronger when she was in contact with the ground, she fell asleep. Sidhari settled beside her in a companionable doze. When Marta woke, the weak afternoon sun was shining in her eyes from low beneath the ever-present clouds moving in from the west, and she was chilled.

"We better get back," she told Sidhari. She closed the Cue and pushed it deep into the bottom of her pack. She took out the loaf of nut bread and the piece of hard cheese she had pilfered from the guild house kitchen. "But first I'll eat. From the looks of the ground around here, you've had your snack already." Indeed the ground around them looked like a large animal had been rooting in it. Sidhari leaned her head over Marta's shoulder and looked longingly at the bread. Marta laughed and broke off a piece of the moist nut bread for her. Sidhari took it delicately in her huge beak.

Marta finished her snack. "That's not going to hold me for long, especially since I had to share. It's getting late—we need to hurry. I don't like flying when it's dark, and we've a long way to go."

Sidhari stood, lifting her wings slightly so Marta could tighten the girths that held the saddle to the broad back of the Karda. The saddle's pommel and cantle were both high. The pommel had an arching handle that extended into broad horns on each side to lock her thighs under. The high cantle was designed to support her back during the often-rough flights. Both were needed as the Karda's body surged and fell with the strong beat of her wings tossing the unwary rider back and forth with neck-snapping force.

She mounted, pulled tight the leathers that wrapped her legs, and leaned forward as Sidhari cantered across the meadow, finally lifting into flight, huge wings thundering with every stroke. They circled, brushing the treetops, searching for the updraft that would take them ever higher in the miracle that was their flight.

She wouldn't be sad to leave the unsettling intrusions into her mind, but she would definitely miss Sidhari when she finally left Adalta.

I need to guard my emotions more carefully. I'm in danger of growing too attached to her.

CHAPTER SIX

M arta hurried through the growing darkness, cloak wrapped around her against the chill and drizzle, hood up, glad for its heavy wool. And glad for the long wool divided skirt and high necked jacket of her blue uniform. It would be good to be inside a warm tavern.

Was it summer? Did this planet even have a summer? The red sun gave far less heat than most of the planets she'd been on, and it rained three out of five days of the long four-hundred-thirty-two-day year. *Well, maybe that's an exaggeration. But surely not by much. I may never dry out.* At its best, summer was less cool than the frigid winter season. And a little less wet, though the wet of winter was snow and ice.

The lamplighter hadn't gotten to this part of the Prime yet. The narrow street she turned into was dark between the tall buildings and smelled of too many people in too small a space too often. She walked faster, careful on the wet, slick stones, still mindful of the lighter gravity on Adalta.

A prickle of warning sent her hand to the hilt of her sword. Quick footsteps sounded from behind her. She pushed the right side of her short cloak over her shoulder, flipped the hood back, and loosened the weapon in its scabbard.

Whoever followed closed fast, too fast, and threatening intentions battered against her shields. The street was too dark and too empty to be careless. She turned.

Two men—hats pulled down, faces half obscured—approached and separated as they got close. She nearly stumbled at the feelings of cold malevolence swamping her.

Swallowing hard against the upsurge from her stomach, she forced the malignant emotions away and slammed her brick wall up, sealed her mind, and scrambled for clarity.

The taller one grinned a happy face with too many teeth. "I'll handle this, Juke. She's only a girl. How hard could this be?"

"She's a Mi'hiru. They train as much as any guardswoman," the other warned, but the first was already stepping toward her, sword up. Marta stepped to the side and drew her sword and yelled as loud as she could, "Patrol! Patrol!" And said, keeping her voice low and calm, "You better go on your way, both of you. They'll have heard me and be here any minute."

"Now do you need help, Cale?" the man called Juke jeered.

They must mean to kill her if they could be so free with their names. She relaxed her body into a loose stance and watched both of them with practiced awareness, blocking everything from her mind but the two men and her physical surroundings.

"Oh, I don't think so," said Cale, the larger one. "Leave her to me, Juke. I don't need your help." He lunged, over confident, overbalanced, and his powerful arm thrust his blade toward her stomach.

She parried, slipped his blade to the side, and stepped off the line, raking his forearm with the tip of her sword before he recovered.

"Shit!" he said and stepped back, his face reddened with fury and surprise.

"I told you, Marta's a Mi'hiru. She won't be easy," said Juke, laughing at him. He leaned, one leg cocked, against the wall of one of the buildings crowding the dark street and tapped his sword on the side of his shin.

How did they know her name? They'd caught her in a deserted area of warehouses. If the patrol wasn't nearby no one would hear her yell. She brought herself back to a ready stance.

She was trained to fight off more than one assailant, but it wouldn't be easy. They were both bigger than she was. Not as agile, but bigger and stronger, though the narrowness of the street gave her a slight advantage. They had to come at her one at a time or get in each other's way.

Cale attacked again. He was strong, and she parried his fast, hard strikes with difficulty, taking care not to block his sword directly. His reach was longer, and he was stronger. A hard block to his sword would numb her arm, maybe break her blade.

She'd have to work to get close to do any damage. And she couldn't forget there were two.

He struck again, and she leaned back. The tip of his sword almost caught an edge of her short cloak, but he overreached.

She stepped into him, and her sword slid into his unprotected side.

He stumbled back and stared down at the gush of blood and the gaping flesh under his sliced tunic. He switched his sword to the other hand and rushed her again, slow now and clumsy with that arm.

She stepped out of his line, whirled, and kicked out hard as he rushed past. His knee crunched. Marta heard it. He fell, and his head bounced off the street.

She shoved away the sudden absence of feeling from him. She didn't stop her turn until she faced the other man. He already moved toward her, his sword up.

She stepped to the side and backed away so he couldn't trap her between him and the unmoving body on the ground.

Her heart fluttered like it was trying to escape its cage. She forced slow, even breaths, made herself ignore the emptiness that had been the man called Cale. She smelled the sharp metallic smell of blood and the death stench of voided bowels.

Juke was smaller, wiry, and agile. She worked hard and fast to keep turning away his flurry of sword strikes. She let him push her back down the street, not attacking, defending with as little effort as possible.

She watched, alert for opportunity, knowing she was tiring despite the flood of adrenaline. She waited, parried and back-stepped, parried and back-stepped.

"Give up, little girl," he taunted, breathing a little fast, trying to muscle her sword down. He disengaged and stepped back. "I can kill you quick and fast, or hard and slow—in Cale's memory. You choose."

"Why are you attacking me? Who sent you?" Her voice was too high, too shrill. She hadn't wanted to kill either of them. She wanted to know who'd sent them. Faint light gleamed on the polished leather of the man's scabbard and belt, and his close-fitting jacket was well made, his boots well polished. These weren't ordinary street ruffians out for fun—twisted fun. They knew who she was. She was their target.

Marta parried his next stroke. She felt his anger grow, felt his thrusts and parries become erratic, and watched for his first mistake. She let her sword tip drop. He would make one. His training was adequate—hers was better. And he was angry.

Then he made it. Lunging to take advantage of her dropped sword, he left himself open, and Marta had a clean shot at his shoulder. She took it, felt the ragged scrape of sword against bone.

He fell back, dropped his sword, and stared, unbelieving, at her, hand clapped over his bloody jacket.

She stepped on his sword. "I'm going for the Prime Guard. You better take your chance and get yourself away from here. Your friend is dead. If you insist, I can make you dead, too. Who sent you?" she said between fast breaths.

"You'll be a long time finding any guard. Next time you won't be so lucky." He disappeared into the darkness of the narrow street.

"Who sent you?" she called after him. But then the windows to her empathy broke wide open. She gagged at the absence that once had been a swirl of emotions, of life. Marta braced a hand against the wall and bent over, hands braced on her knees, her breath hard, quick, and painful in her throat and chest. Who wanted her dead? Why?

She had a feeling the man called Juke was right—there wouldn't be a patrol anywhere close. Marta forced herself to move and walked the rest of the way to the tavern without seeing a single one.

She stood in the shadows just outside the light from the lanterns on either side of the door to pull herself together, to let her breathing ease, to let her heart slow. Adrenaline drained from her body, and she leaned against the wall for several minutes, head down, her cloak pulled tight against the sudden chill to her skin.

When she was steady again, her empathic dampers firmly in place, she pushed her hood back, opened the door, and stepped inside the warm room. She'd had to fight before. She'd had to kill before. The thought didn't make her feel any better.

Readen sat at a small table near the large chimney-less fireplace, a bottle of wine and two translucent green glasses in front of him. A richly dressed man, probably a holder, with two of his guards flanking him, stood talking to Readen. He laughed at something Readen said and turned back to his table.

"I am glad you were able to come, Marta." Readen rose to pull out a chair for her. "I had hoped you would when I sent you my note."

"I appreciate the invitation, Readen. I am sorry to be late, but I had a little difficulty on the way here."

He raised a brow in question, and she told him about the attack. "Excuse me for a moment, Marta." He walked to the bar to speak to a tall man, one of four guardsmen in their green uniforms. The man glanced at her, nodded, and left.

Readen sat again, poured her a glass of wine, then leaned back, idly fingering a silver medallion on a chain around his neck. "I've sent someone to find the guards who should have been on duty in that area. I'm sorry about what happened. Perhaps the wine will help you forget about it for a while."

"I haven't been to this place, but I've heard about it. Their roast lamb with marjoram and sage and orange potato casserole have quite a reputation. And also their wine."

"Shall we see if it lives up to all the talk?"

Her eyebrows rose as she took a sip of the wine. "This is very good. And I'm glad. It's been a long and tiring day." Wine and cuttings of new varieties of grape vines were excellent trade goods.

He spoke for several minutes about the vintage, which she made note of to add to the information on her Cue later. Then he asked, "Karda being difficult?"

"Not the Karda. They are always easy. Young cadets are too often not. I worked all afternoon with a young woman, a cadet. She thought she already knew everything about Karda and refused to listen until the Karda snapped its beak at her when she pulled on a covert feather too hard. She listened after that, but not happily. A Karda's beak is very sharp."

A hint of discomfort tinged his laugh, and Marta remembered too late that the Karda refused to carry Readen. She changed the subject and asked about his hold in the north. They talked about nothing much for a while: the weather, mutual acquaintances, the food. "I understand in addition to being commander of both the Mounted Patrol and the Prime Guard, you have charge of the mines to the north."

She knew how to draw people out—that was a good part of her job—gathering information about influential people—and Readen, son of Restal's guardian, was certainly that.

He sat back. "It's difficult work. Our tools are primitive—the few machines we have break down far too often because it's difficult to get good engineers to live so far from anything civilized. So the work is done by minor Earth talents. And shovel and pick. The miners are difficult. Feeding and housing them is expensive."

There's that word again. Talent. She'd watched everyone closely, searching for some evidence, but whatever talent was, it must be subtle. She'd found nothing. Earth talents obviously work with earth. How? Doing what? Chewing minerals out with their teeth? Farmers? Probably.

He smiled with one corner of his mouth. "Work goes slowly at the best of times. Not just in the mines, either. Many of the large holders have the same problems. Production all across Restal would greatly increase with more efficient tools and machinery. But it is difficult with the laws and restrictions on technology."

"Mmm," was all Marta could reply.

She listened as he talked more of the mines that were the source of much of the quadrant's wealth—of Readen's wealth, taking mental notes for Kayne. The consortium could manufacture machinery that would make the mining more productive and profitable. Readen would be open to that trade.

Marta had heard stories from others about the primitive conditions and hard lives of the miners. What wealth derived from the mines, judging by what she had seen of the quadrant—and she'd flown on patrol over much of it—was not used to make the lives of Restalans easier.

"I would be happy to take you on a tour of the mines when your duties bring you that way," he offered.

Kayne would appreciate that. He wanted more information about the strange magma stones they hadn't been able to burn but which glowed hot in every fireplace and stove she'd seen.

"I'm not sure when I'll be sent to that area, but I'll let you know. It would be interesting." And she'd like to see for herself what the conditions for the miners there were. She remembered Philipa talking about a potential revolt against what she termed the aristocracy of talent and that Readen might be involved. The consortium would want to know about that. Spending time with Readen should be educational.

Readen could be amusing, and the conversation turned to his sharp-witted comments about the people of the keep. He made her laugh. She could understand his popularity with his men. His charm was considerable. *Why, I wonder, will the Karda not carry him? It's odd.*

Readen left before she did, citing a long day ahead and a need for an early night. He promised her way back to the guild house would be well patrolled. He apologized again for their absence when she was attacked. She enjoyed her wine and decided to stay to enjoy a little more of it.

Over the next six tendays, Marta fought off two more attacks. One, she barely escaped with a shallow cut on her side that only recently healed. She would not have fared well either time had she been alone, which she took care never to be. Whoever wanted her dead had sent more than two assassins after that first time.

She'd been lucky. Someone underestimated her. She hoped Toldar Prime was different. The Mi'hiru were supposed to be universally respected, even loved for their singular relationship to the Karda, and they were politically independent of the quadrants. When the guild mother complained to Guardian Roland, she received only a cursory reply that it was being looked into.

Now she was on her way south, glad to be leaving Restal. Her three-month stay had seemed forever, and she welcomed the coming harvest season in Toldar. The whole atmosphere in all of Restal was edgy and uncomfortable. Sidhari's flight had labored wherever they went.

But as they moved across the border into Toldar, Sidhari's flight grew less labored. She moved from updraft to updraft, spiraling high, gliding long kilometers down to catch the next, seldom seeming to move her wings. But what looked like barely noticeable movements of wings and hind legs from the ground required the rider's constant adjustments in the air that made legs and body collect aches and pains over long flights.

It was one of Adalta's rare sunny days, though a dark gray bank of clouds to the west threatened. Sidhari wouldn't fly directly toward Toldar Prime. She detoured several times around circles surrounded by wide forests. From high in the sky they looked like shallow bowls with the trees graduating in height from the inside out.

They stood out on the barren plains of Toldar. The circles were smaller and less frequent in the centers of vast forests. The new plantings around them were evident, where they hadn't been in Restal. Yellow, red, and bronze flecked the forests of late summer, early fall. Summers were all too short on Adalta with its cooler red sun.

Toward evening Marta began to look for a place to land for the night. They flew over unreclaimed land interspersed with irregular areas of prairie surrounding small watering holes. The slanting light from behind gleamed on the long bronze flight feathers of Sidhari's wings. Their shadow was no longer beneath them but moved across the ground way to the east.

They each spotted a small herd of red-striped, dun kurga at the same time, and Sidhari headed toward them. Marta unstrapped her short recurve bow, strung it, and pulled the top from her quiver, carefully locking her empathic senses behind walls. Their shadow flashed over the herd, startling them into a graceful leaping dash.

Marta singled out a doe lagging behind. The Karda held her wings steady in a glide close behind the fleeing kurga. Just as Marta shot, Sidhari hit a pocket of turbulence, and the shot went wide. The kurga disappeared into a thicket of the short evergreens that dotted the barren land. Sidhari's wings moved in powerful thrusts as they surged back up. She would have to hunt for herself in the morning.

Far from any villages or handy traveler's hostels, she and Sidhari would need to rough it again. Probably in the rain, she thought ruefully, looking to the west. She spotted a small grove of cottonwoods with a brief flash of blue that meant a water source—one of the oases that dotted the sterile lands that covered most of Adalta. She leaned forward and concentrated on projecting a picture of landing there to Sidhari, and they flipped into a steep dive.

Wind tore through Marta's hair, and the ground rushed to meet them. Sidhari tilted and twisted her wings and tail to level out and her feet fisted into landing mode. Marta grabbed the pommel handle and leaned forward, hairs from the long mane whipping her face. She lifted in the stirrups, taking her weight on her ankles and calves and doing her best to absorb the shock of landing without banging her seat in the saddle or bloodying her nose on the crest of Sidhari's neck and throwing the Karda off balance.

Sidhari's wings flared, and she met the ground on her hind feet, then her forefeet hit, momentum carrying them into a lope that slowed to a trot. Marta posted on weary legs in the saddle, and they came to a stop near the cottonwoods.

Landings are rough however much Sidhari tries to make them smooth.

Marta unbuckled the flying straps from her legs, tossed her heavy packs to the ground and slid off, rubbing her numb bottom when she landed. She stripped the saddle off, pulled out hunks of dried meat from the canvas sack tied atop her saddlebags, tossed them to Sidhari.

"I apologize for missing the kurga. Dried meat is a poor substitute for a fresh young kurga." She found a place under a spreading cotton- wood, the largest of several softly chattering in the light breeze, stashed her packs and went back for the saddle rigging.

A small stream hidden in tall reeds appeared and disappeared through the grove of cottonwoods, sometimes running above ground and sometimes below, disappearing before it reached the end of the little valley. At least it was rock-bottomed, not mud. She would lose her taste for water if she had to strain the mud through her teeth as she had last night.

Dry downed wood was easy to collect. She cut away a circle of sod and dug a small pit for her fire to keep sparks from flying. Toldar was not as barren as Restal. There were wide swaths planted with a variety of grasses, and hectares of grain fields surrounded villages. The prairie was golden—grass heads hung heavy with seed—and ripe for burning.

The small fire she kindled was comforting as the wind picked up and the sky darkened. She balanced a small pot of water for tea on the creek rocks she'd placed in the pit and filled another with more water, chopped up dried meat with a mixture of dried vegetables and herbs and set it to simmer into a thick stew. She let the tea steep for a few minutes, poured herself a cup, and sat back, leaning against the tree, waiting for her supper to cook, listening to the musical murmur of the cottonwood leaves in the quickening breeze.

She was finally adjusting to the feelings she always sensed around her, the small consciousnesses of the animals, the distant, deep, steady thrum from the trees and the prairie, and the quietly insistent aware- ness of expectation that surrounded her when she loosened her shields.

Sidhari wandered up and lay down beside her, blocking the cool wind. Marta reached out and scratched the feathers on the top of her head.

"I wonder what it will be like, Sidhari," she said. "I hope Toldar is a nicer place than Restal. The land is richer, at least. The people should be more prosperous if it's governed well at all."

A flash of lightning fired the darkening sky, followed by a sharp slap of thunder. "Uh oh. I think we'd better get ready for rain. You can't fly when there's lightning. We'll not be going back up for a while." She pulled her blanket and a small waterproof tarp out of her pack and moved away from the big tree. Cottonwoods were brittle, and the chance of the storm sending a limb crashing to the ground on top of her was too likely to ignore. She anchored the tarp at one end with a few large rocks she carried up from the tiny stream and propped the other end on a couple of stout sticks she braced with rope and stakes. It made a decent shelter if a tight fit. The air stilled. The sensation of other consciousnesses that were constant background noises in her mind calmed, as if the creatures around her pushed aside hunger and fear in the wait for rain. The prairie lit with gold-green light. Lightning cracked, and thunder boomed frequent and close. Hurriedly walking out into the prairie, she tore bunches of tall grasses to soften her bed. She covered the pile with her blankets and decided her stew was ready.

Marta picked the pot up, pulling her jacket sleeve down to shield her hand from the heat. She ate quickly, watching the sky. It was almost full dark by the time she finished. The wind started again, blowing hard, carrying the sweet smell of rain on the prairie. She made her way to the creek in the growing dark, washed her utensils, and stumbled back to the fire just as the clouds opened and the deluge began. She didn't worry about putting out the remains of her tiny fire. It wasn't going to last in this.

She wormed her way under the shelter, wedged herself between her packs with Sidhari's saddle at her feet, and pulled the blanket around her. Rain pounded the tarp. She heard Sidhari stir and tuck herself close to the opening. The pelting of the rain on the tarp was a lullaby.

She sighed and burrowed deeper into her bed of grasses. It wasn't that comfortable, but she didn't care. She was so glad to be out of Restal. She hadn't realized how tense she'd been until she'd put enough distance behind her to relax. Tomorrow she'd be in Toldar Prime with a whole new set of challenges.

She lay awake for a long time, listening to the rain and the wind, reveling in the sounds and the fresh, clean smell of late summer rain. She was getting practiced enough at keeping up the walls in her mind that the surrounding consciousnesses were nothing more than soft brushes across her thoughts. They were almost comfortable. She wondered if she'd miss them if they went away.

She opened her mind bit by bit. The grass trembled with every lightning strike. The leaves and roots of trees and grass drank in the sweet clean rain. The prairie knew. It feared the terror of fire brought by lightning and at the same time welcomed its cleansing force and the promise of life-giving moisture.

What a potent place this is. I can almost hear it speaking to me, to muscle and bone, a force seeping into me from rain and rocks and dirt and trees. I felt nothing like this in Restal.

At the edge of sleep, she worked her hand out of the blanket and wiggled it down through the grasses piled under her, pushing her fingers into the cool, damp soil, the energy tingling up through her hand and arm. *I am imagining this.* She fell asleep, connected, and had a long conversation with Adalta, the beautiful creature who had welcomed her when she arrived. But in the morning she didn't remember.

CHAPTER SEVEN

The dining hall at Toldar Keep was more welcoming than the one in Restal Prime, Marta thought as she looked around. Polished red granite walls, paneled above in rare pale bleached walnut, glowed in the golden light that streamed at a low angle from the tall windows on the far side of the room.

A steward lit bronze oil lamps in ornamental brackets on the walls. Several large round tables with chairs stood in no particular order around the room. No head table on a dais separated the "important" from the "unimportant." It was a room designed to make people feel comfortable, not to impress or intimidate as Guardian Roland's hall in Restal had been.

The boy manning the door was as awkward as Marta felt. He blushed as he asked her name, though she knew she was the only Mi'hiru invited for tonight. It was her introduction to Toldar, to Guardian Me'Gerron, and probably at least some of his councilors. Certainly Altan Me'Gerron, heir and Commander of the Karda Patrol, whom she hadn't met yet.

She'd only arrived four days before. They were more prompt to welcome her than had been the case in Restal. She hoped it was indicative of better relations with the Karda. The boy stumbled over his too large feet as he led her to a table at the far side of the room and introduced her.

Guardian Stephan Me'Gerron smiled and gave her the traditional greeting, "Welcome to Toldar, Marta. May our table provide you sustenance, may our land provide you work to suit your heart and hands, and may you find safety within our walls in your rest. We are glad to have you." He grasped her forearm. "Our Mi'hiru are too few for the work they have, and we need you."

Tall, broad in the shoulders, with silver-streaked blond hair, laugh lines creased the corners of his eyes. Elegant in an informal crisp linen shirt, fine black wool trousers held by a wide, tooled leather belt with a brass buckle shaped like the head of a deer, and a long vest of heavier wool—he carried a confidence that stated his rule here was in no doubt. Stephan turned to introduce the tall woman next to him. "This is my bonded, Elena."

Only a hand shorter than the Guardian, Elena's long lighter blond hair was pulled back in a soft twist at the nape of her neck. Her face would have been severe in its classic beauty but for the light in her intelligent eyes. Silver streaked her hair, too. Her simple dress, the same color as Stephan's vest, was long and high-necked. It draped elegantly over her shoulders, full sleeves coming to a point on the backs of her hands.

She held out her hand and grasped Marta's forearm in welcome. "I hope to see much of you, Marta. I look forward to getting to know you and Sidhari." At Marta's look of surprise that Elena knew her Karda's name, she said, "I was once a Mi'hiru, and I miss working with the Karda. I spend as much time in the mews as I can spare from my duties."

That's why she looks familiar. I've seen her there.

"Sometimes I think Mother would like to escape all this and go back to her life as Mi'hiru entirely. I'm Altan Me'Gerron." The young man who appeared behind Elena was tall, with a body and carriage that showed the physical strength and grace of many hours of flying and weapons work. Marta watched as he wrapped an arm around Elena's waist and kissed the top of her head.

"Welcome back, dear," Elena said. "I hope your patrol was uneventful."

"Mostly," he replied. His eyes scanned Marta, his mouth curled into a smile, and his eyes flashed approval. He wasn't looking at her face.

Just which part of me is it he approves of? All he knows of me is what he sees. Is he that shallow? That arrogant?

Red-blond hair curled softly around his face where short strands slipped from the long tail hanging down his back bound with several bands of silver. His sculpted cheekbones, high forehead, and clear green eyes were a combination of both parents—his mother's beauty and his father's confident air. He wore clothes similar to his father's, brown trimmed with green braid. Full shirtsleeves didn't mask the strength in his shoulders and arms.

He and Marta clasped forearms a moment too long. An electric shock of power surged up her arm. His eyes widened, and she dropped his arm. She rubbed her tingling hand on her skirt. Her arm was numb, and she moved her fingers with difficulty.

"I'm Altan, their son," he repeated, after a moment. "Welcome."

His polite expression didn't change. He must not have felt the shock. He waved a hand at the table next to the guardian's.

"Come sit at my table, please. Away from all the old people here."

"Jenna will be glad to see you are back. She asked when we expected you this morning," Elena said.

"Um."

Marta was sure his eyes rolled. He started to take Marta's arm, then just gestured. A brief frown flicked his forehead.

Maybe he did feel it. It hurt, whatever it was. Yet another strange something from this world to make her think she was going crazy. If it was something in the water, maybe she'd better stick to wine and ale. Being drunk all the time couldn't be any worse. Except for those next mornings.

Altan introduced the group at the table. Commander Jaden, in the dark green uniform of Toldar Guard, sat at her left. They clasped arms, and he smiled his welcome.

A dark-haired beauty in lace-embellished green velvet sat next to the empty chair that could only be Altan's. She gave Marta a long, cool look, and didn't offer an arm clasp. Marta felt plain and uninteresting in her burgundy dress uniform with its split skirt, its short, fitted jacket, and neither braid nor embroidery.

"I don't know how you can be around those creatures all the time. They look at you like you're cake on a plate." She shuddered and turned a brilliant smile toward Altan. "Welcome home, Altan."

Altan nodded with a half-smile and continued introducing Marta. The young woman, Jenna Me'Nowyk, flushed and turned to her opposite dinner partner, Ashlyn, a petite girl with wispy brown hair and a sharp face.

Amused, Marta concentrated on remembering the rest of the introductions. Mostly young people—in fact, mostly young women, she noted. Five of them, all daughters of holders in Toldar. Mistra, a short and very young girl, with a round face, kept her head down and picked at her cuticles. Cori, bland, blond, and bored. Andra, whose brown eyes never stopped moving, flicking from face to face, teeth chewing at her lip as if she were frantically trying to think of something to say. And Staci, whose face was too red, whose laugh was too loud, whose pale blue silk and velvet dress was loose where it should be tight and tight where it should be loose.

Six females and only three males. The oh-so-way-too-handsome Altan and Commander Jaden, with thinning hair and shoulders almost as broad as he was tall. Across from where Altan was seating Marta, Counselor Jeffreys, a slight young man with pale grey eyes in a sharp, thin face was trying to talk to Mistra, his expression patient. Altan introduced him as the counselor from Toldar's coastal holding, Jenna's father's holding.

The heir's table seemed very popular among the younger female set. There were none anywhere else in the room.

She glanced at Altan, then away quickly when she found him watching her, a puzzled twist in his expression. She could hear Kayne's voice in her head. "Use your sex, Marta."

But she couldn't. She just couldn't. The thought was ugly. She picked up her glass of wine, staring down into the clear amber liquid for a moment, then drank. She wished I could just have another glass and then another and forget about what Kayne expected of her.

She looked up and met Altan's eyes for too long. He turned away to Cori and murmured in her ear. She almost lost her studied blandness.

She'd concentrate on his arrogance. Ignore the rest of him. Playing with women is something he enjoyed, maybe more than he should. Marta could play, too.

A quartet of musicians entered carrying stringed and wind instruments. A fifth followed with a small hand drum swinging from one hand. They set up without fuss at the north end of the large room. The soft music they began to play muted the sound of silver on fine china and the clink of crystal glasses.

Stewards moved silently between the tables carrying large platters and bowls, serving orange potatoes with caramelized onions, chopped spinach in a creamy, nutmeg flavored sauce, and small stuffed birds Marta recognized as a cross between quail and a native bird she couldn't remember the name of.

The smell from a basket of warm bread permeated the air as a server set it in the center of the table with a china bowl of pale yellow butter. Marta was hard put not to start right in and tear the bird apart with her fingers.

The four days since she and Sidhari had arrived had been long busy days—getting to know her way around the mews and familiarizing herself with the Karda, the various Karda Patrollers, and the Mi'hiru—and she was hungry. She ate every bite on her plate and two thick slices of nut bread generously smeared with butter.

She saw Jenna glance at her empty plate and sniff, brows raised, mouth twisted with satisfaction as if she could dismiss Marta as a threat. Apparently, Marta's appetite was too hearty to be correct. She noticed Jenna's plate was lightly touched as were those of most of the other young women, except for bland, blond Cori.

Between bites, Marta and Commander Jaden discussed the Karda serving Toldar, with Altan adding a few words from across the table. Altan's and Jaden's knowledge about the individual Karda impressed her. In fact, they gave her useful information about some she had met and several she hadn't—whose feet needed more attention, what patrollers certain Karda preferred and vice versa, whose rigging required checking more often because their turns were sharper and hard on the straps holding the rider secure.

Altan paid close attention to her conversations, glancing her way often. His intensity made her uncomfortable. Especially as she was aware, every time he spoke to her, of the tension from the distaff guests at the table, despite her tight shields. Mainly from Jenna, sitting next to him and playing the part of his very own queen bee.

Marta watched Altan banter with the women. He was skillful at steering his attentions evenly, though Jenna tried to dominate the conversations—touching him often with a proprietary air. Marta felt his amusement.

He'd do better to be alarmed. If he isn't careful, she'll have him caught before he even knows there's a trap.

But the longer she watched, the more she noticed the skill with which he handled the flirting. He was very practiced, never paid more attention to any one person than the others. He wasn't about to fall prey to one of them, especially someone as predatory as Jenna. Marta pointedly ignored her relief at that.

"How is the harvest in Restal, Mi'hiru?" Counselor Jeffreys asked her, speaking across the table. "How welcome will trade for Toldar's surplus be to them this year?" He was young for a counselor. Eyes sparkling with wit and intelligence behind wire-rimmed glasses lit his narrow face. He watched the interplay between Altan and the five young women at the table as well, amusement adding savor to his dinner.

"I know little about that," she informed him, though she did know more than she wanted to admit. She was glad to have something take her attention away from the flirting before it drowned her. "Just that their land is rough and poor in most places, so their harvest can't be substantial enough for the population. Don't you usually trade with them for the foodstuffs they can't raise?"

"Yes, and it would be helpful to know just how much they'll need this year. It's difficult to find out, and knowing would make bargaining much easier." He smiled. "We'd have an edge if we knew how needy they are. It's difficult to find out before the negotiations begin."

That surprised her—until Jaden, seeing her confusion, explained in his deep baritone, "Our people are seldom welcomed across their borders. The relations between our quadrants is uneasy. Too many raiders find refuge in Restal."

Dessert arrived, cherry apple tarts laced with a potent brandy sauce. Servers removed the dishes and platters, and the music grew louder, increasing in tempo. Jaden stood and held his hand out to Marta, smiling.

"May I have this dance, Marta? It would be an honor to be the first to dance with our newest Mi'hiru."

She saw Jenna stiffen. Marta wondered if the haughty young woman expected to be the first to be asked. "No, the honor and pleasure would be mine. Thank you." And they moved out into the open space on the west side of the room where a group was forming.

Marta loved the dancing popular in this culture. Old-fashioned waltzes, slow and intimate, mixed with more prevalent group dances she thought copied ancient country dances, moves called by one of the musicians. Couples came together and moved apart in fast, breath-stealing swirls.

It surprised her that the guardian was not the first on the floor. In Restal no one dared ask another to dance until the guardian and his sons took the floor. It was more informal here. Altan leaned across the table in furious, friendly debate with Jeffreys, moving implements and glasses around the table to illustrate. Jenna glared at the counselor.

When Jaden returned her to the table, Altan appeared at her elbow before she took her seat. "Could I share my first dance with our guest of honor?" he asked, his mouth curved up on one side in a slight smile. The music started. Her stomach clenched. *Oh, no. It's a waltz.*

Marta felt Jenna's glare hot on her back and glanced around at her. *If she isn't careful, her face is going to get stuck that way. Oops. It already has.*

"Guest of honor?" Marta was surprised.

"Of course. We always honor new Mi'hiru with a dinner when they rotate in. You're important to Toldar. We want you to know that."

He took her arm, and again a surge of energy shocked her, just short of painful. His green eyes lingered on her face an instant too long, and a frown flashed so quickly she wasn't sure she even saw it. His expression gave no hint that he felt anything. He took his arm away and bowed slightly gesturing her toward the dance floor.

The strange energy dissipated. They moved seamlessly together, their bodies seeming to coordinate each movement with only the slightest pressure on her waist from his firm hand as they circled the floor to the ancient music.

The tune was slow, almost dreamy, and Marta caught herself wishing he would pull her closer so she could rest her head there in the hollow where his neck met his broad shoulder. His arms tightened around her, and she relaxed against him. Then she realized what she was doing and pushed away, the movement abrupt. He stiffened and loosened his hold, looking down at her, confused. She looked away.

This relationship would be professional—Mi'hiru to heir, like her casual friendship with Daryl. That would be close enough. Kayne would have to be satisfied with that. She looked up at Altan, ignoring the pull of those green eyes and asked him about his Karda, Kibrath. "I've been told you were chosen. Men aren't favored that often."

"Not so, Mi'hiru." His voice was cool. *Apparently, a professional relationship was what he wanted, too.* He made no effort to flirt as he had with the others. "Some holders and most guardians are chosen. There are several female holders but only one female guardian now, so, yes, men are sometimes favored. Restal's Armsmaster Krager is bonded also."

Bonded, chosen, favored—a litany of words to describe this relationship I have with Sidhari. And they don't help me at all to understand what it is.

For the whole dance, Jenna glared at them from the arms of Counselor Jeffreys, whose clamped lips failed to hide his grin. *I must be poaching in her territory.* Marta pulled herself back together, and they talked about the Karda and her stay in Restal. He spoke with surprising insight about the Karda.

"You seem to know the Karda very well," she said.

He looked down at her, head tilted. "Well, of course. I'm Commander of the Karda Patrol."

"Oh! Yes, of course." She flushed. She knew that.

"I guess that shows you how important everyone thinks I am. No one thought to mention it." He laughed.

She grinned up at him. "They take you for granted, do they? That must be hard on the ego."

"You can't imagine. I suffer from it daily." He tightened his hold slightly, then loosened it, as if he'd just noticed how close he held her, and changed the subject. "What have you seen of the Circles of Disorder in Restal? I've heard from several traders that they are growing almost unchecked."

Marta didn't quite know what to say. She still didn't understand about the circles. "I did notice that they are bigger than the ones I saw in Toldar as I flew over, or rather around them. Much bigger. And there aren't as many new plantings there as here. Well, actually, none that I saw. That's all I know. And Sidhari refused to fly over any of them, there as well as here."

Altan looked surprised. "Of course she would."

Marta stiffened slightly. *Once again I put my boot in my mouth, and the polish tastes terrible. What in the world are those circles?*

"They never do," he said.

"I've always wondered why?" said Marta, trying to recover from her gaffe.

"Don't you know? You're a Mi'hiru. You're supposed to know everything there is to know about Karda." He raised an eyebrow at her, and the corner of his mouth tilted up again.

"Oh, yes," she retorted. "I do. Just not that."

94

"Or where they come from or why they consent to let us ride them or where they go when they disappear."

"That too." She laughed. *He's so easy to talk to.* Then she realized he was holding her closer again. Her head could rest in that spot between his neck and shoulders if she let it. She pulled away slightly, and he let her, after a moment. A bemused look flicked across his face. *He doesn't realize we're dancing too close.*

Marta glanced around to see if anyone noticed. Jenna glared at them from the arms of Counselor Jeffreys, who watched her, looking amused. *Uh oh. She noticed. I'm in trouble here if I don't stop this right now.* She started asking him about Toldar's traditions for celebrating the upcoming Harvest Festival.

"I'm usually exhausted by the time it comes around. The harvest is hard work, but the festival is great fun, even for the tired and weary. And sore. We work hard, and we pay for it." He smiled down at her.

"You work the harvest yourself?" Marta was surprised. She didn't think either Daryl or Readen had ever done that in Restal. She couldn't imagine Readen laboring in the fields and raising a sweat.

"Of course. We sometimes have to rush to get it in when there's a break in the weather. It takes all of us. When you're free, you'll prob- ably be called out to help, too." He quirked a brow and looked down at her. "Are you up to that?"

"I think I could handle it. It'll be like going home again." They looked at each other for a long time. Then she lowered her head. Her false history left an acrid taste on her tongue. She avoided his eyes for the rest of the dance. He did the same. Their graceful and too-intimate coordination made it difficult.

The music ended on a soft note, and they stood, holding each other for just a moment too long. Not touching, they walked quickly back. Counselor Jeffreys stood immediately and came around to ask her for the next dance.

She looked at Altan as he thanked her for the dance. A strange expression pulled at his face. Hers probably matched it. She was so confused.

"I enjoyed that," she said, her words soft.

Three tendays later, Altan walked through the streets of Toldar Prime, a pack slung over each shoulder. He hardly noticed the people he passed, nodded without thinking when someone spoke to him, dodged bicycles, horses, hawker's carts. He walked past the shop he was headed for and had to turn back.

Stepping up the worn stones of the entrance, he greeted the shopkeeper, "Hey, Eiryk. Kibrath and I need trail grub for about three days. We'll be gone for a tenday or so, but we'll hunt for most of what we need." He grinned. "Just in case, we still ought to have some supplies. I don't want to dig for tubers like Kibrath does. They taste like old straw. What have you got for me?"

Eiryk grinned back at him. "Hey, to you, too, Altan. Good hunting weather now. And the weather watchers say the rain may hold off for a few days. Where you headed? It'll be snow soon in the mountains." He began packaging slabs of dried meat in two evenly divided large packets.

"Up the Crescent River to a small valley below Adjuna Mountain. The valleys and canyons up there are good hunting. The young barla should be a perfect size by now. And they are good eating. About right for a meal for Kibrath and me."

"But not easy to hunt. Summer's long gone, all too short, and we're well enough into fall for early storms. Hope you packed warm cloth- ing. That's pretty far into the mountains. I don't know anyone else who ventures in that far." He added several packets of dried vegetables. "Be careful. I wonder if we'll ever know what the interior of the mountains is like, inaccessible as it is. I've heard the Karda won't fly over them."

"Sometimes we see Karda there from a distance, but Kibrath won't talk about it. None of the other Karda, either." Altan tossed a couple of bags of dried fruit onto the pile collecting on the counter.

"What are you going to do besides spend most of your time chasing goats and casting seed?"

"Barla taste a lot better than goat, Eiryk, and hopefully there'll be deer. I'm going to hunt and think. I started building a small cot below Adjuna mountain when I got old enough for my parents to let me go out on my own."

He laughed. "I didn't tell my parents about it until last year. I don't think they'd have let us fly so far if they knew. My first efforts were pretty pitiful, and it fell down as fast as I could put it up. It's habitable now. A great place for thinking."

"Now what do you have to think about, young Altan? Women, probably. You should be thinking about marriage. Starting a family." Eiryk stretched to reach packets of tea from a high shelf, looked over his shoulder and waggled his eyebrows.

Altan caught the packets he tossed. "I'm too young for a family."

Eiryk cocked a fist on his hip and looked at him. "You're old enough. You just don't want to be. You'd have to slow down and get caught."

"I'm still raising myself. I don't need to be worrying about raising young ones yet. And there are too many pretty women to settle on one."

There was silence for a few minutes. Altan stuffed purchases into his pack. Eiryk turned away from the shelf with soup packets, holding on to them when Altan reached out.

"You need to think about letting one of them catch you. You are the only heir to the guardianship. No one wants a talent fight between holders if something happens to you and your father. Look what the last one did for Restal. They never recovered, and you know what their current guardian is like." He let go the packets and turned back to find something else.

Altan winced. Rumors were already rife about the number of holders with daughters visiting in the last few months. And several guardians with marriageable daughters had happened to mention them to his father in their correspondence about the upcoming assembly in Rashiba Prime. He didn't need to encourage them—just enjoy them.

He ignored a twinge of guilt and picked up two containers of clarified butter, matches, four sleeves of travel biscuits, and a bundle of small candles for his travel lantern. Eiryk helped him stow everything in his two large packs, already heavy with seed for the tough mountain grasses he would scatter.

"Four argents and three coppers. Do you want me to put it on the keep account?"

"Thanks, Eiryk. My personal account will do."

"If you want to sell the hides when you get back, let me know. There's always a demand for barla hides."

"Thanks, but I need new winter riding gear. I'll take them straight to Rodrig myself."

Eiryk laughed. "Good hunting, Altan."

Altan hefted the packs, headed out the door and down the cobbled street, dodging carts, wagons, bicycles, and horses, the crowd of shoppers, and kids darting every which way between them. Even the occasional beggar.

As he neared the edge of the town away from the market, the crowds thinned. Here were residential houses, compact buildings of two and three stories with red sandstone walls decorated with narrow courses of dark yellow or red-orange brick, arched windows and doors—even an occasional squat tower rose above gabled roofs.

The first settlers on Adalta had included several consummate, inventive masons, and the skills had been handed down in their families for centuries. Wood was long gone when they landed, and the planted forests were still considered a precious asset and carefully harvested. Building was always with stone or adobe, slate or clay tile for roofs, iron and metal salvaged from the Ark Ship for gates and supports.

Small gardens rested behind the short front walls, with tidy straw and compost mulch covering harvested rows of vegetables and berry bushes. Espaliered fruit trees spread against the side fences. The occasional withered cherry apple still hid on a branch here and there. A few fall-bearing bushes drooped with not-quite-ripe berries. Altan hoped he could find wild ones, but at that altitude it was probably too cool for them this late in the season.

He made his way through the outskirts of town to the small gate beside the women's guild house that led to the Karda mews.

Kibrath waited for him in his roomy stall, head looming high over the sides.

Altan reached up and scratched the bronze head of the giant Karda. "Someday you'll have to tell me how you always know to meet me when we're going to fly out." He ran his hands over the huge copper and brown wings, down the slender legs, and checked for cracks or nicks in the long, sharp black talons and the horny pads of landing mode. He found a currycomb in the tack cabinet on the wall of the stall and began to untangle Kibrath's mane.

"How do you get so tangled from one time to the next? You look like you've been rolling in thistles."

~I work hard at it. If you didn't have to brush me occasionally, you'd get in even more trouble than you already do,~ Kibrath telepathed to him. He made sharp clicking noises with his vicious beak and crooned with content when Altan started on his shoulders.

Sober and distracted, Altan didn't answer Kibrath's jibe. He looked up. Marta worked on the other side of the aisle. He stared at her. Her body leaned into the Karda she was grooming as she occasionally brushed her long mahogany hair from her face with the back of her hand. She stopped for a moment to pull a clasp from her pocket and gathered her hair into it, her body arching as she reached back.

His breath caught. His fingers itched to catch in her hair. He wanted her to turn and smile at him with the warm, open smile she directed at others. She bent over to check the horny hoof pads on Sidhari's feet.

He jerked his attention back when she glared over at him as if she could read his mind. Uh oh. He was caught. He looked back at her, his expression bland as he could make it. If she thought he was having prurient thoughts, she was right. But that's all it was. All thought, no action.

The big Karda nudged Altan with his head, half knocking him off his feet. ~Pay attention to what you're doing, not the girl who won't have you.~

Altan laughed and brushed harder. ~Hey, now. Be nice. We're almost done here,~ he replied silently to Kibrath's pathing voice in his head. He finished the grooming, pulled the saddle rig from its stand and began strapping it on. Kibrath held his wings out from his body as Altan pulled the cinches and straps around his powerful breast and shoulders. ~It's just that she's new,~ he pathed to Kibrath. ~I'll get over it.~

~Of course you will,~ Kibrath pathed back and butted him with his head. ~Get over what?~ Altan felt him shake with laughter.

CHAPTER EIGHT

Altan and Kibrath spent their first night on the bank of the southern fork of the Barleyn River and a lazy morning waiting for the air to warm enough for thermals to form. He sprawled against his packs drinking tea, relishing growing warmth from the sun moving up the cobalt sky. The sound of the river flowing noisy and icy cold out of the craggy mountains to the west carried away thought. They weren't far from the southern pass through the mountains to the Coastal Holdings.

The energy of Adalta beneath him was tangible, the gentle force that always pulsed through him. He pulled on it and pinched a tiny mix of Earth and Air to form a ball of fire between his fingers. He set a water shield and played with the flame, passing it back and forth between his hands, rolling it from the fingers of one to the other, keeping it small as a match flame.

He let it go after several minutes and it floated away, fading as he withdrew the tiny tendril of his talent connection. He rolled to kneeling and spread his hands flat on the ground in front of him. He stayed that way for a long time, feeling the power curl through him.

Kibrath looked up, his beak stained from tearing at clumps of succulent green grass. ~Let's go, lazy one. It's warm enough by now.~

Altan laughed and stood, grabbed the saddle and tossed it up on the Karda's back. He was practiced at keeping all the straps and buckles in order. Packs loaded and Altan strapped in, Kibrath loped up the riverbank, took off, and found a thermal that lifted them high. Altan didn't have to think about moving with the vigorous surges of their takeoff—he'd been flying since he was big enough to fit the small saddle his mother had made for him when Kibrath appeared and announced Altan was his.

It was second nature and left him free to think. Not that he wanted to think right now. Contrary to what he had told Eiryk, and much as he didn't want to, he was going to have to resign himself to giving up his freedom and finding a life mate before much longer. He could put it off a few more years, but the pressure was increasing.

Every time he turned around, his mother was behind a curtain pushing Jenna Me'Nowyk at him. She was pretty enough, if a little short for his taste. Her family connections would be a tremendous asset to Toldar. Holder Me'Nowyk had brought her to Toldar Prime for the month to meet him, hoping for just such a match. Altan blew out a hefty sigh. Summer had brought a plethora of visitors with young girls to Toldar Prime, starting with Spring Planting Festival. He shuddered.

Jenna was intelligent enough, he supposed, and her political connections were an advantage. Her witty comments about people, too often aimed at the other visiting holders' daughters, cut a bit deep. He hadn't found her remark about the new Mi'hiru's sinewy arms and "mannish uniform" funny.

His mind wandered to the way Marta looked in it, the freedom with which she moved and the grace with which she danced. The clean herbal smell of her hair. Lavender. He rubbed his arm. Those strange shocks when he had first met her. What had they been? It hadn't been ordinary static, and it never happened again.

When rotations put them together on patrol, she kept a professional distance. He couldn't get serious about her. No political connections. No advantages to Toldar. And her lack of interest in a more casual relationship was so evident it glared at him.

Jenna could draw a little power, and her Air talent dominated. Probably why her humor was so barbed. Sarcasm and hot temper plagued Air talents with not enough Earth for balance. When the once-a-tenday dinner and dancing was over last night, he was relieved. She pouted when he told her he'd be away for the next tenday or so and complained to his mother. Jenna spent a lot of time with his mother. That worried him.

~Yes, it probably should,~ said Kibrath, who waggled his wings, and Altan had to grab the pommel. ~You were about to fall off.~

~Sorry. Wandering thoughts. And I never fall off.~ He felt the big Karda rumble with a laugh. ~You're not supposed to listen to my thoughts, chicken head. Do you know your beak is green? What have you been eating?~ Altan retorted.

He sucked in a long, deep breath and let it out slowly through pursed lips. ~I'm afraid she expected a declaration of undying love last night. And I haven't done a thing to bring that on. I've been more than proper with all of them. Why is it when you finally reach the age of freedom-from-parents there is so much pressure to mate? For women and men alike?~

It wouldn't do to raise expectations or hurt anyone. Or cause political problems. His mother was already pressuring him to choose.

Altan sighed again, and a picture of Marta wiggled into his thoughts. She was currying her Karda in the stall across the aisle. Auburn hair hung loose down her back and brushed against her tall, lean body as she reached up to groom Sidhari's shoulder, small breasts straining against her sweaty work shirt. He blinked the vision away, frowning. Embarrassed, he could feel Kibrath's laugh through the saddle again.

~If you don't want me to hear your thoughts, you need to stop thinking so loud.~

He and Marta were thrown together often. Altan spent a lot of time in the mews, caring for Kibrath, flying with his wing of the Karda Patrol, checking with the Mi'hiru about rotations and the

Karda's readiness to fly. He'd assigned Marta to his patrol several times since she arrived to deflect attention from his efforts to avoid her.

~Oh, so that's why you've been doing that.~

~Stay out of my head, you overgrown turkey. That's not funny.~

She usually ignored any attention he directed her way. To the point of being rude. Unlike too many others.

He wondered if he wore a sign on his back that said in large letters, Open Season on Altan. There had been at least ten willing and unwilling young women visiting the keep with their parents in the last six months. He laughed. He'd become proficient in acrobatic conversation, keeping to the thin line of courtesy without straying into the broad spaces of particular interest.

Marta intruded again. Last night he caught her laughing at a sharp interchange between Jenna and Ryba when all the Mi'hiru came to Toldar Keep for dinner. Her eyes met his, and her mouth quirked up into a smirk before she looked away. Was it disdain or amusement? He shook his head, half angry at the thought, determined to think about nothing but the enjoyment of flight.

He and Kibrath scanned the countryside below as they rose farther into the mountains. The trees hadn't begun to lose their leaves yet, and the rising foothills below were a riot of red, gold, and russet punctuated by spires of dark green conifers. It was the dry season, brief as that was, and the air was crisp and fresh. The thermals were strong, and Kibrath took one up so close to the bottom of the low clouds mist beaded on his feathers and Altan's clothes and face. A pair of Karda glided into view below them flying low, hunting, a small sorrel male with a bigger female gold. A pale, shining gold he'd never seen before. They skimmed the foothills, wings moving only to adjust direction and altitude.

He started to comment to Kibrath when the couple veered up, startled by something below them in the trees. The sorrel Karda screamed and tumbled over and over to fall in a tangle of legs and wings into the top of a tree. A branch speared through one wing, and his head hung limp and twisted to one side. He didn't move.

The female followed him down, wings drawn close in a stoop, her cries high and sharp— kee, kee, kee.

Her flight faltered. Kibrath screamed and jerked. She pulled up, beat her wings to gain altitude in an awkward spiral, one wing not moving right.

Altan saw several men ride through the trees toward the fallen Karda. One of them raised something long and narrow and pointed it at the big female. She jerked again, faltered, and kept climbing, heading into the mountains. Kibrath screamed again.

~Drop down, Kibrath. I need to see who those men are.~ Fury flooded Altan. ~And I need to kill them.~ But Kibrath refused and flew after the gold, wings pumping furiously. Altan yelled at him and jerked his body to the right, trying vainly to turn the Karda to go after the men, but Kibrath ignored him, intent on the female.

Altan hoped the male Karda was dead and not dying for lack of help. *What in the world killed him? He was flying too high for a crossbow bolt to reach him. Who were those men? Raiders? Who would kill a Karda?* He'd never heard of that happening before, not for centuries, and never by a human. Karda were revered.

They flew for most of an hour. The beautiful gold labored more with every wing stroke. Kibrath positioned himself ahead of her, reducing the wind resistance, easing her flight as much as he could. Altan realized they headed toward Mounts Diriga and Adjuna above the valley where his cot stood.

She was tiring. One wing couldn't fully extend, forcing her to adjust her path constantly. But she labored on, relentless.

Altan pulled all the Air he could, pushing it up under her wings, hoping to help her stay aloft until she reached wherever it was she was headed with such desperate determination. His heart burned with pain for her. His body ached with the effort of pulling so much Air.

Finally, she started a glide toward a steep-sided, flat-topped quartz and sandstone spear rising eighty meters high at the head of a valley near the base of Adjuna mountain. He recognized this place. He'd planned to scale the tall rock this trip. His small cot was in that valley. He released the Air he pulled and took several deep breaths.

She glided, wings unsteady, toward the open bowl isolated on its top. The wind-twisted trees that circled the clearing restricted its size. The Karda began her approach. It would be a short, tricky landing.

Kibrath screamed in his head, ~She's too low. She's too low.~

He circled, uttering short, sharp cries, as they watched her touch down, falter and fall mid-landing in the center of the small meadow. She didn't get up. There wasn't enough room left for them to land. The gold lay in the center, blocking the short landing space.

Then Altan saw the large nest of sticks under the trees at the edge of the tiny clearing. He could see at least two nestlings beating their immature wings, bashing themselves against the walls of the nest again and again. He couldn't help staring.

No one had ever seen young Karda. The nesting grounds were secret and hidden, the Karda's homelands a mystery. They came into human inhabited Adalta fully grown and of their own free will. He couldn't imagine why the couple had built the nest here, at the edge of the mountains. The birth must have been early and unexpected.

The babies' shrill screeches reached him as he and Kibrath circled. The gold Karda raised her head and looked straight at Altan as Kibrath flew low over her, calling to her with soft cries, so close the air from his passing fluttered her mane. Her large, pleading eyes watched them. She was communicating with Kibrath, but Altan couldn't hear their speech.

Then Kibrath sheared off, folded his wings, and dropped in a stomach-lurching stoop for the valley below. They landed with a flurry of wings and a very short run.

Altan dismounted and looked at the steep sides of the tall mesa. Twisted trees wedged themselves into the rock in several places. Isolated tufts of wiry grass grew here and there in crevices and on narrow ledges.

If he couldn't heal the mother, if she died, and he had to, he could lower the babies from one ledge to the next. It would be grueling, especially because he'd have to do it twice, but he could do it. He could find or make enough hand- and footholds. What other choice did he have?

Kibrath butted his head against Altan's back. ~You need to hurry. She's lost too much blood. You won't be able to heal her. The nestlings will be helpless up there. They're far too young to fly.~

The nestlings would starve in the time it would take to get help from Toldar Prime. At their age, they'd be growing fast and as voracious as baby birds. He couldn't bear that. He wished he knew something about how Karda raised their young, what to expect if he went up there. Kibrath was reluctant to talk, even now. Altan had never known him to be this distressed.

Kibrath butted him again, pushing him toward the steep mesa.

"Ok. I won't try to climb up. I can drop off of you on the fly like we practiced when I was younger. And stupider. We haven't done it in a long time, but I think I can still manage. I'll have to climb back down. If I can leave enough food and I can heal the mother, then maybe we'll have enough time to go for help. It must have been the father who died back there. I wonder what kind of weapon brought him down from that far up."

He knew he was babbling while he decided what to do. He'd worked at dropping off Kibrath from a hover for a long time when he was younger, but he hadn't done it for several years. He was a good deal bigger now. Could he do it without breaking a leg?

Kibrath looked toward the top of the mesa, making agitated clicking sounds with his hooked beak. ~She's almost gone.~ Kibrath's distress was palpable. ~You'll have to bring them down.~

Altan decided.

He unbuckled his packs and the large packets of dried meat from behind the saddle and dropped them to the ground, sliding off behind them. He emptied one pack and stuffed it with some of the meat, a couple of packets of dried vegetables, two long coiled ropes, a small hammer, thirty pitons, his traveling med kit, and two blankets.

~I'm glad I'd planned on some climbing on this trip,~ he pathed to the worried and impatient Kibrath. He started to fasten it shut, then stuffed in two water bottles, his largest pot, and a ball of stout cord. He hoisted it up and secured it behind the saddle, then unclipped his sword from his belt, leaving it propped against his other pack, checked that his belt knife was secure, and mounted Kibrath.

The Karda took off. Altan didn't bother to buckle himself in, just gripped Kibrath tight with his legs, wedged his knees under the horns of the pommel, and grabbed the handle with both hands. Kibrath's body rose and fell, wings beating hard and fast in a steep ascent to the top of the mesa.

Altan unfastened the six meter length of knotted rope he kept coiled and fastened to the saddle out of old habit. As Kibrath spiraled up to the top of the rock formation, he tied one end to the handle, dropped the coil and watched it whip out behind them. They'd done this many times before. Kibrath wasn't going to let him fall. His confidence in the great Karda was absolute. They flew a slow circle over the small meadow.

He dropped his heavy pack as close to the nest of the agitated fledglings as he could and looked for the best place to drop himself. The softest place, though soft wasn't likely. At least there didn't look to be too many rocks. Finally, Kibrath made a last slow approach and Altan readied himself. He slipped off the saddle, balancing with one foot in the stirrup, both hands on the knotted rope. Kibrath back-winged and hovered as close to the ground as he could, and Altan let himself down.

Kibrath hovered. Altan swung and twisted round and round on the rope.

~Now!~ said Kibrath.

Altan swung his legs and body back and forth to stop whirling, then on a forward swing, he let go and dropped, tucked his shoulders and rolled to an uncomfortable stop in the long grass. It knocked the breath out of him, and he lay on his back, recovering, and watched Kibrath circle back up above him. The big fat chicken was probably laughing.

He got his breath back and ran the short distance to the big

Karda lying with one leg twisted wrong. Blood soaked her breast and one golden wing, running into the crushed and stained grass.

Her great head was down. Large soft eyes held his for a long moment, judging him, measuring him. Then she sighed. Sharp pain jabbed his chest, and he stretched his hand toward her. Absence swamped him as her eyes closed and she died.

Kibrath screamed above them, diving to swoop low, then making tight spirals up above her. He did this for a long time, diving down and spiraling up high into the clouds in an aerial dance, tolling deep, wild, melodious cries, his mind closed to Altan.

The nestlings were frantic with fear and wild grief, their keening loud and shrill. They shoved again and again against the sides of the nest, a tight barrier of interwoven sticks filled with a thick pile of soft dry grass. Altan recovered his pack, poured water into the pot and cut small hunks of dried meat into it to soften, then tossed the bits toward their open beaks, hoping food would calm them. Hoping they would eat it.

At first, they balked at the strange taste, spitting the pieces out, but they were hungry and their hesitation didn't last long. They stopped keening and started pushing at the high sides of the nest to get closer to him and the food. They didn't settle until they had eaten almost all the meat. He cut more to soak. They needed the moisture. He couldn't let them get dehydrated.

Kibrath flew small circles above them, uttering low, intense calls Altan had never heard him make. Altan kept his movements slow and careful and climbed over the side of the nest. They were unafraid, almost as though they looked to him for rescue. He reached out and scratched the head of the nearest, its—her, he noticed—golden feathers soft and unfinished under his fingers. Her body was long and gangly, not much bigger than a newborn foal. She held her stubby wings out as she maneuvered closer to him, making soft, crooning noises.

He felt the grief in her. The smaller brown male held back a little, not quite so willing to trust this strange un-winged creature on only two legs. Finally, worn out from fear and grief, the two settled down close together on the soft grass of the nest, their eyes moving back and forth between Altan and Kibrath above.

Altan walked over to the edge of the meadow. The sides of the tall mesa looked steeper from the top than they had from the bottom. How, by the grace of Adalta, was he going to get them down?

CHAPTER NINE

Altan picked up the heavy pack and carried it to the nest as close as he could get without agitating the babies more than they already were. How could he calm them enough to accept his touch? He'd have to handle them a lot, and it wouldn't be gentle if he were to get them off this narrow mesa. He started singing a song his mother sang when he was little. They watched him, heads cocked at the same angle.

But as soon as he approached the nest again, they scrambled to the other side, stumbling and climbing over each other. They snapped at him with shrill, agitated cries.

"Ok. I know I'd starve if I had to sing for my soup, but I'm not that bad."

~Keep singing, perhaps it will help calm them. They've never seen anything like you,~ spoke Kibrath. ~They are too young to understand when I talk to them, but I'll comfort them as well as I can.~

Altan pulled small pieces of the soaked meat and vegetables—which they weren't too sure about—and tossed them into the fledglings' mouths, moving a step closer each time. They squabbled and pushed at each other like "me first, me first." He ran out of the soaked morsels and couldn't cut more fast enough.

Were they ever going to be satisfied? He didn't think he'd brought enough. Each toss a little shorter, he coaxed them closer and closer. There was little left when they approached close enough he could touch them over the sides of the nest. They let him scratch their heads, fingers gentle in the soft feathers. They butted against him, knocking the side of the nest, trying to get closer, wanting more food. They probably thought he was a crippled Karda with no wings and not enough legs.

Kibrath circled above, crooning the low musical sounds. They watched, agitated when he flew too far away, calming when he wheeled back.

Altan unloaded his pack. He cut narrow strips from the sides of one of the blankets and rolled eight separate rolls. Twisting more pieces into two thick ropes, he used the stout cord to fasten one end of each at opposite corners of a rectangle folded from the other blanket, pulling hard to be sure they'd hold. He cut two more lengths of the cord and wrapped the loose ends of the ropes tight leaving long tails.

Uncoiling first one and then the other of the two ropes from his pack, he looped them back up with close attention. A tangled rope to fight with could mean disaster. He sang softly and had to stop and clear his throat several times when it thickened with uncertainty. If he stopped to think about what he was trying to do, he'd never be able to do it.

The fledglings listened and watched. Heads twisting back and forth, their eyes moved from him to Kibrath flying close circles above them and crooning the odd notes Altan had never heard him make.

Ready as he could be with his preparations, he packed the rolls and the pot with soaking food into his emptied pack and hung it from a stout branch on the nest. He scrambled over the tangled sticks and slowly eased himself toward them, singing nonsense words. They backed away with soft, agitated cries.

Kibrath circled close above and called with a clear musical cry.

Another sound Altan had never heard from him. The two fledglings looked up at him and settled down, one with his head on Altan's knee, letting him stroke them with gentle hands. He kept humming and talking in a low, soft voice.

He reached for the pot and began feeding them from his hand, holding his palm flat, praying he wouldn't lose a finger or worse. They picked the food delicately from his palm with their wicked sharp little beaks, jostling and pushing each other. When he stopped to cut more, they got impatient and butted him. "If we're going to get along, you're going to need to learn better manners." Finally sated, they curled their legs beneath them, put their heads down, and closed their eyes.

"Now if you'll just stand up,"—he tugged on the little female —"I'll wrap your legs. We don't want scratches and cuts on the way down."

He tried picking up one leg, but she flapped her short, barely-fledged wings and hopped away, crying out. He moved to corner her, but she got more agitated, and the little male snapped at his arm, tearing his sleeve. Finally, she began to settle. He showed her the wrappings, letting her explore them with her beak, cocking her head back and forth.

Moving slowly, he knelt by her shoulder and picked up a front foot, placing it on his knee. She was taller than he was when kneeling down, and he struggled to hold her still, talking the whole time. Moving bit by bit, he wrapped and tied the strip around her lower leg from knee to ankle, pushing the curious male's head out of his way again and again.

"Now, that wasn't too bad, was it?" He was sweating in spite of the cold when he finished, and there were three more legs to go. They went faster, and by the time he got to the male, they were both tired and less curious, and the wrapping wasn't quite such a struggle.

Altan thought about the distance he needed to cover to get them down the cliff and swallowed. But their delicate legs would be protected. There was not much else he could do. He'd just have to trust any damage would be something he could heal. There wouldn't be much energy left in him for that by the time he got

both of them down. He wouldn't allow himself an If. It was
When.

He wiped sweat off his face with his sleeve and climbed out of
the nest. Fishing the belt with his pitons out of the pack, he tested to
be sure they were secure in their pockets, buckled it on, stuffed the
hammer through it, and began untangling one side of the nest. It
wasn't easy, and he had to do it so he could put it back up again
before the male could escape.

Blocking him with his body, he pushed the female through the
gap, followed her out and wove the sticks back together as best he
could.

The female butted him from one side, and the male tried to
scramble past on the other.

Kibrath swooped down so close Altan could feel the wind from
his wings, and the Karda called out in that musical voice. He did
this several times until both fledglings looked up, heads cocked to
listen on a frequency he couldn't hear. They settled down, the
female leaning against him, pushing as close as she could. The male
circled and circled inside the nest and watched him, making soft
distressed sounds Altan heard in his head. The male was trying to
talk to him, but it was like trying to make sense of a baby's nonsense
sounds.

"I'll be back for you. I promise," Altan told him, feeling a lump
rise in his throat at the fear in those wide rolling eyes. Kibrath flew
over low again, calling, and the little male settled down on the soft
grass and hid his head under a wing, his whole body trembling.

Altan pulled the blanket sling around his sister's belly, threading
the ends of the thick twists of blanket through a loop at the end of
one of his long ropes, crossed and fastened them at opposite
corners, testing his knots several times. "Let's hope this sling holds,
girl. I can't get you down any other way. You're too big and
awkward to carry with those long, long legs."

Holding the hammock-like sling snug to her belly with one
hand, he maneuvered her to the edge of the mesa, looped the rope
around a stout tree, and tossed the loose end over the side, watching
the coils unfurl. "Here we go, baby girl," he said. She was trembling

but calm, as he lifted her over the edge and lowered her down to a narrow ledge about five meters below.

Amazed she hadn't panicked, he fastened her rope with a quick-release knot, clenched his fists, then straightened his fingers and lowered himself down the side of the mountain. He searched for each toe- and handhold, using Earth talent to secure a rock for a foot, widen a cleft for his fingers, strengthen the grip of the roots of a small tree he braced against.

He talked to her the whole time, his voice calm and low, using nonsense words or "Where is my next handhold? Will this tree hold? Will this never end?" Kibrath circled, soothing the one left behind, calming the little girl on the ledge in the same low, musical tones.

A rock broke loose, clattering down the mountain, and one of her back feet slipped off the edge. She screamed in panic, and Altan watched, frozen and terrified, as she scrambled and clawed, her backend swinging over empty air.

Frantic, he closed his eyes and reached his way into the rocks of the ledge, firming and shoring up the crumbling edge. Finally, one clawed foot found a secure hold. She pulled herself back up and stood, feet splayed, body shaking all over, eyes wild and clamped on Altan.

"Good girl," Altan called, his foot searching for its next hold. He cursed to himself. He should have checked the ledge before he let her down. It would only have taken a few moments of concentration to stabilize it.

"Good girl. I'm coming. It'll be all right, you'll see. It won't take me long." He talked to her all the way down. The side of the mesa was fissured with crevices, some with small stout trees wedging their roots deep and tight. He tested each one he grabbed, carefully sensing each foot- and handhold with his Earth talent, firming the rocks and trees where they were unstable, never taking his weight off more than one at a time, working his way down toward her, talking, talking. He could hear Kibrath calling to the little male and flying tight circles above them.

When he found himself just a few feet above her, he hammered in a piton. The first he'd had to use. Unwinding a short rope from around his waist, he pushed it through the loop on the end of the spike and tied another quick-release knot, tossing the ends down, careful not to startle her. He squeezed himself down beside her on the ledge and scratched under her chin for several moments, catching his breath. He held fast to the short rope, wedging her between himself and the cliff face, stroking her until her trembling eased.

He reached for the bag he'd sacrificed a shirtsleeve to make hanging from his belt, pulled out a few small pieces of dried meat, and offered them on his palm. She hesitated, then plucked them up and swallowed, turning her head to look at him. "You're a fine brave girl, you know. We'll make it." He rubbed her head again, and she twisted against his hand, butted his arm, then very deliberately looked over the edge to the valley far below and back at him. Altan swallowed against a hard bubble in his throat at the trust in her eyes.

He fastened one end of the short rope from the piton around his chest and leaned in, making sure she was secure between himself and the cliff face. He reached for the loose end of the long rope tied five meters above them and jerked. It fell loose, slithered down the cliff, threatened to catch on a small tree, then slid free and pooled at his feet. He hammered a second piton into a narrow crevice just above them and tested it with his hand and with his talent.

He figured it was six or seven meters down to the next ledge and thanked Adalta for the Karda's light honeycomb bones. She weighed little more than half what a foal her size would. Drawing the rope up, he coiled it on the ledge. Looping it through the end of the piton and wrapping it once around his waist, he nudged her off the edge. She panicked again, scrabbling against the side of the mountain, and he lowered her as fast as he could.

Seven times he repeated this. Several times he had to swing her back and forth to reach the next ledge. They weren't all lined up conveniently one beneath the other.

His hands bled, and his arms and legs shook with the effort of each small movement to the next crevice, the next rock, the next small, twisted tree. The rope scored his hands deeper each time he lowered her, and he couldn't afford the energy to keep healing them. But she fought him less and less. He hoped it wasn't from shock.

At last, he lowered her down the final stretch to the floor of the valley. He rappelled down on her rope and fell, exhausted, to the grass beside where she lay. She rested her head on his outstretched arm and closed her eyes. He didn't know how long they slept that way, but the sun was well past its high point when he woke. He groaned and sat up. He was going to have to do this all over again.

Touching the pulse point in her neck, he felt the beat steady and strong—her breathing was even. He didn't see any blood, so checking her for cuts and bruises could wait. He had to go back up.

He groaned and rolled onto his knees. His body screamed its protest. Both hands flat on the grass in front of him, he reached down through the ground, searching for one of the streams or pools of water that ran deep through the bedrock of Adalta. The energy of Adalta surged up into him. He directed it to sooth his strained muscles and ease the pain and raw, scraped flesh on his hands. It didn't completely erase his exhaustion, and he couldn't afford the energy it would take to heal his hands completely—healing took as much out of the healed as it did the healer, and he was both—but when he finally sat up again, he'd found enough strength to go again.

He sat for a while, watching Kibrath circle, trying to comfort the little male up there alone with his dead mother. Then his little girl began to stir, and he untied her sling. He stood, and she stood, too, never taking her eyes off him. She started making hungry noises. He found his other pack and pulled out more dried meat and vegetables. Her eyes flicked back and forth between him and the food.

He headed for his small cabin, and she followed, tromping on his heels all the way. Pushing her inside, he tossed the food to the center of the packed dirt floor and closed the door. Her distressed cries followed him back to his packs. He stuffed more food into the makeshift pouch hung from his belt and headed to the landing strip. Kibrath was already touching down when Altan looked up to call him.

It was late and closing in on dusk when he got down with the little male. There wasn't time for rest, exhausted though he was. He opened the door to the cabin and the female dashed past him, almost knocking him down. The fledglings huddled together, trembling with exhaustion themselves, heads up, frightened eyes darting everywhere. He was afraid they would bolt and hurt themselves. Kibrath settled them down, and they curled against him as close as they could get under his broad outstretched wing.

Altan started gathering sticks, carting them to where the fledglings lay. Two hours later he had a crude nest. Not as sturdy and well made as the one their parents had constructed, he thought as he stood back and surveyed it. But it would do. He threw himself down on the ground beside it, groaning as he heard them start to click their beaks and make hungry sounds. Yes, they were truly voracious. All the time.

He lay there with his head pillowed on his hands for several more minutes, then dragged himself up to find the pack of dried meat and vegetables to soak. He would have to gather a mountain of dried grass to line the nest, but that could wait until he fed them —again—*and* he and Kibrath ate, *and* he got some rest.

His torn hands smarted, his arms and legs ached, his shoulders were wrenched, and his head pounded by the time he got them fed, but Altan couldn't help but smile as the fledglings, beautiful even with their stunted, immature wings, settled, making soft, sleepy sounds, easing toward contentment.

He stumbled his way to his packs, picked them up, and headed for his small rough cot, limping. Somehow he'd gashed his calf, and it was bleeding. Dropping them inside the door, he hobbled to the narrow bed on one wall. He managed to draw enough power, moving his hand in a circle around him, to chase out any vermin who might have taken up residence in the cabin and fell onto the bed. Sleep hit him in the head.

Three hours later, loud insistent cries from the nest woke him. He sat up too fast and had to put his head back down until the world stopped swimming. He scrubbed at his face and winced. His mangled hands were bleeding. He blinked his eyes and stretched. *I better take care of these, or they'll get infected. I should have done that before I slept. But I don't think I could have.* He spread them palms up and reached his mind down into the ground at his feet, feeling the force of the planet move into his body.

He concentrated on his hands, smoothing the energy across and into them and watched as the bleeding stopped, a little pus squeezed out, deep rope burn gouges pulled together, pink scar tissue formed, and the skin firmed.

He was still too tired. Even this little effort made his head ache. He got up, groaning. There wasn't enough energy in him to do anything about his aching muscles. His leg threatened to collapse under him. Somehow he needed to find the talent force to do something about the gash on his calf, he decided, and sat, concentrating on his leg. He drew power from Adalta again. He had used all his reserves on his two descents with the fledglings. He needed to build himself up.

That would have to wait. The cries from outside were growing more insistent. He finished, stood, waited to see if he got dizzy again, lit the small lantern on the rough mantle—using a match, not the twist of Earth and Air talent that created fire—cut up more dried meat to soak for next time, and headed back out to feed them.

He smiled. *If I weren't so exhausted, I'd enjoy feeding them. They are so beautiful.*

~Please hurry with their food. While you're feeding them, I'll go hunt. I'm hungry, too, and all of us could use fresh meat. They won't get enough moisture even with the soaked meat.~

It took another day and night to line the nest with grass, rest enough between feedings to stand without passing out, and convince himself that if he left extra meat in the nest with them, they wouldn't overeat but could ration themselves. They always fell asleep as soon as their bellies were full, so he didn't think he needed to worry about that. In the dim light of approaching dawn, he cut up what was left of his supplies in small pieces and piled it in a corner of the nest on fresh grass with the three, summer-fat, long-eared birbirs Kibrath had caught.

He finished the unpleasant job of cleaning up after them, piled in more fresh grass, and called Kibrath down from where he was circling low, scouting for predators. Altan carried the saddle and one pack out of the cabin after pulling the heat from the magma stones in the little stone stove on the hearth.

He watched the big Karda land and head to the nest. Kibrath lowered his head to the fledglings and began the clicking and crooning that he used to communicate with them. He held their eyes for several long minutes, turned, and headed toward Altan and the saddle and pack at his feet.

~Were you telling them we're leaving for a while?~ Altan asked.

~They understand. At least I think they understand. But we'll need to get back as fast as we can.~ Kibrath's voice radiated concern.

The agitated fledglings watched Altan's every move, heads poking up over the sides of the nest. Altan strapped the saddle on Kibrath's back and headed for the landing meadow. Kibrath cantered across the field and took off toward Toldar Prime and help. They circled once, Kibrath calling, and the anguished cries of the fledglings echoed in Altan's ears long after they were out of range.

It was late. The sun had long set. The large half-moon was a quarter of the way up the sky, and a thin sliver of the small moon was just cresting the horizon. Altan leaned over the pommel handle and patted Kibrath's neck, ignoring the strands of mane that whipped against his face. ~Not much farther, old friend. We're almost there.~

Kibrath's wing beats were slowing. He struggled to gain height. His glides were shorter. The cold night air offered no thermals. Altan knew Kibrath didn't like to fly at night. Finally, a faint light appeared in the distance, and he heard loud cries from the skies around them.

Two Karda swooped down and took position in front of them, breaking the wind for Kibrath. His wing beats strengthened, and they gained a little more altitude. Altan spotted four more Karda headed toward them, silhouetted against a dim glow ahead. The Karda circled them. As they flew closer, the light grew into flaming torches marking the long runway outside the mews.

Kibrath dropped, and they lined up with the lights. Soon they were on the ground, cantering to a stop just outside the mews, more Karda coming in behind them. Every Mi'hiru in the place was there. And every Karda was calling out to them. It was pandemonium.

Guild Mother Solaira was there almost before he dismounted. Her tiny figure vibrated with even more energy than usual, her blue healer's cape thrown over a worn dress, red hair falling out of the bun at the nape of her neck. Mi'hiru Rayna and Mi'hiru Jordana began unsaddling Kibrath almost as soon as Altan dismounted. Marta grabbed his pack, glancing at his face, concern showing on her own.

"What is happening, Altan?" asked Solaira. "Every Karda here has been in and out all night, agitated, circling above, even in the dark. That's why we had the lights on the runway. What are you doing flying in after dark? You're both exhausted. Why would you push Kibrath that hard? What's wrong?"

The guild mother had a habit of peppering questions without waiting for answers. She put her hand on his arm and sent healing energy through him. Altan gave her a weary smile. He glanced at Marta, whose eyes flicked back and forth between him and Kibrath, her face white as she checked the Karda for damage.

"I've found two Karda fledglings in the mountains. Someone killed their parents, and I need help getting them back here." He watched Marta, her incredible blue eyes wide with shock. He was so tired he wasn't even aware that he was talking to her, only to her, his hands on her shoulders, as much to hold himself up as to hold her attention. "We haven't much time. I left them food enough for two days, I think, but they're babies. I don't know how long they can last without care or how safe they are from predators." He stumbled from exhaustion. "We have to leave at dawn. I expect you to be ready." He kept on, issuing orders for what she needed to pack, leaning on her as they headed out of the mews.

Solaira tucked herself under his other arm and frowned. She asked permission and sent her healer talent questing through him, shaking her head. "Now, let's get you to a room and cleaned up. You'll need to sleep here. You're too tired, and you have to leave too early for you to go all the way up to the keep tonight. You need healing, and you're too exhausted to do it yourself. We have a guest room for the occasional male. I'll send word to your parents. Your mother and Guardian Stephan will want to hear about this as soon as possible. I'm sure they'll be down at dawn to see you off."

"But...," Altan faltered.

~I'm fine, Altan. Get some rest. I'll be ready in the morning.~ Kibrath's eyes were already drooping shut, even as he ate what Marta piled in his manger.

Before Altan could say more, Solaira bustled him off to the baths. Fortunately, they were empty. He had little doubt Solaira would have pushed him in even if they were full of women. She left him there and went to make sure the room was ready and to send off her messengers. By then all he could think of was that hot bath and a bed with actual sheets. The stubborn set of Marta's jaw at his peremptory tone when he was issuing orders finally registered. He smiled.

CHAPTER TEN

Marta looked at the tall rock tower at the head of the valley she and Altan flew toward. The steep, craggy sides glowed pink in the soft light of early evening. Was that what he climbed down with the babies? Twice? Then flew all day and into the night —a distance that it had taken them nearly two days to travel back? She was impressed. Eanna and Darta, the two unpartnered Karda who volunteered to carry the babies, circled up above the two of them, waiting their turn to land. Kibrath and Altan landed first, cantering toward the nest.

Marta and Sidhari followed. She looked across the clearing where the two small fledglings peered over the rough nest of sticks Altan had built beside a small crude building in the shelter of low trees. She dismounted and headed toward the babies' nest, so eager to see them she didn't unsaddle her Karda. The babies' shrill cries echoed through the valley.

"Move, Mi'hiru. They're probably more than a little hungry by now," Altan said. "They're going to be cross. And they're scared." He grabbed her arm as she headed toward the nest, nearly forgetting where she was in her eagerness. "You get the gear off the Karda and brush them down. Carry the saddles in there." He pointed to the small cot near the nest. "I'll feed the hungry babies. They won't know you."

Altan grabbed one of the packs stuffed with fresh vegetables and meat, tossed it over his shoulder, and strode to the nest. Marta glared at his back. Now she remembered why she should have protested his autocratic order that she come. She unbuckled the saddles from Sidhari and Kibrath, coiled their long straps, and carried them to the small cot. Then she took the rigging off Eanna and Darta and fished through her saddlebag to find the brushes.

Why was he so rude? She paid more attention to him and the babies than to her brushing until Sidhari swiped at her with a wing. "Sorry," she muttered and went back to brushing.

When Sidhari and Kibrath were brushed, and she'd checked the wing feathers of all four, the Karda took off to hunt. Altan called, "Let's get this nest cleaned up. They're tired, hungry, and sleepy. And so am I."

"You're certainly cross enough," Marta muttered to herself. And he left the dirty job until she could help. They worked together, tossing soiled grass out of the nest. Two days was too long, as was evident from the smell.

Altan laughed when she slipped on a smelly mess and went down on her behind right in the middle of it. She made a face, which amused him even more. She started to brush at the back of her skirt and stopped, looking glumly at the mess on her hand. "I'm going to smell as bad as this nest now."

"And unfortunately, we have to share the cabin tonight." He smiled.

She gritted her teeth.

They cut fresh grass and piled it thick in the middle. Or tried. The curious fledglings wouldn't stay out of their way, nudging Marta, exploring her clothes, stretching their necks to Altan for a head scratch, scattering the grass as soon as it piled up until they wore as much grass as feathers.

By the time she and Altan finished, Marta was hot and itching. Bits of grass pricked inside her divided skirt and blouse and down the tops of her boots. The babies crooned, circled the nest, and settled, eyes drooping, tangled together. She glanced at Altan. He watched them, the planes of his face soft with affection.

She tucked herself as close as she could get, letting their quiet sounds soften her mind. The little female laid her head on Marta's knee, begging for a head scratch. Even after working with Karda for a full season, her empathy honed by contact with so many different animals on so many different planets, she still had difficulty melding with the Karda. Others insisted she was one of the best, but there was always a veil she couldn't pierce, as if they spoke to her, but she didn't hear. She seldom skipped an opportunity to work on deepening her rapport. She looked down at the fledglings. She could feel their hunger dissolve into well-being after their meal, their feeling of safety centered on Altan and Kibrath, their wary acceptance of her.

The four older Karda, replete after their successful hunt, brought three fat birbir for the babies and settled themselves around the nest as afternoon darkened the valley. Altan opened the door to the stone cot and carried both packs inside. Marta stayed, stroking the babies for a long time, then climbed out of the nest and went to the small creek below the meadow. She washed herself and the soiled back of her riding skirt in the icy water. She wrung it out as best she could, headed for the cot, and picked up the packs of feed on the way. They shouldn't leave them outside. The adult Karda would guard against predators that might be attracted but, why leave bait?

A small sandstone chimney-less stove centered the back wall. One narrow, rough bed with a coarse canvas mattress stuffed with grass stood against a side wall. There was no other furniture, only a couple of hooks and crude shelves on one wall. She dropped the packs in a corner and looked around, feeling awkward in the small space. Altan added a couple of round, porous black stones—like volcanic rock—to the ones in the stove. Then he stood and held his hands, palms out, toward it. The stones began to glow red. Marta stared. How could he do that? Her face smoothed to bland when Altan turned around. He apparently thought nothing of starting a fire—or whatever made the stones glow—with a flick of his fingers.

"Sorry, I don't have the energy to warm the room otherwise. The magma stones will heat it up soon. I've used too much..." He stopped and looked at the one bed. "One of us will have to take the floor, I guess." He waved a hand at the small bed.

What was he talking about, warming the room otherwise? I can feel the heat from the stove. That's strange enough.

"We'll draw straws for it." She worked a stiff piece of grass out of the mattress and broke it in two uneven lengths, holding them out to him in her fist. "You pick."

He picked the long twig, rubbed the back of his neck, and gave her a rueful I'm-sorry-but-not-sorry-enough-to-give-up-the-bed grin. He removed his sword belt, twisted back and forth, stretching his back, and sat on the bed to take off his boots.

I guess it's only fair. He's got to be exhausted, three long flights in four days. And rescuing those babies, carrying them down that cliff. I'm surprised he's in as good a shape as he is.

Marta caught herself looking at his "shape" and flushed. She ducked her head and went to find grass or leaves to soften her floor bed.

A distant scream sounded, as from a hawk high in the clear air. Sidhari responded with an ear-piercing trumpet of distress. The others screamed, heads up, searching the sky.

Marta stood still, intent, her head back, trying to see where the sound came from, her heart lurching to her throat. Then, "Altan!" she screamed. "He's dying." She ran for the landing meadow.

Deep trumpeting distress calls from a strange Karda echoed through the valley. Marta's veil pierced. The cries slammed into her head, pounding terror and distress. The four Karda behind her screamed in answer. She stopped dead, and an enormous sorrel Karda crashed in a heap at the end of the grass clearing less than two strides in front of her. She doubled over, feet spread to keep from falling, and wrapped her arms tight around her. Her chest tightened with the terrible pain and intense grief that pounded into her and shattered her shields.

The Karda raised its head, its amber eyes found her, and a wall of fury smashed into her head, snapping it back. The Karda collapsed. Dead.

"No, no!" His sudden deep rapport with her tore loose, ravaged her mind. Rage echoed inside her head, sheared away thought, filling her with the immense void of death. She dove toward him. Altan grabbed her from behind and swung her away. "Wait. Wait, Marta."

Blind to everything but the echoes of the dead Karda's pain and fury, she struggled to jerk loose, but Altan's hand was a tight band around her arm, and he didn't let go. She stood, shaking, until her mind became her own again. He let go.

He was right. She shouldn't touch the Karda unless she had to. It was dead, and Karda had their own way of grieving. There was nothing she could do.

The two of them stood side by side for a moment. Then Marta heard a rustling sound from the ornate rig on the back of the collapsed sorrel. A small child in a rose-colored robe trimmed with heavy ivory lace struggled out of a large pouch in the rigging. Golden hair swirled in a soft halo around the beautiful creamy pink face streaked with tears. The little girl raised her arms to Marta with a piteous whimper.

"A child," Marta whispered, and moved to catch her before she fell. Altan hesitated for a moment then reached a long arm to grab her again.

"Don't," he said. He threw Marta behind him and drew his sword with his other hand. The child cried again, a soft, beseeching sound, her small arms still stretched toward Marta.

"Barra!" he shouted and flicked his sword so quick it was but a gleaming blur and took the child's head off.

Marta screamed, and he grabbed her as she tried to get around him. "What have you done?"

"Wait," he said.

She stopped struggling at the fierce note of command in his voice and looked up, astonished at the intense mix of anger and horror on his face, then back at the child's body.

The little girl started to fizzle. A thick, black cloud breathed out through the small body's pores. Dark fingers eddied out as if searching. The dense miasma, strange and terrible, swirled around the tiny disintegrating girl-child and stretched toward Marta.

She clapped her hands over her mouth to keep from vomiting. Her stomach lurched at the sick, sweet, rotten smell of long-dead things. She stood, paralyzed.

"Look away! Now!" Altan jerked her around and forced her face into his chest, his arms hard around her. She fought to breathe. "Close your eyes and keep them closed." His mouth pressed close to her ear.

She couldn't struggle. Her mind, torn by the sudden wrenching loss of rapport with the dying Karda, was overwhelmed by the skin-crawling evil that emanated from the body of the child and swirled around them. Altan held her face so tightly against his chest she fought to breathe. His face pressed against the top of her head, and his breath blew strands of her hair across her cheek. A shrill, high keen of fury and frustration shoved sharp needles into her ears.

Sidhari screamed a long, trumpeting tenor call. Kibrath answered, then Eanna and Darta. Altan's grip on her relaxed, and Marta stood still, her legs trembling, his arms wrapped around her for several minutes or an age. Then he carried her, nearly comatose, to the trees at the edge of the meadow and sat, settling her in his lap, arms still holding her tight against him.

The four Karda stepped up the grassy meadow, no longer screaming, moving slowly, wings mantled, crests upraised, with a solemn grace. The black cloud was gone—the child thing, a dried nothing of grey dusty skin and bone folded in crumpled rose velvet and ivory lace, lay on the green grass next to the dead Karda.

Kibrath and Sidhari, Eanna and Darta walked in solemn unison around their dead kin and the small withered body of the child. They moved in a slow circle, wings mantled, trumpeting deep, clear tenor harmonies that carried through the valley to rebound from the surrounding mountains like tolling bells.

They turned, cantered down the meadow and rose, one by one. Wide wings snapped out and beat in unison, and the four Karda circled up in two rising spirals over the sprawled body. They flew in a double helix that rose and fell, rose and fell for a long time while the song of their grief echoed through the small valley.

Marta and Altan sat clasped together watching the beautiful aerial dance until Marta, embarrassed, moved away and sat apart, hugging her knees, her eyes on the Karda's mourning dance. Altan finally stood and reached to pull her up. She ignored his hand and forced her stiff body to stand.

He stared as if seeing her for the first time. "It came for you," he said. "Blessed moons of Adalta, why did that Tela Oroku come for you?" He reached his hand out as if to protect her, to pull her to him again then dropped it, his expression tight and puzzled, and they walked slowly back to the small cabin, not speaking.

They sat side by side on the one bed, as far away from each other as they could get without falling off the ends, eating salty stew and drinking the strong herbal tea Altan brewed in a small metal pot on the stove. The travel lantern on the floor in front of them cast a glow on the sharp planes of his face. Marta ignored his stare as best she could, but she could feel his curiosity and alarm.

What is a Tela Oroku? Marta racked her brain trying to figure out what it could be. What kind of horrible thing had inhabited the tiny body of that beautiful child? She knew better than to ask. She'd expose her ignorance of something everyone else knew.

Altan broke the pregnant silence. "Why you?" he said, wiping out his cup and stowing it back in his pack. "Why was the Tela Oroku aimed at you? Who have you angered so much?"

"How are you so sure it was me it was after?"

"Don't be dense. It went straight for you—you can't deny that. And why didn't you protect yourself? You were looking straight at it. You nearly let it grab your eyes before I took off its head."

"I've never seen anything like that before."

He stared at her, his green eyes narrowed. "But you should have known. How is it that you don't know about the Tela Oroku? I don't think you even knew what it was. Granted, it's been a long time since anyone made one, not since the battles with the Larrak. But everyone knows the stories about them."

"It's late, and I'm tired. I'm going to sleep now. We have a long

trip tomorrow to make it even halfway, and we both need to rest."
She moved to her pitiful makeshift bed on the floor, wrapped herself
in her trail blankets, wiggled out of her cold, damp skirt, and
reached to get it near the fire to dry without uncovering herself. He
took it from her and stretched it over their packs next to the stove.
She lay down with her back to the room and him, leaving him to
put out the lantern, her mind in turmoil.

*Why me, indeed? What in this strange world is a Tela Oroku? And what
are the Larrak? I'm not doing my job right if the stories are so well known, and I
haven't heard them. I'm supposed to be collecting ethnographic data, not just
relying on the black hole incompetent data mavens on the ship. My ignorance is
going to kill me. Are the others having this much difficulty?*

This wasn't the first time she'd been caught with too little of
what was common knowledge. Usually ignoring the questions
worked—she was skillful about turning people's questions back on
them—but she had a feeling this was different. Altan's attention had
gone beyond his casual interest in her in a way she didn't like. She
needed to communicate with the ship or one of the other agents.
Chances were there wasn't any information on Tela Oroku in the
data banks anyway, and she didn't have her Cue with her to see if
there was anything on it.

She was tired, and not just from the events of the day. She'd
done this kind of work since she was three when her mother died,
and her father started taking her with him on-planet when he
worked. The excitement of learning about yet another world, yet
another culture, was fading. She missed him terribly. She wanted so
badly to be able to talk to him now. But he was gone, and she had
no one left—no family, few friends, and those few scattered across
the universe like fading stars. She had only her job and the
consortium.

How could she report magic? Inevitably, what appeared to be
magic turned out to be an unexplained or undiscovered technology.
In theory, the rule about exploring a new planet was, "Remember,
anything is possible, even fairies, elves, and Yetis." But that saying
referred to alien life forms, not magic.

Marta and Altan both agreed that the Karda had recovered overnight from the shock of the day before. Marta wasn't at all sure she had, but she wasn't about to say so. Her head was splitting, and the walls she had so carefully built were crumbling.

~The young ones are ready.~ The reassuring words came from inside her aching head, which made them not reassuring at all. Where had they come from? Her head felt like there was something inside kicking its way out with pointy-toed shoes. Or boots. She could scarcely think, and now she was hallucinating.

Altan pulled out the straps and carrying harnesses they'd brought to hold the fledglings on the backs of Eanna and Darta. Lost in their own thoughts, they spoke little, working together with an ease they hadn't had before—oiling the leathers, straightening the straps, fitting them to one and then the other Karda. Avoiding even an accidental touch.

Altan tore down one side of the stick nest he'd so carefully constructed only four days before. They wrapped each small Karda in a blanket, careful of the un-fledged wings, tucking the delicate legs gently inside the wrapping.

~Calm, little ones, calm. Have care for that wing, Marta.~ More words that came from nowhere.

She shook her head and was immediately sorry. It hurt enough to bring tears to her eyes. She was so tired and emotionally drained by the death of the Karda. And Altan watched her every move, deep worry lines between his eyebrows. Or were they lines of suspicion and distrust? She ignored him. Or tried to.

Together they lifted the gold female, her nares flushed, and her wild eyes darted from Marta to Altan to Sidhari to Eanna. They ran straps through the rings of the carrying harness and secured the small body on Eanna's back. Always in the back of Marta's mind was that voice.

~It will be all right, little one, little Irnini. Eanna will carry you safely .~

"Her name is Irnini," Marta said.

He looked at her. "What? Her name?"

She glanced away. She hadn't intended to say it aloud. Sidhari nudged her back. Marta turned and rested her aching head on Sidhari's shoulder. The voices stopped.

When they had the male fledgling safely installed on Darta's back, they saddled Sidhari and Kibrath. Marta almost fell when she stepped from Sidhari's knee to the saddle, and Altan started toward her. She waved him away. "I'm fine, Altan."

He watched her mount then jumped to grab the saddle pommel and swung himself to Kibrath's back and buckled in. The Karda loped in a line, working up to a canter and lifted into the air, circling once above the lifeless body of the big Karda and the small dusty pool of rose and cream silk.

Despite her headache, Marta reveled in the thrill of the steep take off as they circled up a thermal to make altitude before heading north on the long flight to the fields outside the massive walls of Toldar Prime.

They flew for about three hours, and then Marta heard a clear, firm voice in her head. ~Marta, Eanna and Darta are tiring. The little ones don't know how to balance. We need to look for a safe place to land and rest.~

She gasped. The pain stabbed behind her eyes. That was not her thought. She froze. Her hands gripped the pommel in front of her so tightly they ached. "Who...who are you?" she stuttered, afraid she wouldn't get an answer and afraid she would.

~Sidhari, of course. I was beginning to wonder if you would ever wake up.~ The calm voice went on, ~How about over there to the east? There are trees, and I seem to remember a water source.~

Oh, galaxy of the damned, I hear voices in my head, and I'm talking back. What's next, fairies and gnomes? Marta's laugh was too wild, and she clamped her teeth on her bottom lip till it hurt, and the berserk laughter that wanted to erupt stilled. After a confused moment, she signaled to Altan, pointing to the small copse of trees she could barely see lying some way to the east.

I'm going mad.

~Of course you're not,~ she heard in a pleasant, matter-of-fact tone.

It was too much for Eanna and Darta to try to make the trip home in two days. Long before evening the second day, Marta and Altan both noticed the two females tiring, the bundles on their backs struggling to get loose. Marta could hear Sidhari telling her they needed to stop. She was getting used to the voices in her head, and the aching subsided a little.

Maybe whatever that strange creation had been, the thing Altan called a Tela Oroku, had done something to her after all. All those times other Mi'hiru had said something about talking with Karda were apparently not hyperbole.

They followed a small winding stream for an hour and finally landed on the plains close to a cottonwood grove. They unbuckled and unwrapped the little ones and watched them run, flapping their short, stubby wings, butting each other, and getting in the way as she and Altan unbuckled the harnesses on Eanna and Darta and unsaddled the other two. Eventually, Sidhari had enough and scolded them, or that's how her sharp cries sounded. They quieted down, hanging their heads a little. Marta laughed aloud, then grabbed her head when pain flashed.

Altan looked at her. "Are you all right? What's so funny?"

She looked at him, confused for a minute. *Of course. He can't hear them.*

A brief sensation of amusement flashed from somewhere. ~Of course he can, but only when we choose.~ Who was that? Kibrath? Sidhari? Who?

Both of them wandered to the small stream to drink. "Nothing. I'm just glad to be on the ground." She ducked her head to fish in her pack for a brush, feeling his eyes still focused on her. She hadn't heard anything but the Karda in her head all day. Hearing Altan speak aloud felt odd. Too loud.

She was aware of his close attention all evening. He did almost everything to set up their camp. He dug the fire pit, put the stew on and the water to boil for tea. He forced her to sit and work on reinforcing one of the straps from Darta's harness he claimed were coming apart. Marta could find nothing wrong, but she worked over the stitching anyway. He refused to let her help feed the Karda, ignoring her when she tried. He even offered to get her a blanket as the air began to get colder.

She finally snapped. "I have a headache, that's all. And whatever that thing was, it didn't hurt me. I am perfectly capable of taking care of myself, Altan. I'm not an invalid."

CHAPTER ELEVEN

Six Karda met them when they were miles from Toldar Prime. They settled into a V formation around the four weary travelers to ease their flight. When they landed, the mews were a madhouse of Mi'hiru, Karda, as well as Guardian Stephan, Elena, and others from the guild house and the keep. Marta was glad to get away when things settled enough to leave the babies under the care of a tired Eanna who assured her they would be fine for the night.

She pulled off her soft riding boots and found a pair of slippers on one of the shelves in the entryway to the long central hall of the red stone building. She followed Mother Solaira across the flagstones through an archway to the right into the dining room filled with heavy worn, polished benches, chairs, and wooden tables with bright pottery vases of fresh flowers. The two walked through into the big kitchen that adjoined it. A cheerful fire of magma stones glowed in the big metal cooking stove, and the smell of fresh baked bread from the hot adobe oven filled the kitchen. Several large loaves cooled at one end of the big, worn central table. Piles of papers littered the other. Solaira dropped her healer's cape on the back of a chair.

"I'm doing triple duty this afternoon. It's too late to have much traffic at the door, and I'm not expecting anyone to pop out a baby tonight, so I'm helping with the baking and getting some paperwork done." Solaira did duty as a midwife as well as a healer. "Are you hungry?"

She didn't wait for an answer—she seldom did—and cut a couple of slices of warm bread, passing Marta a spreading knife and a bowl of buttery cheese. Marta mumbled a word of thanks, spread the cheese on the bread, and took a big bite. She almost melted at the taste. Solaira poured two mugs of hot tea from the steaming kettle on the back of the stove and sat to join her.

"I love fresh, hot bread." She cut herself a piece. "How was your flight? Did the babies take it well? How old do you think they are? How was the handsome Altan? I wouldn't have minded a long trip with that one myself. He's way too young for me but sooo charming."

Mouth full, Marta held up her hand. She swallowed, took a long drink of hot tea and said, "The nest they built in the mews was just as Altan asked. You're very good at asking questions when my mouth is full. Which do you want me to answer first? The fledglings took the flight well."

Marta gave her report on the Karda to the guild mother while they ate.

Solaira got up and refilled their mugs. "Something happened, didn't it? What went wrong? Did Altan misbehave? I know he can be arrogant."

Marta flashed back to the dinner in the keep with six women to three men. *He probably has to be to protect himself. But how can I answer her? Altan expected me to know about the Tela Oroku. Do I dare expose my ignorance to Solaira?* She bit her lip. "There was a Tela Oroku. Altan said it came for me."

Solaira gaped at Marta. Her cup stopped halfway to her mouth. "A Tela Oroku? What happened? How did you escape it? Oh, Sorrows of Adalta, a child has to die for a Tela Oroku. And a Karda." She put her hand over Marta's, her sharp little face wrinkled with compassion.

Marta told her what Altan had done. "I was almost unconscious.

He dragged me out of the way of the other Karda's mourning dance." Marta told her of the dying sorrel, the little girl, the mourning flight of the Karda—what she could remember of it.

Solaira sat for a long time, staring at Marta. She tilted her head back, eyes on the ceiling. Then she asked the question Altan had, "Why you? Why did it come for you?" adding, "Who would want to kill you?"

The guild mother poured more tea. "Did something else happen on this trip?"

Marta held the cup to her face, giving herself time to control her voice. The heat settled deep in her belly. *Save me from the black hole of relationship. I can't think of Altan this way.* "No, it was pretty straightforward. We flew up to get them and flew back. The only unusual thing was the Tela Oroku. And except for Midsummer Festival, I've either been here or on patrol. I haven't encountered anything odd, nothing that would get me killed, for sure."

"Maybe it was something you overheard or saw in Restal. Someone there is fostering a movement against what they call the rule by talent." She finished her tea. "We're not going to figure it out tonight, but if something occurs to you, let me know."

"There's nothing I can think of, Solaira." But, of course, there was. Assassins had come after her three times in Restal Prime. After she saw Galen with Readen. Marta was too tired to think. She had to rest. Then, she had to get somewhere she could use her Cue.

"You were very fortunate. Your short sword would have allowed it to get too close to you. It's good Altan was with you. It's a clever weapon—you would never suspect a dying Karda and a beautiful child."

"Altan was surprised I didn't recognize it for what it was."

"That's ridiculous. You're from the eastern hill country in Akhara Quadrant. The wars were a long time ago and a long way from there. Stories of them have become just that—stories. They were used by the Larrak in Restal Quadrant, anyway, not by humans. If someone discovered how to create one and had the strength it requires, who would have such dedication to pure evil?"

Marta finished her bread and drank her tea, then rose to go.

140

"I'm falling asleep in this chair, and I need to get these flying clothes off." Her skirt still smelled of baby Karda shit. "I'm ready for a bath and sleep. Do you have what you need for my report?"

"Yes, of course, Marta." Solaira shook herself out of her thoughts. "I need to finish this paperwork before the cooks need the kitchen. I'll see you at dinner."

Marta was stumbling with fatigue by the time she got to her small room, stripped off her riding clothes, wrapped herself in her thick robe, and made her way to the baths. Several healers, a couple of weavers, and one other Mi'hiru filled the steamy room. All with questions about her trip and the young Karda until Jordana, her fellow Mi'hiru, recognized her tiredness and chased them out.

Left alone, Marta soaked for as long as she could in the steaming water, feeling her muscles and her mind relax for the first time in four days. She had been on her guard even before the Tela Oroku incident. Since that first attack in Restal.

What had she heard that threatened someone? The data she'd gathered hasn't been unusual. Well, except the Karda's intelligence and telepathy, and they're not the first intelligent species the ship had encountered. The only thing she could think of was Galen. He may have a legitimate reason for being in Restal, but why be so secretive?

She got out of the tub and shivered in spite of the heated room and the warm robe. Her intuition was screaming. It wasn't just the several attempts on her life. A more substantial reason hid behind them. She could almost feel it through the stones under her feet. Something was wrong in this land she was growing to love, something sinister. She'd felt this way in Restal. But not here in Toldar, not until now. She shook herself and wrapped her hair in a towel. There was nothing she could do about her fears, so she dried them away along with the bath water and stumbled her way to her bed.

The next morning, she clambered over the sides of the nest with her bag of food and began to feed the babies. She laughed as Irnini snatched the morsels out of her hand. Altan climbed over the side of the nest. He settled down beside her, reached for a large tuber, brought out a small silver knife and cut off several slices, tossing them to the male. "I wonder what this one's name will be?"

"What are you doing here?"

"Checking on my babies."

"Your babies?"

"I found them, so they're my responsibility." He pushed Irnini's curious head away from the knife. "At least till they're grown."

"Don't you trust me to know what I'm doing?" Marta demanded. She knew she was irrational. He had every right to be here. Maybe more than she did. She just didn't want to be around him. And she didn't want to think about why.

"As I said, I'm the one who found them. I want to know them as well as anyone who is not Mi'hiru can. So here I am." He smiled at her. His voice dripped honey sweet condescension. "And you're unreasonable."

She looked away. "This isn't going to work."

"Why not?"

She didn't have an answer.

They worked together feeding the hungry fledglings, sitting inside the nest across from each other. The little, relatively speaking, Karda climbed all over them.

Sidhari wandered over, her head appearing over Marta's shoulder.

~You could let me feed them. I've never been a mother, but I know how to do it.~

The words appeared in Marta's mind. She looked up at the beautiful mahogany head with its fierce raptor beak. Hearing Sidhari's voice in her head was becoming less strange. "I want them to get used to me—to us."

"Of course you do. That's what we're doing here. I know that." Altan's tone was exasperated. "I'm not an idiot."

Marta blushed, realizing she spoke out loud to Sidhari, forgetting herself. He couldn't hear Sidhari.

142

~You don't have to speak aloud,~ Sidhari said in her mind. ~Just consciously think the thoughts. And when I choose, he can hear me.~

I'm going crazy.

~No, you're not. I assure you.~

Marta heard Sidhari's amusement. ~I didn't mean you to hear that,~ she concentrated on sending the words.

~Then you need to work on shielding the thoughts you don't want anyone else to hear.~

The male fledgling's loud screech let her know he was still hungry, and she was not doing her job fast enough. Talking out loud to one person and in her head to another made conversation confusing.

She climbed out of the nest and told Altan, "I'm not going to be here this afternoon. I'm escorting Judiciar Raynol. He has three villages to visit before nightfall. I'll have to miss their next feeding, but Jordana will tend to them."

"I'll do it." He climbed out behind her.

Marta looked at him for a long moment, then said, "All right," and walked away down the long aisle of the mews. She was too aware that Altan stood for a long minute, watching her leave, then let himself out the big doors at the other end of the mews.

Late afternoon, the last case before the judiciar wound to a close. A farmer's bull went to visit the neighboring farmer's bull, and things did not go well. A simple enough matter to resolve with the exchange of a well-bred yearling to replace the injured bull, which would be slaughtered and the meat shared between the two farmers.

It was one of her duties as a Mi'hiru to accompany the traveling judiciars to care for the Karda who volunteered to carry them. The judiciars handled small disputes like this on regular monthly routes. Atan or one of his parents adjudicated major issues, or the disputants traveled to Toldar Prime. Marta gathered invaluable information on the culture, potential trade opportunities, and politics on these trips.

Her patrol duties in Restal had been more difficult. When she accompanied their judiciars on rare visits to the countryside, the disputes were nasty, and the judiciar's judgments met with sullen resignation. Guardian Roland heard most claims in Restal Keep. Travel to the prime was expensive and inconvenient for villagers, which meant too many unsettled disputes smoldered in the countryside. Toldar was far more peaceful. She heard no remarks about a rebellion against the aristocracy of talent. That seemed to be a Restal issue.

It wasn't late when they landed back at Toldar Prime, and Marta took the opportunity to use the time to try to communicate with Kayne on the ship. She groomed the judiciar's Karda, checked it over, then she and Sidhari took off again. They flew for a good long while, enjoying their free time in the air before Marta found an open space away from prying eyes to land and use her Cue. She hadn't gathered anything that needed to be picked up by a drone, so she just sent her data and asked to be connected to Director Morel.

"I didn't expect there to be anything in the database about the Tela Oroku. But there should be, so I think you should make an entry and warn the other scouts. I had a difficult interview with Guardian Stephan. He couldn't imagine why anyone would send it after me. And neither can I." Marta chewed her lip to keep the exasperation out of her voice.

Kayne was being obtuse. "What you are describing doesn't seem possible, or even plausible. It must have been a mechanized doll or a hologram. No one is going to cut the head off a real child. You were upset by the death of the Karda." His voice was heavy with concern. "You are a powerful empath. To have one of those animals die almost at your feet must have sent you into overload. That's what it was. Your mind picked up on a tale you heard somewhere and built a hallucination brought on by the sudden death. And the death of what appeared to be a child, too." The concern in his tone sharpened. "Besides, their beliefs, magical or otherwise, aren't what you were sent down there for. Let someone else study their mythology. You stick to commerce and politics."

Marta wanted to throw her Cue across the meadow. What was wrong with Kayne? He'd never been this way before. *Why am I even out here if you're going to discount whatever I say? And gathering ethnographic information is part of the job you sent me here to do. How can we understand their politics without studying their belief systems?*

"Do you need to be recalled or can you get over this ridiculous nonsense?" Kayne's voice from the box went on. "We wanted you there for at least another half year. We plan to make ourselves known just before the Greater Council meets next year."

Being recalled was the last thing Marta wanted. "No, sir."

"You're not trying hard enough to involve yourself in their politics. You failed in Restal, and it seems you're failing where you are now. Your position assures entry into circles of the quadrant's leaders, and training the Karda with young Me'Gerron will allow lots of contact with him. Take advantage of that. Make use of your looks as well as your wits. You're not there just to play with those flying beasts. You are there for a job. Do it. We'll need their influence when we make ourselves known." He was silent for a minute. Then, "Those infant Karda might be something we can trade. I know at least three collectors who would pay a fortune to have something like them."

Marta's body went cold. His next words went unheard. "Do you not understand, sir? The Karda are sentient beings. They are as intelligent as humans, perhaps even more so, with abilities I haven't begun to plumb. They are not things to be traded." She couldn't even imagine what regulators from the Trade Alliance would have to say about that.

It was as if she hadn't spoken. "That will be all, Marta. Report again as soon as you have something—and there needs to be progress soon. Those repressive anti-tech laws must change, however we have to do it." Kayne clicked off, and the box went silent.

Marta kicked a rock across the runway, stinging her toes. Well, now he thought her a complete fool. He hadn't believed anything she had told him. "Get thee to a black hole, Kayne." She couldn't even imagine the uproar any suggestion of selling a Karda to a collector would create if Kayne mentioned it to someone on Adalta. How clueless could he be? *It's as though he's lost touch with reality. He doesn't hear anything I say unless it fits what he wants to hear.*

She sat cross-legged under a tree and tried to calm her thoughts. Several things didn't make sense. Waiting a year or more to make themselves known, for one. The longest it had ever taken before in her experience was the Earth equivalent of six months. Of course, the other planets she'd infiltrated had been eager for the technology the consortium offered. On the colonized planets, life was difficult. Survival had been the focus for most of the centuries since the Ark ships left Earth, and their inhabitants were eager and ripe for goods that made life easier.

Adalta was different. She agreed with Kayne on that. The colonists had been Luddites determined not to follow the disastrous example of Earth's degeneration into catastrophic wars over religion and resources. Technology had developed beyond the human ability to control unforeseen or ignored consequences, and by the time of the collapse, the biosphere could no longer support the exponential population growth.

The colonists' decision to limit technology and outlaw weapons beyond that of bow and sword had been the result. It didn't end war, but it made it more personal and far less devastating. The guiding philosophy was that socio-cultural developments must keep pace with technological ones. Social mores must be the ground from which a society develops, not technology. This was how they hoped to avoid the failures that devastated Old Earth, now all but uninhabitable.

Weapons? Importing advanced arms would not further trade interests—it would disrupt them. Kayne's earlier slip about the weapons deeply disturbed Marta. The Trade Alliance overseeing all the trade ships forbade trade in weapons. The wars that devastated Old Earth were a lasting lesson. No one wanted that to happen ever again. Every planet of the Diaspora remembered that lesson.

She rubbed her arms and looked down the runway at the big

bay Karda, digging with her fierce talons for the small tubers she loved. Sunlight gleamed on the bronze of her wingtips. "You're going to make holes in this runway that'll take hours to fill if you don't stop, Sidhari, you greedy thing."

~They are very nourishing,~ Sidhari retorted.

Marta laughed and walked across the meadow to the tall Karda, kicking dirt back in the holes she found. She mounted, stepping to Sidhari's extended knee, jumped to grab the saddle, pulled herself up, and tightened her leg straps. Sidhari took off at a canter down the runway until her enormous wings caught enough air to lift them into the deepening blue sky.

~Let's go home, Sidhari.~ She leaned forward to catch less wind and relaxed into the incredible ride through the cooling air of the late afternoon. Sidhari circled up the thermal that rose over the valley surrounded by forest ablaze with red and gold in the slanting light of the late afternoon autumn sun.

CHAPTER TWELVE

~H is name is Baltu,~ said Sidhari. Her head hung over Marta's as she and Altan groomed the little male. Marta handed Altan a soft cloth and the green bottle of the oil she used on wing feathers. She scratched Baltu's head to keep him calm. Altan worked, crooning softly to the little Karda. They ran loose in the mews when they weren't being fed or groomed. Baltu followed Altan everywhere he went, his cries piteous and his immature wings beating futilely whenever Altan flew off on Kibrath. Despite herself, she had to admit Altan was good at soothing the skittish baby.

Marta scratched the downy feathers under the fledgling's neck, irritated that Altan was so close to them. He was there every moment he could spare. She couldn't complain that he was interfering. He knew what he was doing. It was just so—irritating. Her fingers tangled with Altan's as they both reached to scratch the same soft spot under Baltu's beak.

Coruscating blue light surrounded them. Marta jerked away. Needles of fire pierced her hand. She grasped it with her other hand, and sucked breath in between her teeth, clenched tight against the pain. She bent over, her hands pressed tight to her diaphragm, her eyes clamped shut against intense blue spears of light piercing her head.

Altan slumped and fell to his knees. The fledgling jerked back, hissing, and mantled his wings. He was distraught and butted Marta with his head until she knelt beside Altan. Marta's hand stung. Her head pounded.

~Well, well. How interesting,~ said Sidhari.

"What is it? What happened?" Marta blinked her eyes, and her vision began to clear. One hand, afraid to touch him, wandered above Altan's body. The other, still stinging, she clutched to her chest.

"My head," he said. "You're in my head." He pressed the heels of his hands to his temples, obviously in pain. "I can hear your thoughts, I swear. Inside my head." His face was tight, lips clamped, sweat beaded on his forehead.

He could hear what she was thinking? Oh. No. No. Marta helped him up and over the side of the nest. His body shook, his muscles slack with shock. "Yes, I can hear you." He leaned on her —*Grace, but he is big.* She lowered him to the ground, propping him against the wall.

"Will you be all right while I get Solaira? I don't know what to do for you. She's a healer, she'll know." Marta tried to keep her voice steady, though she shook with fear and pain. There was a fierce ache in her head, but at least she wasn't helpless on the ground. *I better hurry.* "Yes, please hurry," he answered her thought, his voice tight and low through clamped teeth. "Kibrath's voice doesn't hurt like this. I'll just sit here for a bit." He leaned back and closed his eyes, hands pressed hard against his temples.

She stared at him, then left at a run, head pounding with every step. Solaira came running back with Marta, knelt beside Altan, and pressed her hands to the sides of his head. "What happened?" She dropped her head and concentrated. "I can't feel anything wrong except the pain in your head, and I can't feel a cause for that, so I can't fix it. Can you make it inside?"

He opened his eyes. "Yes."

When he tried to stand, his knees buckled. Marta caught him and stumbled with the weight.

~I'm not that helpless.~ Marta heard a voice that was neither hers nor Sidhari's. It sounded just like him.

~Oy, my head hurts.~

Oh, not more voices in her head. He wasn't talking out loud. She knew he wasn't talking out loud. Hot shards of pain bounced around inside her head.

~You're in my head again. How can you be in my head? What's happening?~

That couldn't be anything but Altan's voice. Inside her head.

~Shield yourself, Marta,~ said Sidhari.

~What's happening? Is this real?~ she asked the Karda. Marta forced back her panic and struggled to hold up Altan's weight. And to block the strange voice in her head.

~Yes. And isn't this unusual.~ Sidhari's voice was so calm and matter of fact, Marta relaxed a fraction. If she could hear Sidhari, maybe it was Altan in her head. Perhaps it was something that happened all the time on this strange world where so many used what she could only call magic.

She shut off her confusion and helped Solaira get him across the wide courtyard that separated the mews from the back of the guild house. Progress was awkward and lopsided. Solaira was much shorter than Marta. They made it down the long flagstone hall to Solaira's study and eased him into a chair. Solaira busied herself at the small stove, fished about on the shelf beside it for herbs, and rubbed the small of her back.

"He's heavy." She divided a handful between two cups and poured hot water over them. "Here, let this steep for a minute until it cools a bit, then drink it slowly. Aspirtea will make you feel better. It'll take a few minutes, so just sit there for a while." Then she moved behind her carved desk and sat, looking at Marta, concern shadowing her eyes. "What happened out there? I need to know so I can treat him."

Marta tugged at her earring and looked down into her cup. "I don't know. We were grooming Baltu, the little male. I was scratching him. And Altan's fingers sort of tangled with mine." She looked up and shook her hand. It still tingled. "There was a flash of light so bright it was painful, and it seemed to last forever. I felt like our hands seared together, and then he dropped to the ground."

She turned to Altan who was taking a sip of the hot infusion, staring at both of them. "I heard you," he said. "You have to be the strongest Air talent in centuries."

Marta just looked at him. Air talent? "Of course you heard me. I was standing right there. What do you mean you heard me?" She was afraid of what he was going to say next. "What's going on? I didn't do anything to hurt you. You just collapsed." *I can't take another voice in my head. And somehow I have to figure out how talent works.*

Solaira sat silently for a moment while Altan drank his tea, eyes closed. She looked back and forth between them several times, then busied herself at her desk writing a long note. She sealed it and left the room, leaving Marta with Altan. "Drink your aspirtea. It should start working in a little bit. I'll be back in a few minutes."

Marta stared after her. It was all she could do not to jump up and follow her.

Altan sat with his head in his hands, his empty cup crooked on his little finger. "You don't have to stay if you don't want to."

But his voice was so shaky Marta hadn't the heart to leave. She steeled herself. "Would it help if I rubbed your head?"

He looked up then winced at the sudden movement. "Yes, maybe. If you don't mind."

She stood and walked around behind his chair, put her hands on his broad shoulders, and rubbed her thumbs hard up the back of his neck to the base of his skull. *What if he actually can hear me in his mind?*

"Yes, I actually can. You sound different from Kibrath. It must be you. You might try shielding yourself. It hurts."

Marta threw up her stout wall of red bricks and closed all its windows. He'd know who she was and what she was doing on Adalta. How could she hide it if he could hear her thoughts? She couldn't hold them back all the time.

He leaned back into her hands, groaning. "That helps."

She heard his thought. ~Her hands feel so good.~

In spite of herself, a smile twitched her mouth. His thought tilted toward erotic. He was going to have to work on his shields, too.

Readen Me'Vere paced the round tower room at the southeast corner of the keep in Restal Prime, his steps controlled and angry. His hand gripped the silver medallion hanging from his neck. Shelves filled with books, containers of all sizes and shapes, and a multitude of arcane artifacts lined the walls. Stacked papers littered the table in the center of the room.

He shoved his long brown hair away from his face, loosing and retying it at the nape of his neck. His eyes burned, and his face was slack with fatigue. He threw himself into the large upholstered chair beside the small fireplace opposite the door to the chamber.

Why did the Tela Oroku fail? The Itza Larrak forced Readen to take the backlash, and it almost killed him. In spite of the amplification from his medallion, the gold Karda fought Readen's control until the animal died. For two days Readen could do nothing, unable even to think. He needed to replenish his strength, but he couldn't find enough energy to build the illusion on himself he'd need to go hunting for someone to use to rebuild his power, much less ride out to the nearest Circle of Disorder.

A fist rapped on the door. Readen composed himself. "Enter."

"I came to say goodbye," said Galen Morel, dressed in clothes for the trail. Tall, sturdy boots, heavy canvas trousers, thick wool vest. He carried his all-weather cloak hooked with a finger over his shoulder. "I can't be gone from my territory any longer, and I finished the assessment of your mines."

He tossed the cloak across a small table near the door. "There's no question that we can provide equipment to improve production and to survey for other minerals besides copper and iron. Gods of the galaxies. Your methods are unbelievably primitive—picks and shovels. Once we solve the problem of what works here and what doesn't, we can begin production. You can get rid of most of your miners. You won't need them."

Readen didn't ask Galen to sit, but he did anyway. He moved to the opposite chair, leaned back and stretched his legs toward the fire. His gaze wandered the room without interest.

Readen cocked his head, a half-smile on his face. *Galen's too beautiful for a male, or would be if that face ever showed anything but boredom and disinterest. He didn't do much of a survey if he didn't discover miners with minimal Earth talent doing the mining—some of whom don't need picks and shovels to extract the ore. If I could hold onto miners with stronger talent, I wouldn't need him or his machines.* But educating Galen about talent wasn't in Readen's interest. And the pretty man was too self-absorbed to discover it on his own.

Galen laced his hands behind his head, watching the fire. "You can't use the weapons until we figure out what to do about Marta. She'll only be in Toldar for a couple of months before she moves on to Akhara Quadrant, but you're running raids well into territory where she could fly with their patrol. The chance that she'll run across a raided village and recognize the damage they do is too great."

He yawned and stretched his arms, fingers laced, in front of him, rolling his broad shoulders. "Father won't send more until she's safely away. He says if even a hint of this reaches the guardians or the consortium, the directors will put an end to it. The Trade Alliance regulations on dealing in weapons are strict. The fines, if we get caught, would finish the consortium and end my father's career. Probably won't do a lot for mine, either."

Readen nodded, his expression a cordial mask. "When will you be back?" Morel's casual indifference infuriated him. "How many weapons will you bring? The two we have are running out of power, and they don't recharge like you said they would." The Itza Larrak was working on a spell for Readen to recharge them from the Circles of Disorder. Readen was frustrated. The Itza Larrak couldn't exist outside the cavern. Even inside it was only able to work when Readen was present and could manifest it. Otherwise, the symbols inscribed on the pillars in the cavern beneath the keep held it trapped in limbo.

But it had given him the spell to create the Tela Oroku. It would have been nice to give the problem of Marta to the Itza Larrak and forget her. But it could only work through an agent as long as the Larrak was held by the cavern. Learning that had given him a gleeful sense of control until he learned that something else the Itza Larrak could do was cause pain for its disciple. A great deal of pain.

Galen scooted forward in his chair, hands on his knees, and pushed to his feet. "I told you, no more weapons until Marta's away from Toldar and your borders. Don't use the ones you have. We're taking a risk in this deal as it is. Consortium management is content to work within your current laws, but that's not enough for Father—he wants more. Don't mess it up for him." He headed for the door.

Readen ground his teeth. He would like to strike the man dead—or better, invite him to a circle—but Readen needed those weapons. He didn't want to move against Daryl without them. Expanding into Toldar would be even riskier. Readen relaxed his shoulders and forced a smile.

"She'll be gone soon enough, I guess. I hope the weather holds till you're back in Anuma." He clasped Galen's forearm and opened the door. Galen flipped his cloak around his shoulders and sauntered out.

Readen kicked a footstool across the room.

The long central chamber of Restal Keep was chilly in the late fall after- noon. The stone floors and walls echoed as the latest supplicants argued querulously in front of Guardian Roland, indolence and irritation warring for prominence in his expression. His white hair was pulled back into a braided tail, its end wrapped in silver wire. Heavy silver embroidery embellished the high collar and wide cuffs.

Readen sat beside his brother, Daryl, bored but holding himself erect, his expression one of careful attention. His tunic, of the same high-necked style, was unrelieved black. Daryl wore the simple blue uniform of the Karda Patrol and not a new one. At least this time he hadn't brought books with him. Books, plural. Daryl was never happy with just one book.

The afternoon was interminable. The tendayly round of audiences was an onerous duty at the best of times, but today was worse than usual. The one before them now was a petty squabble between two red-faced smallholders doing their best not to shout at each other. They weren't succeeding. Readen amused himself by drawing on the anger and frustration of the two men, storing the charged energies. He rubbed his fingers across the medallion beneath his tunic and gave a push to amp their anger into fury. Then he sucked it in with a shiver. This was better than getting drunk.

As always, their self-indulgent, capricious father's arbitrary judgments frustrated Daryl. Roland treated these tendayly sessions as personal entertainment. Daryl took them seriously. Or would if his father let him.

So long as Roland and Daryl were alive, Readen would never be required to pay serious attention to these problems. When, not if, this became his duty, he'd make short order of such irritating complaints. He quit listening, shifting in his seat and sucking on the anger and frustration—a sweetness tangible to him—in the room. Roland finally made his judgment and sent the two holders on their way, neither satisfied.

Holder Connor Me'Cowyn strode into the hall, still in flying gear, carrying himself with the self-assurance of the most influential holder in Restal. Black hair striped with gray topped a hawk-nosed face reddened by the legendary choleric temperament of a powerful Air talent without enough Earth for balance.

"The Circles of Disorder are increasing again, Guardian." He didn't wait to be acknowledged. "Restal must start planting trees again. You have let the neglect go on too long."

Daryl started to speak, but Roland cut him off.

"Good afternoon to you, Connor," Roland said, breathing out a long, loud sigh. "I'm pleased to see you in Restal Prime. It has been too long since you've visited. How is your family? Your lovely daughter?" His words were precise, petulant snaps.

Me'Cowyn was not intimidated. "Yes, it has been too long. And the circles have continued to grow unchecked since I was last here."

Readen considered the holder a resource in waiting. A firm believer in feudal government, the holder was wary of Daryl's views on giving a voice on the council to the larger villages of the quadrant. If Readen were skillful enough, the stories he was spreading about an imminent revolt against the aristocracy of talent would eventually take root and put an end to the feudal system that let only strong talents rule. And Daryl would be hard-pressed to defend himself against rumors that he was fostering the unrest.

Perhaps Readen should convince his father to invite Me'Cowyn's extraordinarily beautiful daughter, his only child and his heir, for an extended visit and whisper these rumors into one of her delicate ears. Me'Cowyn so wanted to catch Daryl for her.

"The circles are not a danger. They are still well contained. But, of course, you are quite free to plant trees around the ones in your holding." Roland looked down at the papers in front of him, flipping the top one to the next pile. "I've told you this before."

"I am as I can. But what of the other holdings? The circles are the responsibility of the guardian—mostly unmet since your father. And if you had bothered to visit one, as you promised to do last time, you would know what I'm talking about."

"You overstep yourself, Me'Cowyn. Have care how you speak."

"This is not an autocracy, Roland. You still answer to your holders. Though lately, it seems as though an autocracy is what you want." Connor's voice rose. "Your Mounted Patrol oversteps itself, arresting villagers for speaking out about the increasing bandits on the borders and the dangers of the growing circles. Accusing them of supporting some ridiculous revolt against rule by talent."

Roland looked past Daryl and said, "Readen, I'll let you answer to that as Mounted Patrol Commander."

Readen smiled, leaning back in his chair. "We've been fighting raiders on the borders for some time now. They cross from Toldar, attack, and then disappear back across the border where we can't follow."

Me'Cowyn shook his head. "They're raiding too far into this quadrant for them all to be from Toldar. People along the borders are terrified. Terrified of the marauders and terrified to speak out." His words were choppy with frustrated fury. "What of the arrests, Readen? What purpose do they serve? I have a list of people arrested from villages on the edges of my holding. Some of these I know personally. They're simply worried people, angry about the circles. Livestock gets sucked in, crops stunted. There's more illness. They are concerned about their children. Several have been born horribly disfigured. This is not something you can expect people to keep silent about. And they're certainly not involved with some imaginary revolt."

"Livestock is always getting lost, crops fail from time to time, sometimes the result of lack of diligence by the farmers themselves. And we can do nothing about inbreeding. These things will always be. If the people of Me'Cowyn Holding are dissatisfied, it is not the guardian's responsibility." Readen's words were measured, his tone reasonable, calm as though soothing a fractious horse.

Me'Cowyn pinched the bridge of his nose with his thumb and two fingers. He looked up, his voice calmer. "We need help, Roland. I continue to plant where circles abut my holding. I have the resources. Others do not."

Daryl leaned forward, his hands on the table. "Father, I've mentioned this problem to you several times. I've seen they're growing. Karda Patrol fly farther and farther out of their way to avoid them. And the power from the land between them fluctuates, so it can be difficult to draw talent. Karda tire more easily on long flights, and they're not happy here. We have fewer and fewer who stay for more than a couple of months at a time. It's getting to be a serious problem."

"You're always so concerned about your Karda, Daryl. Karda come and go as they will." Roland smiled at him.

Readen idly moved a pen back and forth on the table with one hand and clenched the other into a tight fist under the table. *Father can't look at Daryl and not smile.*

Roland turned back to the holder. "We'll take your concerns under advisement, Me'Cowyn. These hearings are at an end."

The angry holder glanced at Daryl, gave a slight nod and left the chamber, boots ringing harsh on the stone floor.

Guardian Roland led his two sons to the study in his private apartments. He walked to the massive carved cabinet against one wall and poured wine into three cut crystal glasses. Feet apart, the guardian stood in front of the tall narrow windows, sipping from his glass, looking out over elaborate gardens where a bevy of gardeners mulched beds and trimmed formal borders.

The wood fire in the stone fireplace—an indulgence he allowed himself despite the scarcity of timber on Adalta—the thick rugs on the floor, and the heavy drapes and tapestries on the walls made the room comfortably warm after the long afternoon in the cold hall. The two brothers waited, but Roland just watched the gardeners outside.

Daryl cleared his throat. "In little more than a tenday it will be Fall Harvest Festival, and we expect the trade delegation from Toldar shortly after, Father. I'm sure you won't want them to stay any longer than they'll want to be here. Whatever reassurances we can give them, we should try, don't you think? We need their grain badly this year. They're beefing up their border patrols—that's probably most of what they want to talk about. Raids along our border with them are increasing, as Me'Cowyn said."

Roland turned and said in a bored voice, "Me'Cowyn is an alarmist. The raiders probably come from Toldar. We want to be sure the talks are over in good time. It would be uncomfortable to have them stuck here longer than is necessary by an early winter storm. It's too cold too early in the hills this year—the lovely fall color is almost gone." He turned back to the window. "Is that all?"

"The bandit problem, Father. It's real."

Readen hid his amusement at the controlled frustration in Daryl's voice. There was nothing that entertained him more than to see his so-talented brother frustrated. "I'll see to the borders

personally, Daryl. We don't want to anger Toldar now. It will do me
good to get out of my tower for a tenday or so. I've been cooped up
here too much lately." He grabbed and squeezed Daryl's shoulder as
he walked past and raised an eyebrow in his father's direction as if
in commiseration. Readen fed off Daryl's frustration at their
indolent father. As he left, he heard Roland's voice, his tone
petulant, "What is all this on my desk, Daryl? Surely we don't need
to go over all these today."

A rough and uncomfortable tenday on the border was
convenient right now. Readen opened the door to his rooms in the
east tower. But riding with his pseudo-bandits was an indulgence he
enjoyed, and he'd be able to test for himself the effectiveness of
Galen's weapon. Besides that, he had some "bandits" to pay.

However, tonight there was time for something else he needed.
He grabbed his cloak, wrapped it close around him, and left for a
stroll through the less salubrious taverns of Restal Prime. He moved
the fingers of one hand to cast the spell that changed his
appearance and gripped the medallion through his tunic to give it
power. It wouldn't do to be recognized when he found another girl,
or perhaps he'd find a boy this time. His power needed
strengthening. Perhaps he'd take the child to a circle in honor of
Connor Me'Cowyn's delicious anger.

CHAPTER THIRTEEN

M arta breathed in the brisk upper air of the foothills as
Sidhari circled up the rising thermal. She'd fought to be the
Mi'hiru for this expedition. Altan was taking Guardian Stephan's
place in the annual trade talks with Restal, and Marta knew her
assessment of the politics between the two quadrants, as well as the
outcome, would be information Kayne would relish. Restal and
Toldar were both her territory.

But it was difficult to keep her mental barriers up when she and
Altan were together so often. She was still getting used to hearing
Sidhari in her head. Altan's voice brought on vicious headaches—
and the occasional doubt about her sanity.

Altan and the other two Karda Patrol, Captain Dalt and
Patrolman Lyall, circled with her, gaining altitude to make another
sweep of the borderlands between Toldar and Restal. Her cheeks
were tight with cold, and tendrils of hair escaped her braid and
blew across her face. Grateful for her long sheepskin vest and heavy
flying clothes, she pulled her hat tighter over her ears, tucked the
stray hairs in, and bent her mind toward the Karda, focusing on
Sidhari's vision, so much sharper and far-reaching than her own.
One of the many benefits of her expanded link with Sidhari was

the ability to share her sight and sometimes her sense of air currents.

A fragment of Altan's thoughts touched her mind, and she slammed her mental walls up immediately. She looked over at him and saw him grimace with pain then wave his arm toward a narrow valley to the northeast. A roiling plume of dirty grey smoke rose out of the red and gold autumn-hued trees.

The four fliers wheeled as one on Altan's signal and headed for the valley. They swooped closer, and a small village came into view. Several structures burned. Fierce flames blazed from windows of the stone buildings, and thick smoke roiled up from burning thatched roofs. Fat columns of smoke rose straight up into the still, cold air.

They dove for the ground. Sidhari swept up behind a raider aiming a weapon at a big villager laying into another rider with an iron bar. Her talons ripped into him, tore him from his saddle, and she beat her way back up. The man screamed as they climbed, and he struggled to force his weapon around to Sidhari's breast. Marta looked over Sidhari's shoulder and gasped. Was that what she thought it was?

~Drop him, Sidhari. Drop him right now!~

Sidhari released him, and he fell, screaming, arms whirling, grab- bing at empty air. They'd been high enough. His career as a murdering thief was over. He was a dead heap on the ground.

The giant Karda dropped one wing to go vertical and wheeled back to the village, pressing Marta hard into the cantle. Karda and riders swooped and tore into the men, talons ripping. The ones they didn't haul into the air and drop they knocked to the ground, blood spraying from long gashes. Villagers swarmed the fallen with knives and cudgels. She grimaced when one almost severed a raider's head with a hoe.

She saw Kibrath sink his terrible talons into a rider's head and lift him from the saddle. He flew high over the woods beyond the village and dropped him. The raider fell and was impaled like grisly fruit hanging on a stark, dead tree.

Three raiders, hunched so low in their saddles they looked like lumpy packs from above, spurred their mounts frantically for the trees where the Karda couldn't reach them. Marta gasped as a streak of fire from Altan set one aflame. *Oh, gods of the galaxies. I'm going to have to find time to think about what that was.* Altan signaled for Dalt to follow the other two who were too close to the trees for fire.

The other three fliers circled down to the grassy meadow outside the village and landed. They tore away saddle straps, leapt from the Karda, and ran toward the buildings. The villagers passed slopping buckets along a line from the well at the center, trying in vain to control the blaze consuming whatever was inside the most prominent building.

Too many bodies lay still at the edge of the central square. Several women huddled near one building wrapped in blankets, their faces bruised and shocked, eyes blank and staring. Other women, skirts belted up, bandaged wounds and tended to those lying on the ground or leaned against one of the unburnt houses.

Altan went directly to the wounded. Marta and Lyall went to the bucket brigade. By the time Altan joined them, she had blisters forming in spite of her gloves.

He stepped to the side of the bucket line, not joining them. "The wounded are stable enough for the moment. I need to help here first."

To Marta's surprise, he knelt with his hands flat on the ground, as close as he could get to the fire. As she passed heavy bucket after heavy bucket, she watched him, mystified. His head down, he concentrated, his shoulders tense. The fire damped down, flames slowed. She stared, transfixed, until the person next to her bumped her with a full bucket, and water slopped on her skirt. She reached for it and passed it on.

The flames slowed but didn't go out, and he sat back on his haunches, face pale. He turned to a man in the line who wore a burn- marked leather apron and watched Altan with hopeful eyes.

"It's too fierce. If I'm to help the wounded, that's all I can do here. I'm sorry."

The man closed his eyes, nodded acceptance, and went back to passing buckets. After a long hour of trying, it was clear there was no saving the burning structure.

Marta went with Altan to help with the wounded. He knelt beside a young boy, unwrapped his bloody bandages, and held his hands over a slash high on the boy's arm. Marta watched in disbelief as the wound slowly knit itself together from the inside out. Altan focused, his face intent, until a narrow red weal was all that remained of the ugly sword cut in the boy's arm. He went in turn to three other wounded, pulled back bandages, held his hands over each wound for several minutes, then nodded to the woman caring for them. A fourth man leaned against the house, in great pain, his shoulder drooping wrongly, his other hand clasping his upper arm. Altan gently moved his hand away and held his own hands to the shoulder.

After a moment, Marta heard muffled popping sounds, and the shoulder snapped back into position. Altan instructed one of the women to wrap the man's arm in place with a sling, then he stood on wobbly legs.

Marta grabbed his arm to steady him. It was the first time she had touched him since she'd begun hearing his telepathic voice. Heat bloomed inside her, and she let go, rubbing her hand on the side of her skirt. Altan was looking around for more wounded and didn't notice. Marta stared at him, shocked beyond words at what he had done. *He healed all those wounds, some of them terrible, in half an hour.*

Altan found the village headman, the blacksmith, Matyn, among those drinking deeply at the well in the dirt square that was the village center.

"They had some kind of talent weapon that killed from a distance. Warn't nothin' we could do. They went through all the buildings and every house, takin' what they wanted, then set fire to the big store- house and two other houses. If you hadn't come. " Matyn looked at the burning building. "Our winter supplies, our seed stock…"

His voice trailed off. He looked over as a roof beam crashed down into the still burning hulk, the winter stores for the whole village flying up as bright embers into the afternoon sky. "Would'a been worse if you hadn't come when you did." He stared into the dying fires. "My wife." He shook his greying head and looked away. His broad shoulders hunched forward, girding against pain.

They walked across the dusty square, gray ash swirling around their boots, to a row of bodies, some lying too still, their faces covered. Altan knelt beside the body of a young man and pulled the crude bandage around his chest aside to look at his wound. He frowned. "What kind of weapon did this?"

"A talent weapon." The man held his hands out with forefingers crossed in a warding-off gesture. "Most on 'em had swords and bows, or crossbows. But one just squinted down a funny kind of stick thing at Merl here, and he fell—made that hole in him. Him and several others just fell when he pointed that stick thing at them. A terrible talent weapon. Just killed everyone he aimed at. Didn't make a sound."

He paused and looked at Altan with questions in his eyes. "Don' think they were ordinary bandits. It would'a been much worse. They'd 'a stole more. They didn't want supplies—they just wanted to kill,"—he looked down—"and hurt our women."

Altan nodded, and the blacksmith went to comfort a man standing and staring, shoulders slumped, at the smoking blackened stone ruins of a house. A heavy beam fell with a crash. Sparks and soot flew.

Marta looked more closely at the wound as Altan held his hands over it and closed his eyes. The narrow oval hole that pierced his chest had leaked too much blood, and the skin around its edges was heat-seared. It smelled of burnt meat. Her eyes widened. She knew what weapon made that kind of wound, and she knew there were not supposed to be any on this world anywhere. But that's what the bandit she and Sidhari dropped from the air had been carrying. She hadn't wanted to believe it.

Altan laid the young man back down and pulled the rough blanket back up to cover his face. "The wound is a mess inside for such a small entry hole. How is that possible?" he murmured.

He moved to the next of the dead who were laid carefully in a long row under the eaves of the large inn. He knelt, pulling back the first man's shirt to show the same kind of hole in his chest. He laid his hand on it and bowed his head.

Altan frowned and sat back on his heels. "Behind the small entry hole, there is a much larger wound. Half his thorax is a scrambled mass of blood, tissue, and bone. The boy's wound was like this. I've never seen anything like it."

Marta thought he was talking more to himself than to her. How could he see inside the body? She swallowed her question.

He turned to the next body, that of a young girl. A hole gaped in her throat, her rough tunic soaked with blood, her fair hair matted with it. Her face seemed surprised, almost smiling. Her wide-open blue eyes stared up into Marta's as if to say, "What happened?" Marta was trapped by those eyes for several minutes, then tore her gaze away, confused and frightened. What was she to do? She knew what had caused these wounds, these deaths. And she couldn't say.

Marta watched her feet kick through the tall grass as she walked toward the meadow where Sidhari waited with the other Karda, several buckets scattered around them. Someone had brought them water. She felt guilty for not thinking of it herself. She leaned into Sidhari's muscular shoulder, thinking furiously. It could be some time before she would be able to get off by herself and use her Cue to report what she'd seen. The man she and Sidhari dropped from the air lay just inside the trees at the other side of the meadow. She walked toward him, searching the grass. The akengun lay about four meters from where his body was crumpled, one leg bent at an impossible angle behind him. She tried not to look.

~They were murderers,~ Sidhari said.

~I know. It's just gruesome. You've killed before, too?~ It wasn't quite a question.

~I've lived a very long time, Marta.~

Marta turned to look at Sidhari in surprise. Sidhari had never said anything remotely personal to her before. Her origins, like all Karda's, were a close secret, which was a big part of what made finding the fledglings so special. Sidhari's feelings, other than her love for her rider, were carefully shielded, seldom leaking through her iron control.

A sudden flash of green light, a jolt of disorientation, knocked her to her knees. Her head filled with the vision of another village engulfed in smoke, people running for shelter, women screaming, children snatched up and thrown down again by rough, laughing men from the backs of their horses. Women ran, men on horseback running them down. The heat from burning buildings and terror from panicked villagers scalded her skin.

She felt held against something warm and hard. She looked up to see concerned green eyes looking down at her. She was lying in Altan's lap, his arms holding her tight. She looked around wildly— no horse- men, no bandits, only smoke from the smoldering buildings and villagers staring at her.

She stood, not sure her legs would hold her, and moved away from him, embarrassed. Confusion warred with an unwanted desire to stay right there in his lap.

He stood with her, his sword-calloused hand circling her arm. "What is it, Marta? What happened? You were standing here frozen, and then you sort of went blank and collapsed. Are you sick? Was this fight too much for you?"

She looked at him in confusion, still caught in terror, unable to push it away from her. "I'm all right," she finally said, words croaking out of the thick clog in her throat. "Just dizzy for a moment. It's been a long time between meals." She stepped away from him.

Not convinced, he waited for a better explanation. She didn't offer any, and he finally let go of her arm. If it was another attack on a village, there was nothing she could do. No landmarks, nothing that would tell them where—or even when—it was happening, if it even was. She hated this. Too many odd happenings too fast.

~How long are you going to be able to hold yourself between your two worlds?~ Sidhari asked her.

Marta looked up in surprise. ~What do you mean?~ she asked her Karda, her best friend.

Sidhari said nothing, just put her head down and continued stripping plump seed heads from the ripe grass. Marta gave up waiting for an answer she wasn't sure she wanted and walked back to the village square. She left the gun lying where it was. Its front flange was crumpled, so it was useless. When they found it, the blacksmith could use the metal. She needed to report this. And soon. The only akenguns she knew of were locked in the ship captain's gun locker. A seldom-used precaution against an emergency.

She walked back, her steps slow, her thoughts racing. She helped villagers move wounded inside the houses. Some stood staring hopelessly at smoking ruins. Altan talked with the headman, running one hand through his hair, pulling it from its tail. The leather tie fell to the ground.

He reached down to pick it up. "You won't starve over the winter. They didn't burn your mill. Guardian Stephan will send wagons with grain and seed for spring planting. Tell me what you think you'll need. We'll send what we can. It will be a while before I'm back in Toldar, but I'll send word to Father. We're on our way to Restal Prime now for trade talks. And talks about these border raids. You aren't the only ones hit."

He reached out and grasped the man's forearm. "I'll take care of it as soon as I can. And I'll make sure your healer has help dealing with the women who were forced. It takes a special kind of healer— and time."

Matyn expressed his gratitude for their help. They watched Dalt land, and Marta, Altan, and Lyall headed back to the meadow.

"They rode off to the northeast, toward Restal and the edge of the mountains," Dalt told the others. "I got one with my bow, but the other headed down a brush-filled ravine. He got away. I figured one wouldn't be a threat. I doubt he'll be back, anyway." The wiry captain's smile was a grimace showing too much tooth.

"Matyn says they were hooded and masked, but he isn't sure they were raiders. If there was a strong talent with them, they were very successful raiders. Too successful. He also said they were too disciplined, at least before we got here," said Altan. "And they burned the grain in the storehouse. Raiders don't do that. They want to come back in the winter for more."

He turned to tighten the straps of Kibrath's saddle. "It's time to go. We're to meet the pack train at Bardil at dusk, and that's coming fast. We've done what we can here." He looked at Marta for a long moment, then shrugged, put his hand on Kibrath's shoulder and jumped from his knee into the saddle. The other three mounted, and they cantered down the meadow, shadows from the tall trees stretching across it. They took off one after the other and circled high into the darkening sky.

CHAPTER FOURTEEN

"R eaden has assured me that there are no groups of marauders sheltering inside our borders." Roland looked to Readen. "Tell Altan what you found when you took the Mounted Patrol out there." He looked back at Altan. "He spent two tendays in the most deplorable conditions." His steward entered the room and stood behind him with a handful of papers. Roland flapped his hand at Readen in a come-on- tell-all motion and started going through the papers, carrying on a sotto voce conversation with the steward.

Altan sucked a long, hard breath through his nose and held it until he had to let it out. But slowly. Two days of trade conversations with Roland, Daryl, and Readen eroded his patience to a thin layer. But at least there'd been progress on the exchange of Toldar's grain and cotton for the wine, wool, iron and copper ore produced in Restal. He even managed to talk them out of some of the rare waterproof wool that formed a flexible armor when woven with spider silk. He could take that back to his father with pride. They touched lightly, and gingerly, several times on the issue they were attempting to finalize this afternoon—the bands of raiders.

All three of the Restal men were lined up in a row on the other side of the table from him. He tried unsuccessfully to change the seating each day. They outnumbered him and made him feel more petitioner than participant. He could only be grateful Roland hadn't raised their seats so they could peer down on him.

Readen leaned forward, forearms flat on the table in front of him, slender fingers laced together, his expression radiating patience and goodwill. Practiced patience and goodwill. "Although I didn't cross the borders with my troop," Readen paused his slow, deliberate delivery. "Of course, Altan, it is easier to pay attention to borders when you are on the ground. Flying allows more latitude." He looked back and forth between Altan and Daryl as if they violated borders every day on their Karda, but he would forgive them. "I spent a great deal of time in the villages, particularly the villages hit by the marauders. Altan, every place I stopped, the story was the same. These bands are coming from your side of the border, Altan."

"What do you base that on, Readen? That's not the conclusion my father and I have come to." *In fact, it's the very opposite.* Altan struggled not to show the anger threatening like a flash flood headed for a weak spot in a beaver dam.

Readen shook his head, and his expression changed to concern. "Riding between villages all along our border, I saw no evidence of any encampments, Altan. No hidden caves, no secret deep canyons where such bands could have set themselves up a permanent camp. On the other hand, Altan, I saw plenty of clear evidence of mounted men coming from your side of the border where they crossed into Restal."

Altan interrupted him. "I'm afraid we're going to have to agree to disagree." *I think if I charge him every time he says my name, I can pay for this frustrating trip, the condescending…*

Then Readen began listing villages near where he'd found evidence of raiders crossing from Toldar. Villages on the Toldar side of the border, which, according to him, had no problems with raiding bands and villages in Restal which, again according to him, *had* suffered attacks. Altan started counting every time Readen used his name. He stopped at eight.

When Readen finished, Altan kept the tone of his voice even, the pace of his words steady as he answered. "Which direction are they coming and going from, Readen? How many raiders did you see? Did you find tracks leaving Toldar overlapped by tracks coming back? Or the reverse? Readen."

Anger flashed on Readen's face and disappeared so fast Altan wasn't sure he'd seen it.

"It rained too often, Altan, during the time we were out there, for us to be certain. The trails were a mess. But I am convinced they are coming into Restal from Toldar, Altan. And so were the villagers I talked to." Readen's slow, too-quiet voice shouted patience. His head tilted as if to say: I'm truly sorry to have to tell you these things but...

Altan looked at Daryl. Why was he not saying anything about this? Dalt told him Daryl's Karda Patrollers said he is out with them all the time. He has to have seen something.

"Daryl, what have you seen when you fly your patrols along the border. What of the fourteen villages attacked on our side of the border? Did you see smoke from at least some of them on your over-flights? Have you seen no evidence of the bandits crossing from Restal, as our villagers report to us? The village we came upon during an attack as we flew here was definitely invaded by men crossing from your side of the border. The holder where we stayed sent men to back-track them, and those tracks led to Restal. They weren't the first he'd seen in his holding."

Daryl straightened in his chair, his face pink beneath the sun bronze. "Readen and his Mounted Patrol are the ones who police that part of the quadrant. The Karda Patrol's territory is the central part where most of our population is. Readen says our side of the border is not populated enough to waste Karda time on patrols there, so I'm afraid I can't add much to this conversation. And he keeps track of what goes on in the north as his holding and mines are there."

He abdicates his responsibility to Readen. He doesn't even consider it a dereliction of his duty. And I wonder whose idea it was to separate their areas like this. Readen's holding is where the mines are. And he is the one patrolling their southern border with us where it's apparently not a waste of time to send

171

their Mounted Patrol. Hmmm. Altan gave up. Readen wasn't going to admit the raiders were Restalans.

Altan looked from Daryl to Readen. "There was some unfamiliar long-distance weapon used in that village that caused wounds I've never seen before. It did far more damage than the strongest crossbow. The people who witnessed its use described it as a long stick-like thing that the user simply pointed, and it killed, silently, with no arrow or bolt. The headman of the village called it a talent weapon. I've never heard of anything like that. Have you had any reports?"

"Altan, I'd be the last person to ask about a talent weapon." Readen's smile was the most twisted and insincere smile Altan had ever seen.

Daryl bit his lip, looking back and forth between the two of them.

Oops, I forgot. Father told me and told me. Never mention talent anywhere near Readen. Or Roland. Readen is the only person he's ever heard of who has no talent at all.

Altan looked at Roland, who was gathering his papers together and handing them to the steward. *And Father claims Roland is misusing his so egregiously he is weakening it all over Restal. From the look of the country-side, I don't think he's mistaken.*

Roland slapped both hands on the table, and all three of the others jumped. "Well, I think we've had some fruitful discussions these past two days. Now it's time to enjoy ourselves. You three amuse yourselves this afternoon, and I'll see you tonight at the dinner honoring our visitors from the south. I look forward to it. My steward and I have just been going over the menu, and I think you'll be very pleased with the wine selection alone. We've produced some excellent vintages in the last few years, and as a special treat for you and your party, Altan, I've told him to bring up one of the fine vintages from six years ago. If you like it, Altan, I'll be happy to send some back with you for your father."

Altan had to work hard to keep his shoulders from slumping. *I guess we're finished talking about border incidents. Readen has produced more fertilizer than fruit, but it seems that's all we're going to get. I'll have to be satisfied with the trade agreements. I think I won there. I hope Father agrees.*

Marta sat on the dais overlooking the large hall of Restal Prime, uncomfortable in her floor-length, low-cut dress of embroidered green silk, her auburn hair in loose curls down her back. She fiddled with one earring, pulling at it, realized what she was doing, and dropped her hand. This was their last night in Restal. As Altan's Mi'hiru she was treated with the courtesy and respect due her as his peer, unlike the few times she had attended when she was posted here. It was not a position she was comfortable with, especially wearing this too-revealing dress. Though she had liked the look in Altan's eyes when he'd seen her. There was nothing wrong with feeling pleased about being noticed.

She sat at Altan's right and Altan to the right of Guardian Roland. On her other side the guardian's elder son, Readen, kept her in conversation. Daryl sat to the left of Roland. Altan was icily polite, dancing with her once to satisfy protocol, then all but ignoring her for the rest of the evening, except for the occasional cutting remark. She sensed his stiff displeasure through her shields, and it made her furious. Her behavior was fine. Certainly no discredit to either the Mi'hiru or to Toldar. She started to pull at her earring again and dropped her hand to her lap.

Readen was a good distraction. She tightened her shields further. Whatever it was about Readen that was pushing against them, she refused to acknowledge. She was uncomfortable enough with block-of- burning-ice Altan on her other side.

Readen tilted his chair back, legs stretched in front of him, shoulder length hair brushed back from his high forehead. He swirled dark red wine around in the bowl of his cut crystal wine glass. She had to turn her back to Altan to talk to him, which was fine with her.

"I shall provide you with a map of who is who tonight so you won't get lost. Or caught by someone tedious, which would be worse." He lifted his glass to a woman across the room, who lifted hers back with a bright smile. "That's Easily Eleanna. Of course, I never call her that to her face. Or at least since she married Battering Baylee, who earned that name in the early days of their marriage."

Readen's solemn tone mocked that of a pedantic professor. "And the tall man at the table next to them with non-existent muscles is Garrulous Gardner to whom I shall not introduce you as it would take the rest of the evening. The small but rotund woman he's talking to, or at, is Querulous Corra. I think their names, as well as their shapes, make them well suited for each other, don't you? I expect good news from them any day now. He shall tell me about it with verve, volume, and verbosity, and she shall be petty, petulant, and, well, not pretty, is she?"

He tapped a cheek with his finger. "Let's see. Over in the corner, cornering someone I can't see as he takes up so much space, physically as well as verbally, is Jocular Joseph. Wetly, too, as he tends to spray with enthusiasm as he talks."

"How do you think of these names?" Marta was finding it hard to breathe, trying to keep from laughing out loud, afraid if she took a sip of wine she'd spray it across the table.

I think I'm getting hysterical. Cool, insouciant Readen on one side and Altan-I-am-a-volcano-about-to-blow scorching the other would make anyone want to scream. Then she saw the man Readen had so lightly named Garrulous Gardner walk away from Corra, devastation naked on his face and in the sharp slope of his shoulders, and her laughter wilted. She raised her glass and drank to cover her sudden mood change.

"I pass the time at these interminable dinners—dinner with you, of course, will not be long enough—by making up names to suit each one in the room. It's so easy I often wonder if their parents chose their names to suit their personalities."

"I'm afraid to ask what name you have for me."

"Madly Marta, of course, as I am fast falling madly in love with you and intend to take you away from Ardent Altan, who is gloriously glaring at me."

"Ah, and I shall call you Riotous Readen. I think you've earned it." She turned her head slightly to glance at Altan, and yes, he was glaring.

"And now, I am afraid I am called to duty." He glanced around her at Roland, who was gesturing insistently toward the dancers on the floor, and pulled his face into a pout. "Father is pointedly pointing me to Angelic Angela, who is twice my age and whose wings are slightly tarnished. But Father likes to keep her happy. He has been trying to get her to give him a cutting of one of the few roses he doesn't already have, and they are in the middle of some very delicate negotiations. I shall return wearing her halo." And Readen stood, leaning close, and murmured in her ear, promising to send her tens of tens of roses if he succeeded. He flicked her earring and left the dais.

Marta turned to Altan, but he ignored her, purposefully leaning around Guardian Roland to say something to Daryl she didn't catch. She sucked in her breath angrily and turned away, looking out over the hall. A movement at the entrance opposite the dais caught her attention. A tall blond man stood in the doorway, looking startled at the festivities. It was Galen Morel. She looked away in confusion and saw Readen notice him, also.

His sudden fury blazed like fire even from across the room and was just as suddenly extinguished.

She dropped her gaze just as he looked from Galen to her. She took a sip of wine and ate a small savory to cover her confusion, pulling at her earring. *I have to break this habit. My ear is getting sore, and it shows I'm nervous. Not a good thing. What is Galen doing here again? Restal's far from his assigned territory.* Agents were always notified when someone changed from one section to another. She could see no reason for him to be here in her territory twice.

Galen jerked his head at Readen and walked away. Marta didn't know if he'd seen her. What should she do? Make herself known to him, or not? Providing she could find him. *I can't leap up from the table and go chasing down the hall after him.*

Readen returned and leaned over her shoulder, his face so close she could feel the heat from his cheek. His long hair brushed her neck. He tugged at her earring again. "If you don't leave this pretty ring alone you'll pull it out of your ear. Please excuse me, Marta, something has come up I must attend to. I hope to see you again before you leave on the morrow, but if I am not able, it has been a pleasure, and I am sure we will meet again before much longer."

He touched her shoulder, the gesture uncomfortably intimate, and left. It was too much coincidence to think that Readen's sudden need to see to something was unconnected with Galen Morel's sudden appearance.

Altan interrupted her thoughts. "So, your friend has abandoned you, has he?" With a raised eyebrow and a mocking smile, he invited her to dance.

"My friend, as you call him, had something to attend to more important than dancing, but yes, I would like to dance." She smiled back at him as sweet and innocent a smile as she could manage.

Dancing with Altan was uncomfortable. As hard as she tried, she couldn't build her walls thick enough, and his irritation leaked through. Though she couldn't imagine why he was irritated. Her body was so stiff it was difficult not to stumble, and he seemed the same.

"I'll be glad to be in the air tomorrow and on our way back," he finally said by way of some kind of conversation.

"Yes, I have missed Sidhari. It is difficult to be away from her for so long."

"I thought you tended our Karda every morning?"

"A few minutes in the mornings are not enough. I especially miss the young ones we left in Toldar. I hated leaving them for so long."

He looked down at her, his face softened, and he pulled her slightly closer. "Me too."

Silence settled between them, and the dance ended with a little less tension.

CHAPTER FIFTEEN

G alen Morel sat, tiredness tarnishing his too-handsome face, and took a big gulp of the wine he poured for himself. His boots were muddy, and his damp, travel-stained jacket hung on the back of the chair. A pair of wet leather gloves lay balanced across one knee.

"It's a galaxy-be-damned long way for me to come here because you couldn't resist using those guns. Marta reported finding one. How could you have been so irresponsible? I told you not to use them." His voice rose, and he slashed an arm out in front of him. "Now you've lost one, and she found it."

Readen fumed and paced the round tower room before the fireplace with its cold magma stones. He kicked at them, irritated that he was going to have to call a servant with talent to heat them. Wood was still too scarce and precious to use for fires. Roland, all too willing to indulge himself with wood fires, refused to allow them anywhere but his apartments.

"Me'Gerron and the villagers thought they were some magical weapon," said Galen. "Father sent me on this be-damned long trip to tell you: Don't do that again. He went to a lot of trouble to hide her report." He paused. "If someone finds it, they're likely to remember her reporting I was here before. If they go snooping, they'll uncover my trips here, and Father won't be able to field that. I have no official reason for coming, especially not so often."

Readen just looked at him, his eyes colder than usual, and sat in the opposite chair, propping his elbows on his knees, hands steepled under his chin.

Galen crossed his legs. His lips were tight in a hard line. He took a sharp breath and said, his tone curt, "I've been riding for days." He looked up, irritation drawing his brows into a frown. "And I had to ride hard dodging one of those 'bandit' groups you're financing. I have other work I need to be doing. Being gone so long and so often takes too much of my time. Someone is going to notice how little information I'm sending. I can't even fake it. If I send data from anywhere but a few kilometers from where I'm supposed to be, that, too, would raise flags. Galaxies, Readen. Use some self-control." He stood abruptly and started to pace across the room. "I'll have to leave again first thing in the morning, and I'm already exhausted. I hate having to make this trip so soon after I got back."

Readen forced himself to calm until he could no longer feel the pulse pounding his temples. *The arrogant coward can't even admit we have to kill the Mi'hiru. It will be more than a year before the consortium ship announces its presence, and I'll need every bit of that time for what I plan. She could spoil things any moment. Do they think I'm going to wait?*

"Sit down and relax for a minute before you go, Galen. Have another glass of wine." He thought about the young girl awaiting him in the cells below and power moved smoothly up his body and into his voice. The fingers of one hand resting over the medallion he wore beneath his tunic, he began murmuring, voice soft, mesmerizing, relentless, never letting Galen's eyes move from his.

When Galen finally left, the confusion and uncertainty in his demeanor were barely discernible, Readen noted with pleasure. He still showed a facade of cocky attitude, and his pupils were only a little dilated. No one would notice. Readen was well pleased with his work. Coercions that left some independence in the subject were difficult. Coercions that didn't created an automaton. That he didn't need.

Marta stood at the edge of the long clearing in the woods, fuming, staring at the Cue in her hand, wanting to throw it as far as she could. Sidhari dug for bulbs at the edge of the trees, nearly bare of leaves. Damp cold wind whipped the bare branches, and gray clouds scudded across the sky, racing swiftly from the north. They'd been back in Toldar for a few tendays, and she was the support Mi'hiru again for the patrol wing of Altan, Captain Dalt, and Lyall. She'd taken the opportunity to find this remote clearing where she could use her Cue unnoticed.

"Galen was just where he was supposed to be all that tenday." Kayne's words from the data-com unit were studied and patient. "You must have been mistaken. I talk long and hard to keep them from recalling you for assessment. I know you're working hard, and your job is not easy. Do you need to come back up here for a time?"

"Do you think I imagined seeing him, sir? I wasn't mistaken, and I didn't imagine it. The job is no more difficult than I thought it would be. I'm fine."

Kayne cleared his throat. When he went on, his tone went from warm to cool. "You're spending too much time with those flying creatures and on useless patrols out in the middle of nowhere. You're supposed to be insinuating yourself firmly into the guardian's politics. You've reported no progress in developing a close relationship with the Me'Gerron son, Altan." Kayne's voice went on and on, finally ending with, "Do you want to be recalled? Is that what this is? A failure would not look good on your record. And quite frankly, it wouldn't make me look good either. I've been standing up for you, Marta."

Standing up for me? What does that mean? To whom? And why? "I'll report again in a month. The weather's looking bad, and I need to get to shelter soon." She didn't answer his question. It was rhetorical anyway. The consortium needed her where she was. In spite of her determined reluctance to entangle herself with Altan—and in spite of Kayne's accusations—she provided a mass of data about the quadrants and their people. She'd sent reports on trade goods, resources, culture, the relaxed political atmosphere in Toldar, the unease and distrust in Restal. She'd collected what seemed like bushels of seeds, plants, soil samples for Cedar's bio-systems drones to pick up. And after the Tela Oroku, she was more diligent about collecting legends and stories about the colony's early days, however fanciful they sounded. She was doing her job and doing it well, no matter what Kayne said.

She ended the communication and walked back to Sidhari, idly kicking dirt over the holes Sidhari had dug under the immense spreading oak at the edge of the meadow. She sat at the base of the wide trunk on one of the buttressed roots, leaning back, watching dark silver-edged clouds fly through the lacework of bare black branches above her while Sidhari dug and scratched nearby.

~I am sorry, Marta. I know how difficult this is for you. Torn between these two worlds. I can feel the pain pulling at you.~ Sidhari's voice was a soft whisper in her head.

Marta jerked up. ~What do you mean? Two worlds?~

~Did you think I wouldn't know what has been bothering you so? You have been conflicted since the beginning.~

Marta stared at the Karda for a long time, not sure what to think.

Since the beginning? Sidhari has known what I am since we met?

~You are going to have to choose soon.~ Sidhari's tone was matter- of-fact.

~I'm not ready to choose. And it's my problem, not yours.~ When did she start admitting to herself that she had a choice? She didn't, did she?

~No, you are wrong. It is very much my problem.~

~What do you mean?~

Sidhari walked away toward the edge of the woods, found some late-bearing berry bushes to strip and didn't answer.

Marta sat leaning against the tree until she was nearly frozen. She let its deep calmness soothe her distress, grounding her. It no longer startled or frightened her to feel the tree's remote consciousness.

Sidhari nudged her leg, nibbling with her curved predator's beak at Marta's flying leathers. ~It's getting late. And sitting here feeling sorry for yourself isn't doing either of us much good. I'm hungry, and so are you. Let's go before the weather gets too rough to fly, and we are stuck here.~

Marta pulled herself up, smiling ruefully. ~That's the best idea I've heard all day,~ she pathed back at the beautiful Karda, looking with love and appreciation at bronze wing tips ruffling in impatience, shining even in the dull light of the cloud-dreary afternoon. They had three more days of patrol before they had to be back in Toldar, three more days to decide what to do. But for now, it was time to find the Me'Byrhn Holding where she and the Karda patrollers were staying tonight.

She looked forward to an evening spent with Holder Me'Byrhn's sizable and unruly family. With gruff Dalt, young Lyall, and even Altan—her patrol partners again. Marta was surprised that her discomfort during the occasional patrol with Altan's unit was no longer quite so strong. Maybe this would be a fun evening. Dalt had a way of pricking at Altan's arrogance that made her laugh, and he indulged in it often. Plus he usually punctuated his comments with the title Guardian Heir, which Altan hated.

Her anger and confusion about the conversation with Kayne Morel dissipating for the moment, Marta mounted, hooked herself into the stirrups and leg straps of her rig, and the two of them cantered through fall-browned grass to take to the air with thunderous snaps of Sidhari's wings. They circled up into the afternoon sky and headed north and west for the last part of their patrol. Marta leaned forward into the cold wind, grateful for her leathers and the sheepskin vest, melding her mind with Sidhari's, working into the hawk-like vision of the Karda, so much better than her own.

They flew for about an hour before Marta began to sense several sizable beings ahead of them on the ground. Maybe a herd of deer or the native elk-like creatures called orda, but it didn't feel like that. It radiated intense danger, and a prickling spread across her neck and shoulders.

~Drop down a little, Sidhari. I sense something ahead. Let's check it out.~ She scanned the scattered trees beneath them for activity and found it. A band of horsemen made its way out of the foothills on Restal's border. ~I can't see well through the trees. Can you? Circle down a little more, but be careful. We don't want to get too close.~

~There shouldn't be that big a group of horsemen here.~

~There's a village about two miles from here. If they look like raiders, we'll have to find Altan.~

~Or you could just call him.~

Marta ignored that. As they glided lower, the horsemen saw them, pulled up, and several pointed toward the flyers and raised crossbows. Sidhari started beating her wings to gain altitude, but it was too late. She screamed in pain. Horrified, Marta watched blood fly from her wing, a crossbow bolt poking up through it.

The Karda struggled up, trying to gain altitude, veering away from the horsemen who disappeared from view as the two of them sailed awkwardly over the thick forest. Marta searched desperately for a safe place to land and found nothing open enough. Sidhari struggled to stay aloft. Her pain and effort pounded at Marta through their bond. It pierced her upper arm and wrenched at her heart.

Fighting the fear for Sidhari that shivered through her, she finally spotted a narrow rocky ridge to the west, its top mostly bare of trees. She pointed Sidhari toward it, urging her on, doing her best to keep the terror making her hands shake and her throat clench from leaking through their bond. They circled down, Sidhari struggling to move her wing. Fighting the sharp gusts of a crosswind at the top of the ridge, they barely cleared the few straggly trees before they hit the ground. Sidhari stumbled to her knees, her wounded wing outstretched in pain. Marta felt her leg straps give, and she hit the ground, hard, banging her head on a rock. There was a sickening crack, and pain seared her right arm. She tumbled to a stop, dizzy. Something dripped down the side of her face, and she wiped at her forehead with her left hand. It hurt. She blinked at the blood on her fingers.

Sidhari's distress pounded through Marta's senses. She forced herself up, agony sharp in her right forearm. She clamped her teeth together and worked her broken arm out of her vest—breath hissing through her clenched teeth—then buttoned her arm inside to support it against her chest. She had to sit for a minute before she unbuckled the saddle and packs off Sidhari using her good hand. Sidhari limped painfully down off the ridge to the edge of the trees, her wing dragging. Marta hoped they'd managed to fly far enough to elude the bandits. She carried one pack hooked over her unbroken arm.

The Karda stood head down, breathing heavily, injured wing outstretched in pain, the bolt poking through at an angle in the leading edge, blood dripping much too fast. Marta examined it closely.

~I'll have to pull it out and find something to pad it with to stop the bleeding. I'm afraid I'll hurt you more.~

~There isn't any choice. You are the only one here with two hands. Do it quickly.~ Sidhari's voice was strong, but Marta heard the pain in it.

~One of them nearly useless,~ she said, cradling her throbbing arm. ~I'm pretty sure my arm is broken.~

Marta cut the tail off her long sheepskin vest to make two large pads. Working as gently as she could, she drew the bolt out of the wound. Sidhari hissed. Marta fought dizziness and pain, both her own and the Karda's through their bond. Teeth gritted and jaw clenched, she pressed a pad to the top side of the wound to slow the blood loss.

She moved under Sidhari's wing and used the shoulder of her broken arm to hold a pad to the underside of the wing, pressing as hard as she dared. She wouldn't even think about broken bones. She held them for several long minutes, hoping to at least slow the blood flow, nearly biting a hole in her lip from the pain. It finally began to slow enough she thought she could leave it to find something to secure the pads to the wing.

She cut two more pads, holding the vest with her feet and sawing at it 2i5h the knife she pulled from the sheath strapped to her leg. She trudged back up the ridge to find where her other pack had broken loose from the back of the saddle. *Probably what broke my arm.* She dragged it back to Sidhari. Fumbling at the buckles with her one able hand, she was crying with frustration before they finally came undone. She pulled out her blanket and tore it into long strips, tying them together as best she could with one hand and her teeth.

She looked at Sidhari. ~This is going to hurt, but I have to wrap it. The pads won't stay on if I don't, and we don't need for you to lose any more blood.~

Working together, they managed to get the pad on the underside of Sidhari's wing firmly held as the Karda folded her wing to her body, hissing with pain, Marta supporting it as best she could. She tossed one end of a blanket strip over Sidhari's back and crawled under her belly, having to stop halfway and breathe for a few minutes before she could place the other pad, pull the ends together and tie them, again with one hand and her teeth. It wasn't a pretty wrap job when she finished, but maybe it would keep the pads pressed firmly enough against the wound that Sidhari wouldn't bleed to death. Marta stomped on that thought.

Finally, she stepped away. Sidhari's head hung low from pain and loss of blood. She'd stopped hissing. Carefully she lay down, front legs folded under her massive chest. She rested her head on the ground, long graceful neck stretched out, eyes closing.

~I'm sorry, Marta. I have to rest. I think I strained some important muscles when we fell. And I'm a little light-headed.~

Marta smiled a shaky smile and scratched Sidhari's head. *Even when she's hurt, she's so formal.* ~I wish I could do more.~ She watched for a moment until Sidhari's breathing smoothed. *I hope those bandits are far away and black hole bound, because we're helpless here. My bow broke in the fall, and I couldn't draw it anyway. I have no weapons besides a sword I can't use and a little knife.* She dropped down onto a large rock, head swimming. Pain surged with a vengeance, and she fought to keep from passing out.

Heavy clouds blotted out the late afternoon sun, and it was turning colder. The air smelled of rain. She would need to do something soon to keep herself from freezing. Sidhari wouldn't be able to fly, maybe not even to walk very far. Karda's wings were fragile despite their size. Losing much more blood would be dangerous. Her efforts had only slowed it, she knew, not stopped it. The vessels supplying the wings were large. Flying took a lot of energy. She couldn't know if any of the delicate bones were damaged, and she hadn't looked for broken feathers.

Marta wasn't sure where they had landed in relation to the band of men she had seen. She wasn't sure where the border was either. She didn't know how much blood Sidhari had lost. Lots, from the look of her wing. Blood soaked the feathers on its leading edge for half a meter each side of the wound. Trying to walk out would be painful for Marta, but it could be fatal for Sidhari. If she were even able.

She went to her pack, struggling to pull out her short, warm cloak. It wouldn't cover much of her. The shreds of the blanket left after tearing off the strips to wrap Sidhari's wing were useless. Altan and the others would be looking for her if she didn't come in, but they probably wouldn't worry until late, and Karda didn't like to fly in the dark. They were stuck up here on this windy ridge until the next day, and she wasn't sure how far outside her assigned patrol area she was. She'd been on the very edge when she'd seen the band of men. They'd flown even farther into the hills. The border with Restal was close, whichever side of it they were on.

The emergency rations in her saddlebags held enough for herself and Sidhari for the night and morning, but that was all. This rocky forest ridge wouldn't have any of the bulbs and tubers that might have helped, and she hadn't seen any water. Her water pouches wouldn't be nearly enough. It could be several days before anyone found them. If those men were raiders, they could be looking for them even now. All she had was her sword and a broken arm. Marta was frightened. As frightened as she'd ever been.

Wrapping herself in the cloak, shivering, she curled up on the ground as close to Sidhari as she could get without disturbing her. At least the break in her arm wasn't a compound fracture. It was secure enough buttoned tight to her chest. As long as she didn't move, the pain was almost tolerable. The air was colder, and she was sure rain was coming, probably with ice. Snow would be better.

Freezing rain was more likely. She was in trouble. She couldn't build a fire with one hand and shouldn't anyway. The smoke would show those men exactly where to look for her. The stunted trees on this windy ridge offered little shelter.

She needed help. Marta dropped her head, fighting tears. She had worked so hard at keeping Altan out of her head, out of her thoughts. Now all she could think about was how much she wished she could reach him, mocking, insolent grin and all. She hugged her broken arm to her chest, pulled her heavy cloak tight around her, and pillowed her head on her pack. The rocky ground was cold. Low clouds blanketed the afternoon sky. Marta fell into an uneasy sleep of exhaustion and pain, calling to Altan. *Find us. Please find us*

CHAPTER SIXTEEN

Altan circled high, at the edge of Restal territory, rising up a thermal. Kibrath's body jerked beneath him.

~Something's happened to Sidhari and Marta.~ Kibrath's tone was distressed. ~Can you feel it?~

~Shock. I sense shock.~ They were at the edge of the territory he'd assigned Marta. A memory of Marta—hot and dusty, sweat-dampened auburn tendrils escaping the braid down her back, concentration on the Karda she was grooming so intense she didn't notice him until he cleared his throat. She jumped, spilling the small clay bottle of oil she was using down the skirt of her work clothes, and glared at him with the intense blue eyes he couldn't get used to.

Where was she? His mouth went dry, his neck and shoulders drew up tight. Intense awareness of her fear tightened the muscles in his stomach. ~Any sense of their direction, Kibrath?~

~To the north and east. Closer to the mountains.~

They searched the deep ravines and sharp ridges below them, flying a zig-zag pattern. Kibrath flew so fast that every time he dipped a wing and changed direction, the force jabbed the cantle of the saddle into Altan's back. His hands gripped the handle on the pommel until they ached.

Where was she? Confusion, fear, then a jab of sharp pain in his right arm doubled him over.

Kibrath screamed.

He forced the pain away. The clouds were lowering, and the air grew colder with the sharp promise of icy rain. He was cold despite his flying leathers and sheepskin vest. They had to find them soon. They were almost over Restal's border. ~Let's head more north.~

Kibrath refused, turning farther northeast. ~I think they've landed.

Sidhari is badly hurt. We're close.~

It was hard to concentrate past Marta's pain and distress pounding his shields. Another shooting pain stabbed his arm. Fear, pain, cold flooded his body. She was hurt. And scared.

Altan had worked so hard keeping his mental barriers up against Marta, it terrified him he might not be able to find her.

He spotted a group of eight mounted men below, coming from the direction of the Restal border. One of them lifted a crossbow and fired. The bolt arched beneath them. They were too high.

Alan could see these were no ordinary raiders—too organized, too disciplined, too well equipped. Was Roland provoking war? The men were headed deeper into Toldar territory toward a small village.

Fury bit hard. Adrenalin flooded tension away.

~Sidhari is hurt. She's been shot,~ Kibrath said and dove at the riders faster than the stoop of a hungry hawk.

Cold, screaming air blew tears from Altan's eyes into his hairline. He leaned into Kibrath's neck, mane lashing him. The force of their speed pulled at the muscles of his face. He clamped his eyes and lips tight. The Karda ended his dive in a stomach-lurching swoop that clipped the top needles of a tall pine.

Altan shook out his right arm, drew on the energy from the black clouds above, and aimed a fire bolt at the men and horses below them. The spear of fire struck the lead horseman. He and his horse went over in a smoking tumble and didn't get up.

He threw another bolt into the riot of terrified men and rearing, bucking horses. Screams rose in the cold air. Fire flashed, dirt and rocks flew, and three more horses and riders went down, bodies smoking on the ground. The rest of the men struggled to control their frantic mounts and raced for the trees.

Altan and Kibrath circled for a few more minutes until he was sure they headed down the hills away from the direction he felt Marta. He couldn't throw bolts through the trees for fear of fire, so they circled back up and flew farther into the foothills. They couldn't chase the men and look for Marta too.

They flew their zig-zag pattern for hours or an eternity. Finally, ~Look down, Blessed Adalta, look down here,~ the words shouted in his head. Altan saw her at the same time Kibrath did. Relief swam through his head. He sucked in a deep breath to still its swirl. They circled too fast down to the ridge, fought the fierce crosswind, and landed in a flurry of back-winging, dodging rocks and low bushes. Altan tore off his saddle straps and hit the ground running before Kibrath came to a halt, not stopping until he reached Marta.

"You're hurt!" He grabbed her close as she stumbled and nearly fell. She gasped with pain, and he released her, looking her over frantically, wiping at the blood on her face. "Your arm!"

"Sidhari's shot. Please, help her. She's bleeding, and I can't stop it." The words tumbled out of Marta.

"But you're hurt." He could hardly stand for the feelings of hurt and panic coming from her.

"Help Sidhari first," she insisted, dragging on his arm with her good hand.

Altan went to the Karda. Kibrath followed close behind, keening concern to Sidhari. Altan loosened the crude strips binding Sidhari's wing. ~May I, beautiful one?~ he asked Sidhari politely. ~I need to check the bones and see to the bleeding.~

~You are always so charmingly polite with all the ladies, Altan. We are so very relieved to see you and Kibrath. I don't think anything is broken other than a few small feathers, maybe a covert, though I am still bleeding.~

Despite her precise, polite words, he heard the weakness in her voice, sounding too faint in his head. He peeled blood-soaked pads away from her wing. Stretching it out with care, he placed his hands above and below the wound. Eyes closed, he concentrated and pulled energy from the ground beneath them, from the trees and brush and boulders surrounding them, from the lowering clouds above them pregnant with icy rain. His hands rested still and firm around her wound.

Then he slumped, breathing hard, and turned to Marta. The pain and worry creasing her face made him want to hold her close and assure her everything would be all right. *And she wants it, too.* Then he felt her shields snap up. He winced. Maybe he'd imagined it.

"I've stopped the bleeding and healed the muscle. No broken bones, thank Adalta. It will be at least a day before she can fly and then only in short hops. She has some damaged feathers, but not enough to inhibit flying once she recovers her strength. You'll be able to repair them once we get her back to Toldar."

Together, Marta doing the best she could with the pain of her broken arm tightly buttoned inside her vest, they bound Sidhari's wing to her side again with the bloodstained strips from Marta's blanket. The finished job was neater than the one Marta had done. She refused to let him look at her arm or her head until they finished.

He put his hand on her shoulder, grasping it when she pulled away. "I need to see about your arm, Marta." He held her still and sent his attention to the break. "It's broken."

She cocked her head and gave him an I-know-that-and-you're-an- idiot look.

"But it's stable for the moment. Sit down and stay quiet. I need to make us a dry place, and then I'll need to replenish my talent before I can help you." He held her gaze for too long and looked away to hide the heat rising in his face.

The sun was setting, and a freezing drizzle started to fall. Altan cut saplings to make a rough lean-to beneath the overhanging limbs of a spruce, piled boughs on top to keep out the drizzle and inside to keep the two of them off the cold ground. He gathered enough dead wood for a small fire near the front of the lean-to, set it alight with a flick of his fingers, taking care that it was far enough away so no sparks would fall on the resinous branches above. The drizzle and the dense needles of the spruce would hide the smoke if the mounted men managed to get reorganized and come looking, which he doubted. They were far away by now.

Altan fed the two Karda half the rations from their saddlebags and crawled into the tiny lean-to where Marta huddled under his blanket, shivering, her face white with pain.

Gently he cradled her arm in his big hand, holding the other above the swollen break, and closed his eyes. He drew power from the ground around them, pulling it from deep in Adalta. He moved the bone, fit the ends together, fused them, eased the swelling, and repaired the damaged blood vessels. Marta fainted when he wrapped splints around her arm.

Her body would have to work to finish the healing, and she was exhausted from the pain. He cradled her head in his hands, concentrating, searching for signs of concussion, drawing the edges of the small cut on her forehead together and sealing it, taking pains to make sure there would be no scar.

He moved her into a more comfortable position against him, drew enough power to warm the ground beneath them, and watched her. The firelight played on her peaceful face and the hair that came loose from its braid. He had no control over the hand that reached out to smooth it back.

When she surfaced again, Altan's kettle was on the fire with water and tea leaves, and he sat close beside her in the small space. The sharp scent of broken spruce branches mingled with smoke and the smell of the thick soup of dried meat and vegetables heating in his iron pot. Her arm was splinted and wrapped in a sling. Her headache had eased, and she was warm. His blanket covered her. She looked around wildly, hissing when she jerked her arm.

"Where is Sidhari?"

"Kibrath is practically curled around her on the other side of the fire. They're both asleep."

She leaned out of the tiny space to look and sighed in relief. "Will she be all right?" Marta fought the tremor in her voice.

"Yes. She will. As I told you, she's lost enough blood to weaken her, and it'll be a day at least before she can fly. She's also tired from the healing. It took a lot out of her. How are you feeling? You don't have a concussion, but you hit your head pretty hard."

"My arm still hurts, but it's better." He was watching her closely. She was confused. He had stopped the bleeding in Sidhari's wing, closed her wound, and set Marta's arm barely touching it. The swelling in her arm was down, and it itched as if it were well on its way to healed. Just like he had done for the wounded at the village where the bandits had attacked.

And he sounded sure she didn't have a concussion. *It isn't the first time he's used medical terms that seem at odds with this primitive culture. Maybe I need to redefine primitive culture for my next report to the ship.* She rubbed her temple with her good hand. Her head was splitting again.

"What primitive culture?" His loud words scraped the inside of her head like diamond on glass. "What report to what ship?"

Oh, black holes and exploding suns, my shields are down. He heard that. She didn't answer. *What am I going to tell him?*

~Yes, what are you going to tell me?~

His voice in her head was a grating pain, her thoughts like snapping wolves, chasing her secrets out of the corners where she tried to hide them. She turned her head away from him and shut her shields to close him out.

They watched the fire for a long time in the small space, their arms touching. The heat from his body burned her with icy fire.

He waited.

The fire popped.

Altan found both their cups and poured tea. They sat close together and kilometers apart in the small space, drinking hot tea.

He waited.

Marta hunched under the blanket, her good arm around her knees, furious with herself. Furious for letting her shields down.

Furious at the relief that threatened to soothe the anger. "I need to think."

"Yes, I imagine you do. I'm not going anywhere." He waved his arm. "There's nowhere to go." His voice was colder than the icy rain that hissed in the fire. He shifted away from her as far as he could without knocking their shelter down, helped himself to the hot stew of meat and vegetables simmering on the fire, and started to eat.

Her stomach growled. She couldn't serve herself with one arm, and he didn't offer. She thought about her father and what he would expect her to do. *First, don't get caught like this. Well, ok. That part's already in the fire.* She heard his voice. "No attachments, Marta. No attachments."

For the first time, she realized that the reason he insisted on taking her on his every mission even when she was young and it was dangerous was because she was his attachment. Without her, his life would have been emotionally empty. When her mother died, he started taking Marta with him. He, no more than she, couldn't live in the claustrophobic confines of the consortium ship. And his job demanded emotional distance.

Acquaintances were good because they were useful. Friendships were not because they created ties. Even then, leaving a planet when their job ended was hard. She remembered how wrenching it had been when she was young. How difficult it had been to train herself not to care.

She thought about her connections to Sidhari, to the planet, to its people and creatures. She couldn't think about the man calmly eating next to her, so close she could feel the warmth of his body through her clothes. "I love it here," she murmured.

"Well, it's a little cold and damp for me, but I'm glad you're happy." "Not *here* here—in Toldar, on Adalta. Even though I'm not from here, I've grown to think of this as home."

Altan looked at her. She almost flinched at the hard way he held his face. "You're from Anuma Quadrant, right?"

She thought furiously for several minutes, then said, slowly and deliberately, "No. I'm not." She paused. "If I tell you this, you will hold my future,"—she paused again—"maybe even my life, in your hands."

She looked at him for a long moment, then stared at the fire for even longer. "I'm not even from Adalta."

Silence. She risked a glance at him. Still no expression. Or rather, still grim expression—pulled down mouth, pulled down brows.

She shifted away from him and sat straighter, careful of her arm, and stretched her legs toward the little fire, looking at him, watching his eyes. "I am an agent of the trade consortium whose interplanetary ship has been circling Adalta for almost a year now. It has special mirror shields so even when the sun shines directly on it, it can't be seen from the planet and at night it doesn't block the stars. I...we...people like me are sent to discover what we can about your quadrants, your resources, your government, your culture. To help decide the best way to let you know we are here. And to find ways for the consortium to garner support so you will agree to trade negotiations,"—she paused—"without letting anyone know what we are doing. But this time it's different. They want to change your laws and attitudes about the things we have to trade. Highly technological things, the very kinds of things your traditions have banned since your ancestors left Earth."

"That isn't possible. Our history is clear that all records of the Ark Ship we arrived on were erased." He frowned at her.

"Well, we're here, so it is possible. There were enough traces for our agents to find evidence to extrapolate where your colonists might have gone. It took years for the consortium to locate you. Being the first to find a lost colony is extremely profitable. Adalta is not the only lost world. Other Ark Ships went astray. The diaspora was a confusing time."

She heard him draw in his breath, then tense silence. She clenched the fist of her good arm. Her fingernails cut into her palm.

"I have done this kind of job—gathering information—on several worlds since I was a small child traveling with my father. Almost fifteen years. We were very good at gathering information." She smiled, thinking her face should shatter, she felt so frozen—

inside and out. "Who would suspect a father and daughter of being anything other than the traders they pretended to be? Or whatever role we assumed."

He said nothing, his face a mask, so she went on. "I have decided not to do this anymore. So, unless you decide to kill me"—she risked a shaky smile—"or turn me in as a spy, I will find my way somewhere with the Karda I love and stay on this world. I'm good with Karda, and I should be able to find work anywhere. And I think Sidhari would go with me. If you don't kill me." She hoped he thought that was a joke, feeble though it was.

He filled his bowl again, held it out to her, and fished in one of the packs he'd shoved behind them for a clean spoon. She looked at him and back to the bowl. A muscle in his jaw bunched, and he propped the bowl on her knee, holding it so she could eat.

"Thank you."

He jerked his head slightly.

He waited for her to finish, handed her a cup of hot tea, wiped the bowl and utensils clean, and stored them back in the pack.

Finally, through clenched teeth, he asked, "What have you told them?"

She propped her aching arm on her blanket-wrapped knees and looked sideways at his profile. His lips formed a tight, straight line, a muscle in his jaw clenched so hard it bulged—a vein in his head pulsed.

"My brief is to collect social, cultural, political, and resource information to aid the consortium in forming a trade relationship." She laughed, her laughter sounding too shrill, too forced, even to her. "And I was supposed to seduce either Daryl Me'Vere or you."

His muscles were hard as rocks, as was his face.

"We are forbidden to trade in any weapons on any planet with prohibitions against them. So, I did report finding the weapon used in that village we found on the way to Restal where raiders had attacked." She bit her lip. "Oh, and about the Tela Oroku, which I didn't know anything about until I figured out it was a bizarre assassination attempt." She looked up and attempted a smile. "They don't believe me about that."

"The weapon," he said flatly.

She turned her face away and looked into the fire, wishing there were someplace else to look, wishing she were someplace else, anyplace else, anyplace larger so she couldn't feel the tension in his body pressed against her. "Yes. I recognized the wounds we saw in those people. They're distinctive. They were made by an akengun, which must have been smuggled from the ship by"—she hesitated —"another agent. I spotted him in Restal several times. He always disappeared before I could talk to him. I think he's working with Readen Me'Vere."

"I thought you liked Readen. Or were you trying to seduce him, too?"

She looked up at him, startled, a little angry. She felt his tension increase again. "So far, I haven't tried to seduce anyone, and I've stayed as far away from you as I can. Readen is an arrogant ass and may be dangerous as well. I've survived four assassination attempts. I'm not too sure they weren't his doing. Probably because I know about the guns."

"Four." If anything, he looked angrier than ever. He reached for the kettle and refilled their cups. He stared at his steaming tea for a long time, the light from the tiny fire highlighting the bronze in his hair.

"I guess you can solve anything with a cup of tea," she finally said, her tea untouched, the cup warm in her hand. "You're not going to kill me right away then?" Yes, all right, was that ever a feeble attempt at a joke? She stared down into her cup like it held some fascinating object.

"No, I may need you to keep me from freezing tonight, and your body would cool off too fast."

She hoped it was humor she heard in his voice. Marta didn't want to think about the strength of the disappointment leaking through the iron shields he'd erected.

He got up and put two more logs on the fire then faced her. "Well, I suggest we get as much sleep as we can. We'll have to share the blanket. I'm sorry—my gallantry doesn't extend to freezing so you can have it to yourself. I'll try to gather enough energy to keep us some-what warm, but I've expended a lot healing you and Sidhari. At first light, you can ask Kibrath to fly you out to Me'Byrhn Holding and let Dalt and Lyall know where I am. I'll need to stay with Sidhari until she can fly." His flat tone gave her no clue to his thoughts, and he kept his mind heavily shuttered.

"I can stay," she said, keeping her head down so she didn't have to look at him.

He ignored her. "Kibrath can lead Dalt back with more provisions— and another blanket or two—and keep watch for the men who attacked you. But I think they headed north away from here. Besides, I hurt them enough they'll take some time to recover." His smile was fierce.

And that was that. *Am I relieved at having it all out in the open, or angry that I got caught?* She fell asleep without deciding, in spite of the uncertainty of her future and the uncertainty of her feelings at being wrapped in the blanket and wrapped in an angry Altan's strong arms. The tension in his jaw, where his cheek rested on the top of her head, eased.

Marta dreamed a long and complicated dream of pain and terror until a beautiful Karda encircled her with bronze and green wings and whispered urgently in her ear. In the cold, growing light of morning, the dream faded into her very real fears for the future.

CHAPTER SEVENTEEN

It was a tenday after Altan got back before Marta got the expected summons to Toldar Keep. She'd seen him several times working with the fledglings and stayed away. He hadn't approached her or made any indication he even saw her, nor had she sensed him in her thoughts.

She changed into a plainly-cut, green woolen dress with a narrow geometric band embroidered in dark gold on the bodice and draped a delicate ivory shawl around her shoulders and the sling for her arm. Solaira insisted she'd need it for a couple of days more. She couldn't make herself wear her dress Mi'hiru uniform. She felt dirty enough as it was.

The days had been interminably long. She felt eyes on her even when there weren't. No one said anything to her. No one acted awkward or angry or curious. No one knew. She almost wished it had been shouted out at dinner. She'd have something to react to, something to hit back at other than her insecurity.

Several times she fought a wild urge to saddle Sidhari and fly away. But Sidhari had been uncommunicative since she'd gotten back. And Marta wasn't sure how healed the Karda was, though she didn't complain. She didn't say much of anything—kept her emotions to herself. But then Sidhari always did. Marta felt more alone than she ever had. She ached with it. Her bones ached with it.

Donning her heavy cloak, Marta walked up the winding, narrow cobbled streets past rows of neat stone houses and crowded shops to the inner gate of the rambling red stone keep. The noise of the crowds and the smells from street grills surrounded her. The cold morning was busy with well-wrapped women carrying baskets and parcels, men pushing carts, wagons crowding people into doorways and side streets as they passed.

A messenger on a bicycle nearly ran into her as she dodged a mule top-heavy with loaded packs. A cacophony of emotion battered at her imperfect shields, and she stumbled more than once on an offending cobblestone.

A small boy met her at the tall, banded iron doors of the keep entrance and escorted her up wide stairs and through several hallways to the guardian's study. Thick, richly colored rugs covered the floor. Heavy drapes bordered tall, narrow, leaded-glass windows. Polished and carved dark wood and leather chairs, well-used and worn, surrounded a large, battered but polished table in the center. Two bronze lamps hung over it, their pleasant yellow glow augmenting the fractured sunlight from the windows. Shelves of well-used books lined the side walls.

Guardian Stephan rose as she walked in. Altan leaned on the stone fireplace behind him, one foot cocked across the other, his face bland. He wore a severe plain tunic. *It's almost the same color as my dress.* An irrelevant thought to calm her nerves. Which didn't work.

The guardian was as tall as Altan, though a little heavier. A loose vest covered a linen shirt open at the neck. More silver than gold showed in his hair. His tanned face was broad, and lines of laughter and care surrounded sharp brown eyes and a generous mouth.

"Mi'hiru," the guardian said. "Please, sit." He indicated the chair opposite him at the table. He offered tea and asked her questions about the fledglings.

Marta wasn't sure how she answered. Her throat was so tight she didn't dare touch her tea. A painful eternity went by before Stephan put down his cup. "My son tells me you have asked for sanctuary in our quadrant."

Marta looked at Altan in surprise, but he didn't so much as twitch. Her thoughts, already confused, went wild, scattered like quail rushed by a fox. What was it she wanted? Was this it? What did sanctuary mean? Refuge? Belonging?

Her voice answered before her thoughts settled. "Yes, sire. I suppose I am."

"You suppose?"

"No, sire. I am. I am asking for sanctuary." She had to work hard to keep her voice from quavering and tears from her eyes. *Sanctuary*.

"Do you know what it means, to be given sanctuary in Toldar?"

Marta felt pinned by his eyes. It was an effort to keep insecurity out of her voice. "No, sire, I'm not sure I do. My information about it is limited to what was in the data banks on the ship. I'm afraid I didn't pay much attention to that custom when I was learning about Adalta."

"Data banks?"

"Library, sire. Data banks are like a library of information collected about this planet. And other colonized worlds."

"Umm. An archaic term." He frowned at that information then went on, "Are there oaths you will foreswear to ask sanctuary from us?"

"No, sire. I am free to leave at any time, or they are free to ask me to leave if my work is not satisfactory. Although usually when an agent leaves, it's to work for another trade consortium, not to stay on a planet. They call that *going native*—it's a pejorative term."

"Have they asked you to leave, then? Is that why you ask sanctuary?"

"No, sire." She looked at the floor. "It's rare for a consortium agent to stay on a planet. To leave their employment and the society on the ship. I only know of one other, and that was a long time ago. They felt he betrayed them. He's thought of as a fool. Which is what they will believe of me." She risked a glance at Altan. "The story is that he was killed to keep him from spreading information about them. I think the story's apocryphal, but then it wasn't a friendly planet." She attempted a smile and failed. "The consortium is very intent on opening trade relations with the people of Adalta. They seek every advantage they can, search jealously for any bit of useful information. They are desperate for trade." She paused, her voice almost a whisper. "I won't be allowed to jeopardize that."

"Apparently they are hiding in orbit." Stephan hesitated over the unaccustomed word, one only found in legends and old histories on Adalta. "Why is it they haven't made themselves known, and what is it they want to trade?"

"In addition to trading unique goods from other planets our specialty is technological tools, communication, and information storing devices—many things not allowed under your current laws — in exchange for raw materials on scarcely populated, primitive worlds like Adalta." She stopped. "I'm sorry for the word *primitive*. To us— them—you are. The fact any advanced technology is forbidden is mystifying to them. They want to change your laws and break your customs. My director has intimated more than once that he, at least, considers using force."

She reached up to pull on her earring but stopped herself and fisted her hands in her lap. "We're called subtle agents, and for a reason. We keep ourselves and our purposes secret while searching out markets for our goods and attempting to learn what reception we will have when we make ourselves known. But I've been told to do things that suggest some in the consortium want to undermine your laws. Even force change. That's against the rules of the Trade Alliance, which oversees all consortium ships. I assume that's why they don't want to be discovered too soon. They aren't ready to act. I fear someone is after more than ordinary trade."

Marta stopped, looked down at her tight-gripped fingers, then back up to meet Guardian Stephan's eyes. "I can't believe this is coming from all the directors of the consortium. It's too extreme. I don't know if it is the consortium, a small faction, or if it is only the one director willing to try force."

Stephan turned to look out the windows for several long

minutes. Marta waited. Sweat trickled between her breasts. She resisted wiping her hand on her skirt.

He turned back. "Altan seems to think you are in some danger for your life."

She thought for a moment. "I don't think the danger is from the consortium. I think it's from someone else. Altan told me the Tela Oroku we encountered when we went to bring back the fledglings was aimed at me. That couldn't have been the consortium. Neither they nor I knew what it was, or how to fashion it. I was attacked several times on the street during my time in Restal. I didn't dare go into the Prime alone at night." She had a hard time keeping her voice steady.

"From whom are you in danger, then, if not them?"

"Someone is smuggling advanced weapons to Restal. I recognized the wounds an akengun makes on the bodies at the village where we interrupted an attack, supposedly by bandits." Her eyes flicked to Altan. His expression hadn't changed. "I also recognized another agent twice in Restal Prime whom I believe to be in contact with Readen Me'Vere. I reported it, but my superior, who is that agent's father, refused to believe me, or admit to it. But I know what I saw. I think someone has been at work undermining my reputation and standing. My credibility with them is less than what it had been, especially after I reported the Tela Oroku. They didn't believe me when I told them what happened. They accused me of being infected with what they called the superstitions of a backward planet."

Both Altan and Stephan stiffened at that, then looked at each other with a brief flash of humor. Altan dropped his head for a moment as if hiding a smile. Then his face resumed its impassivity.

"Is this why you want to leave your work with this consortium, why you ask for sanctuary? Because your reputation is not what it was?"

"No, sire. That is not my reason. If I wished, I could repair any blot on my record with time. Despite my age I have a long history with the consortium. A good history."

He was still for a moment, then cocked his head in question.

Marta looked down. She clenched her good hand into a tight fist, digging her fingernails into her palm. The words she wanted to speak would open her to exposure like nothing she had ever done before. She took a deep breath and brought her gaze up to meet his.

"I have grown to love this quadrant, this planet, to love its hills and valleys, the distant mountains so mysterious and inaccessible. To love
the people in the small villages and towns I visit with the judiciars or on patrol. I am fascinated by the animals, like the fat birbir, I've never seen before. I love the Karda, working with them, flying with them. I have never known anything like them. I've grown closer to Sidhari than I.... I can no longer bear the thought of leaving her when the mission is over."

She loosened her fist and brought her hand up to rest on the edge of the table, forcing her fingers to relax. "I have not known a real home since I was a small child. I have been doing this kind of work, making my way into alien cultures, making temporary homes in strange new places for a very long time. Fifteen years, from when I was very young, following my father after my mother died. He died only three years ago."

She raised her hand to wipe her forehead, changed her mind and dropped it. "I have few friends and many of them are scattered through the stars on worlds far, far away. I want to make a home here, on Adalta. I want friends in Emi House among the healers, the weavers, the Mi'hiru, not acquaintances to exploit for information. I like the people I've met in the Karda Patrol. I want them to be my friends. To be a friend to them. I want this to be my home."

She looked straight at Stephan. "I have always taken what I needed from any society I was in, done my duty with honor and done it as well as I could. But what I've been asked to do here isn't honorable. I can't do it."

She stopped, swallowed, and took a deep breath. "I want to belong here." Her voice was barely more than a whisper. "I want to find a home."

She blinked furiously and looked at Stephan. "I'm sorry to have gotten emotional." She tried a smile. "It isn't at all like me. I never get so emotional."

Stephan watched her for a long time.

"Sanctuary is granted. I do not offer you a home—that you will have to make for yourself. Welcome to Toldar, Mi'hiru Marta of Emi Guild House." He stood and clasped her arm across the table. It was done. Altan still stood leaning with one arm stretched along the mantle over the fire. Expression impassive.

"Are you willing to talk to the Council in Rashiba about what you know?" Altan asked as he walked up behind her. She jumped and whirled. He hadn't spoken to her for the tenday since she had been to the keep, ignoring her altogether though he was in the mews every day—sending off patrols, coordinating the Karda Patrol schedule with the Mi'hiru, playing with the fledglings.

Then he just walks up like nothing has happened? Well, what did I expect? Instant rapport? Instant acceptance? I lied to him for a long time.

"Of course, whenever the guardian wants. I thought he might want me to go with him to the Council Assembly."

"He's not going this time. I am. We leave in a tenday. You will need court clothes, so see Solaira about that. The guardian account will pay for them. You or Emi House will not be saddled with that expense." He turned and walked off.

Marta stood with her mouth open. She neither felt nor heard anything from him but a roiling of emotions she couldn't identify and was irritated with herself for even trying. He was the one who said they needed to deal with the ability they shared, and now he was his arrogant self again.

Push me, pull you.

She went back to oiling Sidhari's flight feathers.

CHAPTER EIGHTEEN

The ground beneath Marta and Sidhari was a gentle rolling landscape, sometimes barren and riven by deep gullies and washes, sometimes dotted with stone-walled fields and occasional copses of trees. And, of course, broad, deep bowls of forest surrounding circles.

Icy winter wind blew tendrils of hair from her braid into her face, and she tucked them back behind her ears and up under her wool cap. The village she and Captain Dalt headed for appeared in the distance, and they began to circle down toward the landing meadow adjoining a cluster of stone houses and cottages. Marta sighed. She wondered, not for the first time, if this was what birds felt like. If they just wanted to stay in the air forever and never land. Except birds didn't have to land to empty their bladders. She shifted in the saddle.

Marta could see evidence that this central part of Adalta had once been plains. Even now the barren areas were less gullied and rough than in Restal, and it looked as if more of the barrens were restored. Bleached gold stubble of wide harvested grain fields poked through the wind-blown snow cover.

They were on their way to Rashiba for the assembly. The pack

SHERRILL NILSON

train loaded with the inordinate amount of clothing they had to carry to this formal event, not to mention the boxes of papers Altan would need, was much slower than the Karda, so they stopped in the villages along the way as if they were on regular patrol. Lyall and Altan flew one tangent, and Marta and Dalt the other.

Dalt and Marta walked through the light covering of snow to the edge of the field to greet the two men and the woman who had come to meet them. The taller man wore a wide-ribboned baldric across his chest—his puffed out chest. The woman, the long skirts of her dress covered with a stained white apron, pulled him across the rough field with no regard for his resistance or his dignity.

Marta hoped the villagers didn't have much business for them to handle. She was tired and cold. It had been a long day of a long journey.

"Greetings, Mi'hiru," the taller man said, and bowed slightly toward Dalt as well. "May I introduce myself? I am Karl, headman of Mill Valley. May we invite you to lunch with us at the Water Wheel Inn?" His manner was polite and formal. "Then I'd like to show you around my fine village. I have—" He continued to talk as they walked to the inn, his words heavily sprinkled with "I," "me," and "mine." Finally, the woman sighed in exasperation and jerked at his arm.

"Oh," he said, as if an afterthought. "And this is Lil, our healer." He ignored the other man who stepped out from behind him.

"Bren!" Marta exclaimed. "What are you doing here? I didn't ever expect to see you again."

His smile was broad. "Recognized you when you came in, lass. Passed through Rashiba a while back and heard about the new Mi'hiru. I remembered you almost fallin' off m'wagon when we spotted those Karda in the air. Suspected then where you were headed. I knew you'd do well. Congratulations, lass."

"But you're a long way from Akhara. What about your farm? And your onions?" She laughed.

"T'wasn't my farm. T'was m'brother's widow's. My idiot nephew's woman trouble got solved by a quick weddin', and he figured bein' a farmer was better for a new baby's daddy than

206

chasin' girls. I went back ta bein' a travlin' trader. Suits me better'n bein' a onion farmer. Them onions give me the itch. Just now gettin' that smell outta my wagon."

Marta hadn't forgotten the first person she'd met on Adalta, and how much she had learned from him. They talked all the way back to the village. Or Bren talked, and she listened. But she noticed how he slipped in the occasional idle question about where she'd been. He asked a number of questions about her time in Restal.

"I be headin' that way, and any bit of information you give me'll be a help in my tradin'."

By the time they reached tiny village, she suspected he knew more about her than most people did, never overtly showing curiosity. She wondered how much he'd learned about her on their trip to Rashiba. She shuddered, remembering how assaulted she'd felt when her empathic senses exploded, grateful for the shields she'd developed. Now she had choice. Usually.

A large mill on the bank of a small river dominated the village, hence the name of the village. The countryside was peaceful this far inside Toldar away from the threats that plagued those near the border with Restal, and with Akhara to the south. The farming villages and small market towns they visited had few problems that needed the attention of the guardian in Toldar Prime. The holders were prosperous, their homes and the towns surrounding them alive with activity.

So far their visits had been little more than courtesy calls. Karda Patrol didn't visit here often. But Stephan sent the patrol to the villages and holdings several times a year.

Just as they reached the edge of the village, Lil grabbed Marta's arm in a tight grip and began towing her off toward one of the small stone houses. "We have great need of a healer," she said. "I hope you're one. Young Rob is hurt, and it looks to be bad infected. Come have a look if you will."

"Lil, the Mi'hiru and her companion will need to take a rest and a little refreshment after their long flight. Young Rob can wait," Karl objected.

"No, he can't. He's like to lose that leg if someone don' care for it soon. I've done all I can for him, and he needs help sooner 'an later." She tugged sharply at Marta's arm. "He waited too long to come see me. It's bad infected."

"Of course, Lil. I'll look at him, but I'm not a healer." And the woman led Marta to a house three doors down from the inn, never letting go of her elbow, pulling her all the way.

The young man, still a boy, Marta noted, dozed fitfully on a pallet in the small main room of the cottage, which served as kitchen, dining and sitting room, and treatment room all in one. She knelt down as Lil pulled back the thin blanket covering him and lifted the edges of the bandages. The slash in his thigh was a deep one. Puss stuck to the bandage, and red streaks snaked up toward his groin.

She swallowed her horror as she glanced at the boy's sweaty, frightened, too-pale face. "I'm sure you have done more for him than I could do," she said. "But we're traveling with Altan Me'Gerron, and he's a true healer. He should be here shortly." She smiled at the young man, hoping her face showed more reassurance than she felt. "He can help you if you can stand the pain just a little longer."

"Yes'm. Lil here has some powerful bad tastin' aspirtea to help with that." His words slurred.

As Marta and Dalt walked to the inn, Dalt said, "I thought Altan was headed straight back to Immer Holding, and we were to meet the pack caravan there for the night."

"Oh," said Marta. "I didn't tell you he was going to meet us here and fly on with us?"

"No." He looked at her, his head cocked with a yeah-tell-me-another look. "But I'm not surprised. He seems to be meeting us more and more often. Lyall says that's the only time he stops talking about you. The boy's getting bored."

She kept walking, her eyes straight ahead, ignoring him. Then she couldn't help herself. "I doubt that. He barely speaks to me."

Dalt laughed. He turned to face her, walking backward. "Mi'hiru training doesn't include lessons on how to attract a man? Next time you see Jenna Me'Nowyk, you should ask her to teach you." He batted his eyelashes at her and dodged the blow she aimed at his shoulder.

She ignored him for the rest of the walk to the inn and excused herself for a few minutes to clean up when they got there. The innkeeper's wife brought a towel and basin of water to the small bath- room with its crude toilet and left her alone to wash and do what she needed. Marta stood in the middle of the room and sent a mental call to Altan. They had scarcely communicated with words on this trip, much less mind to mind. She hoped she could reach him. It was past time for them to start practicing and experimenting with how far away from each other they were able to hear. She frowned, concentrating. It was difficult, and she hated it, always afraid she'd give too much of herself away, but his answer came almost before she was finished telling him the situation and their location.

From now on she'd persist. They needed to practice every day. A corner of her mouth quirked up on one corner at all the ways she could pester him, chattering away in his head all day long. And all night, too, interrupting his sleep, irritating him into accepting that they had to practice.

Altan arrived within the hour, again met by the officious Karl. Puffed with importance at hosting the guardian heir to the quadrant, he tried to push away the impatient Lil. In the middle of Karl's speech, the healer grabbed Altan's arm and more or less pulled him all the way to the cottage where Rob lay.

Altan knelt down beside the boy, pulling away the stained bandages, exposing the nasty wound in the leg.

"What happened here?" he asked the boy. "Looks like you mistook your leg for a log. Legs don't make good furniture, boy. Didn't you know that?"

The boy tried to smile. "My ma always told me I had legs like tree trunks. I guess I started to believe her." His voice was weak and shaky.

Altan turned to Lil. "When I start to work, the infection will come to the surface. Take a clean rag or towel and wipe it away. It will take several tries. And probably several towels. Can you support me as I pull the energy I'll need?"

"Yes." Her answer was firm, her face a picture of relief.

Head down, he worked for a long time, Lil wiping away the smelly corruption that surfaced. Then he leaned back with a sigh. The boy's eyes fluttered closed. The pain lines marring his face eased, the ugly wound now a fresh pink scar on his thigh.

Marta could see the exhaustion on Altan's face. She reached for his arm to help him up. He started to shake her off. A surge of power pulsed through her body, and Altan straightened, his expression confused. She stepped back, unnerved, and the pulsing ceased.

"He'll sleep for a long time, and when he wakes, he'll be weak and hungry for several days," Altan said to Lil, still looking at Marta, forehead creased.

Lil nodded. "We can handle that. We thank you, sir. You've saved his life. He waited too long to call me, and we thought he was goin' to go. It was beyond my talent. We owe you a grave debt."

"No, you don't," he replied. "Just as you have your job, I have mine."

They walked back to the inn, Altan as far away from Marta as he could and still walk the same path. "What did you do?" he asked Marta in a sharp voice.

"I don't know. You were exhausted, and I wanted to help you. It felt like—I don't know what it felt like. It was like something grabbed me and then—I don't know how to explain this—it just— you know what a snake looks like after it's swallowed a large rat or something? Like there's a big bump moving through it? That's what it felt like. Only it happened fast. A big ball of something that shot right through me."

Altan walked away, leaving her standing in a pool of puzzlement.

Why is he irritated at me? You could at least say, "Thank you." It isn't my fault these strange things are happening to us. She had to work to keep those thoughts to herself.

Altan made his appearance at the inn where he was called on to solve a few problems that probably would have resolved on their own and to hear several requests for what they needed from the guardian.

Marta and Bren sat in a corner, still catching up, Marta laughing at his stories of his travels as a trader. She kept glancing at Altan, noting, not for the first time, the good-natured respect with which he treated the villagers. A side of him he was not sharing with her.

She quit after Bren caught her at it several times, his eyes crinkling. She hoped she'd see Bren again. But he was headed for Restal, and she never wanted to go there again.

A half-tenday later, Dalt poked Marta in the ribs and said, "There he goes again. He's exhausting me."

She covered her mouth and tried not to laugh. Lyall was disappearing with one of the serving girls, as he often did, ignoring Dalt's jibe, face bright red. The other three sat at a corner table in The Feathers Inn—Marta was losing track of how many villages had Feathers Inns—enjoying their drinks and the quiet after all the villager's concerns and questions.

The threads of tension between Marta and Altan was so palpable that if they could be woven into cloth, it would keep out rain. Altan reached out as if to touch Marta's hand, then drew back.

Dalt tilted his chair back on two legs and asked, "How is it this last couple of days you always show up just when you're needed where Marta and I are patrolling, Altan? It ain't as though you need to check up on us. You never have before." He looked up and waited for the answer, which wasn't immediately forthcoming.

"What are you talking about, Dalt?" Altan finally said.

"I ain't dumb and I ain't gullible like Lyall. All these intuitions and 'I had a feeling there was a problem here, so we decided to fly over' don't set right. I started out thinking you were just aching to be with each other. In luv, or something more like what Lyall is up to."

"There's nothing going on. Nothing like that." Altan's voice snapped like a broken branch. A branch that landed on Marta's head. Hard. She winced.

"Something is going on." Dalt didn't give up. "You can just tell me to shut up and quit asking questions if it's some big secret, but you're hiding something."

Altan looked at Marta. She looked away, giving the problem to him.

The tone of his voice curled cold in her ears. She swallowed the hurt. "This isn't something you can share in the barracks, Dalt."

"I don't share anything in the barracks but ale and food and the occasional good scrimmage. You know me better than that."

"Yes, I do." He bit his lip and looked back and forth between Dalt and Marta. "Do you remember the stories of Cailyn and Donnal?"

"I knew it. You're getting bonded." He grinned.

"No!" they both said at once, not looking at each other, scooting even farther apart. Any farther, and they'd be sitting at separate tables. "Not that story, the other ones, about the struggles of the first settlement and the first Karda," said Altan.

"They had some kind of mind powers. They could hear each other's thoughts, even over long distances...." Suddenly serious, he looked back and forth between the two of them, then his mouth dropped open, his eyes widened.

"You can talk to each other in your minds? You suppose this means there'll be problems like they had?" He was still staring at them both, then he smiled his crooked smile. "Probably telling jokes about us behind our backs, aren't you?"

Altan laughed. Marta relaxed. Dalt's eyes narrowed despite his flip remark.

"Maybe we can forestall whatever the trouble might be. I don't know, but we are going to try," said Altan.

Marta looked at him, unsettled. She'd never heard the legends they referred to. *And who is this "we" you're talking about? You can hardly stand to look at me. And when you do, you're angry.*

"I always thought the prediction that another couple with telepathy would come if the trouble returned was just to make the stories more interesting. Hope so," Dalt said, frowning. "Lyall's clueless, and maybe I can help him stay that way. He's a good boy and can be close-mouthed, or I wouldn't have recommended him to patrol with the two of you," said Dalt. He reached for his hefty glass mug of ale and turned to listen to the violinist playing by the fire.

Marta noted the thoughtful look on his face. Not much disturbed the unflappable Dalt, but she could see this shook him. Marta turned to Altan. "Why did he think there might be trouble just because we've developed this—?" She waggled her hand back and forth between them. "Whatever this is? If that's true, you might have given me some hint."

He moved his chair closer to her and leaned forward, elbows on knees. "When the Ark Ship arrived on Adalta, the colonists discovered they weren't the first aliens to land here. They found enormous Circles of Disorder, covering almost a third of the continent. They were created by the aliens called Larrak, who spawned monsters to fight with them called the urbat. Evil, destructive dog-like creatures, but half mechanical, half organic. Like the Larrak. They almost decimated the colonists, who were struggling just to survive.

"Cailyn and Donnal were the first to be contacted by the Karda. The Karda had fought these aliens for centuries and were losing the battle for Adalta. They instructed the settlers how to contain and shrink the circles by planting trees. Over time, the more trees planted, the more peaceful things became, and the less power the Larrak had, but it takes time. It has been centuries, and still, the circles are not gone.

"The Larrak were hard to kill. They created hundreds of urbat in the circles. The Karda, Cailyn, and Donnal, along with the Austringer and the Kern, other figures from our history, led the final battle with the Larrak. They fought until there was only one Larrak left. The Itza Larrak. Stories vary about what it was, and how they fought it.

So many Karda died that they were never able to destroy it, only contain it. They imprisoned it somewhere only Karda know about. The legend is that Cailyn and Donnal and the Austringer and the Kern, a hunter and a powerful planter, will return if the Itza Larrak ever awakens and escapes its prison.

"The centuries of struggle between those aliens and the Karda decimated Adalta, killing much of the native flora and fauna. That's why Adalta is so much like Earth. The Ark Ship carried enough from the seed and embryo banks to terraform Adalta. That's also why the Karda choose to serve us. It is in return for our help in killing the Larrak and working to bring life back to the planet.

"It wasn't just the struggle with the Larrak that almost ended us before we began. There was discord among the colonists that fractured the original unity of the settlers and still causes problems. Eventually, the Greater Council was formed, headed by the prime guardian, and the laws banning weapons more efficient than swords and bows and those limiting technology were passed.

"The guiding principle that holds us together was decided. That there be parity between technological and socio-cultural development.

"There's a famous scientist from Old Earth who said, 'Our entire much-praised technological progress, and civilization generally, could be compared to an axe in the hand of a pathological criminal.' That axe, wielded by greed and religious fanaticism, destroyed Earth. We refuse to follow that path."

He took another sip from his mug. "Cailyn and Donnal were also the first to discover our ability to draw power from Adalta. Another lesson from the Karda: that Adalta is more than just a planet. She is a living presence in our lives. That's how the governing families are chosen, by the strength of their talent, the strength of their connections to Adalta, and the power they can channel.

"I know you're uncomfortable with what you want to call magic." He held up a hand to forestall her answer. "Your face shows it every time I do something with talent you've never seen. Cailyn and Donnal were my great, great, whatever grandparents, which is why, I suppose, I have the ability you were able to awaken. How you might be a legend returned to Adalta when you weren't even born here is—well, I don't know what it is. Weird, I guess."

Marta bit her lip and fiddled with her earring. She'd read this kind of thing in the vidbooks she'd devoured when she was young. Fantastic, powerful beings, magical powers, chosen heroes who save the world—stories of superstition and exciting tales for children. But how else could she explain the Karda and Altan's no-nonsense expression when he related the history?

CHAPTER NINETEEN

The polished granite walls of the hall gleamed in the light from bronze wall sconces. Three enormous chandeliers hung from the high ceiling on heavy chains. Round tables for each quadrant ranged throughout the room, with a long rectangular table on a dais opposite the enormous double doors to the hall. Marta supposed they were for the first guardian, his advisors, and their spouses.

Stone fireplaces with surrounds carved with bas-reliefs of the huge bear hybrids called medgeran centered three walls, glowing with magma stones to warm the room.

In the corners, copper braziers on beautifully sculpted wrought-iron bases held more of the fiery stones. Pungent smoke from beeswax candles and chips of resinous wood and sage leaves scattered on the magma stones scented the air.

Marta stopped just inside the tall carved doors, self-conscious in the heavy blue silk dress with its narrow waist, long pointed sleeves, and too-low-for-her-comfort neckline with not enough lace. The beautiful dress made her feel plain. Overshadowed.

~I wish you could be with me tonight, Sidhari. This is going to be awful. I feel even less like I belong than I did before I confessed my sins to Altan.~

~The rooms would need to be a good deal more spacious to accommodate all the Karda who would like to be there. Well, no, they wouldn't. We most assuredly don't and won't ever want to be there.~

Marta heard the laughter in her tone.

~Kibrath tells me you look beautiful tonight. I wish I could see you.~

~How does Kibrath know how I look?~

~By the way Altan is reacting.~ Marta heard the amusement in her voice.

She saw Altan across the room, wearing the deep blue tunic with narrow gold piping on collar and sleeves of a Karda Patrol dress uniform. He stopped talking and took a half step toward her and smiled. Then he turned away. Captain Dalt, also in dress uniform, watched with a lop-sided smile. She grimaced and went to join Altan's table.

Altan was talking to a couple she didn't recognize. The man was close to Marta's height, with graying brown hair and a prominent nose under intelligent hazel eyes. His companion was of equal height with coiled up silver-threaded brown hair, a face that spoke of humor, and a figure that promised to be ample sometime soon.

Altan smiled at her again, but his too-polite smile multiplied her misgivings about being here. He started to reach out, then moved his hand to massage his upper arm, then dropped it to his side, then rubbed it on his leg.

"Westlynn, Nerissa, this is our Mi'hiru, Marta. Westlynn and his wife Nerissa are Toldar's representatives to the Small Council. They live in Rashiba Prime permanently, looking out for our interests." He smiled. "And they do it very well. While Westlynn sits in long, boring council meetings, Nerissa picks up information while she gossips. And she gossips well."

Nerissa slapped at his arm. "Now you're just trying to flatter me, Altan. It is good to meet you, Marta. I've never gotten over my younger wistful love for Karda. You'll soon get annoyed by all my questions and start avoiding me."

Marta laughed and clasped forearms with her and Westlynn and sat in the chair Altan pulled out beside him. The captain and two lieutenants from the caravan guard sat opposite her, bracketing the councilors. She sipped at her wine, not speaking, just following the conversation.

Marta noticed Readen enter the long hall and pause in his survey of the room when he saw her. He looked surprised. He wore a black tunic embroidered with an intricate scarlet band down the front and around the hem. Daryl was behind his shoulder in the light blue dress uniform of Restal's Karda Patrol. They looked more alike than she had remembered. Both handsome, Readen's face thinner, his brown hair curlier and tied back, Daryl's hair, long and thick, hung unbound to his shoulders.

Just for a flash, an aura of red surrounded Daryl. She brushed a hand across her forehead and tightened her shields. Daryl moved to greet someone, smiling broadly, and the red haze disappeared. Imagination. Marta's hand drifted up to fiddle with the malachite stones twisted with gold wire dangling from her ear.

It was clear Readen didn't expect to see her here, but he lifted a hand in greeting and smiled, holding her gaze a minute too long. She nodded back. Altan's look singed her skin.

Leaving his brother and their party, Readen wove his way toward their table through the crowd of holders, counselors, guards, and servers, and lifted her hand by the fingers, taking a little too long to brush them with his lips. Then he smiled and reached across her. He and Altan clasped forearms in greeting. She couldn't tell who released his grip first but was sure there would be bruises. Readen stepped back, his mouth twisted in a predatory smile.

"I didn't expect to see you here, Mi'hiru. You are a pleasant surprise," he said.

"We didn't expect to see you here, either." Altan put his hand on her shoulder and leaned around her. "Will you take your father's place in the Council meeting?"

Marta sat very still. The heat from Altan's hand spread to her throat. She shrugged her shoulder. His hand stayed. His fingers tightened.

Altan's words were a polite dig, Marta knew. Readen's smile

grew even wider. A flick of anger crossed his handsome face. Maybe a not- so-polite dig.

"No," Readen answered. "I accompanied Daryl. Father thought a lesson in citadel politics would be good for both of us, I suppose. And you, is your father here also?"

Altan leaned his other arm on the table, and his hand moved from her shoulder to the middle of her back. He was practically pulling her off her chair and onto his. Marta leaned away. His hand curled on her waist, heating her whole body. Anger swelled. *He's using me to get to Reaaen. What is this show of ownership about?*

"No, I sit in the assembly for Toldar this year. My father says he's retiring from politics. He hopes for good."

Readen's eyes flicked to Altan's arm. His smile twitched, and his eyes spoke anger loud enough to be heard. Readen would never replace his father in the assembly. Altan's words were goads.

And Altan wasn't here because his father was retiring. Stephan stayed back because of the continuing raids along the border. Guardian Stephan and Altan had agreed that having both of them away from the quadrant would not be a good idea just now. Sending Altan in his place was also, she suspected, a move to acquaint the other guardians with Altan's strength and knowledge of the politics of all Adalta—as well as giving him more experience in diplomacy.

Readen looked at Marta. "I hope we'll have a chance to talk together, Mi'hiru. I would like to get to know you better. You left Restal sooner than I had thought you would, and I feel I lost my chance. I'd like to make up for it. Perhaps later this evening. I understand there is to be dancing, and I remember you like dancing." He bent in a half bow to the Toldar counselor, Westlynn, greeting him and Nerissa formally, kissed his fingers at Marta, and strolled back to the Restal table.

Altan's emotions were a forge fire next to Marta. She took a breath and tried to swallow the anger and confusion heating her body before their side of the table combusted. She scooted as far from him as she could without falling off her chair. Altan took his hand away and picked up his wine glass, taking a long drink, not looking at her.

"That went well," said Dalt, sitting on the other side of Marta, all spiffed up in his dress uniform.

Altan just looked at him—his head cocked, his mouth pulled into an expression of disbelief. Dalt smiled back. "I wish the two of you would just kiss and get it over with. The tension is upsetting my appetite. I hate when my appetite gets upset."

Westlyn and Nerissa watched the byplay with amusement and more than a little curiosity.

"I'm going to ignore that exercise of your vivid imagination, and I suggest we all do the same," said Altan. His nonchalance was contradicted by the tension in the cords of his neck and the hand holding his wine glass. "You're embarrassing the Mi'hiru, Captain."

Nerissa looked even more interested.

Marta stood. "Would you all excuse me? I need to find the little room reserved for ladies. I think I have a button coming loose." There were no buttons on Marta's dress. She left the table.

Her efforts to cool her body and her temper failed when Readen intercepted her return to the hall and the Toldar table. *He was waiting for me. I don't need this. Why is he so theatrically attentive and persistent?*

"Perhaps I could interest you in joining us at our table for a time, Mi'hiru. I know you enjoyed my brother's company when you were in Restal. He would like to pay his respects to you."

Marta looked back at the Toldar table. Altan was watching her, his face so frosty she was surprised there weren't icicles hanging from his eyebrows. He looked away, smiling at Nerissa, and said something. Nerissa looked confused. *Hot. Cold. Hot. Cold. I wish he'd make up his mind. I think. Maybe. What am I supposed to do now? Give me a clue, Altan. Why do I need a clue? What do I want him to say?*

She turned to Readen and said, "Why, yes, I would enjoy seeing your brother again. I'll have a glass of wine with you if you wish," and headed for the Restal table on his arm, ignoring her discomfort. "Maybe you'll help me with who all these people are. Surely you have names for all of them." It was only after the second glass of wine that she was able to excuse herself to go back to the Toldar table, relieved to do so. Readen could be funny, and he did have names for many, with his kind of insight about each. But too often his insights veered away from humor and toward malice. She closed her empathic dampers against what she felt from him. She didn't want to put a name to it.

Altan ignored her when she came back, suddenly engrossed in something Westlynn was saying. Dalt stood and held her chair.

"Did you enjoy yourself, Mi'hiru?" he asked, his eyes dancing between her and Altan.

She gave him a one-more-word-and-you're-dead look, blew out a frustrated breath, and took her seat.

Altan walked her back to her rooms in the Toldar suite. The two caravan guards went with them and stationed themselves to either side of the door to the hallway. He escorted her to her rooms. "To be sure nothing surprising arrived while we were at dinner."

"Is this necessary?" she asked as they stepped inside.

He waved his hand, making a small gesture at the sconces on the wall and the sitting room lit with soft yellow light. "You've been the target of how many assassination attempts? You are under my protection. I won't leave anything to chance." His posture was as stiff as his stilted words. He walked through the bedchamber and checked the bath.

She stood in front of the small fireplace in the sitting room, suddenly reluctant to see him go. "Altan."

"Yes?" He stopped in front of her, almost but not quite too close. "Sometime would you explain to me how you do that?"

"Do what?"

"Just wave your hand at the sconce, and it lights. And how you healed my arm so fast, and the other healings I've seen you do. And what are talent weapons if they are not just the superstitious imaginings of village folk?"

He looked down at her. "Yes," he said and touched her face. One finger traced a soft line from temple to cheek, an electric line of fire. She sucked in a sharp breath and moved back.

He smiled down at her. "Yes, but later."

He put his hand to the back of her head and pulled her to him, his mouth brushed hers, warm and soft. She raised her hand to his chest to push him away and found herself clutching his shirt and pulling him closer. Her body exploded with the feel of him. Her mouth parted as if by itself, and she felt his tongue hungrily exploring. It was as though every emotion they had used to push away from each other for the past months came flooding in to press them together in a bond of feeling that held no separation.

He finally pulled away, his hands hot on her shoulders. "That was more than I expected," he whispered.

She felt his body tremble. He leaned his forehead against hers.

"I've needed to do that for a long time. I couldn't stand it, seeing you with Readen this evening, no matter that you told me you thought him an arrogant ass." They stood that way for a long moment, their minds entwined in a caress more intimate than any physical one. Then he straightened and said, "Till tomorrow, Marta," and left.

She collapsed in the chair by the fire, unable to think clearly, smiling a smile she couldn't stop. She touched her lips with the tips of her fingers. She sat there for a long time before she finally went to the bedchamber, undressed, and fell in the bed. Marta lay awake, her emotions roiling, not sure whether they were her emotions or his when he knocked on her mental door to say, ~Goodnight,~ with a mental caress. Oh, yes, there were some extraordinarily nice things about telepathic communication.

CHAPTER TWENTY

E arly the next morning, Marta and Altan were in the prime
guardian's study. Hugh Me'Rahl was not at all what she
expected. A large, florid man, his full face and bright green eyes
lined with care and humor, broad shoulders, and a flat stomach, he
looked like a hard-working, prosperous farmer who would rather be
pacing his fields than sitting in meetings all day.

He wore a severely-cut brown tunic with a hint of gold
embroidery at the neck and on the cuffs of his sleeves. A slender
bronze circlet set with a brown topaz held back the silvered chestnut
hair that touched his shoulders. He stood behind a well-used,
highly-polished table of dark wood. A plain sword in a worn leather
scabbard hung on the back of his chair.

Long, narrow mullioned windows of wavy glass on the far wall
bracketed a carved stone fireplace with glowing magma stones.
Cabinets and bookshelves lined the two side walls, and a large
painting of the forest outside Rashiba Prime hung over the
mantelpiece. The chairs beside the fire and around the table were
well-worn leather and polished wood.

Hugh clasped forearms with Altan and gave a half bow to
Marta. "Sit, sit," he said, his voice almost too loud for the room. He

sat, pointed to the tea tray with its basket of hot buns and butter on the table, and asked, "Have you broken fast?"

"Yes, sire," said Altan.

"Then have some tea and tell me why your Mi'hiru is with you for this appointment." He looked over the rim of the cup at the two of them and took a sip of his tea. The delicate cup was incongruous in his big hand.

"Mi'hiru Marta has asked and received sanctuary from Toldar and is here under my protection," said Altan. "She's been through four assassination attempts. We're trying to prevent more."

"And you think I can help." Guardian Me'Rahl raised his eyebrows. "Why don't you tell me about it?"

Altan nodded at Marta, and she took a deep breath. "I'm not from Adalta. I'm a covert agent—a spy, I guess—from a trade ship that's orbiting the planet. I was assigned here to gather information about your culture and to assess the markets for the highly technological goods Alal Consortium trades in."

The prime guardian watched her, turning his teacup around and around in his hands. His face showed not a flicker of anything but polite interest

She forced herself to be professional, detached. It was as if she were listening to a voice outside herself. "And to look for ways and opportunities to change your laws and policies against technology. Whatever it takes."

Me'Rahl's eyes narrowed. Marta was suddenly more aware of how big a man he was.

His voice rumbled low and tight. "I don't like those words, 'Whatever it takes.'" He pressed his lips together and looked back and forth between the two of them. The easy bonhomie left his expression. "Why can't we see this ship? How did they find us? The colonists destroyed the records of our Ark Ship when they left Earth. We've been left alone for five hundred years."

"Traders spend a lot of money on efforts to locate the lost Ark Ships. There were several. Someone found an old diary in some books salvaged from Earth, I think, that gave enough hints to extrapolate where to find Adalta. Finding lost colonies can be very lucrative. The Adalta colonists weren't the only ones who protected their destinations during the diaspora. As to why it's not seen, ranks of mirror shields protect the ship by mimicking its background surroundings, like camouflage."

Hugh stood and walked over to lean on the fireplace. He stared at the glowing stones long enough for Marta to start counting her breaths, then turned back and resumed his seat at the table. He scrubbed at his face. "We had hoped never to face this problem. Your ship's shields are certainly effective. We do keep watch, and we've had no warning."

Altan shifted beside her, leaned forward as if to speak, then settled back.

"What can you tell me about this...consortium's intentions? And your speculations, substantiated or not?" The guardian leaned back in his chair and folded his arms across his stomach. "Just how much danger are we in? What kinds of weapons will we face?"

"We..." Marta's fingers were laced together so tight they ached. "I mean they have never before interfered in a trade planet's internal politics. It's contrary to the regulations that govern the trade ships. And then my supervisor made a comment about trading weapons— a slip he didn't intend me to hear. But I found one of the weapons in a village that had been raided near the Restal border with Toldar."

"Tell me about the weapon. What can it do? What advantage would it give?" His voice was tight, controlled.

"The akengun is designed as a weapon for mobile troops. It fires a pulse of—I don't know how to explain that to you. It's technical, but it can burn a fatal hole in a person from three hundred feet and can be fired repeatedly. As many as fifty times before it has to be recharged— which can be done in a few hours with energy from the sun falling on a special plate attached to it. A relative few of these weapons would be enough to devastate opposing troops. There are shields that can be employed, but producing them is technically beyond your capabilities. It would be disaster," she said. "And not just for Restal or Toldar."

Altan leaned forward. "The wounds it made were unusual. It was as if it made a hole, then opened up and shredded and burned flesh and bone inside. There are certainly no weapons I know of that could do the damage that one did. I know of no talent force that could." He paused. "What I am certain of is that these raiders came from Restal."

Hugh looked at Altan for a long moment. His teeth were clenched and the veins in his temples stood out like pulsing cords. Then he turned back to Marta. "Go on with your story."

She licked her lips. Her mouth was dry, and she took a sip of tea. "The Trade Alliance strictly forbids trade in weapons where the planet's laws and customs don't allow it, but it's happened. Not often, and the perpetrators are fined heavily when they are found out," Marta continued. "According to alliance directives, trade must be openly and freely accepted by a planet. Alal Consortium has always traded high- technology items for raw resources, especially fine crafts and unusual or rare planet-specific products. For Adalta to refuse to trade for such goods would be a devastating blow. Coming here was a gamble."

Marta held her breath in the silence that stretched too long.

Finally, Hugh asked, "Are these guns being smuggled into Restal? And why bother with that? Why not just land and take us over?"

"It's a trade ships so big that isn't possible. The population is made up of families who live their whole lives aboard ship for generations— not troops. Peaceful traders, not invaders. The ship isn't made to land, and it doesn't have weapons that could threaten the planet. It's designed specifically to operate as a factory and trade ship, in space, with shuttles to carry goods and people back and forth. No trade ship, in all the years since the diaspora, has encountered any alien species that would need to be defended against, so the ships carry few offensive or defensive weapons. Some cannons used in asteroid mining, that's all."

Marta unclenched her fingers and took a sip of cooling tea. "The only ships we have ever encountered are, like ours, family trade ships, re-figured remnants of the diaspora Ark Ships. The technology and capability to build more were lost with the self-destruction of Earth. Life there now is harsh, primitive, and violent."

The faces of the two men showed patent relief. "They won't be able to change our laws peacefully. That's why they need to take control of Restal," said Altan. "And if they succeed, why would they stop there?"

"We have sometimes bloody border disputes, and the lady Adalta knows, we have ambitious and opportunistic holders and guardians. We always have had," Hugh said. "However idealistic we sometimes think our founders were about balancing socio-cultural development with advances in technology, we have held to their philosophy in spite of ourselves, and the quadrants have remained in balance, in general, if not in specifics, for a long time."

"Sire," said Altan, "when we visited Restal in the fall for trade and border discussions, it was very evident their Circles of Disorder are growing and have been for some time. They're not planting around them. Maybe you know something I don't, but I haven't heard of that happening anywhere else on Adalta."

"No, and I would know. Why do you think that's relevant? We've known about Roland's laxity regarding the circles for some time."

"It was the circles and whatever fed on them that almost destroyed the first colonists. That they're growing just as this ship has appeared seems too much coincidence. Restal was where the final battles with the Larrak were, and it hasn't recovered as much as the rest of the continent."

Hugh pushed back from the table and started pacing back and forth in front of the tall windows, the slanted sun putting him in silhouette. Marta couldn't see his face for any hint of what he was thinking.

"What are relations between you and Restal like now?" he asked Altan.

"We've had to garrison mounted troops in some of the larger villages to patrol. There are too many raiders along the border that hit only villages on the Toldar side. They hit and run back into Restal and avoid our patrols and towns with garrisoned troops. We complained, but Readen says he's doing everything he can to keep the bandits down, insisting they're based in Toldar. There's little evidence of that."

"They will try to claim too many mounted troops on the border is an aggressive act on your part."

"Yes," Altan said.

"I don't think this situation would benefit from our council knowing about the ship just yet." He looked at Marta. "We need more information. How many weapons do you think Restal might have?"

"I don't know. I don't think Director Morel—he's my supervisor and the director I suspect is responsible for this—would give them more than one or two at first. He'd want to be sure he could trust whomever he's using in Restal to honor their agreement, whatever it is."

Altan frowned. "And I don't believe they've given up on silencing Marta. If they already had them, she wouldn't matter."

"How many people know who Marta is, or was?" Hugh smiled at her absently.

"No one but Father, Mother, and I," said Altan.

"Do your superiors in this consortium know you've defected?" asked Hugh.

"I haven't reported in for a month, but they might not see that as unusual. For some reason, it's increasingly difficult to communicate with the ship. The communication satellites have disappeared."

"Are you willing to continue your association with them on our behalf?" Hugh asked.

"There is one other thing, sire," said Altan, sensing Marta's discomfort. "When the two of us went to retrieve the two fledglings I found—"

Hugh interrupted, suddenly smiling, "Yes, your fledglings. I can't wait to hear about them. You'll have to tell the whole council at once, or you'll be repeating the story over and over. I've heard about little else since you arrived. But go on."

"Marta was attacked by a Tela Oroku."

Hugh stiffened. His head jerked back. "A Tela Oroku! There hasn't been one of those since the colonists defeated the Larrak."

"Yes, sire. I know. But when the carrier Karda died, something happened to Marta. And then to me. We can talk to each other telepathically. With whole thoughts. Over distance."

Hugh looked dumbfounded. "Like the stories of Cailyn and Donnal? And how many people know this secret?"

Altan told him, "Only my parents, Marta's guild mother, Solaira, and my captain, Dalt. It's difficult to fly every day with someone as bright as he is and keep that a secret. He's more than trustworthy."

"So many secrets." Hugh paced back and forth. "Well. This puts an interesting light on the situation. Let's hope it doesn't mean war is inevitable as the stories warn. Or that the Austringer and Kern will suddenly appear."

That's the second time I've heard Austringer and Kern mentioned. Who or what are they?

Hugh sat back in his chair and looked up at the ceiling. "Who's fomenting this border disruption between Restal and Toldar? Do you have any idea?"

He leaned forward and picked up the fragile teacup again, turning it around and around. It nearly disappeared in his big hands. "Roland is getting to be an old man. Does he want to make taking over Toldar his legacy, do you think? I wouldn't have thought he'd have the energy or the interest. It doesn't sound like Daryl Me'Vere. He's young and idealistic. I could be mistaken, but I think his energies are being spent in the effort to ameliorate the damage Roland's excesses are causing the quadrant. Me'Cowyn is the strongest holder in Restal, and his ambitions regarding the guardianship are no secret."

Marta was silent. She couldn't be the one to voice suspicions about one of the ruling houses of Adalta. That was not her place. She looked at Altan.

"It might be an internal struggle, but I doubt it," he said. "I have my suspicions, but they're just that, suspicions, and it wouldn't do to make them public or even to make accusations to you in private. Though I doubt you'd be surprised. All we know is that another agent from the consortium was in Restal when we were there, and he didn't want to be seen by Marta. She tells me she saw him several times when she was assigned there, and he avoided her. He wasn't supposed to be in that part of Adalta. He's Director Morel's son and is the logical one to be carrying out his plans here."

Hugh frowned. "Who is this man? I want his name and description."

His look at Marta let her know he would brook no resistance to this request. In fact, it wasn't a request—it was an order.

"I must think on this for a while. And you—" Hugh turned again to Marta, "I want you to think very hard about what you owe the trade consortium. If they are sending spies into our territory, attempting to influence our laws, bringing in weapons like you described, I need to know everything you know, even things you don't think you know. Where does your allegiance lie? If your communication with Altan is like the telepathy some have with their Karda, you can't lie mind to mind, or I wouldn't trust you at all. But I do trust Altan."

He paused for a moment, scrubbing his hands through his hair in frustration, then said, "We need to know how many weapons there are and who's receiving them. You're the one who can discover that—if you are willing. If this is a struggle for the succession between Daryl and Readen, the council won't involve itself in their internal politics, but if these weapons are involved, this would be an exception." He paused for a moment, looked down at a paper in front of him. "See my steward for an appointment for tomorrow afternoon. We'll talk again then."

He looked at Altan. "One thing we can be grateful for. It isn't Akhara Guardian Turin who was contacted. You and I and possibly Daryl are as strong as he is, but he has something we don't."

Altan looked startled. "Viciousness."

Hugh looked at Marta. "Now, I'll have that description of this agent."

Behind their two guards, Marta and Altan walked down the stairs and across the sunny colonnaded courtyard toward the Toldar apartments. Marta was white and shaking.

Altan took her hand and laced his fingers with hers. ~That wasn't so bad, was it?~

~I'm afraid of what he is going to ask me to do. It seems dirty, somehow. Like my work was beginning to feel to me. That's a good part of why I wanted to quit.~ *And I've betrayed my ship, my community already. Not just the ones who are smuggling weapons. Nothing about this feels good. I had to give him Galen's name. He has to be following Kayne's orders. And that hurts. Both ways. It hurts that he's doing this, and it hurts that I have to betray him. Which is the worst betrayal?*

"Shit," said Altan. "Here comes that galaxy-be-damned Readen. I think he's looking for you."

Marta looked around and took a deep breath, relieved to be brought out of her thoughts. ~Maybe I can make his interest in me work to our advantage.~

~It's too dangerous. This is possibly, no probably, the man who's tried to kill you four times, remember.~

~What can he do if I'm surrounded by people and the guards I'm sure you'll have following me everywhere? It's worth trying.~

"Good day, Mi'hiru, Me'Gerron. I'm glad I found you. I'm going into the market this afternoon and wondered if I could interest you in coming with me, Marta. It's a pleasant day and I want company," said Readen.

"I need to report to the Mi'hiru Guild this afternoon, Readen."

"Well then, we can walk down together. I'm headed to my favorite bootmaker, and his shop is not too far from the guild house. I'd enjoy that. Shall I meet you here after luncheon?"

~I don't like this one bit,~ said Altan silently.

"Yes," said Marta with a sidelong glance at Altan. "I'll see you then." With a nod at him, she walked on. Altan followed, the heat of his disapproval blasting her back.

When they reached the stairs to Toldar's quarters and the guards were safely out of hearing range, Altan turned to her, his face stormy, his eyes hot. "This is not wise," he began.

"Altan, I have been doing undercover work my whole life, with all kinds of people. I am trained in sword work, in self-defense techniques, and if you remember, in equivocation. I can handle myself in all kinds of situations. I'm sure you'll insist I take a guard with me. What could happen on public streets with a guard?"

"I don't like it. It's too dangerous. I don't trust him. He tried to kill you." His voice got louder with every word.

"We can't be sure it's Readen who's trying to kill me. We have no proof. And isn't this what Guardian Hugh is going to ask me to do? Stay undercover, so I can serve Toldar and the rest of Adalta?"

"With the trade consortium, not with someone like Readen. You have no idea what you're getting yourself into. I'm not sure I even know. If he's the one who sent the Tela Oroku, it will be something you won't be able to protect yourself against. It may not be a physical threat."

"Then tell me what I need to look out for."

"There isn't time for that, and you don't have the ability to shield yourself, no matter what I tell you."

"I do have the ability to be in contact with you all the time I'm with him, though. And with Sidhari. Isn't that protection enough?"

She heard Sidhari's voice. ~No. Altan's right. This isn't safe.~

Marta ignored her. "He must have some reason to be so attentive to me." *Other than irritating Altan, which he's doing very well.* "Whatever I can learn will be more information than we have now. It's worth it."

He grabbed her arm and pulled her up the rest of the stairs, opened the door to her rooms, and almost pushed her in. He stood by the fire- place, frowning to himself for a moment, then reached into his pocket for a small black velvet bag and tipped a delicate gold chain into his other hand. A fire opal cabochon clasped between two flying Karda wrought of delicate rose gold hung from it. He held it in his palm, concentrating intently on it, his eyes closed. Fire flared from it as if the stone came to life.

He stared into the fire smoldering in its depths, took a deep breath, and said, "If you wear this, it will protect you and make me feel better. I don't like him. I don't trust him. There is something about him that screams danger to me. It would be best if he can't see it, so wear it under your clothes. He won't sense it—I've made sure of that."

He clasped it around her neck, and iridescent light blazed from within the stone, flashing prismatic colors around the room. That same intense electricity infused her whole body, and she felt her knees start to give. He caught her, turning her to face him.

Marta stared down at the stone then up into his face. He stared at the opal, emotions flashing so fast across his face Marta couldn't sort them out.

The light had not just been in the room. It had been inside her. *I can't think. I can't think. I need to think.* "What was that?" She got her legs under her and pulled away from him, almost afraid. She touched the wings of the rose-gold Karda at her neck. *Do I want to know the answer to that?*

Altan controlled his face. He pushed an errant strand of hair behind his ear, then pulled loose the leather cord holding his hair at the nape of his neck, smoothed it back and retied it, never looking at her. "We can—" He cleared his throat. "We can talk about it later. Right now, it just means you're protected. I have to meet with Nerissa and Westlynn to discuss the issues we're putting to the assembly. I'll send Dalt with you." He kissed her hard and left her staring after him, bemused.

~Well, now. Isn't that interesting,~ said Sidhari.

She'd said those words before when Marta's life changed. Was it changing again?

~Are you eavesdropping?~

CHAPTER TWENTY-ONE

M arta changed into the long, burgundy, wool split skirt, cream linen shirt and green fitted jacket of her Mi'hiru uniform. Her body felt so light she was surprised the uniform didn't hang on her. She was no longer an agent of the Alal Trade Consortium.

And Altan had kissed her.

She was leaving what had been her work, her life, for most of her nineteen years, and her Father's before her. Had he ever been tempted to go native? Raising a child, always on strange worlds, and never a real home?

And Altan had kissed her.

From the coat tree by the door, she grabbed the elegant hooded cloak her weaver friend Kai had woven for her and left to find Dalt.

Dalt raised his eyebrows when she told him they were to meet Readen in the outer courtyard of the rambling citadel complex. His only comment was, "Interesting." But he said it with a smile on the highly-entertained side of interesting. He kept a few paces behind her and Readen as they walked through the streets of Rashiba to the guild house.

Readen left her there. "There's a nice tavern on the next corner. It's close to my cobbler's and the other shops I need to visit. I'll meet you there when you're finished. I have several errands to run for my father, so if I'm a little late, just wait, if you don't mind. I may be longer than you."

Marta found Guild Mother Cailyn, whose usual uncompromising expression broke with a smile and a flood of questions about the two fledgling Karda. She visited with a few Mi'hiru from her training days, arranged times to work out with tall, rangy Tayla, the guild armsmaster, and scheduled sessions with the trainees. Visiting Mi'hiru were always asked to share what they could about the quadrants where they were assigned. No one missed asking about the fledglings, and no one was interested in much else about her life. She felt ego-punctured.

She looked up into the sky as she left. The sun glinted off Sidhari's bronze wingtips as she glided in a circle high above with Kibrath. Marta suspected she was enjoying the opportunity to gather information. Not gossip, of course. Sidhari insisted Karda were above gossip.

~We're going hunting, Marta, and we'll need to range far. There are many Karda visiting here. I'll be back when you come tomorrow.~

Marta walked down the narrow cobbled street to the tavern on the corner, Dalt following her. He refused to walk with her. "I'll just amble along behind."

"You're skulking, not ambling."

He laughed. She paused just inside the door to let her eyes adjust to the dimness and shield her empathy from so many people. She felt the captain's presence move to the bar where he could keep his eye on her.

"Marta."

She searched the room for Readen. It was not Readen—it was Galen Morel, possibly the last person Marta wanted to see, at a table in the corner. He motioned her over, stood until she sat, and ordered her a glass of wine from a passing serving boy.

"You got me in a whole lot of trouble, Marta," he began without preamble, his voice low. "It took me a long time to convince them ship-side that I was where I said I was when you thought you saw me. What were you trying to do?"

"Is it safe to talk in here, Galen?" she asked. She needed time to think.

"Of course. I'm not stupid. No one is close enough to hear, and I come often enough to know people keep to themselves in this place."

"It wasn't you I saw?" she asked, eyes wide. *How can he even think I wouldn't recognize him?*

"No! I was in Anuma the whole time, training and working with the Planter Corps—that's my cover. It allows me to travel, but so far, only to Rashiba. It's difficult to have an alibi when the people you are with don't know who you are and why you need one." He looked at her, jaw clenched with simmering outrage.

How arrogant he is. Is he so self-involved he's delusional? He can't possibly think I'll believe him. She looked closer. Something was wrong about his eyes. The pupils were too dilated even for this dim light. His too-handsome face had a slackness about it, almost as if he were barely conscious. *There's an alien tension around him, as if he's bound with tight strings gripped by a puppet master.*

Empathic senses were so frustratingly vague. She tried to shake the unease away, but it stuck. "Then I am truly sorry I got you in trouble. I hope it wasn't too bad for you, Galen. Our job is difficult enough without causing trouble for each other." She looked down, concentrating on her wine. It was surprisingly good.

She was grateful her relationship with him had ended. He'd always been distant. Cold. Unable to open himself to any emotion that went beyond the surface. *He's so good at manipulating people that he's arrogant enough to think he's convincing me.* "How is your work going? Are you finding it as difficult as I am to get people interested in new technologies?" *Particularly when you don't even try.* A touch of guilt tinged that thought.

He hesitated a minute. Then, at least appearing mollified, he said, "It's like there is an insurmountable wall out there. Their belief that greed and intolerance too often drive technological advances is powerful. And nothing works here anyway. The satellites are gone, everything I bring to the surface eventually fails. Spy bugs just disappear out of the air. The only thing that works is my Cue. And it's not that trustworthy."

Marta frowned, as perplexed as he was and glad it wasn't her problem now. "I know. I haven't had visuals on my Cue since the heli-shuttle set me down. What do the engineers say? I assume you've been in touch with your father."

"Maybe we can talk later." His glance flicked beyond her toward the door. His face went blank, and he blinked several times. After a moment, he stood. "Maybe we can talk later." As if he hadn't already just said the same thing. And he left, leaving Marta with her mouth open to respond. He brushed past Readen who was just coming in the door. Her finger flicked her earring. Galen's more than strange behavior perplexed her.

Readen put a hand out and stopped the boy delivering a meal to another table and ordered an ale. He sat across from her, turning his chair so he could see the door and crossed his legs out in front of him. "Did you get your business done at the guild house, Marta? I was successful. The boots Jand made for me fit perfectly, as always." He waggled his feet. "You must admire them so I know I'm justified in my joy."

She laughed. "Yes, they are very shiny. And tall."

The boy put Readen's ale down on the table, hands shaking, and left quickly. Readen smiled after him, drawing a deep breath as if savoring a delicious scent, and took a sip of ale.

A nauseating mix of fear from the boy and hunger from Readen — not a hunger for food—slipped through her empathy shields. She took a sip of wine and strengthened them, leaving a tiny opening to learn more of him.

They talked for a time about the issues facing the council, his surprise at Altan's substitution for his father, Daryl's concerns about the tax levies. He stopped when, despite his subtle questions, Marta would not or could not reveal anything of substance for him about Altan's positions. He asked how she liked Toldar. Then he fell silent.

She fished for something to say, fiddled with her earring, then forced her hand back to the table. "Do you have an arrangement with the boot maker here in Rashiba?" *What an inane comment.* "Of course you do. He must keep your last. Are there no good boot makers in Restal?" Her laugh felt false. It echoed. Readen didn't speak, just watched her, smiling, his face pleasant.

She glanced around. The room was wavy, indistinct as if she were inside a crude glass bowl looking out. *I haven't had that much wine.* The normal tavern sounds of glasses clinking, people talking and laughing were muffled, confused. The opal on her chest flared hot against her skin, and the room returned to normal. A flash of anger crossed Readen's face so quickly Marta wasn't sure what she saw.

"Even my brother doesn't use the boot makers in Restal Prime. And he's not so picky about his boots as I am, as you surely noticed." No anger showed in his voice. His words were distinct, evenly paced, marching in a monotone inside her head as he talked on about boots.

Marta fought for something to say. "I've missed Philipa and Nuala. Are they still there? I haven't heard." Her tongue was thick, the words hard to form. The sense of being inside a wavy glass bowl came back. Marta watched Readen's mouth move, his voice slid in and out of her hearing.

"Is she the short one? I don't think so. I don't know where she went, but she left a few tendays ago." Sounds linked together, His mouth moved speaking a ribbon of words that flowed on and on with no meaning. She watched them form patterns in the air around them, weaving between them. Linking her to Readen.

She felt her mouth make words, smile. Her hand moved to bring her glass to her lips, but she felt no liquid on her lips, tasted no wine. She watched her hand set the glass back on the table. She tried to see Dalt at the bar through the wavy glass.

~Ground, Marta. Ground!~ Altan's voice shouted in her head.

She forced herself to look down at the table, at the battered surface, at someone's name carved there, but she couldn't read it. The letters scrambled and moved. She heard Altan's voice again. ~Your feet are roots, Marta, reaching into the ground. Concentrate, Marta.~

Then he said something else, but it made no sense. She tried to answer him, but her words floated away in translucent bubbles. She watched them bounce against the ceiling and burst into colorful shards. She looked down at her hands on the table, concentrating. She wanted to look up again. To Readen's eyes. Somewhere far away floated a thought that it wouldn't be a good idea. She reached for it.

She looked down at her feet. Roots. Her boots sank a few inches into the floor. She wanted to laugh, but she was nauseous and dizzy. Feet. There was something she was supposed to do with her feet.

The stone on her chest flared hot, but this time it didn't cool. It burned against her skin. Her mind cleared a little. Ground, she thought. She sent a thought down through her feet, through the dirty, stone floor. She saw a shadowy man lying there, half-in half-out of the flagstones, his face in a pool of vomit and blood. In fact, she could see through the man. She forced her attention deeper. Coolness moved up through her legs, and her nausea eased. Her attention reached further into the ground, through the stone into the clean soil beneath.

Like a root searching for water, she sank deeper. She passed a worm and smiled at it. That wasn't right. There was a sharp pressure on her forehead. A voice spoke, soft and insistent.

"Surface, Marta. Surface. There is nothing for you down there but worms. Have another sip of your wine."

She saw her hand touch the wine glass, and the opal thumped hard against her chest. Pain split her head, and something tried to move inside. She reached again for the coolness of the ground, and this time, she felt herself going deeper, down all the way to bedrock. She spread out on it and grabbed, anchoring herself deep in the rock. Something brushed against her face, and she looked up.

An enormous, translucent Karda stood over her, green-gold wings spread around her, protecting her. ~This is all I can do, Marta. You must resist him yourself. He uses a power foreign to me. I can only touch him through you. You will have to learn.~

A wing brushed her face and her head cleared. Roots grew from her fingertips, and she tied herself firmly to the bedrock. Suddenly she heard Readen's voice, the words clear. His even, monotonous tone sounded wrong, but she didn't know why. It scrabbled at her like hungry crabs.

"You will bend yourself to my will. There is nothing for you in Adalta. You only feel my strength. You only hear my voice. It reverberates in your head, closing out all other voices, all other thought..."

Persistent, seductive, the voice nibbled on and on at her mind. Then another voice rose against it. ~Concentrate on me, Marta. Concentrate on your connection to Adalta. Focus. Block out everything but me and your ground, your strength.~ Altan's voice!

Her being spread further through Adalta, drawing strength from the rocks, the soil, the trees. Floating way above the planet, clouds surrounded her. Suddenly she broke through. Her skin felt as though oily water slid off it, carrying away the ravening crabs. She opened her eyes. The room was normal again. Dalt leaned against the bar watching her, a frown of worry on his face.

"I'm sorry, Readen. My attention wandered for a moment. You were saying?" It was an effort to speak. She had to think about every word.

Readen's eyes widened, and fury flared in them just for an instant. She almost missed it, then he smiled again. Even through her confusion, Marta saw the bulge in his jaw where he clenched his teeth. A single drop of sweat slid down the side of his face.

"It's probably time for us to get back, anyway, Marta." Just the slightest shade of anger thickened his voice, but his rage was palpable. It helped clear her confusion.

"I still have a few errands. Your Captain Dalt can walk you back if you don't mind."

"Of course. I'll probably see you at dinner, then. Thank you for the wine." She left him sitting at the table, his face pale. The surface of the blood-red wine trembled in the glass he held tight in his long fingers, their knuckles white with tension.

Altan spent the time Marta was gone in the arms salon working out against the jovial Rashiba armsmaster, Tomas. By the time they finished, both he and Tomas dripped with sweat. Tomas was broad and thickly muscled for a swordsman, but it didn't slow him. His moves were precise and his footwork fast and graceful. Altan leaned forward, head down, hands on his knees, sucking in air.

"Whatever is bothering you, man," Tomas said, wiping his face with a towel, "you better get control of it. Your anger left you open several times. Be glad we were using practice blades, not live steel. You're going to have bruises you shouldn't have."

"I'm sorry, Armsmaster," Altan said, holding his tender ribs. "May I clean up here and cool down in your bathing room?"

"That might be a good idea." Tomas smiled, and they clasped forearms. "It's good to see you, Altan. You give me as nice a workout as I can take when you aren't thinking about something else. Come as often as you can while you're here."

"I'll do that, sir. I can use the practice. And I will work on my concentration next time, I promise. You won't have it so easy again." He rubbed his arm, sending energy to the punished muscle where Tomas had gotten in a particularly hard hit.

It took only a short time to clean up and tend to his bruises. Altan paced back and forth between the curving staircases that bracketed the long colonnade across from the courtyard gates. His face held such an attitude of fierce concentration that the few people who paused to talk to him changed their minds and walked on. He could feel Marta in his mind without effort. He'd insisted that she keep herself open to him the whole time she was with Readen. He'd felt Readen's efforts to control her.

What kind of force had Readen used? Altan's fingers gripped the fire opal in his pocket until the wings of the gold Karda cut into his palm. It was identical to the one he fastened around Marta's throat. It was warm in his hand from his efforts to shield her. At last, he heard her voice.

~I'm all right. We're headed back. I'm tired, but I'm all right. Thank you.~

Finally, she and Dalt came through the big gates, and Altan

released his grip on the opal, silently thanking it for the use of its power. He'd taken a chance when he gave her its mate. *Thank Blessed Adalta I did.*

"Here she is, back safe and sound." Dalt's voice was not as assured as his words. "I thought for a moment she was getting sick, but she assures me she's fine. It's a good thing. I told her you'd dismember me if anything happened to her on my watch." His usual wit was stumbling.

"I'm not a fragile piece of art to be handed from one caretaker to another, Dalt."

Altan took her arm, and they headed up the stairs. "Something happened. I could feel nasty, greasy fog around you." Marta stood in the doorway to the Me'Gerron apartments. She trembled with an unfamiliar insecurity. He lifted his arm, dropped it, and fisted his fingers against his leg. She hadn't moved from the door, so he took her elbow carefully and led her to her rooms.

"The conversation with Readen was so strange." She looked past his shoulder with a perplexed frown. "It was hard to hold my thoughts together. Most of the time I had no idea what he was talking about. Several times I thought the room was going to disappear. I heard you telling me to ground. What was he doing to me? I thought I could handle most anything, but this was "

"You're all right, though?" He reached for her hand and pushed her down into one of the chairs on either side of the small stone fireplace. She sat on the edge, perched, looking ready to take flight at any moment. He took her cloak, hung it by the door, and spent a moment heating the magma stones to a glowing red. "Your hands are ice, and you're shaking."

"The room kept wavering. It was like looking through a cloudy glass bowl. I couldn't communicate with you. I could hear you, but I couldn't answer." She hugged her arms around her and looked at him, watching him sit across from her as though if she took her eyes away from his, he'd disappear.

"I'm used to taking care of myself in all sorts of situations, but this was terrifying. Nothing in my training prepared me for this kind of attack. That's what it was, wasn't it? An attack?" She didn't mention her encounter with Adalta. The memory of that faded fast into the part of her mind that stored things of imagination and dream. Things she wasn't ready to know.

He moved his chair closer and took her hands, holding them like he'd hold a frightened bird. "I was working as hard as I could to counter what he tried to do to you. It wasn't anything I've encountered before. By Adalta, what a horrid cloud of ugliness."

She shuddered. "I don't want to do that again." She took a deep breath and sat back from the edge of the chair, pulling her hands from his, looking at him, her mouth tight and grim. "At least my empathy was working. I didn't learn much, but I need to warn you that the couple of times your name came up the hatred that came off of him was vicious. He did his best to cover it, but it was there. Whatever you thought he thinks about you, double it. The other worrisome thing was, strangely enough, his emotions about his brother, Daryl. There's something implacably menacing about what he feels when Daryl is mentioned. I think he's planning something that doesn't bode well for his brother."

She shuddered. "That's all I got from him other than his efforts to get control over me. If it weren't for you, it would have worked."

Alton said, "Part of the reason it was difficult for me to counter what he tried was that he used your confusion and fear to augment his attempt to control you. I don't know where he's getting the power he uses, but it has the same feel as a Circle of Disorder."

He looked at her. This tall, slim, athletic woman. Fear for her hit with an intensity that weakened his knees. He pulled her to her feet and held her, tight, resting his chin on the top of her head. He breathed in the herbal scent of her hair. When had anything ever felt so right?

CHAPTER TWENTY-TWO

K ai had done well by Marta in the clothes she brought to the assembly. Kai was knowledgeable about the changing fashions of the assembly halls of Rashiba and took Marta to her favorite dressmaker in Toldar to choose her clothes. She even brought some of her weavings for the dressmaker to use, and Kai could work wonders with cloth.

Tonight Marta wore a deep red-brown dress of finely woven wool with gold bullion circling the neckline and the edges of the long full sleeves lined with burnished gold silk. The same silk, inset in pleats below the tight bodice, swirled gold when she moved, showing up the amber lights in the long hair that hung loose down her back. Gold clasps, with the smallest of Sidhari's feathers dangling, held the sides behind her ears. The opal necklace was beneath her high collar.

Altan wore a dark green tunic trimmed with bronze embroidery down the front and around the high collar over narrow trousers. A dark green velvet baldric with the embroidered badge of Toldar hung from his left shoulder and supported a tooled leather belt and dress scabbard for his sword.

Used to wearing flying leathers and clothes suited more for work than play, Marta was gratified to note that the two of them turned more than a few heads when they entered the room. Remembering Altan's eyes when she stepped out of her room in the Me'Gerron suite, she lost all her irritation at having to wear this less than practical outfit. She felt beautiful—a rare feeling for her.

The others stood as they approached the Toldar table. Councilor Westlynn's sharp brown eyes crinkled at the corners with humor as he took her hand to brush it lightly with his lips saying, "Well met, this evening Mi'hiru. I trust you enjoyed your day in Rashiba. Have you met Jenna Me'Nowyk?" Marta stumbled, and Altan caught her arm, looking at her with concern. "And her father, Karyl Me'Nowyk, of the Coastal Holdings."

"Yes." Marta's throat thickened. "I've met Jenna. But not her father." She exchanged nods with the round, red-faced man with the slightly bulbous nose behind Jenna. Altan's hand tightened on her arm. Then he dropped it. She didn't feel beautiful anymore.

"Altan." Jenna ignored Marta. "I saw you this afternoon coming from the arms salon, all hot and sweaty from your workout."

Marta didn't throw up, but she wanted to.

"I called, but I guess you didn't hear me. I am delighted to see you here. Father said you would be, but I was afraid to hope. We just got here this afternoon after flying all day. For too many days. I am so glad to be off that Karda. I did thank her though. You told me they like to be thanked. I remembered."

Her smile was so bright Marta thought they could blow out all the candles on the tables and still see.

Somehow she found herself seated between Westlynn and Jenna. Altan took the only chair left. On the other side of Jenna. *I better get used to seeing the back of her head. That's all I'm going to get from that direction.* At least she could think again.

Altan, Karyl Me'Nowyk, and Councilor Westlynn spent most of the evening in close conversation about the business of Toldar they were to take up with the Greater Council. Jenna joined in, well-informed and passionate about the issues.

Marta changed places with Dalt to sit next to Nerissa. She looked up across the room, and Readen's eyes found hers. It took her a little too long to look away. This could be big trouble. She caught herself tugging at her earring and forced her hand to pick up her wine glass.

Altan looked at her, saw Readen watching, and looked back at her, a question in his eyes. She shook her head and turned to Nerissa.

"I am glad to talk to you, Marta," said Nerissa. "As charming as these young gentlemen are, I am sure they are running out of things to talk about to a little old lady and would rather swap war stories among themselves. They don't seem to appreciate my lessons in embroidery."

Nerissa smiled at the young lieutenant next to her she'd been talking to. About horses, not embroidery, and said to Marta, "My sister is Mi'hiru stationed in Akhara Quadrant at present and will never forgive me if I don't find out everything you can tell me about the fledglings Altan found in the mountains."

Jenna looked across the table at Marta and put her hand on Altan's arm. "It seems Readen Me'Vere is interested in your Mi'hiru, Altan. She might be a good match for him. I can't think of a single holder willing to accept him with his lack of talent. Father certainly wouldn't. He expects me to marry someone powerful."

Marta watched her fingers squeeze Altan's arm. "Mi'hiru can marry, after all. Your mother did." Marta disposed of, Jenna went on, "I hope you are going to support us when Father submits his petition to the council to make the coastal holdings the fifth quadrant."

Altan's face showed nothing of what he felt. But she heard, ~Readen, over my dead body,~ in her mind. She found she could taste her dinner after all.

~I think that may have been the longest evening of my life.~

Altan's thoughts were a caress in her mind as they made their way behind Dalt and Lyall across the citadel courtyard to the tower that held the Toldar apartments. He took her hand in his. It felt warm. She stiffened, but he didn't let go.

~I enjoyed talking to Nerissa. And you seemed very involved in your political discussions. Jenna is very familiar with the politics of Adalta, isn't she?~ *And with you.*

He looked down at her. ~I don't think you meant me to hear that last thought. And I was so distracted I had to ask Westlynn to repeat himself several times.~

Her face was a glowing magma stone. ~Yes, Jenna's very pretty. I don't blame you for being distracted.~

~Who? Who is it you think distracted me?~ His grip on her hand tightened.

They left Captain Dalt and Lyall at the doors to the main room of the apartment.

"May I come in?" Altan said, not looking at her.

The touch of uncertainty in his words pierced Marta's self-control.

Her voice caught. The words came out rough. "Yes, of course."

They stood facing each other, not speaking, in front of the tiny fire- place. She loosened the collar of her dress and pulled out the necklace. The fiery opal between the gold Karda resting above the curve of her breast shimmered in the firelight. His fingers curled around it, brushing her skin, raising goosebumps on her arm. She tried to step back, but he kept his hold on the pendant.

"We have a problem, Marta. A problem I didn't anticipate when I gave this to you." ~She is so beautiful.~

Marta stared up at him, unsure about the words she heard in her head. "Who is beautiful? Do you mean Jenna? Yes, she is. Did you intend this pendant for her? I can give it back." She reached for the clasp at the back of her neck, not sure she would have enough strength in her fingers to undo it. She was bereft. Pain bloomed under her ribs.

"No. No." Altan took hold of her wrists. "It wasn't for Jenna." His look begged her. "Don't take it off. Please."

"You're scaring me. If you didn't give this to me by mistake, and you don't want me to give it back, what is the problem? Is this your mother's?" She lifted it and looked down. The fire in the stone coruscated—a living prism held in the talons of the two gold Karda.

She couldn't look away.

~You. You are the one who is so beautiful I can think of nothing else.~

They stood for a long time in front of the tiny fireplace. Altan held her face in his hands, kissing her—her lips, her throat, the softness of her neck below her ear. He moved his hands slowly, unfastening the buttons down the front of her high-necked dress. His fingers curled around the fiery opal, brushing her skin. Her nipples tightened, and he circled one lightly with his rough palm. Heat flamed low in her belly, flushing her body. She pulled his shirt loose, sliding her hands up his sides, feeling the solid muscles of his back. He shivered against her. The brown and gold silk slid to pool around her feet, her shift soon joining it. He stood back, looking at her, his breath coming faster, his calloused hands on her waist.

~You are so beautiful.~

~Altan,~ she said silently, cupping his face with her hands. ~Take me to bed.~

For the rest of the night, there was nothing but him, his body, his emotions, his senses, his self, the two of them wrapped in a swirl of oneness with no edges.

Altan sat back in his assembly seat, angry and thinking hard. Prime Guardian Hugh sat in the center at the top of the U-shaped wood table, his chair slightly larger and more ornate than the others. The huge bulk of Akhara's Guardian Turin was next to him.

The sun hung low outside the tall leaded-glass windows and showed weak through thin clouds in the West. The polished granite walls of the room darkened.

The meeting recessed long enough for servants to enter and light the lamps in the ornate iron sconces along the walls. Tapestry banners representing each of the quadrants of Adalta adorned the stone walls above the paneling of rare golden oak, their faded colors highlighted as each sconce was lit.

"Continue, Daryl," said Hugh as the servants made their way out of the chamber.

"I don't know where these bandits are coming from, sire. My brother has spent a great deal of time these last six moons on the borders searching them out. He says he's found only a few small bands and he's taken care of most of them. It's true our towns and villages are not being hit the way Altan says Toldar's are. Whoever they are, they seem to restrict themselves to the occasional raid on a trade caravan or travelers with few guards on our side of the border. But then, to be honest, Toldar's villages are richer than most of ours. The border runs along the edge of the foothills. The rich farmland is all on Toldar's side."

Daryl frowned. "I can assure you that we are not hiding them. The rough countryside on our side of the border is riddled with hidden valleys and caves. It's thick with second growth forest from fires. It's almost impossible to see anything from the Karda, so we depend on Readen's Mounted Patrol."

He paused then said in a lower voice, "We're not blessed with a surfeit of Karda for aerial patrols. We seem to have a difficult time attracting enough Mi'hiru and getting them to stay for long."

Altan looked hard at Daryl. He sounded sincere—there was little doubt of that. But he could feel the man's unease. He wasn't saying something, as though Daryl had his own doubts but wasn't able to articulate them even to himself. Altan sat forward in his chair. There was little point in carrying this discussion further. He didn't want a full diplomatic break with Restal. The goodwill his father worked so hard to foster between the two quadrants was shaky enough.

"I accept your assurances, Daryl. But you must accept mine that the increase in mounted troops along the border is not a sign of aggression toward Restal. They are there for the protection of our towns and villages. For now, we won't ask your permission to chase bandits across the borders, but I can't say that won't come up sometime in the future. We do ask for increased communication with the troops on your side. Maybe that will be enough."

He paused. "I don't think we need to take up any more of the assembly's time. It's getting late. You and I can work this out by ourselves, I think."

Daryl's relief was palpable.

Little other business could be done by the assembly without lengthy discussion, and the session ended shortly thereafter. Altan headed up to his chambers, taking the steps two at a time. Marta should be back from the guild house by now. He was determined to skip the assembly dinner this evening so the two of them could have a quiet supper by themselves.

They'd both worked hard for the past tenday. He was in assembly sessions until late, and Marta worked with the Karda, the Mi'hiru, and their trainees for hours daily. They were taking advantage of her ability to talk with all the Karda, not just empathically, and not only her own telepathically.

He missed her. The little awkwardness they felt at first were fading. He could feel her in his mind, a constant feather-like presence. If it went away, it would be as if he lost a part of himself. Distance seemed not to matter. When they were apart she was there.

When they were together, well, there was nothing in his experience—and he was not inexperienced in relationships—to compare with this. A melding of thought, emotion, and body that surpassed any need for words.

He slowed to a stop. Jenna waited for him at the bottom of the stairs, smiling. "I've missed you these past days, Altan." She took his arm. "Father says you are representing Toldar well. But I'm not surprised. You'll be a good guardian." She looked up at him, tugging his arm playfully. "When the time comes, that is. I haven't seen the gardens here yet. Will you show me?"

In the dark? How much more dangerous can this get? Altan sighed. His father wouldn't care, but his mother would be delighted. If the coastal holdings became the Coastal Quadrant, a union with Jenna would be advantageous. *Oh, Jenna must be the reason mother put the bonding stones in my packs. She's not going to be happy.*

"You seem absent-minded, Altan. Are you talking to that Karda again?"

How could I ever have considered a marriage with someone who could call Kibrath "that Karda"?

~You couldn't. I don't know why you are even thinking about it.~ Kibrath's voice interrupted him.

~You are eavesdropping on me again.~

~Who else is going to protect you from yourself? Why don't you invite her to go flying with us again?~

Altan almost laughed out loud picturing her skidding into an about-face at the invitation. Jenna was not fond of Karda.

Marta walked in the gate. Jenna called out to her and waved. "Here comes your Mi'hiru looking serious, like she has something of vital importance to talk to you about." She pulled his arm down, so her lips were close to his ear. "I'll help you escape. Let's walk in the gardens."

She laughed and pulled him in that direction.

"I'm afraid I can't, Jenna."

She stood still and looked from him to Marta, who turned away and went up the stairs. Jenna's lips thinned, and her face paled. She walked across the courtyard, fury riding double with disappointment on her shoulders.

How could I ever have thought I could marry her? No matter how much political influence she could bring Toldar. Mother will just have to be disappointed. And he took the steps up to the apartment two at a time, impatient to see Marta.

She was there when Altan reached the apartments, watching two nervous young pages set out a small supper of cheeses, bread, fruit, wine, and a simple hot vegetable soup smothering with toasted cheese. Her face was closed, no smile in sight. He felt like she'd slapped him. *Is this about Jenna? Does she think I'd do that to her? That she means so little to me?*

Neither of them spoke until the pages left, then Marta said, "Readen met me walking back up from the guild again."

Altan stiffened. "I felt it."

"He tried to coerce me again. My...the pendant got so hot I

251

thought it was going to burn through my uniform. He's tried it three days in a row now and hasn't succeeded." She looked at him, her face cool, her words crisp. "Thank you. I know it must be difficult for you to have to keep track of me while you're concentrated on assembly business."

Altan felt like pieces of himself were breaking off and shattering against the frozen mask of her face.

She shook her head and changed the subject. "Mother Cailyn says Daryl is asking for more Mi'hiru again."

"You're not going back there." The thought was terrifying.

Marta went on as if he hadn't spoken. "She doesn't like having to replace them so often. I suspect it's Readen. He hates Mi'hiru, and he hates Karda. He can't hide that. I'm sure he makes the emotional atmosphere for them so poisonous they can't stand more than six months there. And she's worried about the growing circles in Restal and how they affect the Karda."

Altan clenched his fist so hard his fingernails bit into his palm. He changed the subject back. "You're too polite to him. If you'd discourage him more overtly—" He stopped. He was getting angry.

"If there is any chance I can learn more from him, I must. Anyway, he's leaving early, probably in a couple of days. Daryl's staying for the rest of the assembly meeting, but they have gotten word their father isn't well. One of them needs to return to Restal." She turned her back and held her hands out to the magma stones.

"I don't understand why he keeps trying to control you."

"I don't know. I'm sure by now Galen's told him who I am. He can't be sure I know about the guns, much less that I've told you and the prime guardian about them. Or about myself. I don't know what he wants with me. Maybe it's just ego. He doesn't seem the kind to accept failure."

She gestured at the table. "I'm sorry you went to all this trouble. I have to go back to the guild house tonight. There's a meeting..."

"Not tonight, Marta. We have to talk."

She turned back around and bit her lip. "Yes, I saw you with Jenna.

I understand."

"You understand what? Jenna's not important. This has nothing to do with Jenna."

She put her hand to her stomach, closed her eyes, and let out a breath so long he thought she might have been holding it all afternoon.

"Sit down, please, and have some supper, then we'll talk."

Neither of them ate much. They stacked the dishes on the tray, and Altan carried it out to the hall.

When he turned back, Marta sat rigid in one of the chairs by the fireplace with its glowing stones. Her face was back in a so-emotionless-it-screamed-emotion mask.

"Please explain to me what this pendant is. The part you don't want to tell me. Besides a way to protect me. It's obviously more than that or you wouldn't be so sorry you gave it to me."

He looked at her, startled. "I'm not sorry. That's not it."

"Then what is it?" Her fingers tapped on the arm of the chair. She was poised to fly out the door any minute.

By the lady Adalta, how am I going to explain this?

"They're called bonding opals. Couples exchange opals when they agree to bond. They almost never flash like these...like this one does." Altan didn't think it was possible for Marta to get more stiff, but she did at the word *bond*.

"You said you gave it to me for protection. So you could sense what Readen might do to me. And it worked. That's all." She held the pendant out and looked down at it. "So when we're away from here, or when Readen leaves, I can give it back to you. I don't see the problem." The flashing rainbow from the opal danced on the planes of her face. She blinked several times, wiped at her eyes with the heel of her palm, and looked at him again. Her expression said, "I dare you to object," so loudly for a minute he thought he heard her say it.

"Mother's and Father's opals flashed so brightly when they were exchanged at the bonding ceremony guests were blinded for several seconds."

Marta blinked again. "What does that mean? I know...I know you can't ask me to join you in a bond, so what does it mean?"

He pulled the matching Karda-bracketed stone from his pocket. Even through his closed fist, the light from its flash was so bright the bones of his fingers glowed through the flesh. The sharp edges of the Karda's wings pricked his palm. "Bonding—sometimes, when the stones flash as bright as yours, ours, it means the connection between two people is so strong it can't be broken, that it is enduring no matter whether they are together physically or not. It means there can never be another true relationship for either one."

Her face changed as comprehension dawned, flashing emotions so fast they were impossible for him to read.

"I'm so sorry, Marta. I mean no, I'm not sorry. I mean... It means you're bonded to me. And I'm bonded to you. It means that...." He stopped.

"What have you done to me?" she whispered.

CHAPTER TWENTY-THREE

N*ext to flying, this is the kind of day I love.* Altan's horse picked his
way behind Guardian Hugh and Daryl Me'Vere through an
open forest of four-hundred-year-old trees crowned with delicate
black tracery of winter-bare branches. They rode up a hill topped
by a grove of towering pine. The sun was warm on his back. For
once the sky was a perfect sapphire dish above them. The only thing
missing was Marta, but she was furious with him and not speaking.

They were hunting. Fifteen assembly members, men and
women, including the prime guardian, were on a well-deserved
break from a tenday of assembly meetings, to help restock the
citadel's larders. They rode hard all day, taking four does past
bearing age and three younger bucks. Now they headed over a hill
to circle back around through the forest to Rashiba Prime.

A big older buck, one many-pointed antler broken and hanging,
jumped in front of the troop of hunters from a tangle of smaller
trees and brush. Hugh and Daryl raised their bows and shot, killing
him with one arrow to the throat and one to the heart.

The stag dropped, and Altan lowered his bow, arrow still
nocked. A fluttering buzz flew past his ear, and an arrow sprouted

from Daryl Me'Vere's back. Altan threw the reins over his horse's head and hit the ground running.

Three long strides took him to Daryl's side, the prime guardian on his heels. They caught Daryl as he slid from the saddle, his mouth a surprised O, his eyes wide, staring down at his chest where a bloody arrowhead protruded. Then they fluttered, rolled back in his head, and he passed out.

"Sire!" yelled Altan, and the guardian whipped his short hunting cloak down on the ground and helped Altan lower Daryl to his side. Altan pressed his hands to Daryl's chest and back. "Help me hold him here." He knelt on the damp ground, lowered his head, and concentrated, ignoring the shouts of men searching for the shooter and the confusion of milling horses. He heard Readen yelling something, felt someone clutching at his back. Then someone grabbed Readen and shouted, "Let him work, man. Let him work."

Altan felt along the length of the arrow, the splintered rib, the hole in the lung, and a tiny nick in the large artery from the heart. And something else, a fierce toxic heat in the wound, fiery and poisonous and spreading. An ugly red and yellow haze burned his mind.

Fistoria —the healer poison. Every healer was taught to recognize it. If Daryl regained consciousness and started healing himself before he recognized it, he would activate a feedback loop that would kill him in minutes.

The hunt master came running with his saddlebag, pulling out rolls of bandages. He held out a couple of thick white pads to Altan.

"Sire,"Altan looked up at Hugh, kneeling on Daryl's other side. "I think you can cut the arrowhead off now. Do it quickly, and sire,"he looked up, his voice low,"Don't take your gloves off. Handle it carefully."

Hugh's eyes widened, and he frowned. His mouth tightened. He reached for his belt dagger and cut away the arrowhead, wrapped it carefully in a cloth from his pocket and put it in his belt pouch.

Altan looked behind him at the closest hunter. "Gavan, when I tell you, pull the arrow out slow and careful. It's nicked an artery, and I need to repair that as you're pulling it away." He pressed one of the white pads against the wound in front, holding the other ready as

Gavan pulled the shaft slowly free. Altan eased up on the pressure, letting the wound bleed freely for several minutes.

He heard Readen say, "What are you doing, man? Put more pressure on it. Stop the bleeding."

He let it bleed a minute more, soaking the white pads through with scarlet blood until he could tell most of the poison left the wound. He hoped it was enough. It was a gamble, but much more blood loss would do the job the poison was intended to do.

He drew power from the forest around him, sent tendrils like hollow rootlets searching down into the ground, felt power flow up through his talent channels. It swirled up from an underground spring, from the hearts of the immense trees, from the rocks and soil of Adalta herself, surging through his channels with all they could take, a minute fraction of her terrible power.

He increased the pressure to slow the bleeding and began to feel his way along the trajectory of the wound, aligned the fragments of bone from the rib, closed off the damaged cells of the lung and cleared it of the toxic blood. Head down, he concentrated, closing the wound from the inside out, feeling the swirl of Adalta's force move through his hands and into Daryl's body.

Then he sat back on his heels and almost fell over, exhausted and shaking. Cold damp from the forest floor soaked his heavy brown pants. He monitored Daryl's heartbeat and breath while the hunt master bandaged his chest, wrapping tightly to hold the newly-healed rib secure and keep the newly-healed wounds from breaking open.

Altan heard Merenya, Anuma Quadrant's guardian, yell something and saw her reach for the reins of one of the beaters. The beater slashed at her with a long knife, and the tall, grey-haired woman jerked her hand back. He kneed his horse toward a break in the circle of hunters, but it closed around him.

His body went rigid—he gave a garbled, inarticulate cry that rang of despair and turned the knife on himself. The point pierced the artery in his neck, blood spurted, and he slid from the saddle.

His body convulsed, his back arched, his heels drummed the torn, mucky ground until he went still.

Merenya spoke into the shocked silence. "Look at the fletching on his arrows. It matches that." She gestured to the headless arrow on the ground by Daryl.

Hugh spoke, his voice rasped with anger. "Whose man was he? I don't recognize him."

No one answered.

Hugh and Merenya organized the rest of the hunters for the trip back while Altan oversaw getting Daryl back to the citadel. Two men cut stout saplings and wove a makeshift litter using the breast collars from several horses and a couple of hunting cloaks. They carefully moved the still-unconscious Daryl onto the stretcher. Four beaters lifted him to carry him back to the citadel. Altan rode close enough to warn Daryl about the healer poison if he regained consciousness. Close enough to block Daryl's talent if he tried to use it.

When the hunters had ridden about half a kilometer, they descended into a tiny valley with a stream at the bottom. Altan dismounted to wash the blood from his hands. Hugh and Readen dismounted with him, and the others led their horses to drink upstream.

"Altan, thank you. I shouldn't have tried to interfere," Readen said. "You knew what you were doing. I was frightened." He turned away for a moment. "I had no idea you were such a powerful healer." Altan and Hugh looked at each other.

"He isn't out of the woods yet, Readen," said Altan, his tone pitched low.

"What do you mean?"

"I mean there was poison on that arrow." The look of shock and dismay that appeared on Readen's face was half a second too slow, Altan thought. And from the tight furrows on the prime guardian's forehead, so did he.

Readen tossed his saddlebags to the floor beside Daryl's bed. "I still don't like this. I don't know whether to worry more about you or Father. I wish we had more information about how bad he is."

Daryl moved himself up higher on the pillows behind him, toppling a pile of books, and grimaced with pain. "He apparently had a stroke. The healers here say this happens with older people, particularly when they're under stress. Sometimes they get over it with little damage. The message the Mi'hiru brought said he seems better, though he walks with a cane and slurs his speech. That's not unusual according to what Corinne tells me."

He looked up at the dark haired older woman on the other side of the bed. "And I know she's a good healer. She's certainly taking good care of me. Thank you, Corinne. If you could leave my brother and me alone for a while, I'll take my medicine as soon as he's gone, without even being threatened."

She smiled, handed him a cup of an herbal concoction, and left the room, saying over her shoulder, "I'll be back to make sure you do, sir."

"And she will, too. Probably hold my nose and pour it down my throat if I don't." He took a sip, grimaced, and reached to set the cup atop a book on the table beside his bed.

"I know one of us needs to be there, but it should be you, not me," Readen said.

"Well, I can't be. Corinne tells me I won't be able to travel for a tenday and a half, and even then, I'll need to take it easy. Altan agrees with her. I don't have to like it, but the fistoria means I can't monitor myself, so I have to take their word for it. I can fly as far as Toldar Prime with Altan and his party. Altan assured me it's not a problem, and I'll be strong enough when they're ready to leave."

Daryl shifted and picked up the mug again. "You can send an escort for me there. I can hobble down to the assembly meetings. You know I can't leave before this session is over. We haven't even begun talking about the tax levies yet. We can't afford for me to miss those negotiations. Restal can't afford for us not to be represented."

"I still don't like leaving you by yourself. Someone tried to kill

259

you, brother." Readen had to work hard to keep his voice calm and his words from racing in his impatience to leave.

"Hugh has cautioned Captain Kendal and his guards not to leave me alone as long as I'm here. I've got two of our best Karda Patrol with me. And I'm warned now. I'll be careful. Go on, now. Be safe."

Readen clasped his brother's forearm, mock saluted, threw his saddlebags over his shoulder, and left, heading down the stairs two at a time to the stables west of the main courtyard. He schooled his face to mask the glee he felt, to contain his malice. He buckled his gear behind the cantle, checked the rest of his party, noted the horses were fresh and stamping with impatience in the cold early morning air with impatience that matched his own.

Readen hoped his guards were ready to ride harder than they ever had before because this opportunity wouldn't wait. He grimaced. Frustration that the damn Karda refused to carry him brought a momentary pall.

But the time he would have saved by flying he could use for planning. It would take a well thought out plan, and he needed the time to refine his tactics and strategy to take advantage of this new opportunity—his father crippled, and Daryl forced to remain in Rashiba Prime, unable to use his talent. Then Daryl would have to fly through Toldar to get home. This could be the chance Readen waited for.

He swung into the saddle, and the party moved out as the citadel guards hauled open the massive, iron-banded gates to let them through. He smiled to himself. He'd spent a great deal of energy trying to put a coercion on Marta with no opportunity to replenish his reserve of power in Rashiba. They'd skirt at least one Circle of Disorder on the way, and he was looking forward to persuading a victim from one of the villages they passed to join him at the circle. He'd have to be careful, but he smiled as avid anticipation swelled low and warm in his groin. The guard next to him looked away from that smile, uneasiness coloring his face, which made Readen's smile broader.

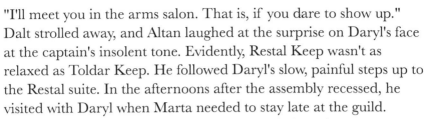

"I'll meet you in the arms salon. That is, if you dare to show up." Dalt strolled away, and Altan laughed at the surprise on Daryl's face at the captain's insolent tone. Evidently, Restal Keep wasn't as relaxed as Toldar Keep. He followed Daryl's slow, painful steps up to the Restal suite. In the afternoons after the assembly recessed, he visited with Daryl when Marta needed to stay late at the guild.

It was an opportunity to get to know the heir to the guardianship of a quadrant that had been a troublesome neighbor at best and at times an open enemy of Toldar. They were becoming friends, which Altan found, to his surprise, he enjoyed. He suspected Daryl was a lonely person in Restal. His men treated him with reserved respect and little of the rough camaraderie Altan shared with his patrollers.

Daryl's recovery was slow. The wounds and damaged rib were healed, but the effects of the poison left him weak despite Altan's best efforts. Prime Guardian Hugh and his men questioned every member of the hunting party, searching for the identity of the man who shot him. No one knew him or would admit to it. Hugh was one of the few whose talent was strong enough for a forced truth spell, but even under the spell, the other bearers knew nothing.

Holders, guardians, and representatives were all questioned, albeit with caution—using truth spell on them would not be tolerated—but no link was found to the shooter. There was no good description of him to circulate—a man of medium height, medium brown hair, medium looks, dressed as the other bearers.

"Do you allow Captain Dalt to talk to you that way all the time?" asked Daryl.

"He has an irrepressible wit and an unruly tongue, but he is as good with a blade and a bow as any man of my patrol and as good a flyer as I am. He's a friend. I enjoy his company. He keeps me honest and humble. Puncturing inflated egos is his favorite pastime," said Altan.

Daryl looked thoughtful. "I can think of any number of inflated egos in our keep that could use puncturing, but the puncturer might not survive the puncturing."

Altan laughed. "That's why he's on patrol much of the time. There are some inflated egos in Toldar Keep that I would enjoy seeing match wits with him, but so far we've protected them from each other. He does know his place. There's no better soldier than Captain Dalt. I would trust him with my life. And have." He paused, unsure of whether to go on in the direction his thoughts were taking him, then decided to continue. "I hope you have men like him in your army and escort."

Daryl looked at him, then what Altan had not said began to dawn. He blurted out, "You think that arrow came from someone in my party?"

"I didn't say that. There's no proof."

"But you think it."

"It isn't my place."

Daryl shoved the heavy door to the Restal suite open, and it slammed back against the wall. He kicked the piece of plaster it knocked loose across the room. Anger and confusion chased back and forth across his face.

Growing up is hard, thought Altan. *He's the same age I am. How can he be so clueless about Readen?* They sat in the chairs facing the carved stone fireplace, Daryl, elbows on knees, held his hands out to the fire.

He was silent for several minutes, then looked up. "I hope I have loyal people like your Captain Dalt. Armsmaster Krager is probably the best friend I have."

He sat back. "Besides my brother, whom I trust implicitly." The defensive note in his voice said he wasn't going to talk about Readen.

"Let's finish our discussion of what to do about the border raids. I think we can arrange better communication between our patrols and yours. We should be able to work out an agreement to allow your Karda Patrol at least some flyovers of our side of the border when you're chasing a band of these outlaws. And I'll talk to Readen about sending Karda Patrols there more often."

Altan kept his mind on the discussion Daryl preferred, hoping he had at least planted some suspicion in Daryl's head. Daryl was an idealist, bookish, almost pedantic but for his wary innocence. Altan hated to be the one to rob him of that, and Toldar didn't need a neighbor torn by a war fought between brothers.

CHAPTER TWENTY-FOUR

I t took more than a tenday to make the trip from Rashiba to Toldar Prime, even without the detours to villages they'd taken before. Three days before they were to arrive, Altan sent Lyall ahead to let his father know they were close and to ask him to relay a message to Restal for Daryl's escort.

"I don't think an escort will be necessary," said Daryl. "I'll be fine with the two men with me."

"That's what we agreed to before Readen left," replied Altan. "You're still not recovered enough for such a trip with only two flyers. When we get to Toldar Keep, I'll flush the remaining poison and ask Father to double-check that the fistoria is gone." He grinned. "I'm getting tired of doing all the work. You can send a message with Lyall to forward on to Restal if you want."

"I'll do that," said Daryl.

Daryl, Altan, Dalt, and Marta sat in the large common room of the hostel where they stopped for the night. The four of them lounged at a table near the large stone stove while their guards laughed and joked at a table nearby. It was snowing hard and piling up. The room was warm and the ale good. They finished a meal of roast lamb with vegetables and a cherry-apple tart with heavy cream and were enjoying cups of hot mint tea laced with a fiery alcohol none of them recognized. They'd been forced to stop early once before because of a snowstorm. All of them enjoyed the leisure time, knowing that things would get rough when they were back on regular patrol—winter had just begun.

Altan looked across the table at Marta. *Adalta, how I've missed talking to her.* She stared down into her cup. Amber strands in her dark hair gleamed in the firelight that shadowed her angular face. He swallowed a sudden urge to shout at her.

~What are you thinking so seriously?~ he pathed to her, taking a chance. She hadn't spoken to him mind to mind since their confrontation in Rashiba. She spoke to him aloud only when immediately necessary.

~It's rude to carry on a conversation like this when Daryl is sitting there waiting for an answer to whatever he is saying,~ she replied.

He let out a long, slow breath that felt like it had lodged in his lungs for days. ~Daryl isn't saying anything. He's lost in his thoughts, and you're avoiding my question.~

She took a sip of her tea. ~I'm thinking this is some potent tea.~

~No, you aren't.~

~Are you sure you want to know what I'm thinking?~

~I'm thinking we need to talk. I'm thinking I'm tired of you avoiding me.~

~What do you want me to do?~ She looked up at him. Her blue eyes reflected the yellow flame of the candle on the table.

"Come on, Marta. I'll walk with you out to the mews to check on the Karda." He stood and waited.

She bit her lip and rose with a short, sharp nod of her head. Daryl didn't look up.

The two of them took their warm cloaks from the hooks on the wall by the door and walked to the mews. Big snowflakes fell perpendicular in the still air, enclosing them in white silence. Marta slipped on an icy flagstone and jerked away when Altan caught her arm to steady her.

It was less cold inside the mews with the large double doors closed. They moved down the enclosed aisle checking each Karda. Marta talked to them, her voice low, asking what they needed. Altan enjoyed watching her. He felt her say something silently to Sidhari, and the big Karda hissed and mantled her wings, butting her great raptor beak against Marta with a gentleness that made Altan smile —the love and trust a tangible thing between them.

~What's going on inside her head, Kibrath? What does Sidhari say?~ Altan stopped by the stall where his Karda was eating.

~You know better than to ask that, Altan. She wouldn't say, and I wouldn't ask. It is for you and Marta to work out.~

They reached the tack and feed room separating the horses from the Karda, where it was somewhat warmer. Marta sat on a tow sack and he beside her. The stacked bags of feed formed a miniature cave around them. Magma stones in the iron stove on the opposite wall radiated heat and soft dim light. He moved close, spreading his cloak over the both of them. She started to pull away.

~Allow me this courtesy, please. I'm not going to assault you, Marta. And I'm cold.~

She relaxed and pulled up her knees, locking her arms around them. They sat together in silence, breathing in the familiar scents of the stable: the hay, the oiled leather, the horses, and the sharp, spicy smell of the Karda.

~I'm ready to listen now. Please explain what it means—that you and I are...bonded,~ Marta pathed, her head turned away from him.

Altan held himself still, trying not to slump in relief.

~Does it give you some kind of rights over me?~

He was appalled. ~No. No. Nothing like that. Is that what you thought?~

~I didn't know what to think. You made it sound inevitable. Like I have no choice. Like you took choice away from me.~ She hesitated. ~Can I even trust what I feel about you, what I think?~ Her fingers found the slight bulge the opal necklace made in her tunic. ~This will change my life, won't it? Will I have to give up being Mi'hiru?~

266

~No.~ He chewed on his lip. He'd never been so unsure of himself. ~A bond can't make you feel anything you didn't feel before. There are bonded couples who seldom see each other—by choice—and there have been those who were separated by force. If you should decide that's what you want...~

She put her head down on her knees. He realized she was crying. Silent sobs shuddered through her body so hard he ached for her. He slid his arm under her knees and moved her to his lap, holding her tight against him while she cried—deep, gulping sounds that threatened to break him.

When she finally stopped, he held her, rocking until her breathing evened. "You are," he whispered into her hair, "the most beautiful, the most irritating, the most fascinating woman I've ever met. Please don't decide to leave me. Please." He pulled the necklace that matched hers from his pocket. "Will you put this on me?"

She pulled away from him and lifted a hand to his cheek. Her fingers moved over his face as if searching for the truth in his words. An almost-smile trembled on her lips. "You think I'm irritating?"

~I think you are fascinating and beautiful, too. Didn't you hear that part?~ He held his breath. His heart pounded so loudly in his ears he was sure she could hear it. Her fingers touched the pulse in his neck.

~No one has ever told me I'm beautiful.~ She traced the line of his upper lip and cupped his cheek.

He shuddered.

~Not unless there was something they wanted from me.~

~Whoever that no one is—he was very unobservant.~ He started to breathe again. ~If you will put this around my neck, I think I want very badly to make love to you.~

Marta took the stone and reached up to clasp the chain around his neck. The light flared around them, fused them into a pair, an unbreakable pair.

Into the silence he thought was never ending, she pathed, ~I think I want very badly for you to make love to me.~

He kissed her long and deep. Her cold hands slid inside his shirt to circle him, holding him so tightly he could feel every part of her tremble against him. Whatever happened, he could never let this woman go. Heart to heart, breath to breath, soul to soul, they were inextricably entwined.

He spread his cloak over the feed sacks and laid her down. His large hand stroked down the side of her face, fingertips feather-light under her chin, he touched his lips to hers. The heat of her spread through his body. Their eyes on each other as if tied by spider silk threads, they removed each other's clothes piece by piece, with movements slow and deliberate, and lay side by side, her cloak over them.

Skin to skin, Altan was aware of every inch of her. Her trembling matched his own. They moved together, for a long sweet time, until they both shuddered in a shared ecstasy of being beyond what any thought, any word, could express. They lay there, limbs tangled, minds tangled until the cold began to penetrate the weight of the cloak spread over them.

Little more than a day outside Toldar Prime, Lyall was waiting as they landed, one after the other, on the runway at the holding where they would stay the night. He had grave news from Guardian Stephan.

"A Mi'hiru and patrol wing were flagged down at the border by three Mounted Patrol from Restal," he reported, looking at Daryl. "Guardian Roland is incapacitated, and Readen declared himself Guardian Regent. He's calling it a victory for those of lesser talent. The end of rule by the aristocracy of the talented."

Daryl grabbed the saddle rig he'd just taken off his Karda, Abala. "I must fly home immediately. How much farther can I get tonight, do you think?"

"Please, sir," said Lyall, his words hasty, his tone urgent. "Read the message from Guardian Stephan before you make a decision."

He handed the message portfolio to Altan who scanned it. "Let's get inside. You do need to read this. And whatever you decide, Abala must rest and eat."

~Yes, I must, and so must you,~ added the Karda. Altan wondered if he'd ever get used to hearing Karda other than Kibrath in his head.

They settled themselves—Marta, Altan, and Daryl—at the table nearest the fire, and Altan read the communiqué more thoroughly. He handed it to Daryl and turned to Marta. "Three Restal patrollers escaped Restal Keep. They intercepted our patrol on their way to find Daryl in Toldar Prime. They advise him not to return. They're sure he'll be killed if he tries. Readen's troops are patrolling the border day and night, watching the skies for him. The Prime and keep are filling with mercenaries Readen hired.

"Apparently Guardian Roland has not been seen since Readen declared himself regent. He was weak and barely able to speak then. He slurred his words. He had difficulty walking without support. The healers don't expect him to live much longer. Readen has the keep manned by those in the guard loyal to him and a great many mercenaries. How far his control spreads beyond the keep is a question."

Daryl put the communiqué down and put his head in his hands, elbows on the table, took a deep breath, huffed it out, and turned to Altan. "How much longer to Toldar if we fly as long and as fast as we can? I want to talk to these men before I make a decision. The Mi'hiru flew Bastin—one of the patrollers—back with her."

His smile held little amusement. "Poor guy was probably terrified. He's never even been near a Karda before. It'll take the other two several days to get there on horseback."

Altan turned to Marta. "How hard can we push? What do you think?"

She did some calculations in her head. "If there is no more snow, or only a few light flurries, if we make few rest stops, carry extra food for the Karda, and the wind is with us, we can reach Toldar Prime by late tomorrow evening. I think we can make it. It'll be a long hard day, Daryl. Are you sure you are up to it?"

"I'm almost back to full strength," he said, his words quiet, firm.

"Why don't we get supper over with, then retire so we can get an early start in the morning?"

Marta nodded and excused herself to check with the Karda and give them extra rations so they'd be ready for the next day's grueling flight. She had the stable master prepare a hot vegetable and grain mash for them and tossed extra meat, grain, and tubers in the mangers. When she returned to the inn, her dinner of hot lamb stew, fresh hot bread, strong ale, with dried berry custard tart to finish waited for her. She and Altan stayed for a few minutes after Daryl went to his room, sitting quietly before the glowing magma stones in the great fire- place of smooth river stones.

"Well," said Altan, "this will give Father something to think about other than our bond, now, won't it?"

"Maybe he'll be so worried we shouldn't tell him at all." *I wish. I wish. I wish.* "Will he support Daryl?"

"I can't predict what he'll do. He'll wait till he gets my report on the assembly before he makes his decision. If he does decide to back Daryl in wresting control back from Readen, I figure we'll need at least six tendays to prepare, and he won't move without consulting the prime guardian and informing the council. Readen must have been thinking about this for a while, biding his time. Otherwise, how did he get so many mercenaries so fast?"

"He wants Daryl dead. We know that. I have no question in my mind that he controlled the assassin. And triggered the compulsion that killed him."

They flew into Toldar Prime in an exhausted flurry of back-winging just at dusk. Guardian Stephan had horses waiting, and Daryl and Altan rode immediately to the keep. Stephan met them at the gate-house and offered rooms in the southeast tower of the rambling keep for Daryl and his men. Daryl excused himself and left to hear what Bastin had to say. Altan walked with his father up the narrow stairs to his study.

Stephan poured wine into a heavy mug, heated it with a hot iron from the magma stones in the fireplace, and handed the steaming cup to his son. "Here's what I've done." He gestured at the clutter of maps on the large table.

"I've deployed three additional wings of Karda Patrol to the border to gather what intelligence they can. I've sent word to the Mounted Patrol troops garrisoned along the border to send back what word they gather from the local folk and what extra activity they observe along the border. There hasn't been time for any of them to report. The guard is on notice, and though it stretches their non-partisan policy, Mi'hiru are taking messages to the border garrisons and holdings to prepare. I haven't moved any more troops yet—it's too soon. I've also sent word to Hugh, who's ordered his closest undercover man, Bren, to get to Restal Prime as fast as he can."

The chair back his hand rested on creaked. He looked down and relaxed his grip, shaking out his hand. "According to the men who came to warn Daryl, Readen won't make any move toward us until he's consolidated his power. They claim he hasn't firmed his hold on the rest of the quadrant and isn't likely to do so soon. There are too many powerful holders he must appease or coerce, and he is taking hostages. Several holders' daughters. Not a smart move."

"I have little doubt that his ambitions extend beyond their border to us. And perhaps even beyond," Altan said. "He must not have those weapons from the consortium, or he would already have moved. There's probably still some time, but how much is impossible to know."

"We have a decision to make. Do we support Daryl or do we stay out of it? If we don't support him, it might give us more time to prepare for Readen's inevitable invasion. If we do, and Daryl fails, will we give Readen an excuse to invade?" Stephan looked more closely at Altan. "But you're exhausted. You need to get some rest. We need clear heads to decide this. I called our council. I've sent word to all the holders and town representatives who currently serve."

His hand on Altan's back, he herded him toward the door and said, "I need you rested and clear-headed. You and Daryl both. You must have flown hard and fast to get here so soon. We'll talk in the morning. Not much of a welcome home for you. And you have a report from the assembly to make."

Altan turned to leave then paused. "Father, if you would call Mother to join us, I have something I need to tell you both."

His father looked at him, frowning, then went to the door to call a page to send for Elena. "Is this something I am going to like hearing about?"

"I don't know. Let's wait for Mother. Do you suppose I could get another mug of that hot wine and something to eat to tide me over? I am not just tired—I'm hungry. And I think it would be appreciated if you had something sent to Daryl and his men, too."

"Yes, of course. I should have done that immediately. I was so relieved to see you I didn't think of it. I must be slipping in my dotage." Stephan moved to the door to summon another page and send him for food. Then he heated Altan another mug of wine.

Altan heated the magma stones to flame to chase the chill from the room, and the two of them sat quietly waiting for Guardian Elena. Altan stared at the flickering stones, nerves taut.

When she arrived, she wore a fur-lined dressing gown. She crossed to the fire and hugged her son, touching his face gently.

"I'm sorry, Mother. You had retired. Were you asleep?" Altan asked.

"No, I was reading. I was too agitated with the news to do much else."

"Now, she's here. So what is this all about?" asked Stephan.

"I found what you hid in my dressing-case, Mother," said Altan. He pulled the fiery opal necklace from beneath his tunic.

Elena put her hand to her heart and smiled widely. "And you're wearing it." She moved to him and hugged him hard and long. "I am so happy for you, for us all. Thank Blessed Adalta. This is a good thing."

Stephan frowned, watching this. "What's a good thing?"

Altan turned so his father could see the pendant. Stephan's frown disappeared into relief. "I hoped when Me'Nowyk stopped here on their way to Rashiba and Jenna was with him that this would happen. Congratulations. It is indeed a good thing."

"I admit I've been a little worried about the mind talk you share with the Mi'hiru," Elena said. "But Jenna is the right choice. She—"

Altan held up a hand, palm out. "No. No. You've jumped to the wrong conclusion." He watched his mother look back and forth from him to his father. Her face switched from happiness to puzzlement to disappointment with a light salting of anger.

Stephan leaned forward, hands on the map-covered table. "Not Jenna? Holder Me'Nowyk was of the opinion that the match was all but settled. What happened? We can ill afford to antagonize him. If his proposal to make the coastal holdings independent succeeds, we'll need his good will. We'll be landlocked on all sides." He stood.

Altan was stunned. His eyes followed his father who paced in front of the thick drapes closed against the night and the cold. Nothing had been settled between Altan and Jenna. How could they think that? Tendrils of anger began to take hold of him, growing into thick, thorny vines that threatened to strangle him.

"You'll just have to reconsider your hasty action. I'm assuming you brought this to us before you made any public announcement." Stephan looked at Elena.

"It doesn't have to be a disaster," she said, arms crossed in front of her chest. "I'm disappointed you acted so precipitously, but this can be handled..." Her tone was slow, steady parent-patient.

Altan looked at her, his jaw muscles clamped against his fury and disappointment.

Her words faltered to a stop. She bit her lip.

Stephan turned back to Altan. "So who is she who wears the other opal? If it is the alien Mi'hiru we offered sanctuary, you've carried it a little further than I intended." His attempt at a smile only added fuel to Altan's fury. And his mother's disappointment clawed gashes in his control.

The parents who had fostered his strength and independence were now trying to take them back.

Altan ran his hands through his hair, pulling most of it out of the leather thong that held it back. "I was hoping you would be happy for me, Father." His teeth clenched so tight the words had to be forced out. His fingers twisted the leather tie until it broke.

Stephan dropped his eyes to the stone on Altan's chest. "I have seldom seen a bonding opal with such fire. It will be difficult for you, for both of you, to separate."

"It won't be difficult at all. There will be no separation."

CHAPTER TWENTY-FIVE

Marta sat up in bed, her head foggy with sleep. The short, sturdy teacher, Janaya, stuck her head in the door. "Didn't you hear me knock? You have a visitor."

She looks smug and happy, Marta thought when the teacher left and when the sleep-fog lifted enough for her to think. *I wonder why? Her usual attitude is waspish at best.* Marta suspected a disappointed attraction to Altan.

Marta dressed in the cleanest riding clothes she could find, grateful to have them. They'd outrun the pack train on the way back, and she was limited to what she could carry on Sidhari. Her clothes had long since given up cleanliness.

She ran down the stairs debating whether to go by the kitchen on her way and decided not to. Solaira bid her enter when she knocked. She stopped dead just inside. Elena, Altan's mother, sat next to Solaira's desk. Marta swallowed nervously. Elena's face was stiff, unhappy, and unwelcoming.

"I wonder if you could give us a little privacy, Mother Solaira." It was not a question. She didn't take her eyes off Marta.

Solaira looked from Elena to Marta. "If there is a problem with one of my guild members, perhaps I should remain."

SHERRILL NILSON

"It is a private matter. One that does not involve the guild."
Elena waved Marta to a chair facing hers and waited until Solaira
had closed the door behind her.

Elena reached over and pulled the chain and pendant from
beneath Marta's tunic. She dropped it when it flashed. It was so
bright Marta had to blink before she could see again.

"Oh, dear." Elena bit her lip. She clasped her hands together in
her lap, so tightly her fingers were blotched red and white. "This is
not going to be easy for you."

Marta dredged words out of the pit she was falling into. "What
is not going to be easy?" Her head felt too light, her body too
heavy.

"Of course, you know this cannot be." She waved her hand at
the pendant. "It is difficult and painful to leave a bond, but you must
be strong. For Altan's sake. It will be difficult for him, too, but you
can make it easier."

It was as if Elena's words floated in the air between them,
visible, coming toward her like glinting, slow-moving arrows aimed
directly at the pain crushing her chest.

"I...I don't understand." She had to force her words to come out
above a whisper.

"Of course. You couldn't have known. The match between
Altan and Jenna is already decided. She and Me'Nowyk told
Stephan and me when they stopped here on their way to Rashiba.
Altan should never have given you this." She reached for the
pendant, and Marta jerked back in her chair, crossing both hands
over the opal, unable to breathe through the pain radiating from the
stone.

Elena dropped her hand back to her lap. "All right. I won't take
it now. You have the right to give it back to Altan yourself. I am truly
sorry, my dear. I know what it is to be bonded. And I have known
those who chose not to be with their bonded. It is a hard choice, one
you know you have to make. But you are a strong young woman.
I'm sure you will do what is right for your adopted quadrant. And
for Altan."

Elena's words pinged Marta's ears like cold sleet slung by a hard north wind. She forced herself not to wrap her arms around her, forced herself not to shatter into flying shards of ice.

"Altan must make a political match. I know you have feelings for each other." She glanced at Marta's hands covering the pendant. Her cheeks flushed pink, she shifted back in her chair and crossed her ankles.

"The political and economic ramifications if Altan refuses the match with the Me'Nowyks will be felt for years if the coastal holds gain independence. I know only too well that Mi'hiru are not allowed political alliances. It was difficult for me to leave the Mi'hiru when I bonded with Stephan. But remember, you have a bond with your Karda — Sidhari, is it? That bond will be your strength." She shifted and uncrossed her ankles, scooting to the edge of the chair.

The Me'Nowyks. Match with the Me'Nowyks.

"I'm certain Mother Cailyn in Rashiba will be happy to assign you elsewhere. It would be difficult for you to remain here, for both you and Altan. I'll speak to Solaira."

She stood, hesitated. Her face flashed pain for an instant, then her lips tightened and settled into resolve. Marta looked away, and after a moment, Elena left, easing the door closed behind her.

How long it was before Solaira backed through the door into the room with a tray of hot sweetbread, butter, cheese, and fresh fruit compote, Marta didn't know. The guild mother put it on her table, then busied herself with making more tea. For Solaira, tea could solve any problem. She sat in the chair Elena vacated and poured two cups.

"Drink that while it's still hot and tell me what's wrong." Then she saw the pendant lying outside Marta's uniform jacket. "Oh, dear." She looked at Marta's face. "Oh, Adalta. What has Elena done?"

Marta looked at her. Elena's words hung, persistent, in the air of the room. If she let them in, they would split her chest wide open.

Solaira picked up Marta's hands and folded her fingers around the cup. "Take a sip. I'll be here when you're ready to talk. Just sit here and drink your tea. I'll be back in a moment."

The tea was so hot it burned Marta's tongue, but the pain didn't register. *Who am I now? I have left everything I was. Where do I belong? I can't stay here in Toldar.*

~Marta, no one can break a bond, and no one can force you to separate once you bond,~ Sidhari's pathed words burst into her head. ~No one. No one can make that choice except you and Altan, Marta.~

Marta heard the sharp note of Sidhari's distress and the piercing cries of several Karda from the mews.

"My mother what?" Every Karda in the mews raised a head. Kibrath echoed Sidhari's piercing scream. The pendant on his chest burned, and he jerked it out, pricking a finger on one of the Karda wings. His whole body shook with pain so deep he grabbed Kibrath's mane to hold himself up. It wasn't his pain.

"I'm not sure exactly what she said to Marta, but I saw the pendant. And I saw Marta's face after Elena left. I don't know what Marta will do," said Solaira.

Altan ran. Through the main hall of the guild house where men weren't allowed. Several women looked up, and Janaya started toward him, a smile on her face, then backed away. He slammed open the door to Solaira's empty study. ~Where is she Kibrath? Sidhari, you know. Please, where is she?~

~Sidhari says she is in her room, packing.~

Altan pounded up the stairs where men certainly weren't allowed. He didn't even think about it. He was shouting her name before he hit the first stair. Red-headed Rayna stuck her head out of her door. "Rayna, where is she? Where is Marta? Which is her room?"

Rayna held up a hand, frowning, and opened her mouth to say something.

"Don't tell me I'm not supposed to be here. I know that. Where is her room?" He could hardly speak for the pain—his and Marta's.

Rayna pointed.

Her door was open, and she stood inside in the middle of the room, a jacket hanging from her hand, her face paper-white.

"What did she say to you? What did my mother say to you?"

Marta's mouth hardly moved as she spoke. "I assume you came to tell me about Jenna. Don't worry, I have been alone before, and I can be alone again."

"What about Jenna? What do you mean you can be alone again?" He was vaguely aware that what doors weren't already open in the long hall, opened, and ears sharpened. ~What about Jenna?~ he pathed, ~Jenna is nothing. There is nothing to tell you about Jenna.~

Marta folded the jacket and stuffed it in a saddlebag. ~It was decided before you gave me this.~ She reached to the back of her neck to unclasp the gold chain of the pendant.

Altan closed the distance between them with one long stride and grabbed her wrists. ~No.~

~I understand, Altan, I truly do. A good relationship with her father is important to Toldar, and...~ She wouldn't look at him.

~Karda shit on that relationship. You are the only relationship I can ever have.~

She stood still, her head down.

~Look at me, Marta. Look at me. Losing you would be an amputation I could never survive. I would bleed to death. Look at me. Mother had no right to tell you about Jenna. It isn't even true. Don't let Jenna— don't let the maneuvering of that scheming bitch destroy us. Don't let my mother's over-developed guilt at not being the political match for my father she only thinks he needed destroy us.~

He put a finger under her chin and tipped her head up. ~There are no bonds that can be broken without breaking the bonded. There may be bonded who choose not to be together. There may even be bonds that form for something other than love. This is not one of those. I am tied so tightly to you I can't move without knowing which direction you move.~

Her face began to relax. The terrible grief contorting it faded. She reached out and closed her hand around the opal pendant on

his chest. She leaned into him, and his arms went around her.
~Tighter, Altan. Hold me tighter.~

Marta wound her way up the crowded, twisty streets of Toldar
Prime for her meeting with Mireia Me'Rahl. She was more than a
little nervous. Altan made the appointment for her and insisted she
go. She walked up the cobbled street dodging through the crush of
people. It was market day, and people with oversized baskets
maneuvered around carts, displays outside shops, and running
children.

   She watched a skinny girl filch an apple from a grocer's, toss it
underhand to an equally skinny boy who darted behind a man
selling sausages. Then she looked with pleading eyes and a penny at
the grocer, who handed her another apple and waved her off,
smiling after her.

   A young boy opened the door of the small, two-story red cut-
stone house. "M' name's Oreon. I looks after Finder Mireia. Who
sent ya here?" His half-belligerent words left Marta in no doubt that
he looked after the finder very well.

   Assured by the mention of Altan Me'Gerron, he showed her
into a small room at the back of the house. Sunlight streamed across
brightly figured rugs from the tall windows looking into a tiny
garden, mulched and winter dormant. Floor to ceiling bookcases
flanked them. Magma stones in the small fireplace flickered. Green
plants trailed from stands at the windows.

   A tiny, rounded woman crowned with a drift of fine white hair
stood as Marta entered, motioned to a chair in front of the fire, and
sat across from her. A writing table and more bookcases stood
against one wall, paintings of the countryside lined the opposite. It
was a cheerful, well-used room. Marta took the cup of tea Mireia
offered and sat on the edge of her chair, warming her cold hands.

   "I'm sure you're wondering what this is all about, Marta," said
Mireia. Her voice was unexpectedly strong for such a tiny woman.

   "Yes, Oreon called you Finder Mireia. Alton only insisted I

come— he didn't tell me anything about you. I recognize the name Me'Rahl. I've met the prime guardian, but I have no idea what a finder is."

"Hugh Me'Rahl is my second cousin. A very commanding and determined man who would rather I lived where he could take care of me. I would rather not. So I moved to Toldar many years ago. They needed a finder, and I needed a place to live independently."

Marta was sure there was more to Mireia's tale than that. It was too practiced a story.

"A finder determines the strengths of your talents and the direction they will probably take. It is how we decide what to teach children about using their talents. Finders also do that. Altan said you know little about talent, and he explained why."

She set her cup on the little table beside her. "Here's the basic introduction. Talent is the ability to draw and manipulate the elemental forces of Air, Water, and Earth that come from Adalta. Strength in talent is what distinguishes the leaders of Adalta and is believed to be inherited. Though everyone has talent to varying degrees. Well, with one tragic exception. Daryl is his father's heir in Restal instead of his older brother because Readen was born with no talent.

"But Daryl's talent is strong, perhaps as powerful as Altan's, and Altan is the strongest talent born on Adalta in many generations. They are the only two I know of who are equally strong in all three elements of talent—Earth, Air, and Water. Most have one dominant talent— village healers in Water, the most successful farmers in Earth, weather watchers in Air, for example." She stopped for a sip of her tea.

"Talent is the ability to draw power through the rocks, the water, plants, the very air itself. The way it is manipulated—used—is different in each person according to individual personality traits and abilities in the same way innate intelligence or physical prowess expresses itself differently in individuals. Training, upbringing, family, opportunity, necessity—all influence how the talents are combined and used."

"I can't imagine I could do that. It sounds impossible to me," said Marta.

Mireia smiled. "You are probably a strong Air talent, all Mi'hiru are. We'll see." She laughed. "We could use someone to help with the weather. We haven't had a good weather talent in twenty years."

Manipulating the weather? People can do that?

"You'd already have had some disturbing incidents if you were." Mireia reached over and patted her knee. "In combination with Earth and Water talent, Air can be used to control the weather, to foresee, or far-see. An unusual facility with growing things, a connection with animals, the ability to sense the unseen presence of other beings. The ability to manipulate soil, stone, rock, minerals— those are Earth talents."

She sat back in her chair and smiled. "Isn't it interesting that although we left there centuries ago, we still say Earth? Earth combined with Water enables healing, though some healing is possible with only Water talent. Everyone has enough Earth and Air talent to do simple things with fire and heat, such as light candles or lamps, warm a room, or trigger the heat in magma stones. Twisting Air and Earth talent, Altan has the rare ability to draw and focus fire from the center of Adalta. That makes him a very powerful warrior talent. Through his Earth talent, he can draw strength and enhance his quickness and agility, which is what helps him be a superb swordsman."

Marta was silent. She looked down into her cup. The visions she had from time to time that were so disorienting, was that foreseeing? The consciousness she felt from her surroundings? Could those be a kind of talent ability?

"I see I have hit a nerve," said Mireia. "More tea?"

"Yes," said Marta. "Please."

Yes to tea? Or yes to struck nerve?"

"Both, I think."

Mireia poured them each another cup of tea. "Altan sent you here because my Air talent manifests as the ability to be a Finder. I identify and teach the manipulation of talent, how to draw power from Adalta, how to make your capabilities more controllable and predictable, even to bring them out if they're hidden. These are the things I help you develop once I have identified what talents you might have. When I've identified someone's major talent and taught the basics, if they are particularly strong, I pass them on to a teacher with their particular blend of talents for further training."

By the time Mireia finished taking Marta through an exhausting series of exercises and questions, Marta's head was spinning. Mireia sat back, her fingers steepled under her chin. She was silent for a long time. Marta grew more and more uneasy at the finder's steady gaze.

The Finder moved her chair a little further from the fire. "If you don't mind sitting on the floor in front of me—this kind of testing takes something out of one, and I would rather sit than stand. I don't want to fall over on you. I don't usually have to do this. It may disorient you some, too, so let's make ourselves comfortable."

Marta self-consciously, and with not a little fear, moved to sit on the cushion Mireia placed on the floor. She could sense Mireia's—it wasn't exactly concern, maybe confusion? *Probably because I'm not from Adalta, I don't have talent. I'm not sure how I feel about that.*

"Just lean back against me and relax as best you can. Take some long, slow breaths and expand your shields to include me inside them, like an elastic bubble. I can't intrude on your thoughts so don't worry about that. Altan is the only one who could do that, and incidentally, one day I would like to explore the ability you two share. I understand you are plagued by a great capacity for empathy, but there is no one else here with emotions you might have to contend with, and I'll keep mine to myself." Mireia's voice was calm and patient, soothing Marta like the experienced teacher she was.

Mireia cupped her hands on Marta's temples. They felt cool at first. Then they began to warm. She moved her hands away from Marta's head a little, but the heat continued, growing uncomfortable. Marta's mind began to swirl. Colors formed and moved in strange patterns behind her closed eyelids. Her breath grew short, blackness closed in from the outer edges of the bright swirls of color, and then there was nothing. When she recovered, she was leaning back against Mireia's knees, nauseous and disoriented.

She blinked and focused her eyes on the leaf and vine carvings in the granite surround of the chimney-less fireplace. She took several deep breaths, then sat straighter, away from Mireia.

"Better?" asked Mireia. "Can you get up and move to your chair now, or do you need a few more minutes?"

"I think I'm fine." Marta stood and almost fell into the chair opposite Mireia, who looked as exhausted and disoriented as she felt. "What did you do to me?"

Mireia didn't speak for several minutes. "I don't often have to do that. It's usually when there has been some trauma that blocks channels, and I have to work to open them."

She took a sip of her tea and made a face. "I need to heat some water—this is cold." She moved to the fire, poked a few stones into blue and yellow flame, and swung a small, brass kettle on its hook over them. Marta stared at the hearth with its intricate flowing pattern of color in an inlay of tiny ceramic tiles.

She took a deep breath and closed her eyes for a moment. She was exhausted, and her thoughts swam around in her head like minnows flashing in a small pool. There was a sharp ache in the middle of her forehead as if someone had pushed a thorn into her head just above the bridge of her nose.

Mireia took the teapot to another room to empty it, taking her time she added fresh leaves, and poured the now hot water over them. She waited for them to steep, then poured both a cup and looked at Marta, frowning.

Marta sat up straight, panic pounding. There was something wrong. Fear pinched her breath, then Mireia smiled. It was a little forced, but Marta's panic eased somewhat.

"I've never found anything like what I found in you." She put her hand on Marta's knee. "Relax, dear. Nothing's wrong, just puzzling. You look like a rabbit who's just seen a really big coyote coming for her in full leap. Take a sip of tea. I'm sure you have a headache, right here." She touched Marta's forehead just above the bridge of her nose. "This tea will help. Though it has a bitter taste. Add some honey if you want."

Marta smiled weakly and nodded. She was almost—actually

more than almost—afraid to ask. "What did you find?" Panic began to roll again.

Mireia sipped at her tea and looked at her over the rim of her cup, her head tilted as if she could see better that way.

"I'm not sure. Like I said, when I do this, it's usually because something blocks the channel or channels, and power builds up behind the block. If it's not cleared, sometimes the channel burns out. That's not good, to say the least. But yours...there are no blocks. The channels are wide open, all three."

She sat up straighter. "Strong wide channels. Almost as strong as Altan's. But they're like a precocious infant's. Trickles run through them, like a broad valley with a small stream meandering through the middle of it. Mind you, those trickles are larger than most ordinary channels, particularly the Air talent that, with a trickle of Water, enables your extraordinary empathy and the mental connection with Altan.

"What you opened in Altan is between the two of you. No one has had this ability for centuries. I've certainly never seen it before. It's beautiful, by the way—all gleaming turquoise shot with gold. Strong and solid." She looked into the distance for a moment.

She shook her head and looked back at Marta. "You definitely have foresight, and you've developed some ability to control it. Although, I imagine it acts in a random, rogue fashion. I expect you've had visions of some sort all your life, but you didn't know what they were."

Marta nodded. "I thought it was imagination triggered by stress or my empathic senses overloading."

"You have an extraordinary ability of empathy, but you already knew that. You can't be Mi'hiru without that ability, and at least that one ability is well developed. I suspect you can feel intentions as well as emotions. I have a feeling the two abilities are linked, somehow, and your foresight links to intention through empathy. But that's just a guess. Teaching the talents is more art than science. Everyone's talents, strong or weak, manifest in ways that are as particular to them as their differing personalities."

Mireia held up the teapot and nodded to Marta's cup with a

raised brow. Marta shook her head and took a sip from the still full cup. It needed honey.

Mireia went on, her tone matter-of-fact. "It's your own unique twist of all three of those trickles of talent that enables you to sense the emotions of people and animals around you, even those you don't see, and to communicate with growing things. You can draw strength from them. But it is precognition and empathy you need to work on first, or they will overwhelm you if your talent channels begin to fill. Individual manifestations of talent show as brilliant threads of color braided together in strands. But you don't just have room in your talent channels for strands—you have room for cables like ship hawsers. Perhaps because you are new to Adalta, they are not filled yet, as with a child. But you need to prepare for them to fill. Let's just hope it is a gradual process, and your talent doesn't flood you in a sudden surge."

Marta had begun to recover from her puzzlement and uncertainty. Somehow Mireia's calm tone made the extraordinary things she was telling Marta seem ordinary. Something she could learn to manage.

"I'll give you exercises to do every day. And you must be diligent about it. We start learning to recognize and control our talents as children. You are not a child, and I have no idea how your talents will manifest other than that they will be powerful. These exercises will enable you to have some control when they do. And when they do, you must find someone like me soon. An out-of-control talent the size of what you have the potential for is dangerous.

"But for now we'll begin with learning control of what you have. Altan told me you need to work on grounding yourself in Adalta. The exercises will help. The shield you are using to control your empathy is primitive and either too dense or too open, with little subtlety. It feels like a stone wall with holes that can open and close. There are two ways in which you'll have to learn to improve your shields. Probably the most important right now is to learn to recognize when the foresight is happening, to shield against it. You have no shields at all for that."

Marta started in surprise. "Shield against it?"

"Yes. If, or rather when, those trickles begin to expand, you won't want to be bombarded with all kinds of visions—that would be useless and more than disorienting, not to mention intrusive. And I'm certain they will expand. Let's hope it's not in a flash flood. We'll work a little on shields before you leave today. You don't want your shields to block everything. They need to be porous, for example, like a fire screen that blocks sparks and embers but doesn't keep out what is important —the heat."

What a helpful way to describe shields. Marta felt the tension in her shoulders begin to dissipate, and the pain in her head eased.

"It may take a while for this to become automatic and for your visions to happen when you intend them to happen. But you won't need to know the future of every shopkeeper you meet or the love life outcome of every friend you have a conversation with. Practice the grounding and centering exercises I'm going to show you. Your shields are not grounded as they need to be. I'll help you with the foundations, and you can go from there with just a little help from Altan and me over the next tendays. Today is Tuesday. By Noviday, you should be well on your way to good shields if we work hard. Which we will."

She smiled and reached across to pat Marta's hands, which were clutched tightly in her lap. "You won't have to do this by yourself. Why don't you sit here for a few minutes? I have some correspondence to catch up on. Just drink some more tea, and I'll have something brought in for us to eat before we begin. Even if you don't feel like eating, you need to. I don't want you passing out on your way back to the guild house. And I'm tired and hungry myself."

CHAPTER TWENTY-SIX

Daryl hesitated when he entered Stephan's study, looking back and forth between Marta beside Altan and Elena, who stood on the other side of the room,. There were no women in influential positions in Restal, not even on the council. Marta ducked her head to hide a crooked smile.

Daryl's men persuaded him that if he tried to get into Restal, he would be killed, so he agreed to stay, spending his time trying to figure a way to restore his position. His sense of duty to his quadrant was evident to Marta in the constant frown of sick worry he wore. The Restal patrollers who escaped to warn him told him about the hostages Readen held from the more powerful holders, the people he imprisoned, the repressive hold his guards and mercenaries had on the keep and the prime. Marta suspected only Daryl's innate good sense kept him from leaping on a Karda and flying off. Instead, he asked for another meeting with Stephan.

"I know it is not possible for you to field an army to support me in Restal," he said to Stephan. "That's unthinkable. I don't want to involve my people in a war. Even in a quadrant-wide conflict with Readen. Bastin tells me that so far, Readen only controls the keep.

His position in the prime is uneasy, and I can't allow him time to secure his hold any farther. No matter that he's my brother, and I trusted him and loved him." Pain flicked across his face so fast Marta almost missed it.

Restless, he paced back and forth in front of the windows. "But my blindness isn't the issue here. It's what I do now. I will not abdicate. Readen would be disastrous as guardian. The holders will never accept him with no talent. They would be in revolt already, but for the fact he's holding some of their family members hostage.

"The quadrant...I have disagreed with much of the way my father governed us for some time. Readen supported him, encouraged his self-indulgences, and advocated even more repressive methods. I cannot live in exile and accept that." He stopped pacing and faced the others. "I'm also concerned about my father. I do not want him to die believing I turned my back on him and my responsibilities to the quadrant."

Marta watched the keen appraisal on Stephan's face as Daryl stopped speaking. The guardian didn't say anything for a long time, staring past Daryl, unseeing. His words were slow when he finally spoke. "I am not sure what we can do for you, Daryl. If we do nothing, there will eventually be war here, I'm certain. If we help you, there's a strong possibility war will come sooner."

"I have an idea." Marta and Altan spoke at the same time.

Marta was embarrassed. "It isn't my place," she murmured, looking down.

"It's very much your place, now, Marta," said Altan.

Stephan added, with a glance at Elena, "We'll hear Altan's idea, then yours."

Elena's look was not a happy one. Marta chose to ignore the waves of tension and disapproval radiating from her for the whole meeting.

"No," shouted Altan, and he slammed his mug down on the map

table, sloshing tea across the papers. "I won't permit it." The glowing stones in the carved stone fireplace behind him blazed hot and popped. The lamps around the wall flared.

"You won't permit it?" said Marta. "Who asked you for permission? This is the best solution, and you know it."

"I'm your commander, that's who I am," Altan replied, his eyes snapping as furiously as the fire behind him. The others in the room stood back and let them argue.

"No, I'm Mi'hiru. Mother Cailyn in Rashiba is my commander. You are my bondmate, and that's how you're reacting. This is a policy decision."

"Yes, I'm your bondmate, and I say I forbid it."

"You are my bondmate, not my bondmaster. You can't forbid me to do anything. This is the best opportunity we have. It's a good plan. In fact, it is the only plan that has a chance of doing what needs doing."

"Let someone else do it, then."

"Who of us has the most experience penetrating alien territory and not getting caught? I have been doing this kind of work since I was a child. I'm good at it. You don't have anyone else who is as good as I am, and you know it." The two of them glared at each other.

~Oh, I wish I could be a mouse in the corner for this meeting,~ Marta heard Sidhari path.

~This isn't funny.~ Marta worked to control her breath—and her temper.

~Yes, it is. Kibrath and I are greatly amused.~

~I think you and Kibrath spend too much time gossiping about Altan and me. And you're too big to be a mouse.~

Stephan reached over and picked up Altan's cup to refill it. "She has you there, Altan," he said. "We had no idea who Marta was before she told you."

"Readen will recognize her the minute he sees her," said Altan.

Stephan put his hand on Altan's shoulder. "You can take care of that," he said, his voice soft. "You can make her look like anyone you want."

"No, Stephan." Elena's hands covered her mouth; her eyes widened.

That frightened Marta. *Why is she frightened and what does Stephan mean—Altan can make me look like anyone he wants?*

"He'll see through a talent illusion," muttered Altan.

"He won't see through it. Not if he doesn't have any reason to suspect her," said Stephan. He walked over and leaned against the fire- place, waiting for Altan to respond.

Altan stood, his head down, hands scrubbing at his face. He looked out the window at the bare, winter-resting garden, dull in the cloudy grey light.

Daryl looked back and forth between the three of them. "Talent illusion? You can disguise her with a talent illusion? You can put an illusion on someone else? Not just yourself?"

Marta watched flickers of hope and incredulous disbelief flash across his face.

"I've never heard of anyone who could put an illusion on someone other than themselves. Can you do it? Could I do it?" His head turned sharply toward Marta. "Would you be willing to let him? Or me?"

Altan took a deep breath, looked at his father, who inclined his head, and at his mother, who shook hers. "I have the ability and the knowledge to cast an illusion on another—a willing person—and change his or her appearance completely. The spell has been in our family for generations, but it takes more talent than most have."

"It's dangerous knowledge," said Elena. "How could you trust anyone to be who she says she is if this ability became widespread?" She looked at Marta and Daryl in turn, fear pulling at her face. "It's after the fact to ask you to respect this secret, but I ask anyway. No one must know Altan can do this. No one. He already must be careful about revealing how strong his talent is, so he isn't feared. If this became known he would be." The look she gave Marta could fry her toes in her boots. Elena bit her lip and turned away to look out the window, hiding her face.

"It's your choice, Altan. And Marta's. It's a good idea. It's a way to let Daryl's supporters know he isn't a prisoner here, to expose

Readen's lies," said Stephan. "Daryl can't do it himself until someone lays the groundwork. It's too risky. You know that. Readen knows Daryl won't sit still and be satisfied with exile. He knows he'll try something. He'll be watching every border and have spies everywhere. Flying in unnoticed will never work. Going before Daryl's supporters are alerted would be disastrous. He'll need safe places to meet with them—safe places for his loyal guard to gather."

Elena turned back around. "But, Stephan, Hugh sent Bren. He can do all that."

"No, Mother." Altan rubbed his temple with the heel of his hand. "Bren doesn't have the access a Mi'hiru has."

"He won't recognize her if she goes as a Mi'hiru. He seldom goes near the Karda or the Mi'hiru unless he has to. And they are desperate for Mi'hiru. Bastin says all but one of them left, and the Karda Patrol is all but grounded. Philipa went back because the guild at Rashiba insisted someone had to. Sending Marta can easily be arranged." Daryl was pacing now, already thinking of possibilities.

Marta touched Altan's hand. "I can be in contact with you anytime I need you. You know that. Bren will be there, and you won't be that long in arriving. You and Daryl will be close behind me."

"Not close enough to help if he discovers you. The illusion isn't foolproof," said Altan, "and it will take more than four tendays for us to get there if we use Daryl's plan. I can't help you if you get in trouble and I'm miles away, even if you can reach me."

"Thanks for the vote of confidence!" Marta pulled her hand away. Daryl looked puzzled at this exchange. "First, she'll need to establish contact with Krager, my armsmaster. He works to keep Readen's trust. He always has. He's never trusted Readen." Daryl looked down at the maps, then up to meet Altan's eye. "He'll know who is safe to contact. Krager visits Tarath, his Karda, even when he can't find time to fly. He'll eventually come to Marta—she won't need to risk going to him. He'll know who to trust, and he and Marta can visit the holders who support me. Readen is still using the

Karda Patrol, though I understand their cooperation is reluctant. They don't fly without a Mi'hiru for each wing, so more Mi'hiru will be welcome. I know you don't want her to do this—"

"Ha!" Altan threw his arms out then propped them on the table, his shoulders hunched, head hanging, and blew out a breath harsh with frustration.

Daryl went on, "I wouldn't ask it of her, but she volunteered. I can't think of a better way. She'll be well placed to assess how far Readen's influence goes. Someone has to find my supporters and tell them I'm on my way. When they're alerted, we can arrange discreet meetings for planning to retake the keep. But Marta and Krager are the only ones who can lay the groundwork. He has the contacts. She'll carry our plans."

~I don't need your permission, but I won't go without your blessing.~ Marta took Altan's hand in hers and looked up at him. He met her gaze steadily, his green eyes fierce.

~I'll never forgive you if you get killed,~ he finally pathed.

She smiled and touched his hand. ~I love you, you know.~

"Yes," he whispered aloud.

~I will miss you, Marta. I know you don't want to leave me behind, but you must,~ Sidhari said as Marta groomed her wing feathers, touching them lightly with oil here and there and thinking of Altan.

She started at Sidhari's words. ~What do you mean, leave you?~ she asked in surprise. ~Aren't you going with me? Certainly, you are. You can't think I could ever leave you behind.~

~I won't be far away. I can't go on this journey as your partner. I am too recognizable as yours. You just haven't wanted to admit it. You need to choose another to bear you. I have already spoken to Keidar. She is more than willing to partner you.~

Marta realized the truth in what Sidhari said. ~How do you mean to be not far away from me if you are too recognizable?~

~Unpartnered Karda watch the skies even over Restal. Kibrath and I will join them. Restal is not a comfortable place to be. It is tiring to fly there. The land is poor in power, reluctant to let it go, and the Circles of Disorder are becoming more virulent, but we watch anyway. There is not a place on Adalta we do not watch. I will always be aware of you, Marta.~

~I am very fond of Keidar, but she is not you.~ Sidhari was silent.

Marta stood for a long time. Then, without speaking, she went back to grooming the Karda, checking her talons and the callouses on the long digits that were hoof-hard when she fisted her feet to land. There was a slight pressure in the back of her mind on her shields, but she ignored it.

But a lightning flash of bright color struck her mind. She cried out. Her hands grasped her head, and she dropped to her knees.

A vision of the hall outside Daryl's quarters emerged out of the flashes, overwhelming her view of the small paddock. A man opened the door and moved silently toward Daryl, a garrote stretched between his hands. He slipped it over Daryl's head. Marta stood abruptly and staggered. The vision dissolved then coalesced to repeat.

~Altan, there's an assassin heading for Daryl's rooms. I think it's Sebyn. Hurry. Daryl won't suspect Sebyn.~

Marta's voice shouted in Altan's head. He leaped up from the table where he was going over maps with his father, grabbed his sword from where it hung on the back of his chair, and headed for the door, shouting for the guards outside to follow him.

He took the stairs down three at a time and ran across the courtyard toward the southeast tower and Daryl's quarters. He passed Bastin and Hart, two of Daryl's men, grabbed one by the arm, and shouted, "Where's Daryl? Where's the other guard? Why aren't you with him?"

"In his study," stammered the flustered man. "What's wrong? He sent us out for food. He's fine. Sebyn headed up to be with him. He's guarded."

Altan let go of his arm and yelled for his guards to take the two surprised men into custody. He ran for the tower stairs, slammed open the door, and grabbed it before it banged the wall. He stopped outside Daryl's study and listened, but he heard no sound. He motioned for quiet as two of his guards came up the stairs behind him. He opened the door. Short, dark-haired Sebyn reached up to slip a thin leather strap over Daryl's head and pulled hard on the crossed ends.

Daryl didn't even have time to gasp. He struggled to get his fingers under the strap around his throat, rising to his feet, fighting for breath.

He jabbed back with his elbows and kicked hard. But Sebyn held tight. Altan was across the room in three strides and struck Sebyn hard behind the ear with the pommel of his sword. The man slid limply to the floor. Daryl struggled, choking until he finally got his fingers beneath the strap and pulled it away from the deep red line that marred his neck.

He sucked in a gulp of air and stared at the man on the floor. He looked up at Altan. "What happened?" His voice rasped, hoarse, and he stared at the thin strap in his hands. "Never mind. I can see what happened." He shook his head in denial. "He tried to kill me." He fell into his chair coughing and rubbed at the vivid mark on his neck.

Altan sheathed his sword in the scabbard he hadn't taken the time to belt on. The two men who followed him up the stairs carried the unconscious Sebyn to the guardhouse cells. He heard their grunts and complaints as they maneuvered the big man through the door and down the narrow stairs.

"You seem to be making a habit of saving my life. I think I would rather you find another hobby," said Daryl, rubbing at his throat, his voice like gravel. "Don't get me wrong. I'm grateful, but I hope this is the last time you have to do this. I'm fast running out of ideas on how to pay you back. I'm going to have to be your devoted slave for a long time."

His mouth quirked in a parody of a smile. "This could have been an unfortunate incident not easily explained. I thought Sebyn was faithful. Where are his two companions?"

"They're in custody. Apparently, you sent them after food."

"Yes, I did. And Sebyn stayed to guard me." He laughed. "Some guard. I think I will check out my other guards a little more thoroughly. Though that Karda has already flown, maybe it's time to shut the mews doors on the others."

Stephan strode into the room. "Altan, what in the world is happening here?"

Altan explained.

"I used truth spells on those men. How could this have gotten by me?" Stephan asked.

"You were interrogating them about the affairs and sentiments at the keep and Readen's intentions, Father. I would guess you took their loyalty for granted since they left Restal to warn Daryl."

"Apparently I assumed wrongly, Daryl. I am sorry."

"It never occurred to me to test them further. I made the same assumption you did. I should have been more suspicious of troopers from the Mounted Patrol. Readen is their commander. It's still hard to believe he wants to kill me."

He rubbed gingerly at his neck. "My death would be difficult to explain to Hugh and the council at Rashiba, and it would have made Readen's assertions against Toldar legitimate." He paused, gesturing over his shoulder in the direction of the guardhouse. "How did he expect to get away with it and make it look like a Toldar assassin?"

Stephan looked at the thin leather garrote dangling from Daryl's fingers. "I expect he was going to knock himself out and claim to have been unconscious when it happened. It would probably have worked. Even if we truth tested him then, the deed would be done, and Readen would make the most of it. You're here under our protection. It would be impossible for us to explain."

After a long silence, Daryl looked up quizzically and asked, "But Altan, how did you know? You didn't just happen to be crossing the courtyard with all those guards. And you took the other two into custody before you got up here."

"Ah, that," said Altan. "Uh, that's going to take a little explaining. Why don't we let Father question your other guards under truth test, unless you want to do it yourself, and then we'll talk about that." He hoped Daryl would forget about it in the confusion.

"I'd rather take care of it myself, I think. Not that I don't trust you, sir," he said, "but it's my responsibility. They're my men, and I want to be sure there are no future surprises or assassins. Although, I think it might be wise if one of you or your officers attended, don't you?"

"Altan, why don't you and Daryl take care of that now if Daryl is feeling up to it?" suggested Stephan.

"Oh, yes," said Daryl, his face grim as he massaged his neck. "I'm definitely up to it. And we'll test the flyers who've been with me, too."

The two flyers, Peele and Lange, went through the truth test showing complete loyalty, but the first mounted patroller looked uncomfortable as he entered the room. Hart, ruddy-faced with a too-red, too-prominent nose, sat down across the table from Daryl and Altan. "Why do we have to go through this again? We've already done this once, and you've caught Sebyn."

"It's a precaution, Hart, not necessarily a reflection on you personally. All of you are being tested, including Peele and Lange even though they had ample opportunity to kill me before we got here," Daryl said.

Altan watched as Daryl concentrated, and a barely perceptible haze that swirled green and purple began to fill the room.

Daryl leaned into the table. "Hart, did you know Sebyn was going to try to kill me?" Hart shuddered violently, staring at the table top in anguish, gritting his teeth, trying to resist. His eyes lost focus, his face a rictus of fear. "He'll kill me. Readen will kill me if I tell you." His words grew more and more incoherent. Daryl lifted the truth spell, and Hart slumped in his chair, barely conscious, his blotchy face slack. A thin trickle of blood seeped from his nose and dripped from his chin.

"The penalty for attempted assassination of a guardian heir is hanging in Toldar. If it is different in Restal, we will honor your wishes. But—" Altan stopped.

Daryl's eyes narrowed, cold with anger. "It is the same in Restal. Immediate hanging." He looked at Altan. "This has all the signs of coercion, but with an energy I don't recognize. It's ugly—and it's not elemental talent. There's nothing of Earth, Air or Water in it."

Altan nodded grimly, eying the exhausted Hart with distaste. He had felt that kind of power before. When Marta had been with Readen in Rashiba. His fists clenched just thinking of what it could have done to her. He put his hand on his chest where the bonding pendant lay under his uniform and blew out a long breath. "The seed of treason had to be there for the compulsion to work. Or at least that's the way it would be if talent was used—or misused. I don't want to think what Readen did to him is powerful enough to overcome true loyalty."

"The others will never understand. Sebyn's life is forfeit, I'm afraid. Either by his own hand or by the hand of his companions. He'll have an 'accident' sooner than later," said Daryl.

The other patrol, Bastin, was just what he said he was, personally loyal to Daryl and suspicious of Readen. Sebyn and Hart had come to him with the story of Readen's plans and the idea that they defect into Toldar. He had no reason to distrust them, and the three of them escaped together. He took their deception as a personal failure. Daryl would have no more loyal guard.

For several days, Altan worked on changing Marta's appearance, drawing on Adalta, doing it bit by bit. He set barriers so that a glance at her would slide off, show nothing but a young, round-faced, snub-nosed girl with messy brown curls, a little plump, and with some effort on her part, a trifle silly.

"Will you still love me when I'm short and fat?" Marta asked him, her arms around him, her head resting on his broad chest.

"I'll love you short, fat, plain, even old and gray when that time comes, although it's a little disconcerting to make love to someone who doesn't look like the woman I bonded to unless I concentrate," he replied.

"Maybe we better only make love in the dark, then. I don't want you feeling like you're betraying me. I'd be jealous."

"At least I didn't make you ugly, be grateful for that. And I'm sorry, but I can't make you short."

Marta looked down, resting her head on his shoulder. "It might have been better if you made me ugly, and old to boot," she said quietly .

"Second thoughts?" asked Altan. "It's not too late to back out."

"No. It's just...," she hesitated, not willing to admit her fear of Readen, even to herself, and locked it behind her shields. "We haven't been apart since those first days in Rashiba. This is going to be hard." She grinned. "I sound so...so... Whatever happened to strong, independent, don't-get-attached Marta?"

"Believe me—she's still there." He folded his arms around her, resting his chin on her head. "I'm not going to enjoy it much either. If we can't talk, I don't think I can bear it. There will be a lot of distance between us."

Altan, too, looked different, with his blond hair now dark brown and a scraggly beard beginning to cover his face. He walked with the swagger of a mercenary, and Marta teased him unmercifully about his arrogant stride. "My first impressions of you were right after all. Arrogance comes naturally to you."

"You are mistaking arrogance for complete and utter competence." He raised his head, looking down at her over his nose. One eyebrow wrinkled his forehead to his hairline.

Marta laughed.

A tenday later Daryl, Altan, and Marta spiraled down out of the bright blue sky to a snowy meadow tucked in the forest out of sight from the small town ahead of them. The Karda back-winged furiously to land in the small space. A few green spears of grass that hadn't succumbed to the idea of winter poked through melting snow and wet, sloppy ground.

It was the last town of any size before Rashiba Prime, and it was where Marta would leave them. She would fly in, while they went horseback as mercenaries wanting to hire on as guards for a wagon train to Restal.

"I hope we can pick up some rumors about my father when we get to Rashiba Prime. Readen couldn't have declared himself heir and Regent if Father were at all able to function," said Daryl as they stripped the saddlebags and packs from the Karda, piling them in a copse of small trees where there was less snow on the ground. "He has to be either incapacitated or dead for this to have gone so far."

"We've heard nothing about his death, Daryl," said Altan, "and that would be impossible to keep secret. Why would Readen even want it secret? He'd be in complete control."

"As long as he's satisfied to be regent for Father and doesn't name himself Guardian, the holders might not rebel against him right away, particularly the ones whose families are hostage," replied Daryl, his words clipped. He stamped his feet in the wet snow, shoved his hands under his arms to warm them and walked back to the Karda.

They worked in silence for a while, and Marta told Sidhari good- bye. ~Are you sure you can't come with me?~ she asked. ~I'm sure Keidar won't be disappointed.~ The tightness in her chest felt all out of proportion. Sidhari didn't say anything. Just lowered her head to Marta and crooned, the soft sounds incongruous coming from such a fierce predator.

She fed the Karda the dried meat and tubers they had left. Sidhari was going to Restal ahead of Marta and Keidar, and Kibrath would follow Altan from the sky. Marta would fly to Rashiba on Keidar, a showy red sorrel with bright copper wing bars and copper legs and feet. She loved Keidar, but she wasn't Sidhari.

While the others arranged their packs, Marta walked off by herself and pulled out her Cue. It had been nearly a moon since she had reported. She slipped behind a clump of short evergreens, hoping that the others would only think she needed the privacy for a different reason.

"I will be out of contact for some time, I'm afraid. I had to work hard to have the excuse to get off by myself to contact you now," she told Kayne. She made a cursory report, mostly about the reaction in Toldar to Readen's takeover of Restal. She knew they would have heard rumors, so she couldn't very well not. She didn't mention Daryl. "This has everything in an uproar, particularly along the border, and I'm flying patrols with others all the time. No one is allowed to go out alone."

"Do what you can. Keep your head down. With war threatening, they'll be alert for people who act suspiciously. We don't want you caught," Kayne replied.

"Since I may be flying patrols near the border I would particularly like to know if you have found out anything about the possibility of smuggled akenguns. The thought of being shot out of the sky makes me extremely nervous."

After a too-long silence, he said, "Yes, the purser did an extensive inventory and found nothing. We're still searching manifests, but so far there's no trace. That's the one exception to taking no chances with reporting—if you discover anything that might be an akengun, find a

way to let us know immediately. Let's hope it was only the one weapon. Someone made a lot of money on that."

She signed off, her stomach sour with Kayne's lies, and walked back through the wet snow to the others. She nodded to Altan, drawing him aside. "We have to assume that Readen doesn't have more than the one akengun we found, or he'd already be using them. But he will soon. Kayne is lying. Send a message on one of the Karda saddles for your father. I've told him about their range and the kind of damage they inflict, but he needs to know there's a chance the Restal Guard have them, or will soon."

Altan cursed and went to his pack to dig out writing materials. Marta walked back to the Karda and leaned against Sidhari's shoulder, thinking. This was the first time in a very long while that she had friends and a place that she belonged to, and now she was leaving to be on her own again. She hadn't thought it would hurt so much. Leaving Altan was a hurt she couldn't think about. Awkward in her body illusion, the Mi'hiru put her arms around Sidhari's neck and buried her face in the Karda's mane. Sidhari crooned in sympathy.

How can belonging hurt worse than not belonging?

CHAPTER TWENTY-SEVEN

R eaden shoved the silver scrying bowl across the table, water
slopping over its sides. He cursed and picked up the maps
littering the tabletop, shook water from them and called for a
servant to mop up the spill. The man came in, cleaned off the table,
and left as fast as he could.

Readen glared after him and threw himself into a chair beside
the fire. He hadn't been able to see a thing. The keep and the people
at Toldar Prime were blocked to his vision. Probably Stephan's
interference, he thought. Or Daryl's or—what difference did it make
whose— he was blind so far as Toldar and Daryl were concerned.
He lifted his boot and kicked his footstool. It ricocheted off a table
leg and fell on its side.

It had taken everything he had plus trickery, subterfuge, and a
sedative to subdue and imprison Malyk. The old advisor was far
stronger than Readen anticipated. Fortunately, he was also too
trusting. Readen leaned forward, elbows on his knees, hands
cradling his pounding head. He'd spent too much energy scrying on
top of the tremendous effort he'd expended setting the arcane
defenses around the keep walls, subduing Malyk, and keeping his
father contained. And he hadn't taken time to replenish himself.

He could use the three men currently in the prison cells beneath his tower. They weren't much—petty criminals with little talent to steal—but he could use them if he must. Death and sex didn't bring as much power in the cavern as it would near a circle, but it would have to be enough. He opened his door to call one of his more trusted guards. "Find me a girl. I want her by tonight."

"Sire, it's getting dangerous. People are talking. Girls aren't allowed out by night without someone with them. It may take a couple of days." The guard winced at Readen's answering curse.

Traveling to a Circle of Disorder was out of the question. He daren't leave the Prime. It was a calculated risk just to leave the keep. He didn't think he had enough power now to craft an illusion on himself. But he enjoyed the use of pain and fear. Tonight he would absorb the energy that came with sexual humiliation and the slow, painful death of a man from the cells. He shivered with a trill of anticipation.

"Find one." He shut the door and went back to his chair to fume. He moved to get up and go below to the prison cells, but a knock sounded at the door, and Galen Morel entered at his command, shaking snow from his heavy cloak. Readen noticed with pleasure that this was a very different Galen Morel from the one who had been here last. Beads of sweat shined on his forehead and upper lip, and his hands trembled. Shadows under his eyes marred his beautiful face.

"Welcome, Galen. I'm glad to see you back. I expected you days ago. I assume you have brought me the guns. Sit, sit, man. You look worn."

Galen licked his lips, nervous at this show of amiability, and moved to the chair opposite Readen, lamplight glistening off his damp fore- head. "You have no idea what I had to do to get here, Readen. In spite of Father's efforts at diversion, they're keeping track of me all the time. It took me three days to set it up so I could make this trip. Working as a Planter Corps trainee helps, but it isn't easy."

Readen stood and moved to the chest between the windows on

the wall behind Galen. He took his time pouring two glasses of wine. "And the guns?" he asked, handing him a glass.

Galen held it with both hands to keep from spilling and gulped the wine.

Readen watched with satisfaction. The coercion was working well.

The man obviously didn't want to be here, but here he was. "The guns?" Readen repeated. Little humor tempered his smile.

"Marta's reports have them in an uproar. I can't get near where they're hidden, not until the furor has died down or Father garners more support." Galen's voice shook, his eyes fixed on the red liquid trembling in the glass.

Readen's eyes narrowed as he sat across from Galen. "No guns," he said flatly.

Galen lifted his eyes from his glass. A flare of resistance flashed in them, a brief echo of the brash and arrogant man he had been before his last visit to Restal. "It would have been worth my life to try to get to them now."

Readen held his right hand out toward the man, fingers spread. "Listen to me and listen well. You. Will. Bring. Me. The. Guns. You will have them here within three tendays."

Galen jerked stiffly upright in his chair, his face chalk white. The glass tipped in his hand. Dark red wine trickled over his fingers. Shreds of anger warred with the coercion.

Readen waited—allowed no sign of doubt on his face.

It was a hard fought battle, but the coercion won. Galen slumped. "You will have the guns within three tendays." His voice was hollow, the words uttered at an even pace in an even tone with no inflection. His eyes lost what little light they'd held. His vacuous face was a parody of the arrogant, handsome man he had been.

"Leave, now," said Readen, and he watched Galen go. He stumbled once on his way to the door.

As soon as the door closed, Readen threw his glass against the stone of the fireplace. Red wine splashed across the hearth. More time wasted. Galen was stronger than he'd thought. He'd resisted the coercion to bring the guns, but he hadn't been able to resist coming himself. He wouldn't be able to resist at all now, but half of winter would be gone before he got back with the weapons. At least when winter finally hit with its bitter cold and furious storms, Daryl wouldn't be able to attack. And Readen didn't think his brother could muster his forces ahead of winter.

Readen would have to do a lot of repair work before Galen was worth anything to him again. He'd been surprised at the man's resistance. Readen hadn't thought Galen cared about anything or anyone, not even himself, but there was something at his core that fought for control. *I was too ruthless. I may have broken him with this coercion, but it will get me the guns.*

Readen pulled himself together. He needed to work on his plans. He wouldn't be able to move as fast as he wanted to take the rest of the quadrant. There was planning to do, and then he would descend to the basements to replenish his power. He smiled at that last thought.

Readen made his way down the dank, narrow staircase to the basement cells, breathing in the sharp smell of fear that permeated the stone walls. At the bottom of the steps was a small, lantern-lit room. A man rose from behind a table laid with a meager supper and a large mug of ale. Of medium height, he had a bland face, with dirty brown hair pulled back severely and wrapped with a leather thong. He wore heavy clothes and a jacket against the damp cold. There was little remarkable about him except his massive arms and chest and little black eyes that gleamed with avid anticipation when he saw Readen.

"The one in the second cell, I think, Pol," Readen said. "Bring the light."

The dark hall beyond held several empty cells and four holding a man each, including Malyk. He passed the old man's cell, drinking in his anger. He had hated him from childhood. Malyk had been the one who finally told him what his father hadn't wanted to say. He would never have the talent Daryl had. Never have talent at all. Readen would prove him wrong. He didn't need talent. He had power of a different kind. The kind no one imagined until he'd found the cavern and the Itza Larrak.

"Readen, I implore you," Malyk said, turning his head slowly on the hard bunk of his cell. "You will ruin yourself if you continue with this." He paused for a breath. "You are playing with forces of evil that will destroy you if you don't stop. I've known you since you were a child. You can't contain this. You haven't the ability or the strength however much power you manage to steal. The Larrak is too powerful." His grey hair lay dirty and tangled on the rough blanket. The sharp intelligence in his blue eyes was shadowed. The planes of his face were gaunt from too little food and too many drugs.

"You are a fool, old man." Readen controlled his anger with difficulty. Weak as Malyk was, he could still turn Readen into a child in the schoolroom again. "The Larrak has given me a power source greater than you could dream of. A power greater than Daryl's. I don't need to draw from Adalta." He smiled. "I won't have to listen to you much longer. A few more sessions and I'll have stripped your talent, and you will be silent forever."

Readen pushed Pol ahead of him to the end cell. "Unlock this one and bring the man."

Readen's eyes ranged over the length of the tall man. His filthy clothes covered long, rangy muscles and a broad chest. His dirt-streaked face was handsome. His pale, bare feet were long and narrow. Readen's gaze lingered there for a long moment, and his fingers curled. The man cast an uneasy look at Pol, uncertain of what to do, of what was to happen to him. Pol took his arm and led him from the cell.

"Are you the judiciar, then?" the man asked, looking at Readen.

With relish, Readen noted the growing doubt in his face. The man had been before a judiciar at some time and knew this wasn't usual. "Don't speak. Come with me. He can carry the light, Pol."

The man looked at his chained wrists and began to struggle against Pol. Readen grabbed his face, looked into his eyes, whispered, and made a small gesture with his free hand. The man stilled, his body grew slack, his struggles grew feeble. His wide eyes flicked from Pol to Readen and back. Readen stepped close and brushed his lips against the man's mouth, licking his lower lip. He shivered with anticipation and sucked power from the prisoner's terror.

"Take it," Readen told him. "Follow me." The man, obedient, raised his chained hands and took the light.

The prisoner stumbled along in his leg irons. Only his eyes, darting around in fear, moved with any volition of their own. His mouth moved, but he made no sound, formed no words.

"I will remove the coercion as soon as we arrive at our destination," Readen said in a soft voice. "Some of it anyway."

The man looked at him, a small light of hope in his eyes. Readen leaned close and breathed it in with the smell of the prisoner's fear. Vain hope held a delicious taste of power all its own.

The hall narrowed and sloped as they moved through the twists and turns, deeper into the earth. The damp, worked stone of the walls changed to smooth, more natural curves. They were no longer in a hallway constructed by humans. The man's arms trembled with the effort of holding the lamp high with his chained hands.

"It isn't far." Readen's touch on his arm was gentle and intrusive, sliding across his shoulder and down his back in a caress. The man tried to shift away. "Keep walking." Readen's hand moved slowly, gently down to cup his buttock, and the man's face fired red in anger and fear, but he couldn't flinch away. Readen stepped closer and tightened his hand. "There, just ahead around this little bend," he whispered. His mouth close to the man's ear, his breath tickled the dirty blond hairs. Readen thrilled at the shudder that quaked the man's body.

There was a twist in the hall, more a tunnel now. Obscured in a cavity was a small door of smooth dark wood. Arcane symbols were carved in the stone lintel above it.

Readen held his hand against the lock and whispered several sibilant syllables, and the lock clicked open.

"Go ahead of me. And do not shrink from my touch again." Readen felt heat curl up inside him. Making the man—or, even better, a girl or a boy—compliance against will was the thing that excited him the most. His hands caressed the man, sliding lower on his back. He felt him lean into Readen as though seeking comfort, then jerk away. Shame and self-hatred flooded his face with heat. Readen felt power begin to pulse from the hot anticipation growing deep in his groin, and he licked his lips, tasting it.

They entered the cavern. The ceiling soared, its roof lost to darkness. The light of the small lamp showed little but the area immediately around them. Leading into the gloom were randomly spaced columns of limestone, incised with chiseled symbols, dark with flaking brown stains. Readen pushed the man to a small pile of torches next to the door.

He ran his fingers slowly down the man's face from temple to chin and softly kissed him on the lips, licking between them with his tongue. The man shuddered violently but couldn't move away. Readen himself shuddered in expectation. Sex and fear were immensely powerful reservoirs, like pain and death, and he thirsted for them all. His breath came faster.

"Pick up the torches, light them at the lamp and place them in the holders you see." Awkward, his movements jerky, the man did as told, and the room brightened in the flickering torchlight. Glittering minerals in the walls danced light through the cavern. In the center of the huge space stood a large limestone rectangle, its surface stained brown. Readen led the man to it. Several small, sharp knives lay on a cloth at one end.

"Here is the key to your irons. You may remove them now." The relief in the man's face made Readen smile. The relief twisted into terror as the man looked further into those cold, glistening, avid eyes.

Marta wiped the sweat from her face with a towel, breathing heavily. "Thank you for the workout, Tayla. I needed it." She smiled at the rangy blond and returned her practice blades and armor to the racks at the side of the Rashiba guild arms salon.

"Yes, you did, Robyn. I understand you're new. Mother Cailyn says you got your training elsewhere."

Marta noticed the skeptic glint in Tayla's eye.

"And you'll only be here for a few days. Make time to see me every day while you're here. You're not bad—just a little rusty. A few days' work will start to take care of that as long as you promise to keep it up when you get to Restal."

"No question of that. I hadn't realized I'd gotten so out of shape. I'm wringing wet," Marta's hands were on her knees, her head hanging, her lungs sucking air. Working out with a new body shape was challenging. Her reach was clumsy, her stocky body slower—there was a lot to get used to.

It had taken Altan and Daryl both to persuade her mind to accept the disguise. She still moved as if she were slim instead of round. She needed to make frequent use of the arms salon while she was in Rashiba. Altan had told her tailoring the disguise to make her experience of the body illusion real was difficult but necessary. It was also awkward. She headed for the baths, grateful for the time to soak her aches and pains away.

Mother Cailyn had found three Mi'hiru to send with her to Restal. It had taken longer than Marta had hoped to find Mi'hiru willing to go there. It was an even less sought after place with the Mi'hiru and the Karda than when she worked there before. But being one of four rather than one alone would make her less conspicuous.

When Hugh told the guild mother about the weapons, the threat of war, and the threat to all of Adalta, it was enough to override the stricture against interference in the internal politics of a quadrant by Mi'hiru. And, more importantly, the Karda were insistent. And while they always supported a leader they were bonded to, they never went further than personal support. Until now.

Marta soaked as long as she could justify and finally pulled herself out of the hot bath to dress. She and two other Mi'hiru were going to the cafe at the end of the street for the evening's entertainment. The others wanted to hear the new harper there, and Marta wanted to collect as many rumors about Restal, Readen, and Daryl as she could before she left Rashiba.

She toweled her hair dry and started combing it out, startled again at the unfamiliar round face in the mirror, with its snub nose and wildly curling mouse-brown hair. Marta missed her softer auburn length, and the fingers twisting it into a knot were clumsy. She dressed in a long dark green split skirt, a pale, yellow blouse belted at the waist, and a sleeveless tunic of rusty tweed that reached to mid-calf.

She pulled on her brown leather boots, leaned her head against the back of the bench in the dressing area, and sent her mind out looking for Altan. He and the others had gotten to Rashiba Prime late two nights before. They were to be at the tavern that evening if they were able. She quit trying to path him when he groaned at her with exhaustion. They were loading wagons, and he was too busy to talk. They'd found a caravan more than willing to take on him, Daryl, and his men, Lange and Peele, as guards. The rumors about Restal had worked for them in this case. The wagonmaster was relieved to have four more guards.

Winter had arrived in full force. Cold, dirty snow was piled along the sides of the streets in iced-over slush mountains. The warm room was a relief when Marta and her companions reached the tavern, and they hurried through the door out of the weather, pushing it closed against the wind. A harper sang a lively ballad to an even more lively crowd in the large room.

The round wooden tables were mostly full. People stood along the bar in front of the kegs with their bright polished brass and copper fittings. Shelves of gleaming bottles ranged along the back wall. Marta, rangy Tayla, and Lili—stocky, solemn, dark-haired, eyes sharp and knowing in her lined face—made their way to a newly vacated table. Magma stones glowed red beneath flickering blue and yellow flames in the fireplace of massive sandstone rocks.

Marta shook out her wet cloak and looked up to see Galen Morel across the room, sitting at a small table by himself, a large mug of ale in front of him, and an odd vacant expression on his face. She ducked her head and turned to hide her face before she remembered the face she was wearing wasn't one Galen would recognize.

"Are you all right, Robyn? You look pale," said Tayla as the three of them sat, ordering ale from the serving girl.

Marta pulled at her earring and shook her head. "No, I just saw someone I thought I knew."

"If it's the tall, beautiful one sitting by himself, I wish you did know him so you could introduce me."

Marta laughed. "You're insatiable, Tayla."

She sent a silent message to Altan as the others sat back to listen to the harper. ~Altan. Galen Morel is here in the tavern. If Daryl comes in, he'll be recognized.~

It was a while before Altan answered, and she was getting worried.

~Sorry, it's a little confusing carrying on two conversations at once. He won't recognize either of us. I want to know who Morel is. I'm coming in. Point me toward him.~

The door opened. Altan and a heavy-set, rough-looking man came in with a flurry of wind-driven snow. They hung their cloaks on the pegs near the fire to dry, ordered beer and food at the bar, and moved to a table not far from Galen, carrying beer and bowls of hot stew with thick slices of bread on top. Obviously mercenaries, others watched them for a hint of whether they might be ill-tempered mercenaries. They ignored everyone, eating as if this were their last bowl in this life.

~Galen is at the small table in the corner beside you. He's wearing a brown shirt and a dark green leather vest, drinking ale. Or rather, staring into the mug.~ Marta turned to her companions, ignoring the mercenaries but paying attention as best she could without attracting attention.

The men's conversation turned naturally to the job they'd just taken with the caravan bound for Restal Prime. Marta watched

Galen look up and listen. She got a clear look at his face, and she was shocked. His beautiful face was thin, drawn, his eyes deep-set in bruised shadows. He looked haunted.

He stood, stumbling a little as he left his corner table, and approached the mercenaries. "Did I hear you right? You're headed to Restal with a caravan tomorrow?" he asked.

Altan turned to look him over. "Within a few days if the wagon-master gets enough cargo to make up a full load," he said. "If you want work, you're too late. All the teamsters and guards've been hired. We're just waiting to see if there are more goods to be carried before we take off. Sorry, mate."

"No, no. I need someone to carry cargo to Restal. How can I find your wagonmaster?"

"Well, he'll be right glad to see you. His name is Master Coynar, and he'll be at the east gathering yards beyond the stock pens tomorrow first thing, I'd guess. How much do you have? Will it make up a wagon load or more?" Daryl asked.

"No, just five crates. Heavy, but they won't take up much room, maybe half a wagon."

"Well, mayhap he can fit them in somewhere. Good luck to you." The two turned back to their mugs of beer.

~What are the odds that these are the guns, Marta?~ asked Altan.

~I wouldn't take that bet. I'm sure they are. I wonder if he'll travel with them. And how difficult will it be to get rid of them along the road?~

~We'll just have to be clever about it. It's a long trip.~ He stared at her over the rim of his mug—his eyes flashed with heat. ~I miss you. When do you leave?~

His voice sounded husky in her head. He was so near and so untouchable she ached. She felt the opal hidden beneath her tunic heat. It was a good thing both were hidden. Everyone would notice the wild flash of the bonding opals.

Marta sat back in her chair as if listening to the harper, her arms wrapped tight around her. ~As soon as the other Mi'hiru come in, less than a tenday. It's been difficult finding Mi'hiru willing to go to Restal. I'm not eager to find out why.~

~We'll try to be here every night until we leave. It is nice to at least see you, even if you do look like a stranger. You don't suppose you could get away from your friends for a couple of minutes?~

Marta sent him a mental laugh. ~Only a couple of minutes?~

CHAPTER TWENTY-EIGHT

Half a tenday later, Altan rode beside a wagon along a narrow trail through a heavily wooded valley. The train of thirty big canvas-covered freight steam-wagons, each pulled by six to eight horses, stretched for more than half a kilometer along the trail. Six outriders guarded the sides and six more scouted the front and rear of the train, Daryl's men, Lange and Peele, among them.

Two teamsters rode each wagon, one to drive the horses and the other on the brakes. The lead wagon, driven by the cooks, carried the small two-man tents, bedrolls, trail supplies, the cook's pots and pans and food stores.

Behind that followed the repair wagon, loaded with the needs of the farrier and the wheelwright who traveled with them. Accidents happened on the trail, and there was usually no one to repair a wheel or re-shoe a horse for a good distance.

It was a bright, clear day, but steadily rising wind told Altan a change in the weather was coming from the north. When they crested the hill at the head of this valley, he noted low grey clouds massing, and the wind picked up even more.

How did I think joining a wagon train in the middle of winter was a good idea?

The sun softened the snow where it hit the trail between the trees, muddying the road that the horses struggled through. Mud covered their legs from hocks and knees down and splashed on their bellies. Puffs of steam spurted out of the brass hubs on the wheels, assisting the horses.

The road alternated between deep, rutted, sticky mire in the sunlight and slick, rutted, frozen mire in the shade. The wagons bucked and rolled and slid. The curses and cries of the teamsters filled the quiet air of the valley. White steam rose from the struggling horses' nostrils and backs.

Two scouts rode out of the forest ahead of the wagons, one with a deer slung over the back of his mount. Altan rode up to meet them, catching up to the wagonmaster, who motioned them off the side of the trail out of the way of the slipping, sliding wagons and the laboring horses.

"Roast venison for supper tonight, Wagonmaster," called the first rider when they got close, his black beard white with hoarfrost.

"We got lucky, and it looks like we'll need a good supper tonight because tomorrow's trail is gonna be rough. It winds around the south side of the hills ahead in the full sunlight. If we get more snow tonight, and it doesn't get much colder, we'll be slogging through axle-deep mud above some pretty steep bluffs down to the river below."

His horse sidled, and he turned it back around. "Looks like maybe we can cross the river late this afternoon. There's a good, wide camp-site just across the ford where we can enjoy this venison tonight. There's ice, but the first wagons'll break that. It'll be nothing but mud by the time we get the last wagons across. It's been in full sun all day, I'm afraid, and there's not enough space to camp on this side of the river for several kilometers."

The second rider, broad-brimmed hat pulled down over his ears, added, "There's a blow massing up to the north, and my weather sense tells me it will hit us just about the time we get to the ford. Looks like it will be sleet or heavy, wet snow. That's not going to help."

"Unload that carcass in the supply wagon," Wagonmaster

Coynar, his face like worn, tan saddle leather, told the rider with the deer. "And tell the cooks to move ahead to the ford as fast as they can and start setting up. They're lighter than anyone else, and I assume if you'd seen any sign of human trouble that'd been the first thing you told me, so they should be all right. Go with them."

He turned to Altan. "Ride back along the train and tell the teamsters to start pushing harder. Let's see if we can beat the weather to the ford. Bad enough to have to camp in wet snow without having to set up in it, too. Take Danyl and range out a little behind us. Don't want any surprises coming up to bite us in the ass. You told me you had a bit of Air talent. Can you see enough to set my mind at ease? I got bad feelings, and I'm not sure whether they are ahead or behind us, or if it's just the weather building."

Danyl was the name Daryl was using. Altan went by Arden. He laughed and shook his head. "I don't have that kind of sight, sir. I'm sorry. I don't even know anyone with that talent, do you? I only have a little battle talent."

"Well, let's hope you don't have to use it on this trip, then. Get along and let's see if we can't move these wagons a little faster." Coynar rode back to the head of the train. The supply wagon's horses strained to work up to a faster walk in the heavy mud, stretched its lead over the rest of the train, and disappeared through the trees with the two outriders in front.

Altan moved back down the side of the trail, urging the teamsters to faster speeds. By the time he got to the end of the train, the teamsters were already keeping pace with those in front of them. He waved to signal Daryl to follow him. They rode out from the train, circling wide through the forest—quiet, not speaking, only an occasional cluck to a horse.

This was an old forest, the trees huge, the canopy high above, bare of leaves but there were enough resinous conifers to keep the forest dark even in the rare sunlight of this winter afternoon. Little snow covered the ground under the conifers. The horses moved with almost no sound over the fallen needles of the pines. They startled three deer out of a thicket of berry bushes too thick to shoot an arrow through with any chance of success, so neither tried.

Avoiding drifts, they rode around the back side of a hill well away from the train. Tall trees shaded the snow, and the ground was firmer here, the rocky hillside less muddy. Daryl held up one hand, and Altan stopped, watching as Daryl slid off his horse and walked forward, reins draped over his arm. He studied the ground and waved Altan forward.

"Looks like four riders. They can't be far—these tracks are fresh." He spoke in a low voice. "There's the same track with the off shoe on the left fore. These are the ones we chased off two days ago."

"Where are the other two? There were six of them," Altan wondered. "Let's move out a little more and see what we find."

Daryl mounted, and the two moved farther down the hill to a small creek at the bottom. They rode along it, breaking through thin ice for several hundred feet, watching both sides before they found more tracks.

"Looks like they met up with the two others and headed toward the back of the train. Probably think they can hit the tail end, take what they find, and run before anyone gets after them. Shall we surprise them?" Altan suggested.

"Only six? Do you think that's a fair fight?" Daryl grinned. "We warned them last time. That's enough."

They moved their horses to a trot and followed the tracks. They'd almost reached the train when they spotted the riders moving silently through the trees. They were a ragtag bunch, dressed in a combination of fine but dirty stolen clothes and plain, much-patched garments. The horses weren't much better. Altan pointed to one side of the group, then to himself so they'd approach at two angles from behind the outlaws and dug his heels into his horse's flanks.

One of the bandits looked up and yelled at the sound of the galloping horses. He drew his sword, and the others followed, jerking their horses around.

Altan hit them at the same time Daryl did, slashing across the arm of one who looked too young to be fighting and reaching across himself to hit another a hard slice across his ribs. Then he was through to the other side of the fight and wheeling his horse back around.

The largest man, a rough band across his head covering one eye, rushed Altan from the side as he turned. Altan hit him straight on in the chest with his sword and had to wrench hard to get it loose before the man slid off his horse. Daryl wheeled up beside him and stopped, scarcely breathing hard.

Two men lay still on the ground. The boy Altan hit first grabbed one of the wounded men's reins and jerked the horse around. "Let's get out of here," he screamed. There was no hesitation. They ran, riderless mounts following.

Altan slid off his horse and went to check the two downed men. They were both dead.

"Should we chase them, do you think?" asked Daryl. "I hit two of them pretty hard, probably won't be alive for long."

Altan looked after the galloping horses. "They won't be back. We've done enough damage." Both men stared down at the two bodies—too thin, clothes too ragged. Altan mounted, and they rode silently across the trail to circle back to the train.

Restal was rougher country than Toldar, and much poorer, the soil rocky and thin, the barrens more prevalent. And, he thought, the people hungrier, like these two. He told himself there was no reason for him to feel guilt for the deaths. But these men were nothing like the bandits Altan had fought near the border. Those had been well dressed, well fed, and well mounted. He looked at Daryl. The look on the other man's face as he rode was thoughtful.

They made their way back after another hour of scouting. Nothing else threatened, and they rode side by side along the trail back to the wagons, following the freezing wagon ruts and skirting deeper drifts.

"How do we get to those guns?" Altan asked almost to himself as they rode.

"Morel never gets out of sight of the back of that wagon. I thought he was going to have a fit when the wagonmaster put it at the end of the train," Daryl answered. "As long as he's around, we haven't a chance of getting at them." He frowned. "He's obsessed.

320

He doesn't look good—his eyes are sunk in his head, his face haunted. He scarcely leaves that wagon to get food. He even sleeps under it instead of by the fires with the others. We didn't need to worry about him recognizing me even without this illusion and a new name. He sees nothing but those crates."

Altan was silent for a long time as they rode through the quiet of the stately conifers. A few raucous crows squabbled high in the branches. Finally, he said, a little hesitantly, "Daryl, I've never asked you why you don't want these guns. They would, after all, give your quadrant an edge in any struggle with us, or with anyone else for that matter. You are as determined as I am that they not reach Restal. You could get rid of Morel and me and take them for yourself. It would make regaining the prime from Readen much easier. Why?"

Daryl laughed. "I don't think it would be so easy to get rid of you, Altan. Now is a funny time to be asking me these questions. They might have been better asked before we left Toldar."

They rode on in silence for several minutes before he spoke again. "I know that some people think the stories of our arrival on Adalta are about half legend. But there are some old, old records in the Restal Keep library, copied onto paper and spelled against aging. I have read them, and what they speak of frightens me. They tell of the world we came from and the terrible conditions on Earth when the ship left with the people who were our ancestors. One of them was written by the captain of that ship, Alton Robbinson. Spelled with an O."

"I learned about it in my studies, but I didn't know there was a written record anywhere."

Daryl's saddle creaked as he leaned forward to scratch his mount's neck. "He talks at length about conditions on Earth when they left. It must have been terrible. The history we're taught doesn't say enough about how bad it was. The very air they breathed was toxic. The planet overcrowded with people. Outside the cities, land was either desert or depleted or poisoned. What farmland there was had high fences and guards to keep people from stealing food. Tyranny was absolute. Fanatics ruled the world with armies that fought with weapons that destroyed whole cities and left the land uninhabitable for kilometers around.

"He wrote about the landing here, of the war between the alien Larrak and the Karda. About the reasons behind the laws passed here on Adalta limiting technology and forbidding weapons other than swords, bows, and talent. He kept his log or journal for the rest of his life here on Adalta, and I read all the volumes. They were fascinating.

"Did you know that our talent to draw power was not known on Earth? It caused a lot of consternation when it began to manifest. There was even a faction of the first settlers who thought that those with major abilities should not be allowed to mate so their talent would be bred out. They were afraid of it. That's where the laws requiring the extensive education and training in ethics that powerful talents get came from. It took years to come to agreement. I wish everyone with major talent were required to read these journals. The history books and legends are not the same as reading their own words and the reasons behind their fears."

He laughed. "That's a long answer to your question. I am determined that this world never become what Earth was then. Readen is ambitious. I hadn't realized how far he had gone in his ambitions."

His expression sobered. "Apparently as far as embracing fratricide. Morel's strange behavior—and that of the assassins Readen sent after me—can only be explained by coercion. Readen shouldn't be able to do that. He has no talent."

"He tried it on Marta when we were in Rashiba. I blocked him, but it wasn't easy, and it didn't feel like any talent I've ever sensed."

Daryl stared at Altan, saying nothing. Then he moved his eyes forward and rode on, silent, his face set in anger. And grief.

The two of them rode, deep in thought, through the darkening cold light until they reached the wagon train, which was crossing at the ford. Then they had much to do helping the wagons cross and getting camp established on the other side.

Weather stuck them at the crossing for several days with snow too heavy for them to attempt the steep trail over the hills. It lay deep on the ground, and the road was treacherous, icy in the shade of the dense conifers. Travel was slow once the weather cleared enough to move on.

This was wild country, scarred with deep washes and ravines. Strong wind buffeted them when they had to cross the open expanses of the barrens that ruled Restal. Huge tracts of barrens stretched between the forests surrounding circles and between the fields of farms around scattered villages. There was nothing to slow the icy wind for kilometers.

As they moved further into Restal Quadrant, they passed two Circles of Disorder. Trees—stark, white, and dead—littered the edges. Even with the road a safe distance away, Altan could feel the greasy sense of evil and alien-twisted power. Daryl said nothing, but Altan saw him frown as they rode around them. He looked worried. Very worried. As was Altan.

Altan concentrated on the problem of the guns. They'd argued for an hour over which one of them should destroy them. He won the toss they resorted to. Both of them had reasons to want the guns destroyed. He could wait until the right moment to disable the wagon's brakes and perhaps send the wagon over the side of the trail at a particularly dangerous point, but he had no desire to kill the teamsters or the horses. He would have to wait for another opportunity to present itself.

Marta had described the guns, how they worked, and how they could be permanently disabled. If they could manage to get Morel away from the wagon long enough, they could disable the guns, seal the crates back up, and no one would be the wiser until they tried to use the weapons. But Morel was never out of sight of the guns.

There was another solution, but Altan wasn't sure he wanted to try it.

CHAPTER TWENTY-NINE

The clang and clash of swords filled Restal's women's guild armory as the two Mi'hiru sparred. Marta dripped with sweat, awkward and off-balance. Try as she might, she still too often fought in her own body while her opponent fought the illusion of her 'Robyn' body. After taking a bruising hit to her ribs, she stepped back, signaling a halt, and pushed sweat-soaked hair off of her face. "Oh, Philipa, have mercy on me." She bent over, hands on knees, breathing heavily.

"You've let yourself get out of shape, Robyn. You deserved that last hit. Your right side was wide open. Rest a moment, and we'll have another go." The diminutive Mi'hiru chewed at her lip. "We need to be even more ready than we usually are. The Karda are not doing well at all and are unusually restless. Their unease is making me uneasy. It isn't just the Karda, though. Come with me to the market this afternoon and you'll see what I mean. The whole tenor of this town is unsettled since Readen has named himself Regent."

"Right now all I want to do is get to the hot baths and soak some of what you've done to me away."

"All right. I promised Nyla a bout. I'll find you in a couple of hours after I've had my soak. Maybe Nyla will go with us. We can have supper somewhere. Could you tell whoever is cooking tonight that we won't be here?"

The three Mi'hiru wandered slowly through the market, pausing to look and occasionally buy something. Many shops displayed their various wares under canvas awnings over their entrances. At the center of the open paved square a large fountain splashed. At its center a statue of a nude woman stood with her foot resting on a large rock. Her hair streamed back. Her face looked to the sky. One arm reached out to her side, palm down, and the other stretched in front of her, hand cupped, a flood of water spilling from it.

Next to the fountain, a man held a small pony so it could drink from the basin. A woman filled a bucket at the spilling stream, holding her long skirts back from the splash. Marta would have expected to see children in the square sliding on the ice where the fountain splashed over, but there were none. The ones she saw held close to their mothers or older brothers or sisters.

Nyla's attention was caught by a soft blue silk printed with a swirling design in shades of gold and bronze hanging at the front of a large stall. They stepped under the cloth awning. A voice came from inside the shop behind a stack of bolts of colorful wool, and an older woman wrapped firmly in a shawl peered out.

"Oh, Mi'hiru, are you?" She nodded at their clothes, which were particular to Mi'hiru—long split skirts, short fitted jackets worn over fine, tailored linen blouses. Her face was brown and wrinkled, with black eyes that looked them over shrewdly from behind gold-rimmed half glasses. "Haven't seen any of your kind for a while. New to Restal Prime, are you? I know you travel light, so you'll be looking to have some clothes made for you. Working or dress?"

Marta hoped she wouldn't be here long enough to need more clothes to fit this body. The others were more interested in playing with the various fabrics. Philipa was something of a clotheshorse. Marta could see her avid glee as she pulled out bolt after bolt, scattering them until the small stall looked like a large horse ran through a rainbow, splashing color everywhere. Nyla was wrapping a length of pale blue around her lush figure, holding it up to her round face, electric with energy. She pulled her thick red braid, around against the fabric.

The woman called out to someone behind a stiff canvas curtain at the back of the stall, "Corolie, come and help before someone gets buried in this mess. My daughter," she explained. "A fine seamstress. She can help you better than I. I know fabrics, but don't have the eye to turn them into something fit to wear."

Philipa and Nyla chattered happily with Corolie. Marta left them to their delights and started back out of the shop to wander the market.

The old woman touched her arm. "You'll want to take care being alone here, Mi'hiru. I know you can use that sword well, but stay where there are people." She headed back inside.

"Wait," Marta said. "What is there to worry about? Isn't there a town guard?"

The woman hesitated, looked around to see that no one was within hearing distance. "Too many young serving girls have gone missing over the last months, and the guard is none too interested in finding them. Just say they're runaways. It's been happening more often than usual."

"Maybe they did just run off." Marta frowned at the woman. *More than usual? Usual?*

"That's what the guard says. But two of them, I knew. Good girls, both, and no problems with their employers. They just disappeared running an errand. Their parents were told nothing could be done— but these things can't be kept quiet like nothing is happening. So be careful, and tell your friends in there, too. Things are not as they should be in Restal Prime." She disappeared back into the colorful chaos of her stall.

Marta mused as she walked on around the square. The old woman's words were urgent—Marta sensed the fear running beneath her words. It lay burdensome and oppressive as if it seeped from the stones under her feet.

She wandered the square, noting the meager array of goods

offered. Vegetables and fruit were scarce and often small and misshapen. Fowl hanging from hooks in front of the butcher's shop were thin and bony. There was little other meat hanging but for several strings of sausages that couldn't be called plump. Even the flies looked dispirited. Brass and copper pots in one window hung from a rack with hooks for many more.

No flower vendors tended carts with their profusions of colors like there were in Toldar, even in winter. If she had to name a color for this market, it would be grey. Even the people looked grey, hurrying to get their shopping done. No one lingered to visit as was usual in the markets. No old men sat, gossiping and arguing in the sun on the benches near the fountain.

The narrow streets that led off the square were all but deserted —the few people she saw hurried along with their heads down. Three times, she passed pairs of guards or mercenaries, cold eyes scanning the sparse crowd. Once, two of them started toward her, then their eyes flicked to her sword and over her Mi'hiru uniform, and they passed on.

What is happening in this town? It's much, much worse than before, and that was bad enough. The fabric shop was the only one she had passed with a substantial show of wares. Marta wondered if the people just couldn't afford them, or if wearing bright colors brought too much attention. She looked back at the proud woman of the fountain and imagined she saw tears streaming from her eyes to splash unnoticed in the waters of the basin.

A short, wiry man brushed against her, and she turned. "No onions today in the market."

She stumbled. Then she recognized Bren. She started to grin and greet him, but he stopped her with a brusque gesture and went to drink at the stream from the lady's hand. When he turned away, he brushed against her again and pushed a paper into her hand.

Shoving it into her pocket, Marta walked back toward the cloth merchant's stall, her mood a little lighter, relieved. Bren was Hugh Me'Rahl's agent in Restal. She wouldn't look at the paper until she was alone in her room that night.

How naive she'd been when she met Bren on her first day in

Adalta. How strong had been her self-assurance that she could meet any challenges this new world could bring her. That she knew so much about so many worlds that this one would only be different in the details.

The other Mi'hiru finally finished their shopping, and Philipa led them to a narrow, white-plastered building tucked between two larger ones on a side street. Windows with empty flower boxes flanked the door bright with fresh green paint. Candles and small wall sconces lit the restaurant with soft light. Six polished tables, each with a candle in a polished brass holder, were just far enough apart for a server to pass between them. The tall, thin man who met them at the door beckoned them to a small table beneath a landscape painting.

A couple of well-dressed men held a quiet, deep discussion at one table. At the only other occupied table, an older couple sat, obviously man and wife, eating quietly, patently ignoring each other, the small woman holding herself stiff and upright, putting her spoon down after each bite of soup. The man stared past her shoulder, only occasionally raising food to his mouth. Marta was glad for her strengthened shields. She didn't want to feel the emotional miasma all but visible between those two.

The three Mi'hiru each ordered wine, and when it was brought with fine stemmed glasses not found in the taverns where Marta usually ate, the server told them solemnly, "We have roast fowl with a nut stuffing, boiled potatoes with butter and parsley, and stewed greens."

They looked at him, waiting to see what came next, but he turned and walked toward the door that led to the kitchen. "That's all?" Nyla's eyebrows went up.

"That's all they had when I was here a tenday ago, but it was good—the fowl a little on the skinny side, but good. And the stuffing is delicious," said Philipa.

"The woman in the fabric stall said something bothersome to me," said Marta. "She told me to be careful. Apparently, several younger girls have gone missing here in the Prime. The guard seems to be doing little to find them, or so she said. I find it hard to believe that there wouldn't be a huge outcry about it."

"There's something wrong in this town. You can feel it even in the guild house," Nyla said, her usually mobile face taut. "There's always lots of loud political discussion in the taverns in other places I've been posted to. Not here. No one speaks of Daryl or even Readen. No one has seen their father in several tendays. Then there's our unhappy Karda."

Altan sat leaning against his packs, facing a campfire, staring into the flames raised against the dark and cold, listening to the sounds of the night and the soft voices of the men. The caravan was a few days from Restal Prime. He didn't want to do this, but they were running out of time. He'd be as careful as he could, but still, someone could get hurt. What he planned would be difficult to contain. And this was the first time Morel had been away from the wagon long enough for Altan to work.

Daryl sat next to him—he'd lost the toss. His job was to shield the rest of the wagon.

The land here in Restal was so drained there was little strength left in it for Altan to pull from. It seemed reluctant at best, even resentful. He would have to sink his roots deep into Adalta to find enough potency to do what he needed.

He narrowed his eyes, drawing from the fire in front of him, concentrating on the five large crates stowed in the back of the wagon directly opposite. Sweat beaded on his face. Shudders shook his body. He reached as far as he could into Adalta, drawing energy from her center. It moved up reluctantly, slowly as if the planet herself was laboring—or reluctant.

He twisted Earth and Air talent and aimed it at the back of the wagon. He was sweating in earnest when smoke began to trickle out of the cases, thickened, then flames erupted out of all five cases at once. The entire back of the wagon was afire, burning hot and fierce. He could feel the edges of Daryl's containment field on the rest of the wagon and diverted his energy to help. The fire raged on its own.

Galen Morel leaped up from his blankets on the ground, grabbed one, and raced for the flaming wagon yelling, "Fire!" He beat at the flames futilely. Others ran to help. He gave up beating at the fire with his blanket and climbed up into the back of the wagon amid the flames, fumbling with the latches of the end gate, working desperately to pull the cases out onto the ground

Altan rushed to the wagon and grabbed him, yelling at him to stop, to get away, but Galen threw him off. Galen clawed frantically at the cases, screaming with terror, "He'll kill me. He'll kill me," over and over as he struggled with the burning crates of guns.

Altan tried again, Daryl helping, but Galen's desperation gave him super-human strength, and he shoved them away. It took three men to hold Altan back as the fire grew too hot to approach again.

"He's crazy, Altan. Get away from there before you burn up, too," yelled Daryl.

Daryl was trying to dampen the blaze, and Altan added his talent in the fight to contain what he started.

Galen finally succeeded in throwing one blazing crate to the ground. It burst open, and flames shot even higher as the oily rags wrapping the guns blazed higher. He jumped down from the back of the wagon, his clothes and hair burning, and beat at the flames engulfing the weapons with his bare hands.

Altan ran toward him and knocked him away. Calling on Earth and Water, he rolled Galen over and over in the dirt until the flames went out. Galen's ragged voice screamed all the while, "Readen will kill me. He'll kill me. He'll kill me." Finally, he subsided and lost consciousness, his face, chest, and arms horribly burned.

Altan choked on the air full of the smell of charred meat and burned hair, some of it his own. He retched.

Daryl joined him. "I'll work on him while you rest. We can't both work at the same time. Burns are the worst things to try to heal, but we can keep him alive. He'll be scarred, but he can recover."

He carefully placed his hands close above the center of Galen's chest over the burns. It took a long time, and Altan fed him what power he could draw until Daryl finally sat back on his haunches and sighed a deep sigh. "Let's find a place to move him. He won't be able to ride at all. Tomorrow we can work on him again, maybe lessen the scarring a little." He looked at Altan's expression and frowned. "Altan, this was not your fault. No sane man would have done what he did."

Altan nodded and stared up at the wagon. Neither Altan nor Daryl made any further attempt to contain the fire. Coynar, the burly wagon-master, had managed to climb over the front of the wagon and shove the other crates to the ground with a long, thick branch from the wood stacked for the campfire. The crates lay burning at the end of the wagon. Several of them burst open. He and the others managed to put out the fire in the wagon itself, but the crates continued to burn fiercely, the guns twisting in the intense heat.

"Oily rags! He had those damn crates crammed with oily rags. One spark from the fire—even spontaneous combustion could have set them off. He never told me. I could have taken precautions. What was the man thinking? I'm just lucky none of the other cargo was badly damaged." He'd never noticed the healing Daryl and Altan had done.

Wagonmaster Coynar, his red beard bristling with anger, fumed as his men cleaned up the mess left by the burning crates and tossed them off to the side. "What do you think these things are, anyway?" he asked Altan, who helped as best he could with his bandaged hands. It wouldn't do for him to show they were healed already. That required a level of talent neither Daryl nor he was supposed to have. They itched.

"Whatever they were, they're useless now," Coynar ranted. "He wouldn't even tell me who they were to go to, so there isn't any way I can let them know what happened. Damn man's obsessed with secrecy. Strange fellow."

He and Altan tossed the last of the remains of the guns, mangled, warped, and warm from the fire, to the side of the trail.

Coynar moved away to get the caravan started again and to make what accommodations he could for the badly burned Galen.

The girl on the bed stirred feebly, shrinking from Readen as he stood and laid the silver knife on the table by the bed. He gently lifted her to her feet and rearranged her clothing around her blood streaked body. He looked down and smoothed her dark hair back from her pretty tear-streaked face. Power was returning to him for the first time in several days after all he expended setting defenses around the keep. Not as much as if he had been able to take her to the cavern or a circle, but it helped.

She turned her face with a sob, but he forced it back around and kissed her gently on the lips. She trembled and tried to pull back. His body warmed with her fear. "Thank you, my dear. You've been most helpful."

He drew in a long, satisfied breath and called his servant. "Odalys will clean you up and bring you some food." He patted the girl's hand and pushed her into Odalys's uncaring arms. This girl was strong— with care and patience, she would satisfy him for days.

The dark-haired, statuesque beauty gripped the girl's arm and jerked her toward the door. The girl winced and tried to pull away. Odalys's lovely face smiled with a show of perfect white teeth and no compassion at all.

"Don't touch me. Please." The girl's voice was hoarse from screaming. Odalys pushed her to the tub in the bathing room beyond Readen's bedroom.

Readen frowned and pushed his hair back from his face. He had an appointment to meet two of his most ardent followers and Armsmaster Krager. It was inconvenient to use his tower to work magic, but he hadn't had time to take the girl to the caverns, and the room was keyed to him, set up for him to work undetected. No one could hear the screaming.

He left the room, closing the door behind him. He moved his fingers, forming a sigil, and let a slight tingle of his power slip into the lock behind him. He walked through the empty halls. Servants tended to stay out of his way when they had the choice. He had to work harder and harder to garner power outside the cavern, and he didn't dare leave the keep to visit a Circle of Disorder where he could reap so much more. He had to be satisfied to take it from the young girls and boys Pol brought to him and the few petty criminals locked in the cells in the basement reaches of the keep.

He strode into his father's study. Empty now of his father's things, it had become his own. Maps of Restal and reports from the guard covered the over-sized, over-ornate desk in the center of the room. Armsmaster Krager leaned against it, arms crossed, body relaxed.

Readen suppressed a surge of irritation. The armsmaster had long been a closed book to him. His impassive face seldom showed emotion. The only one to ever break his impassivity had been Daryl, years ago when the armsmaster had accidentally hurt him. Readen had seen the caring and concern on his face for the brief moment it was there. The surge of anger and jealousy he had felt still burned.

He was convinced, however, that what Krager felt toward Daryl now was betrayal. He watched him closely, and he'd seen a grimace, however brief, twist his taciturn face, turning it cold when he heard of Daryl's defection to Toldar.

"Report," Readen said shortly. The other two men in the room with Krager began shuffling nervously through the papers on the table.

"There were three more defections this tenday from the guard and no sign of where they might be going, but the defections are slowing. There were only five last tenday. Hanging the one we caught helped." This was from Samel. The slight, immaculately dressed young man with curling red hair smiled. His eyes were wide with pleasure. The hanging had been his idea. There had never been public hangings on Adalta. Wherever he got the idea, Readen liked it.

Illias, a tall, pale-faced young man, his black curls arranged artfully on his shoulders, spoke. "Me'Feire and Me'Neve have arrived for your judgment on the road tariff Me'Feire imposes on the ores Me'Neve moves through his holding. Me'Kammon and Me'Cowyn are both making ready to leave. All of them have family with them."

"Cancel judicial hearings for the time being." Looking at Illias, he ordered, "Choose which of the family members we will invite to stay in the keep for a while. I'd prefer daughters." He smiled a smile that held no humor. "I am sure they will be glad of such honor to their holdings. Inform the steward of the additional rooms he'll need to make ready in the guest wing. We don't want them to feel slighted in any way." He told Krager, "Send guards to accompany the ones Illias chooses, for their protection of course."

Krager's nod was brusque, his face unreadable.

CHAPTER THIRTY

M arta watched as Jym, the nervous young man hoping to join
the Karda Patrol, approached Kigi, a small light brown
Karda with bright white wing stripes and black mane and tail.

"You say I could fly her all the time?"

"If she agrees," said Marta, amused at his wide eyes.

She watched for a few minutes as Jym started brushing Kigi, his
strokes so tentative the Karda would soon complain. Then she went
back to repairing the bent flight feather on Armsmaster Krager's
Karda, Tarath.

"What's the matter with Tarath's wing?" asked a deep voice
behind Marta. Night black hair, stern brown eyes habitually
narrowed against the sun, large calloused hands Marta was sure
never strayed far from his sword—the tall, lean man stood propped
against the opening to Tarath's stall.

"You must be Armsmaster Krager. Tarath was just complaining
about you. He's agitated. He will hardly stand still for me to repair
his flight feather. I'm sure he damaged it futzing about in here." She
held out her hand. "I'm Robyn, sir. I'm pleased to meet you. I've
heard much about you."

He clasped her arm and looked at her, eyes sharp. "He was

complaining, was he?" He moved to scratch Tarath's head with vigor. "How much damage did he do, the idiot?" The sorrel butted him with his huge head and preened at his hair with his beak. Krager walked around to the Karda's side and examined the wing carefully, tugging gently until Tarath spread it for him. Not fully. That was impossible, roomy though the stall was.

"I've imped in a new feather. He's good as new if you need to fly somewhere today."

"No, I've just come to visit."

Marta felt like a third thumb watching the two together, so she left them for a while and busied herself with chores, keeping an eye on him until the mews was empty of all but Karda and Krager. When he stood from where he had been sitting, leaning on the recumbent Tarath, stroking the great head, Marta approached nervously. Would this be the death of her? She squared her shoulders and said softly, "Daryl sent me."

He stiffened, not looking away from Tarath, and said nothing.

"You and Daryl have been friends since he was seven and you were eleven. He broke his arm falling out of an apple tree when he was ten and the two of you were raiding someone's orchard. He told you to hide so you wouldn't be punished for leading him into trouble. You gave him a concussion in weapons lessons when he was twelve, and you were punished then. Daryl says he's always felt bad about that because it was his fault—he forgot his training and got angry, made all the wrong moves and got in the way of your practice sword just as you swung. That time you were punished even though it was his fault." She took a breath.

The armsmaster didn't turn. "He always felt guilty about the punishment—worse than I did about causing his concussion. I think he still feels he owes me something for that. But you could have heard that story anywhere." He was silent for a long time. "How is he?"

"I think he feels he's leading a charmed life. He's survived two attempts on his life so far."

Krager's wide shoulders tensed and he turned, looking Marta in the eye. "What did you say your name was again?"

"I'm known here as Robyn," she said carefully.

He raised a brow. "And what do you want with me, known-here-as-Robyn? I felt Tarath calling me with more urgency than he usually does. Did he get that urgency from you?"

Marta swallowed. "Daryl's on his way here. With Altan Me'Gerron." He raised the other brow slightly.

Does he ever show emotion? "They are with a wagon train less than a tenday out."

"And you would know that how?"

Marta shifted. How was she to explain knowing where they were, indeed? "They sent a messenger." She regretted the lie.

"To you, not to me." He waited.

She thought furiously. "Tarath needs exercising, and one of the unpartnered Karda also does." She smiled ruefully. "We have quite a few of those. It seems inordinately difficult for them to select riders here. I spend a good part of my days flying with them. If I don't, they get restless. Tarath wouldn't go with me, though. He waited for you. Perhaps we could fly together now for an hour or three."

Krager walked to the rack without a word and picked up Tarath's flying rig.

He flew, Marta noted, as if he were part of Tarath. He reveled in it, totally relaxed, his black hair streaming behind him. She could feel the love and joy in both of them, flyer and Karda. Yes, this man was one to be trusted. How was he tolerating what was happening here in Restal? Several unpartnered Karda circled and dove around them like children at play, clearly enjoying themselves before shearing off and leaving them to their flight. Marta saw Sidhari high above them, floating with the clouds.

Krager signaled, catching her eye, and pointed below, slightly west. A small greening field nestled in a valley between two hills. She nudged Kimli down, and both Karda folded their wings back and dove for the ground. Marta grabbed the pommel with one hand and waved wildly with the other, exulting in the wind whistling past, thrilling to the dive and the gut-churning flare of wings as they skimmed the ground, circled again, and touched down in the small meadow, cantering to the shade of an enormous elm. She dismounted, more than a little breathless.

Krager's mouth twitched slightly as they stood the saddles on end to dry and carefully coiled the leathers. The two Karda playfully struck at each other, clashing beaks, energized by the flight. "That was a fast landing, to say the least. Tarath seldom does that. I guess he didn't want the young one to outdo him."

This was the first emotion Marta had seen on his face. Clearly, he'd needed this respite from whatever his life had been like lately.

He motioned her to sit first. Angling his sword around in front of him he sat cross-legged, put his hands on his knees, and leaned forward slightly, his face impassive again. "Tell me what this is all about."

Direct and to the point. This man is more than a little intimidating.

"First, my name is not Robyn. I am Marta, bonded to Altan, Guardian Heir of Toldar."

"I've met Mi'hiru Marta. You are not her." His face didn't change.

Nor did the relaxed tone of his voice.

"Altan worked hard to make sure my disguise-illusion was as good as it could be."

He looked at her. "Altan disguised you." It wasn't a question. His expression didn't lighten.

"If you'll wait a moment, my proof will arrive. I know you don't speak mind to mind with Tarath, or he could tell you who I am."

They sat silently for several minutes, then Sidhari appeared, skimming the treetops, circling to land almost on top of them, stirring their hair with her back-winging.

~Thank you for coming, Sidhari.~

"Do you recognize her?" Marta asked the armsmaster.

"She was the talk of the Karda Patrol barracks when she was here before. Only Abala and Altan Me'Gerron's Kibrath are as big as she is. She is unmistakable." He faced her. "No Karda partnered with a Mi'hiru will allow anyone else to fly them without permission. Show me."

~Can we fly without a saddle, Sidhari?~

~We've done it before.~ She knelt so Marta could climb up her leg to her back. Marta gripped hard with her legs. It was risky to fly this way, but Mi'hiru trained for it.

They took off, Marta leaning forward, her hands wrapped tightly in Sidhari's mane. ~I wish we could fly like this forever, Sidhari. I've missed you. How you manage to be so close without being seen is a miracle. But we'd better not take much time. The armsmaster can't afford to be gone too long.~

They circled the meadow once and landed again, trotting to a stop nearly at Krager's feet. Marta slid off, gave Sidhari a scratch on her head and a look of longing as the great Karda took off again.

"Tell me," said Krager, as he watched Sidhari circle up.

"They're coming in as guards on a trade caravan from Rashiba and are little more than a tenday out, weather permitting. They're fighting a lot of mud."

"Why is Toldar involved in this? It's none of their affair. Or do they think to take advantage?"

"They are convinced it is of concern to them. Believe me, the discus- sions were long and thorough. And Daryl concurs. Readen is getting access to a shipment of highly technical weapons from a trade ship in secret orbit over Adalta that would make his conquest of Restal and Toldar, and beyond, far too easy. If Readen gains complete control here, Stephan knows it won't be long before he moves against Toldar. Some of your troops, disguised as bandits, have already been used to attack villages in Toldar. Readen's been doing this for a while unbeknownst to either Daryl or, Daryl is convinced, his father."

Krager didn't look surprised, even at the mention of the weapons and the ship. *Does he know about them? How could he? Has he gotten that close to Readen?*

Marta continued, "There is a growing friendship between Altan and Daryl that Stephan hopes will lead to better relations between your two quadrants. As you probably know better than I, it has not always been good. He and Altan both feel this is an opportunity to improve those relations. Daryl said to assure you, which I can do with authority as Altan's bonded, that none of this means that there will be Toldar influence in Restal that goes beyond this help and the friendship between the two heirs. There are no troops coming, and they sent only one other ahead. He's circling through the inns in the lower Prime, listening and learning."

Krager looked for a long time at Tarath, his lips pursed. Tarath and Kimli had quit playing and were industriously stripping old seed heads from the tall grasses of the meadow. "It is good for Tarath to play," he said absently. "He is too serious most of the time."

Marta had to work to hide her smile at this. "No one has ever accused you of being too serious, I'm sure."

His mouth twitched. "Daryl would never countenance interference from Toldar no matter how strong the friendship. He can be very stubborn." He looked at her, his face stony again.

"He was certainly stubborn about refusing to accept that Readen was responsible for the poisoned arrow in Rashiba. He wouldn't believe it till the next attempt nearly succeeded, and the flyer put to truth spell," Marta said, pulling a stem of grass through her fingers.

"Who?" The muscles along the edge of Krager's jaw bunched.

"Their names were Sebyn and Hart. Readen sent them."

Krager rubbed his face and looked away for a minute. "I tried to tell him any number of times that Readen was not the brother he thought he had." He looked back at Marta. "What does he want me to do? I've already begun identifying those in the House Guard who can be trusted. There are more in the Restal Guard, most in our Karda Patrol. I haven't approached more than one or two in the Mounted Patrol. They've been under Readen too long, and he's had time to weed out those he doesn't trust."

"You've already started, then," Marta said, a little surprised.

"I know Daryl," he said simply. "Readen has had me looking at the holders, also." His mouth twisted in a moue of distaste. "He has to trust me. He has no one else close enough to the guard and the Karda Patrol, and he's deluded himself that he can. I've prepared for this for a long time. I not only know Daryl—I also know Readen. Since childhood, he's been devious and relentless in his ambition to displace Daryl, however much Daryl tried to ignore it. And I've been devious and relentless about getting him to trust me." He shifted and stared across the meadow toward the two Karda, now digging for tubers.

"The holders who visit the keep with their families are allowed to go only if they leave a family member, preferably a daughter as 'guest.' He has also 'invited' several more. He tells them he's looking for a wife. He even sent a couple of his mercenaries to collect two of them. Those holders, the halfway intelligent ones anyway, are very angry. How much they'll be willing to help I don't know. They'd be risking their daughters."

He twirled a grass stem still heavy with seed in his hand, "If I can convince them I can protect the girls, a few might be persuaded to bring their personal guard, but they would have to be careful and very, very discreet. There has been unrest in Restal for some time. It was quiet so long as Daryl was heir. He is loved as his father and brother are not. Most were willing to wait for him to become guardian to repair the damage that Roland's done with his excesses. But now..." He shrugged.

Marta handed him the crumpled paper from Bren. It was a short list of smaller holders who could be trusted, and several with lines crossed through them that she assumed could not.

He nodded as he perused it. "Where did you get this?"

"The prime guardian has an agent here. Guardian Stephan borrowed him."

He looked the paper over again slowly, then tore it into small pieces and tossed it into the grass. "Must be a good agent. This is confirmation I need."

"I am at your service and so are the Karda. They're not happy here, but they are willing to stay and serve as they are needed." Marta had seen one dead at a Circle of Disorder on her way to Restal when she was first assigned, and another had died, used as the Tela Oroku against her. Sidhari suspected it was Readen's men who had killed the fledglings' parents also. The Karda were furious, Sidhari reported, and somehow concerned about something more significant, something dire that Sidhari wouldn't talk about.

341

"Yes." The armsmaster looked over at Tarath again. "I know Tarath only stays because of me. They are creatures of talent, and the growing circles are draining talent from the land."

It was late afternoon before the two flew back to the mews. They were unable to meet often. It was difficult for Krager to get away. Readen kept him close. Whether out of genuine need or suspicion, Krager told Marta, he didn't know. But he was occasionally able to relay messages through Karda Patrol members, though they were too often kept busy and out of Restal Prime.

Readen had doubled their patrols in the countryside around the prime. Krager was working on the list of supporters, sending Marta to meet with those he could trust but was unable to meet with himself for fear of being discovered. Neither of them ever put anything in writing. Marta relayed those names to Daryl through Altan in their nightly talks. She never approached anyone Daryl and Krager didn't approve first.

Altan and Daryl walked into the tavern's big common room late in the evening. The two well-armed—and large—men drew a good bit of attention. Daryl's self-administered disguise was holding. They threw off trail-dusty travel cloaks and almost fell into the chairs at a small back table. The serving girl plunked down the mugs of ale they ordered and listed the poor choices for dinner. Bread, cheese, and a thin chicken soup seemed the best option. A couple of wrinkled apples and some rather pungent cheese followed.

"Not much better than trail food. At least we were able to hunt and had better meat most of the time," muttered Altan, searching for the chicken that was supposed to be in the soup. They had helped the teamsters unload wagons all day after riding into Restal Prime late the evening before. Altan was worn out, and he suspected Daryl was, too.

"At least it's food. It's a long time since breakfast. And a lot of heavy work. I'm not made for this. I prefer a more pampered lifestyle." Daryl leaned tiredly on one elbow as he downed soup, the spoon nearly lost in his large, sword-calloused hand. "It seems quiet in here for such a crowded room, don't you think," he said, voice low.

Altan looked around warily, raising the bread he had topped with cheese to his mouth, following the dry stuff with a sip of ale. Several heads turned away quickly. Others surreptitiously stared, only a few with honest curiosity, most with wariness.

A stocky man with unruly dark hair stood from a nearby table, stretched, and made his way to their table. "You fellas come in with that big caravan last night?"

Daryl raised an eyebrow to Altan.

"Yup," Altan answered, looking at the man steadily.

"Guards or teamsters?"

Altan waited a long moment, face impassive. "Guards."

"Staying long?"

"You seem to be awfully interested in us," Altan said, and shifted his sword. "Is there a reason for that?"

The man smiled, raised his hands, and stepped back slightly. "No harm. I just hadn't seen you around before and thought I'd make a guess. Do you know if the wagonmaster is planning on leaving out soon? I'm looking for a job and thought he might want another guard." He lowered his voice. "I don't mind telling you, I'd like to leave Restal." Both men relaxed a shade. "Sit down and have a drink with us," said Altan, making a decision he hoped wasn't a mistake. "You from here?"

"No. Been here long enough, though, I reckon."

"Some reason you'd be thinking to leave we might find interesting?" Altan asked over his mug, his gaze sliding around the room. Most of the other customers had gone back to their own business.

"A couple of big men with business-like swords walking the streets here might draw more attention than they find comfortable 'less you're looking to get hired as one of the mercenaries up at the keep. Even little as I am, I get noticed." He grinned ruefully. He wasn't little—not overly tall, but with powerful arms and shoulders.

And he moved with the easy movements that told Altan he could use the sword at his side. "Rumors are running wild."

"Someone is hiring mercenaries?" Daryl's voice was tight.

"A big shake-up at the keep. One son declared himself Regent for his ailing father and is proclaiming the end of rule by talent strength. The other son and heir is missing. Some say he's dead. Some say he's gathering supporters to take back his position. Some say he's prisoner in Toldar. Some say Toldar is getting ready to attack. Like I said, rumors are rife. The new regent doesn't seem to trust his own guard. That what you're looking to do?"

Altan glanced at Daryl's tight jaw and answered, "Not interested in that kind of fight. You recruiting?"

The man threw up his hands. "Not me. No. Sorry, I guess I didn't introduce myself. I'm Hagyn from the Me'Feire Holding a couple of days riding south of here. The Me'Feires were here, and I had thought to go back home with them. Farming—oh, Adalta!— even herding sheep, is looking better and better to me right now, and I haven't seen my folks in a long time. Seeing the world is not the exciting adventure I thought when I was younger. But they left in a hurry, and I missed my chance. I heard rumors that their eldest daughter stayed—a 'guest' they called her. I have my doubts. Much as I want out of here, I hate to think of her here with no one from her hold left."

"You're not so eager to leave as you want us to think, I'd say," said Altan, watching the man's reaction.

Hagyn downed the rest of his ale and stood. "Maybe if you're here tomorrow night, we'll share another drink. My pleasure then. I guess I'll check with the wagonmaster tomorrow. What did you say his name was?"

Altan said, "I didn't, but it's Master Coynar." He doubted it was Coynar's need for a guard Hagyn would be checking on.

CHAPTER THIRTY-ONE

Marta took off her robe, her body still warm from the bath. The air was cold, and she shivered, rubbing the goose bumps on her arms. She pulled on her heavy linen nightshirt and dove for the bed and its thick quilt. Altan was here. He'd contacted her last night and then this morning. And would again anytime. *He's probably tired.* The minutes stretched into an hour. He'd been unloading wagons all day.

She dozed off in spite of herself.

~Are you asleep, love?~

She blinked awake. ~Almost. You were busy today?~

~That was a lot of wagons and a lot of freight. I don't think I was meant to be a teamster. I'm hoping I never have to be a caravan guard again if this is part of what they have to do.~ He was silent for a long time.

~You can't forget it, can you?~ said Marta. She couldn't either. The images of Galen she'd caught from Altan's thoughts hurt more than she'd thought possible. She'd known Galen all her life, loved him once, and whatever he'd done, she couldn't forget that.

Altan's anguish was palpable. ~We took him to a healing house. In spite of the work Daryl and I did on him all the way here, it will

345

take him a long time to recover. And he'll be scarred. He'll regain the use of his hands, especially the right—they were the worst damaged. That he'll be able to use them at all is not much short of a miracle.~

Marta could imagine him pulling at his hair. ~You couldn't have known what he would do. It wasn't the act of a man who was in control of himself.~

~I recognized the signs of a coercion. I should have known how he'd react. Or Daryl should have.~ He paused. ~I can't lay any blame on Daryl. It was my action that did it.~

~No, Altan. It was Readen's, not yours. And Galen made his choice when he agreed to smuggle the guns in the first place. Let blame perch its bottom where it belongs.~

~I'm just tired. I'm sorry to burden you with this.~

~If not me, then who?~

They talked for a long time into the night. It was the next best thing to being together, and hopefully, that wouldn't be long.

Marta walked down the dark street, her stride confident, her cloak pulled over her head. Dalt, who'd flown to the Me'Fiere hold the tenday before and hitched a ride in to the prime, followed at a discreet distance. She knew she could take care of herself, but the streets were not safe at night, and knowing he was there was a comfort. She slipped into the alley behind The Barred Wing, a tavern owned by one of Daryl's supporters. Another hooded figure waited at the tavern's back door. Marta thought she recognized Bren. Then he disappeared down the alley and around the side of the building.

The door opened. Dim light gleamed across the wet cobbles, and she and Dalt slipped in, Krager close behind them. They went directly to a small room off the back hall. Altan stood as they entered, letting out a relieved breath when he saw her.

Jym, the young rider of Kigi, had developed the habit, like so many young men, of hitting the taverns at night whenever he could, gathering information and acting as liaison between Marta and Krager. Marta hated to use him. He was so young. But he was an unlikely suspect, and he played the role of irresponsible young rake inclined to drink more than he should with such enthusiasm. Dalt commented on his acting skills more than once.

"It isn't acting," Jym retorted. "I like the ale just fine."

"And the girls, I notice," Dalt said.

Jym nodded soberly. "That too."

This was one of the few times Marta and Altan had been able to meet in person, and they sat, shoulders pressed together, at the table. Hastily scribbled lists of who had been contacted and who were to be counted on to provide weapons and/or fighters littered the table.

Marta had flown for hours and days over most of the quadrant, contacting holders and merchants under the pretense of working with the many unpartnered Karda. More than the usual number now populated the skies of Restal.

The heat of Altan's muscular thigh against hers made Marta hope he'd had the forethought to get them a room upstairs. He wasn't going to like her news at all. His large hand moved slowly up and down her thigh, gripping her firmly from time to time as the four of them talked. She laid her hand lightly over his, twining their fingers, squeezing hard. He shifted a little on the bench they shared. She smiled to herself. He was going to be very uncomfortable indeed if this meeting went on much longer.

The conspirators were almost ready with their final plans. That's why they risked meeting together tonight. They wouldn't do it again.

Krager started the meeting. "Daryl is meeting with Holder Me'Fiere. Hagyn is with them. Me'Fiere wants the layout of the guest wing where his daughter and the others are kept hostage. He and Hagyn will go directly there with his Hold Guards. They'll secure the hostages. They're lightly guarded and—"

The innkeeper knocked at the door and opened it without waiting for an invitation. "There are two guards out there. They're not here to drink. They's takin' note of everyone. I doubt but what they'll want to see who's in this room in a few minutes." He hurriedly shut the door and disappeared.

Jym jumped up and unbuttoned his trousers halfway, pulling his shirttail out.

"What are you doing?" Krager looked at him then swept the papers from the table into the fire in the iron stove in the corner.

"You three get in that privy and pray." Jym turned to Marta. "Mess up your hair and unfasten whatever you can of your blouse." His face went fiery red, and he sauntered out the door, fastening up his pants as he half staggered toward the common room.

The three men looked at each other. "After you, Heir," said Dalt, a small twist at the side of his mouth.

Altan glared at him, and the three large men stuffed themselves into the small, uncomfortable, odiferous space. Marta stripped off her vest, threw it partly under the bench, unfastened her blouse halfway to her navel, rucked up her skirt, so too much of her legs were exposed, and lay back.

The door opened. Marta looked up and said, smiling drunkenly, "Oh, you came back, little Jym." She manufactured surprise to see the two guards, who laughed as Jym pushed past them with two mugs of ale.

"Do you mind, gen'lmen?" he slurred and firmly shut the door in their faces. They opened it again, and he leaned down to kiss Marta on the mouth, his lips firmly closed, slopping ale on the floor.

"Just call if you need any help there, laddy," one of them said and closed the door. Marta could hear their rude remarks as they walked away.

Jym blushed furiously and whispered, "I'm sorry, Robyn. It was all I could think of. We're lucky I've run into those two several times. They've seen me drunk before."

"You're a quick thinker, Jym. Your mother would be proud of you, I'm sure," she teased. *Could his face get any redder?* She shook with relief and laughter.

It was several long minutes later that the innkeeper knocked on the door again. Jym was sitting on the bench, Marta arranged

seductively on his lap, thoroughly enjoying his embarrassment in
spite of the danger.

"They's gone." The innkeeper looked around the small room.
"What'd you do with the other three?"

Jym jumped up, dumping Marta on the floor, and rushed to the
privy door to let the suffocating men out. All three leaned down,
hands on their knees, and took long, deep breaths.

"Why couldn't we have found a nice big storage closet? Bad
enough to be stuffed in a small space with you two, but a privy? I've
never held my breath so long before," said Altan. Then he noticed
Marta's disheveled appearance with a raised eyebrow.

"Don't ask," she said, laughing at his red face. "Hard to breathe
in there?"

"What? Do you think being stuffed in a smelly privy with two
giants makes breathing easy? And you two need a bath," said Dalt,
himself nearly as big as Altan.

Marta thought she might have seen Krager's face twitch with a
flash of humor. They were settled back around the table when Daryl
and Me'Fiere walked in, startling them all. "That nearly scared the
piss—Sorry, M—Robyn. What's wrong with you, young Jym?"
asked Daryl. The boy's face was still scarlet, and he couldn't look at
Marta. Or Altan for that matter.

Altan laughed. "He's afraid I'm going to kill him, I think. Don't
worry, boy. I know it was enjoyable. But don't count on me to share
again any time soon." He ran his hand through his hair. He had
done it so often this evening it was standing up in a fair mess.

Marta punched him in the arm.

"We're ready," Daryl said. "Hagyn's cousin is scheduled to be on
main gate duty two nights hence."

"I'll see Captain Kyle tomorrow. What do I tell him?" asked
Krager. "Give him the final schedule. You've briefed him on most of
what we've done. The gate guards need to be ones he trusts. They're
assigned from the guard, not the mercenaries. I get the feeling
Readen's mercenaries are not popular with the guard. That should
help." Daryl answered.

"We'll start passing the word about when to start moving first thing tomorrow. The market will be open so our troop movements won't be so noticeable. I hope," Me'Fiere said.

"Robyn, you stay at the mews," said Altan. Marta bristled.

Altan and Marta lay wrapped together. They'd had their heated discussion about Marta's role in the assault, but Marta's heart wasn't in the fight. She had another matter to discuss, and he wasn't going to be happy. Marta held him tightly, her head on his broad chest as she listened to the steady thump of his heart.

She knew better than to tell him to be careful. They wouldn't see each other again until it was over. She just wanted to lie there all night, awake, holding him. She moved away slightly, smoothing his mussed hair away from his face, and looked at him by the light of one candle.

"What is it, love? You've been avoiding something all evening." He pulled her over on top of him, his body stretched out beneath hers.

"I have to go to the keep for dinner tomorrow night."

"No! Absolutely no!" He was furious.

He sat up so fast she almost tumbled off the bed. "I can't get out of it. I've seen the same watcher outside the guild house several times in the past few days. It took me a good long while to lose him before I came here tonight. I almost gave up. We can't afford to draw Readen's attention. He's invited the new Mi'hiru several times, and we've made too many excuses. It's always done when a group of us are assigned to a new place. You know that. He's going to start getting suspicious." She faltered to a stop, smoothing her hand down his clenched jaw. He didn't speak. "I'm sorry," she whispered.

He reached up and scrubbed at his hair, gripping handfuls and pulling at it. "I don't suppose I can forbid it, or lock you up somewhere?" he said through his teeth.

"I'm sorry, love," she said again. "I'll be all right. No one has the slightest inkling I'm not who I say I am. I've been so careful. Not even the other Mi'hiru, who are the most likely to suspect something, as closely as we work together. I think the wrongness the Karda are feeling is distracting the Mi'hiru empathic senses." She fell silent.

"But someone followed you tonight."

"Altan, remember. This is what I've done all my life. I'm good at it." She smiled up at him tentatively. "I can hold my own with the best of liars."

He closed his eyes. "You'll talk to me all evening. Everything that happens I want to know about."

He wrapped his arms hard around her, his muscles bunched with tension. He pulled her back to the bed, rolled them both over, propped himself up on his elbows and looked down at her. "Don't expect to get any sleep tonight. I'm going to pour my whole self into you." He kissed her hard.

She could feel his desperation through the tongue that searched her mouth and the long body pressed so tight to hers she could scarcely breathe.

Marta and the other new Mi'hiru walked through Restal Prime to the keep. Hard-faced mercenaries lounged at every other corner watching everything. Halfway there, the Mi'hiru came across Captain Kyle sitting on his horse talking to two guards.

He nodded at the women. "Good evening, Mi'hiru." His eyes slid over Marta casually with no sign of recognition.

"We haven't seen you at the mews lately," said Philipa. "I can tell Tukar misses you. He circles the keep every morning."

"I know. I've seen him. Give him extra care, if you will. If he lets you, take him up for some exercise. He isn't getting enough just circling up there. It may be some time before I'm able to come out." He smiled. "Sometimes, I miss being a Karda Patrol more than I can say, and I'm not sure the promotion was worth it." He showed no sign of anticipation or nerves.

Marta was impressed.

She noticed the double guards when they reached the gate at the keep. They were stopped and questioned thoroughly, if apologetically, before they could pass, even though they wore the dress uniforms of Mi'hiru and were expected. There was a tingle when Marta crossed though the gates.

The dining hall was not crowded. Too many empty tables made the dim light gloomy. It seemed many of the holders who were there most years for a couple of moons before planting season called them away had either not come or had left. The steward led them past a table filled with pale-faced young girls and women.

There were only a few people sitting at Readen's head table. Marta was seated too close to him for her pleasure. She spoke a polite greeting and tugged nervously at an earring as she sat, then caught herself and pushed back her hair. *This evening is going to be unending.*

She made desultory conversation with the men on either side of her. To her left was a thin—and gloomy—holder who was more interested in his wine than he was in conversation. On her other side sat a portly man with the look of a fop, but with very shrewd eyes, who studied her with interest. He introduced himself as Illias.

"It must be wonderful being a Mi'hiru. If anything could make me want to be a woman, the possibility of spending all my time flying would be it," he remarked, his voice melodious. He invited her to tell him everything she knew about the Karda. She suspected he wouldn't fight being a woman very hard.

I was right—this evening is never going to end. She started to fiddle with her earring and pushed her hair back instead, again. She noticed Readen watching her. When he turned away, she took the earring off and put it in her pocket.

His cold eyes flicked to her ear and narrowed ever so briefly. She thought she might be in trouble. He nodded and smiled broadly.

The interminable dinner finished. Marta noticed the young girls leaving their table in a close group and with unseemly haste. Readen made it a point to walk the Mi'hiru to the door, nodding to his other guests as they passed.

As they buckled on their sword belts, he said, "Good evening, Mi'hiru. I hope you have a pleasant walk back. It seems a lovely night for it." He took hold of Marta's arm. "I'd like you to stay for a few minutes, Mi'hiru Robyn, if you will."

She swallowed. "Of course."

"You go on back to the guild house," he said to the others. "I won't keep her long." His grasp was too firm on her arm. "Perhaps you'd join me in my study for coffee and brandy —Robyn."

She walked with him, trying not to appear unwilling. The opal against her chest warmed inside her uniform jacket. He commented on every one of the paintings they passed on the way, pointing out ancestor after ancestor. "And this lovely is Daryl's mother. This next is my mother. Amusing how much they look alike. Father evidently had a type."

He's enjoying himself too much. Drawing the suspense out as much as he can. He's trying to frighten me. And, all right, I'm scared now.

He moved his grasp to her hand and drew her arm through the crook of his.

~What's going on, Marta? You're uneasy,~ asked Altan in her head.

~It's all right, love. Readen just wants to talk to me about something. I'll be there soon. Don't worry.~

"What is it you wanted to talk to me about, Guardian?" she asked.

"Oh, let's wait until we've had our coffee before we talk business. And you should call me Readen. I'm still just the regent, not guardian." He smiled at her, pulling her a little closer.

She controlled a shudder. Readen's outward resemblance to Daryl made him feel colder, more sinister.

He ushered her into the room, closed the door, and gestured her to a seat before the fire. He tugged on the bell pull behind his ornate desk, and in a few minutes, a footman entered. "We'll have coffee now." The footman nodded and left. "While we're waiting, why don't you tell me how the training is going. I've sent quite a few of my guard to the mews, but few are accepted. Is there some reason for this?"

"I can't say," she said. "Karda have their own criteria." She looked toward the door, willing the footman to hurry. "How is your father, Readen? Is he recovering?"

The coffee arrived, and the footman arranged it on the sideboard and left. Readen poured them each a cup. He held up a crystal decanter. "Brandy? I believe this one was laid down by my grandfather. It's a fine one."

She declined and took a large sip of her coffee. It scalded her tongue, but she was determined to finish it and get out. The heavy ruby-red draperies over the windows, the massive ornate furniture, the thick rug that silenced footsteps—they were all oppressive.

He smiled at her over the rim of his cup. Ignoring her question, he said, "So tell me a little about yourself, Robyn."

Marta noticed his slight emphasis on her name.

"What part of Adalta are you from? Your accent isn't familiar."

"Dalpin. In Akhara, a very small village." Marta took another large drink of coffee.

"I'm not familiar with it. So tell me, what do they raise in that part of...Akhara?"

He's toying with me. A tremor of fear salted with anger spidered up her back. It was difficult to remember details about who Robyn was supposed to be. Her thinking was fuzzy. Readen's face blurred. Her hand started toward her ear before she could catch herself.

Then he said, quite casually and in the same desultory tone, "You should never try gambling, Marta. You pull at your ear when you're nervous." He waited, smiling.

"Who? My name is Robyn." She'd hesitated too long. She didn't want to hear what he'd said.

~Marta, I can't feel you. What's happening?~ She shook her head, trying to answer Altan. The words wouldn't come.

"I remember that from our time together in Rashiba. That's all it took for me to see through your illusion. I hadn't realized you were talented enough to create such a good illusion on yourself. Without the ear pulling, I could never have penetrated it. Is your ear sore?" His tone was almost concerned. He leaned across and touched it. "They are such lovely earrings. You should put this one back in."

Marta jerked back in the chair, gripping its arms, trying to clear her head.

"I don't imagine being in that body is very comfortable for you. It's not as...appealing. Ah, it's fading. Your lovely hair is starting to break through. Illusions require belief, you know." Readen smiled. One eyebrow arched. He was amused. He shook his head at her with mock concern. "You hardly touched your dinner, I noticed."

CHAPTER THIRTY-TWO

Marta tried moving her legs, her numb, wood legs. Her eyelids refused to lift, and her head ached like she'd been bashed with a club. She rolled to her side. Her wrist bumped on something hard and unyielding. She heard moaning and thought it might be her. She tried to open her eyes. *Where am I?* She gave up and floated back into uneasy half-consciousness.

Sometime later, she stirred and tried opening her eyes, sticky with rheum, again. She wanted to rub at them, but her hand wouldn't move. She blinked. It seemed to take a long time.

Strange vertical stripes across the room wavered in and out of focus. What were they? They curled and twisted in her vision.

A long, lost time later, Marta wiped at her eyelids with the sleeve of her blouse. Now she could move, though she had to tell her hand what to do. Her eyes opened to dim light, squinted hard, and focused.

The undulating stripes settled into bars. Her hand reached up slowly and explored her aching head. Tears welled and dripped down the side of her face into her hair. Pain surged, and her chest clamped tight.

She closed her eyes for another while and woke at the sound of metal grating against metal. Part of the bars moved, and a beautiful woman with the coldest face she'd ever seen swam blearily into view.

"Sit up." The voice was harsh, unpleasant. "Here's your dinner." She clanked the tray down on the floor and went out. The barred door clanged.

Another metallic grating sounded. *Lock. She locked it. I'm locked in.* She sat up slowly, one hand pressed to her swimming head, and looked around the small space. She was in a cell—rough-cut stone wall behind her, a narrow window high up near the ceiling, bars on the other three sides. She closed her eyes, opened them, and tried focusing again. Yes, she was in a cell.

"I see you're awake." On the other side of the bars to her right an old man sat on a crude wooden bunk. She hadn't sensed him. "Where am I?" she asked. Tall and too thin, he had silvering hair and a patrician, hooked nose. She wanted to ask more, but her head hurt, and her voice had trouble coming out.

"My name is Malyk. And I think I know you. What is your name?"

"It isn't Robyn," she answered through her pain. She concentrated.

"It's Marta." What was wrong with her? "What's wrong with me?" She could remember her name but was so angry with herself. *Why am I angry?*

"You've been drugged."

"Drugged? Is that why everything is swimmy?"

"It's in the food," he repeated. "Don't eat it. Throw most of it in the hole in the corner to your right and mess the rest around on the plate. They won't believe you ate it if you scrape it all off. It's awful. The water in the jug is sometimes good. I've been drinking it, and my head almost clears until I have to eat again. I've found I can go for two days without food, just not water. If I go longer than that, I get too weak to resist Readen."

Readen. Clarity froze her body with ice. *Readen.*

"Marta." The sharp command in Malyk's voice jerked her to her feet. "You need to move."

357

One wobbly step at a time, her hand scraping along the rock wall, she made her way around the cell to the door and hung on the bars, looking down at the food. She picked up the tray and did as he told her, scraping away half and stirring the rest around a little. It looked like the hot mash she sometimes fed the Karda, only it didn't smell as good. She dropped the tray with a loud clatter and staggered back to the crude cot.

"Try and sleep for a while. You should be better when you wake up."

She lay back down and closed her eyes. She was beginning to feel her body now. She ached all over, and she realized why she was so angry with herself. She'd betrayed her own identity because she couldn't control her one bad habit. Her earring. Pulling at her earring.

Altan paced the small alley back and forth all night. He looked at the gate of the guild house like he had a hundred times. Marta's mind was a disconnected muddle of thoughts and feelings—when he could sense anything at all, though he never stopped trying, barely aware of his surroundings.

The sky turned pink with the rising sun, and he had to admit Marta wasn't coming. Readen had broken her disguise. Altan ran his hands through his hair for the umpteenth time. The hard ball of fear inside his rib cage made it difficult to breathe.

He left the alley and started back to the inn where he and Dalt stayed, his boots pounding and echoing through the empty streets. He had to find Daryl. Daryl might know where Readen would take her.

It took the better part of three hours for Altan and Dalt to run Daryl down in Factor Hyrt's spacious warehouse where a number of their men hid, waiting. Daryl was passing out bright purple and yellow armbands, his personal colors. He froze, an armband dangling from his fingers. "What's wrong?"

"Marta didn't come back from the keep last night." Altan's voice was tight. "And I can't reach her this morning. There's just a cloud where she should be."

Daryl paced up and down while Altan stood, fisted hands pressed tight against his legs. For the first time in his life, nothing was in his control. They couldn't move up the timetable. Their forces were scattered through the city, waiting for the signal to move the next morning when Captain Kyle stationed loyal guards on the gates.

Echoing his thoughts, Daryl said, "We can't move any sooner. It took too much planning to set it up for tomorrow to change it. We'd never reach all the men, let alone Kyle."

"We'll have to wait," Altan said, his voice low, tight with worry. He was bereft and struggling to fight his feelings.

He walked the city streets all day through the cold mist that fell unnoticed until the light began to fail. Dalt finally caught up to him as the lamps were lit along the busier streets. Wet cobbles in shining pools beneath them glistened in the yellow light.

"If you don't get some rest, you won't be worth anything tomorrow, and what good will that do Marta? You've been up for more than thirty-six hours, and I'll bet you haven't eaten all day, either."

Defeated, Altan let Dalt lead him back to the inn. He finally fell asleep a few hours before dawn. But his sleep was not restful.

Marta felt Malyk's attention on her the moment she stirred. Her head was clearing, but she had more immediate problems. She stood, looking at Malyk with a red face. "If you'll turn your back, please. I need to take care of something necessary." She moved to the stinking hole in the corner of her cell. She finished, and said, "You can turn back around now."

He moved stiffly to the bars separating them, his face and arms marred by varicolored bruises and long, narrow scabbed-over cuts. Too much blood spotted his clothes.

"You're hurt," she observed.

"It's the cold and damp working on old bones and muscles. If you'll come over and sit down in front of the bars with your back to me, I'll attempt to relieve your head pain. Resisting Readen takes most of the talent the drugs leave me, so I don't have enough left to heal it, but I might have enough to help the pain."

Marta grimaced as she sat and leaned back against the bars. "It feels like someone's stomping around in there with sharp nails in their boots." Even speaking hurt.

He put his hands on her shoulders for a few minutes. She could feel his palms heat. It veered toward discomfort. He moved them behind her ears, holding them slightly away from her. Even though his hands didn't touch her, heat pulsed and the pain eased. She closed her eyes. He pulled away after several long minutes.

"You'll need to rest now. That takes almost more out of you than it does me."

She stood and was suddenly dizzy. "Maybe I'll lie down for just a little while. Then I need to figure out what to do."

Malyk laughed. It didn't sound as if he found her words funny. "How long have you been in here?" She looked at the bars and the dim, dirty passage beyond. Marta could smell years of fear and pain steeping the damp stone walls and hardened her shields against it, damping down her returning empathy.

It would not overcome her. It would not force her into despair.

"As soon as Roland declared Readen heir, the guardian collapsed. It wasn't two days before Readen started trying to usurp my talent connections with Adalta. He thinks to steal my talent. That's what he keeps trying. I have powerful shields, but he is using an arcane power I've never felt before. I'm afraid to find out how he's getting it."

He stopped for a moment and took several breaths. "It's malevolent, the same malevolence contained in the Circles of Disorder, but active, not waiting like the circles feel." Almost to himself, he said, "How has he managed to hide this from us? From me all these years?"

He paused. "He's disabled his father. That odious guard, Pol, carries Roland down here every few days. I suspect Readen's stripped him of what talent he has in his weakened situation. I disagreed often with Roland's decisions, but he doesn't deserve that. From his own son." Malyk's gaze lost focus, and he drifted away.

Marta closed her eyes and lay back on the hard cot. She couldn't sleep, but unfortunately, she could think. Her mind was only too clear. *I've lost track of time. I wish I knew what's happening out there. How close Daryl and Altan are.* Her stomach growled. Water wasn't enough. She was hungry. *This is only going to get worse.*

The pain and distress in Altan's voice shouted at her, ~Marta!~

She could almost feel his strong hands grabbing and holding her. Marta wanted to grab back and never let go. Tears ran down the side of her face and into her ears. She didn't care.

~I've been so worried. What's happened to you? Are you hurt?~

~I've been drugged.~ She felt him groan. ~Listen before you panic. Daryl and Reden's old tutor, Malyk, is here with me. He worked on my head. I'm fine. Just tired. Malyk says they put drugs in the food and water, so I'm thirsty and hungry, but I'm alright.~

~Where is Reden?~

~I don't know. I'm locked somewhere beneath the keep. There's a small window, but it's too high to reach. It's dark. And cold.~ Marta didn't want to tell him how foggy she felt and how much her head still hurt. She couldn't seem to stop the tears. She knew there wasn't a reason to feel safer having him in her head again, but she did.

~Do you still have your bonding opal?~

~Yes, it's hot on my chest. I think it helps me clear my mind.~

~Oh, thank Adalta. Whatever you do, don't let anyone take it from you. So long as you are wearing it, the protections I'm putting on it now won't let him physically touch you without your permission. I wish I could have done that before you went without alerting him.~

The stone on her chest throbbed, hot and comforting.

Reden stalked out of his bedroom. The serving girl was worthless.

All she did was lie there, unmoving, while her life's blood seeped out to stain the sheets. No screams, no fight, little resistance. She was dying too soon—little power in that. His obsession with Marta had driven him too far, too fast with the girl.

He couldn't get Marta out of his mind. Her channels hadn't been so obvious when she'd been in Restal before. Now they were immense with potential talent. He coveted them. Through them, Readen could finally free the Itza Larrak from its prison in the cavern pillars, and he'd have access to all the power he needed. The Itza Larrak had promised. But Readen wouldn't go to the cavern until his power was at its strongest.

He slammed the door behind him with such force it split, and he paced furiously across the study. There was a timid knock. He flung it open. "What do you want?"

A small page stood there with a thick batch of folded paper in his hands. The terrified boy thrust the papers at Readen and fled.

He read the long missive from his secretary, wadded it up into a tight ball, and threw it in the smoldering fire. He kicked the logs to get the fire started again so the papers would burn and headed out the door.

One of the hostages, the Me'Fiere girl, had locked herself in her room and was refusing to eat. Two angry holders waited in the reception hall demanding to see their daughters—Me'Fiere and Connor Me'Cowyn. A deputation of merchants brought complaints that his mercenaries were harassing their customers, and the market was nearly shut down.

Even the kitchen was complaining. His breakfast had been meager, and he refused to think about what dinner would be. He would wait to deal with Marta.

The waiting would soften her up. He'd let the drugs work. He'd gotten no word that Daryl had left Toldar. Waiting held no danger, only more time to consolidate his power.

Marta sat again with her back against the bars between her and

Malyk. He slumped a little and took his hands away from her head. The heat finally relieved her pain. "Thank you, Malyk. It's better now. I think my body can take care of the rest."

Malyk had to support himself with the bars to sit upright. "It's a good thing. I'm not sure I could do more. Healing takes effort, and I'm getting weaker. Tonight I'll have to eat the food, drugs or not." He wrapped his arms around himself and shuffled to his cot, his face gaunt and drawn. "I'm sorry."

"Let's just sit for a while and talk," said Marta. "Unless you feel the need to lie down."

"No. I'm tired but not that tired. Besides I've been in here too long, mostly by myself." He went silent for a minute. "It's good to have company, however much I deplore the forced nature of it."

"What do you mean you have been in here *mostly* alone? Have there been others?"

Malyk was silent. He took a small sip of the water and, head down, refused to look at her.

"Why won't you tell me?"

"I don't know whether it is better that you know or not know. This is not the part of the prison where criminals are held. It holds only a special few at a time."

He stopped. His silence was palpable, then he said in a low voice, forcing the words out of his tight corded throat, "They are mostly young girls, sometimes boys. Serving girls. Barely out of childhood. He takes them out of their cells for a few hours at a time. After too few days of that, if they come back, they can barely move, can't talk. They lie on their bunks staring at the ceiling, eyes dead. Blood seeps through their clothes. It's usually only a few days before they don't come back at all."

Marta was horrified. She shook with anger for the children and fear for herself.

It was several minutes before Malyk spoke again, then he whispered, "That's another reason I am so tired and depleted. I try to heal them. I try. But it does no good. Nothing can heal their minds. Whatever it is Readen is doing to them, they are lost." He didn't speak again.

~Marta!~ Altan's voice shouted in her head. ~Your anger and fear are piercing my head. You're terrified. What's happening? Readen is a dead man!~

She held her breath and swallowed her panic. She couldn't tell Altan this. He'd do something crazy like try to break into the keep before they were ready. That way meant sure death for him and failure for Daryl and his forces.

~Nothing is wrong, Altan.~ She sat up straighter. ~I was just having a bad moment. I haven't seen anyone but Malyk all day.~ She wanted nothing more than to see Altan come through the door, sword in hand, sun-gilded hair flying around his head, green eyes firing sparks. She wanted it so badly she ached with fear and frustration.

~Tell me what's going on. I feel so helpless not being there.~

Altan began to talk. ~Daryl has things well in hand. It's frustrating not to be in charge, but it's his quadrant, and he's fully capable. I'm having trouble remembering I'm only here to support him. He's a master at tactics and strategy. Better than I am right now. I can't think of anything but finding you.~ He stopped for a moment. ~Me'Cowyn arrived and his forces are quietly infiltrating the prime, joining the others in the spaces we've secured.~

CHAPTER THIRTY-THREE

Malyk ate the morning meal and was lying insensible on his crude bed, his breath too shallow. Marta missed his company. She paced the square of her small cell. Hunger made it hard to think about anything but—hunger. Sidhari and Altan hovered at the edge of her consciousness.

She sat on the edge of her cot and forced herself into the exercises Finder Mireia insisted she practice every day. She sat until she felt the stones around her, felt their roughness, their structure, sensed the immense pressure that made them. But try as she might, she could not move them. She could feel the metal of the bars, the heat that formed them, but she could not bend them.

She reached deep inside, searching again, as she tried so many times before, for the channels Mireia told Marta were there, reached for the talents to manifest, but she sensed nothing, though she tried for hours.

Finally, she gave up. *I know my empathy works. It has never stopped. If my shields let go for an instant, I'll feel all the rats I can hear. Can I use it to connect to what is around me? I have no idea where I am other than under the keep somewhere. Somehow I need to let Altan know how to find me. He'll come. I know he'll come.*

She pulled her legs up to sit cross-legged and closed her eyes again. She grasped her opal lightly in her hand, comforted by the cool gold wings of the Karda and the heat of the jewel they held. It was warm all the time now. She took long, slow, deep breaths, feeling her way past the square stones of the wall behind her, slowly forcing her consciousness through the fog of her hunger out from the cell into the passageway walls, feeling them come alive in her mind.

The pain and terror embedded there almost broke her connection. Ignoring the rats and spiders and little crawly things, she breathed, forcing her way past them, beyond the walls of the dark underground place, past the few tortured souls she found. She wondered if such pain, such terror, could ever be expunged from these stones.

She felt her way slowly down the narrow passage to the guardroom. Marta shivered at the dirty human she sensed there. Her fog lifted a little. She expanded her way outward. Slowly the whole of the tangled and layered emotions of the keep's inhabitants spread through her mind. Some kind, some confused, some concentrating on a task so intently she knew what they were doing. Some were angry. Many were disturbed. A few made her cringe with disgust and fear worse than the person she sensed in the guardroom.

Around the tower at the end of the east wing, intense feelings of fear and despair struggled against a viscous, voracious hunger for power. Readen, with a small, feeble consciousness—a young girl. It was the same aura of pain, terror, and despair imbued in the cell walls around her, intensified. Marta's muscles tensed with shock and disgust. Her body jerked. Her stomach twisted, and her senses reeled at the anguish and horror of the child's pain and violated trust.

~Shield, Marta.~ Sidhari's voice was sharp and pulled her out before she drowned in the horror. She sat up on her narrow bed and shook her head to clear it. She'd never been able to do anything like that before. She'd connected with the whole of the keep above and around her. And everything in it.

366

It was too much to bear. She closed her eyes against the renewed pain in her head and strengthened her shields, grateful for the increased protection Mireia had taught her. She didn't want to think about what she'd felt.

~Ground, Marta. Ground.~

Grateful for the calm voice of her Karda, she sent her mind down through the rocks and soil deep into Adalta, searching for strength from the heart of the planet. She wished she could draw on it like Altan could. How wonderful it would be to be able to manipulate the stones and water around her. She thought, not for the first time, of the way Mireia had described the channels within her and tried again to sense them, to draw from Adalta through them. But she could not get past the suffocating evil in the walls around her.

Sidhari's voice whispered past her shields, ~Wait, Marta. Wait. Save your strength.~

She fell back on the hard mattress, her body unable to hold her upright, her head fuzzy, her stomach growling. She'd have to eat her next meal.

Altan diverted his panic by working with Daryl, moving through the silent, empty streets of the prime from one group of hidden guardsmen to the next, checking equipment, mending armor, and handing out the purple and gold armbands.

He spoke to Marta as often as he could get through. Her shields held strong and solid most of the time. Altan sensed when she was exploring the keep and followed her thoughts without impinging. He kept his shields tight. She didn't need to know how terrified he was for her.

Daryl climbed to the loft of a dusty stable, talking in a low voice to the men hidden there. Altan heard boot steps in the courtyard. He moved to the wall beside the door and peered out through the space between the rock wall and the partly open door, watching. Voices and footsteps rang across the broken stone of the courtyard outside. "Daryl," he whispered. Straw drifted from the bales stacked around the edge of the loft, and Daryl's head appeared.

"There are two guards in the courtyard headed this way. I don't want to kill them. We don't know whose side they'll take, but we can't afford discovery. When they come in, I'll take care of them, but it would help if you could distract one for a moment." He drew his sword, waiting. There was a stealthy rustle overhead.

The guards laughed as they neared the door. "I don't know why you keep your horse here. Old man Patel can barely keep the horses fed and groomed."

"That's why we're here. I check on him often. They always look well cared for even if the rest of the stable is a mess." He pushed the door. "Hmm. He left it open. Must have oiled the hinges. They usually screech so loud it scares the horses." A tall guard stepped inside.

Altan let him pass, waited for the second man, and aimed the hilt of his dagger at a spot just behind the man's ear. His foot slid in the straw that littered the stable floor an instant before the blow hit. Startled, the man half turned, and Altan missed his target. The man didn't go down. He turned and cried out, lurching back.

The first man didn't even have a chance to turn before a heavy bale of straw fell from above, knocking him to the ground. He didn't move.

His partner stumbled into Altan, who tripped over the high doorsill, and they both fell to the ground, the big man on top. Altan's dagger flew out of his hand, and strong hands curled around his neck. He tried getting his fingers under them. Altan bucked and twisted.

Darkness slid into the edges of his vision. He jerked his knee up and jammed it hard in between the man's legs. The guard rolled off Altan with a groan. Altan grabbed one arm, twisting it behind the man's back.

"Not a sound, or I'll break your arm." His voice croaked, and his chest heaved as he sucked air in great painful gasps.

Daryl slid down the ladder behind him.

"Find something to gag him, and a rope. This one has a hard head," Altan gasped. "The other one?"

"I dropped a bale on him, and he didn't get up." Daryl handed Altan a large handkerchief and cut a long rein hanging from the wall at the end of the stable.

Altan gagged and trussed the guard who groaned and tried to curl up on himself.

"The other one's dead. Must have broken his neck." Daryl scrubbed at his face with a big hand. He took a deep breath. "I know we'll have to kill others this day, but this wasn't even a fair fight. I don't even know if these men would fight against me. They're not mercenaries."

Altan put a hand on Daryl's shoulder then let it drop. "Let's go, friend. We have to get to the rooms overlooking the keep gates and start working on those defenses. They didn't feel easy." Daryl nodded. They dragged the two guards to an unused stall at the far end of the stable and bolted the door. Altan and Daryl left.

Twenty men climbed down the ladder behind them and scattered silently in several directions, blending with the growing market crowd.

Heavy footsteps coming down the hall woke Marta. They weren't the light gait of the beautiful, cold woman who brought her meals. She felt two people this time. One was Readen, and the other had the dirty, greasy feel of the man in the guardroom. The light of a lantern threw bizarre dancing shadows on the dank grey stones of the hallway as they approached.

She stood on shaking legs, swaying and dizzy. There had been drugs in her water this time. She fought her dizziness and raised shields against Altan as best she could. The last thing she wanted to do was distract him now.

Time for the assault must be nearing. He and Daryl would be working on the defense wards soon. He wouldn't be able to come for her before the keep was secured. She tried to swallow, but her dry tongue refused to work.

Readen looked at her through the bars. "Well, I see you drank the water."

How did my empathy fail me? How did I not know what Readen is? Did I ignore my senses because I just didn't want to believe what I felt? That such evil exists?

The large, lumpish man with him grinned, showing two teeth missing. Tiny eyes glinted from his round face. She was already afraid of Readen. Her fear intensified at the sight of the huge man leering at her.

~Courage, Marta. Courage.~ Sidhari's voice was a constant strength bolstering the edges of her shields.

Malyk stirred on his cot. He'd eaten his food. "Readen," he said, his voice slurred. "You don't want to do this. It won't end well."

Readen's eyes narrowed, and he spoke, not looking at Malyk, "Well, old man, I won't kill her. Not yet, anyway. If she's willing to give me what I want, maybe I won't *have* to kill her."

He turned, the silver medallion at his chest shined in the dim light. He looked directly at Malyk who was struggling to sit upright. "I haven't killed you yet, and you've given me nothing. But you never have, have you? You hoard your talent for yourself. Pol, unlock the door and bring her."

He took the torch and walked down the hall in the opposite direction from which he had come.

Marta stepped back as the big man approached. Reaching into her pocket for the earring, she tossed it behind her onto the cot. She fought as hard as she could. He was simply too large, and drugs and hunger slowed her reactions, made her forget how to move. He slapped her, and she fell, hitting her head on the filthy stone floor. She lost herself for a moment.

He jerked her off the floor and shoved her, face first, against the bars and wrapped rough rope around her wrists, rasping the skin. Pol picked her up like a baby, her arms contorted painfully behind her. She twisted her body, kicked with her feet and tried to butt him with her head. He just pulled her tighter and smiled down at her. Marta gagged from his rancid breath and turned her head away.

He carried her into the hall, following Readen and the torchlight. Her stomach heaved in fear and revulsion. She willed her body not to shake, concentrating hard, trying to regain her strength and clear her mind.

They walked a long way through the twisting passage. Marta lost track. She hadn't come this way in her mental explorations. She tried to memorize the turnings in the narrowing hall they passed through, to tell Sidhari, but it was confusing. She was frightened, slipping in and out of pain and a fear-filled drug haze. Pol shifted her in his arms. The defensive moves she knew would help her escape slithered and slid around in her head.

They stopped at a small door hidden in a twist of the tunnel. Pol set her down in front of him, pulling her too close when her knees threatened to give way. She shrunk away, and he followed, jerking her bound hands. She sucked in a sharp gasp of pain. Warm blood trickled into her palms from her raw wrists.

Marta watched with fascination as Readen ran his fingers over the incised symbols on the lintel and traced sigils in the air over the lock. The lock clicked, and the door swung inward. Pol shoved her in the back, and Marta stumbled through behind Readen.

The walls of the passage beyond were not the same worked stone. They flowed in bumps and curves, rough in some places, smoothed and covered with symbols carved by some ancient hand in others. The weight of tons of stone and dirt above pressed her senses. She fought to breathe through the claustrophobia, gasping with growing terror.

She stumbled to her knees. Small sharp rocks on the floor jabbed her. Pol hauled her upright by her bound hands. Pain twisted her shoulders, and she managed to stand before he jerked her arms out of their sockets.

They reached the end of the tight tunnel, and the yellow light from Readen's torch lost itself in vast darkness. The walls of the passage disappeared behind them and opened into an immense cavern. She could sense no ceiling, no walls. The cold air smelled of dampness and sharp, deep-earth scent. She heard the faint burble of water running over rocks.

"Light the torches, Pol." Readen's voice echoed.

Pol shoved her to the ground and grabbed one leg. She kicked at him, but he caught her other foot and wrapped rope tightly around her ankles. Her head swirled, and she turned her head to vomit, hoping it would get rid of some of the drugs.

He walked toward an enormous pale limestone block in the center of the cavern, lighting torches in tall black iron stanchions circling it. Minerals and scattered crystals embedded in the walls glowed and flashed, their colors shifting in the flickering light. Huge stalactites hung from the ceiling, some meeting stalagmites to form thick columns.

Those just outside of the circle of torches were smoothed pillars reaching into the darkness at the top of the cavern. Arcane inscribed symbols, darkened with something flaky and brown, covered the vertical columns that stretched from ceiling to floor.

Marta couldn't stop the violent tremors that shook her body. One elbow banged against a sharp rock, and she sucked in a sharp breath at the jolt of electric pain.

Light flickered and shifted on the limestone block covered with the same brown flakes. Pol picked her up, ignoring her futile struggles, and carried her toward it. She could hear his quickened breathing, feel his rancid breath on her neck, stirring her hair. At one end of the stone block, small silver knives lay in a row on a pristine, white cloth—a neat, precise, terrifying row.

A sharp pain broke through her shield, and the sense of Altan flooded in. She felt the cut on his right forearm, sensed his muscles tightening and releasing as he swung his sword. He fought with steady, practiced moves, sure and skilled. Then he broke into a run, breathing hard. Frenzy and fear beat at her. Her shields snapped up again. The assault had started.

She felt a flash of hope.

Then Readen stepped into her view.

CHAPTER THIRTY-FOUR

Altan sprang up the stairs to the tall arched doors at the front of the keep, Dalt close behind. He heard Daryl and Krager shouting orders and directing men to each side of the house. The guards outside faded away when they saw the two of them. Few wanted to fight Daryl. Several others chose to accept his colors and join him.

Altan put his hand to the door and felt his way into the barriers set on the locks, the thick oak of the doors themselves, and the doorframe. Like the outside defenses, Readen's spells were overcomplicated, shifting layers of strong and weak fields. The energy was malevolent and oddly familiar, like warped, uneducated, and confused talent. The power shifted in Altan sprang up the stairs to the tall arched doors at the front of the keep, Dalt close behind. He heard Daryl and Krager shouting orders and directing men to each side of the house. The guards outside faded away when they saw the two of them. Few wanted to fight Daryl. Several others chose to accept his colors and join him.

Altan put his hand to the door and felt his way into the barriers set on the locks, the thick oak of the doors themselves, and the doorframe. Like the outside defenses, Readen's spells were overcomplicated, shifting layers of strong and weak fields. The energy was malevolent and oddly familiar, like warped, uneducated, confused talent. The power shifted in crude, unorganized swirls from one layer to the next.

He sent careful, narrow tendrils of power around and through the tangled fields. It was taking too long. The junctions where he worked to attach his power lines were slippery and hard to hold. Sweat soaked his hair and tunic when he finally shook off the greasy feel of the defenses, knotted his strands together, and with a plea of prayer to Adalta, wrenched them hard. The spells broke with a loud, electric snap.

The men behind him stepped back.

Altan motioned them forward. "Let's get these open."

Wide iron strips banded the heavy oak doors. It took several men to force them open against the defending mercenaries and the House Guards who had not disappeared. Altan and Daryl burst through, fighting side by side, Krager and Dalt close at their backs, men pouring through the doors behind them.

Altan fought with barely contained fury. His sword flashed as he deflected the first mercenary's thrust, and his blade slid into the man's side. Pulling it free, he blocked another, the blow jarring his arm. He twisted his body and cut low, nearly severing the man's leg. Knocking the sword out of the downed man's hand, he stepped around him. His mind focused on nothing but the men in front of him who blocked his way to Marta and the feeling of sword on flesh and bone.

The world slowed as he turned and twisted his body sideways, minimizing himself as a target, stepping forward one foot at a time, trying not to slip on the blood-slicked stones of the floor. Guarding, deflecting, cutting through the maelstrom of swinging swords and contorted faces. One after another fell until he came back to himself, surrounded by dead and moaning men, and there was no one left in front of him to fight.

He looked around, dazed, his heart beating fast and strong. The sudden silence rang in his ears. The smell of blood and voided bowels was thick in his nostrils.

Men wearing Daryl's purple and yellow armbands carried wounded and herded prisoners to the great hall under Krager's direction. Others did battlefield triage where it was needed.

Daryl directed men down the corridors to the left and right after those who fled or were stationed elsewhere in the keep. He finished and approached Altan warily.

Altan leaned down and put his hands on his bloody thighs. His right hand wouldn't let go of its grip on his sword. He hung his head, breathing hard. When he stopped fighting, his sense of Marta's fear almost overwhelmed him. He struggled to control it.

"I've seen you fight," Daryl said. "But not like that. If I ever do again, I hope you are still by my side and not facing me."

Altan heard him through a haze. Slowly, his head cleared, and he looked up. He wiped his bloody sword on the tunic of one of Readen's mercenaries at his feet. "Where would she be?"

Daryl looked back over his shoulder at the carnage. "Take Willem and his troops and search through the lower halls. The basements are there—that's where you're most likely to find Marta. You'll need to check..."

Daryl stopped at the look on Altan's face. "You know what to do. Krager will clear the guest wing with Me'Cowyn and Me'Fiere. Kyle and I will take the residence and administrative wing and Readen's tower. If she's up there, I'll send someone for you immediately."

"Have you felt any new defensive wards?" asked Altan, his voice scratchy. "All the ones I've destroyed so far have been set for a while."

"No. Readen apparently trusted his wards to hold without him. More than he should have." Daryl paused. "If he set trip wards to alert him when he's otherwise occupied, you must have bypassed them."

Altan felt the blood leave his face—Readen was probably otherwise occupied with Marta. He took the stairs down to the lower halls two at a time. Breath raged through his chest. He tried again in vain to reach her thoughts. All he could feel through her shaky shields was pain and confusion. With Dalt and several men

375

behind him, they rushed the mercenaries blocking the bottom of the stairs.

Sudden pain flashed through him, and his step faltered. Marta, confused and terrified, filled his head, obscured his vision. Dalt shoved him to the side, blocking a sword swipe that would have taken off his arm.

"Altan! Pay attention, man. Are you hurt?"

He slammed up his shields. *Oh, Lady Adalta. I can't let her distract me now, or I'll never reach her.* He barely felt the cut on his arm.

He stormed through the remaining mercenaries like they were standing still, their swords moving as if through thick honey. He directed the men behind him to check each room they passed and sent men down each intersecting hall. When he reached the stairs leading to the basements, he was alone.

He sent the next guard's sword flying with a swift cut to his arm. The man fell, grabbing his arm with a cry. Altan went to one knee, jerking him up by the shoulders, heedless of his cry of pain. "Where is Readen? Where are his prisoners?" he shouted.

The guardsman's eyes flicked to a large door in the hallway ahead.

Altan dropped him.

He ran. No more guards barred the way in front of him. He knew exhaustion was close, but he took the stairs down two at a time. He stumbled twice with a searing pain that was Marta's as if it were his own. It burned through his shields. This he couldn't defeat with a sword.

Marta gritted her teeth, stifling a cry as Pol sliced a sharp knife through the thongs holding her wrists and ankles, nicking her calf. She tried moving her fingers. They had no feeling. She shoved herself away from Pol and braced against the table, kicking out with both feet, hitting his stomach hard. He let out a small "oof" and smiled.

His hand swung and slapped her. Her knees buckled. He

grabbed for her, tearing open her tunic, and his hand closed around her opal. It knocked him off his feet.

She ran for the door, fighting dizziness. Her feet felt as if they were moving through thick mud. Pol caught her, grabbed her arm, and whirled her around. Her body smashed against the table. She fought to keep conscious. His body crammed against her. The stone table bruised her back. She swallowed through her tight throat.

"Pol," Readen said, unable to suppress the excitement in his voice. "Fasten her to the table."

Pol lifted her to the top of the stone with ease. His repulsive touch lingered too long, leaving her feeling disgusted and unclean. *Is this what rape is like? Am I going to find out?* She sucked in a deep breath, fighting the terror.

Her head pounded with every pulse of her blood. She struggled to sit up, kicked at him, struggled to free her arms, struggled against the drug haze that slowed and weakened her.

He ignored her kicks as though they were nothing and strapped her arms and legs to rings on the sides of the stone. He hit her with his fist, knocking her head against the table, which was cold beneath her back. The short thongs let her move her limbs but only so far.

How many had lain here, as she was now, helpless and terrified? Pain and terror seeped through where her skin touched the stone, gritty with flakes of dried blood.

Anger blazed inside her. She would not give in. The opal around her neck burned. She drew courage from the heat. It was as if Altan held her.

Readen approached the table, smiling. "You've grown much more powerful, Marta. What's this? A bonding opal?" He reached toward the stone. The opal flashed, and he staggered back with a hiss.

Readen paced around her, muttering almost to himself. "How are you holding this shield? Who gave you this opal?" He held his hand above her chest, eyes closed, head thrown back. "Oh. Oh, yes. Amazing. And how fortunate. Your channels are wide open and nearly empty, enormous. We have only to break your shields."

He pointed to one of the instruments arranged on the table

above her head. "That one, I think, Pol." He smiled at her. "Pol enjoys administering the little tender mercies for me."

A long pair of pincers appeared, the ends flared widely. Pol slid one flat prong under her left hand. At Readen's nod, he squeezed. Small bones in her hand shattered. She screamed.

~Marta! Where are you? I can't find you!~ Altan's voice echoed loud in her head. She could feel Sidhari's strength reach for her.

Pol squeezed again, increasing the pain. She screamed so loud something tore in her throat. Through the haze of pain, she saw Readen, a look of bliss on his face, moving his mouth in a slow chant of words she didn't recognize.

His fingers drew complicated sigils in the air. He reached his hands toward her, palms up, curled into cups. She panicked. It weakened her shields. The stone grew colder beneath her, and she felt a pull toward him.

"Galal sabitti ata me peta baka."

The opal flared with heat against her chest, and the pull stopped. Marta struggled to ground herself to Adalta, to push through the pain and fear. Her hand pulsed with agony. Her focus wavered. He leaned over her. "Where is Daryl? What are his plans?"

She reached desperately for Adalta, grounding herself, feeling the heat of the opal on her chest intensify, fiercely holding to Altan and Sidhari.

Readen chanted again, "Galal sabitti ata me peta baka." He reached for her opal. It flashed. He convulsed and fell backward to the floor with a garbled scream.

Marta smelled singed flesh, and his fury slammed her shaky shields. He rolled slowly to his knees, gasping for air, and stared at his blistered hand. Pol helped him to his feet, murmuring to him, crooning in despair.

Readen cursed and walked back and forth beside the stone table, his steps uneven, cradling his burnt hand. He drew in a deep breath and picked up a small silver knife. "She won't be able to hold her shield much longer. It's the opal that's binding it to her, that won't let me into her channels." He handed the knife to Pol.

Pol slashed open the waist of her skirt and slowly drew the

instrument across her belly. Beads of blood swelled along a shallow cut. Marta screamed. Three more times Pol sliced her, the movement slow and deliberate.

Altan swore in her mind, his thoughts frantic. She reached for Adalta, and suddenly a searing green-gold light flooded her body, its power pulsing through her. The pain faded, and she heard the words,

~This is why you came, Marta.~.

Readen's questions were muffled by the strange light. "Where is Daryl? What are his plans? Who are his supporters?" He circled the table, whispering "Galal sabitti ata me peta baka" over and over in a low monotone.

Again he grabbed for the opal. It threw him into one of the stanchions, knocking it over. Burning oil spilled in a fiery stream across the floor. He cursed, unable to get up without Pol's help.

Slowly the green-gold light faded from Marta's consciousness. and pain flooded her.

"How is it you can touch her when I cannot?" Readen said, pulling himself up to lean against the table at her feet. He seethed, his teeth clenched, the taut muscles in his jaw bulged. "Blood! I need blood from her. I must call the Itza Larrak. She will not hold against it. I must have her channels, and I must have Daryl's plans."

Pol placed a small silver bowl under her right wrist. He picked up the silver knife and sliced down sharply. She gasped and tried to pull away, but he held her arm tight. She heard the spill of her blood hit the bottom of the bowl.

She floated out of her body. The sounds in the cavern echoed— faint in her head—Readen's breath as he made his way painfully to one of the inscribed pillars, the fast beat of her heart, Pol's excited breathing, the slow drip of her blood into the bowl.

She watched a shudder of revulsion and pain roll through her body as she hovered above it, feeling nothing, floating in the strange green-gold light. She wanted to stay there, looking down, separate from what was happening below.

~Marta,~ she heard Altan's thought, ~Don't leave. Hold on to me. Just hold to me. Hold to Adalta.~ His words repeated in her head. She felt his desperation and turned, drifting toward it. Sidhari's wordless crooning surrounded her like warm downy feathers.

"Don't let her bleed to death, Pol. We want to control her, not kill her." She heard the faint shakiness in Readen's voice.

He held his burned hand with the other, breath hissing between his clenched teeth. Pol wrapped her wrist tightly with a strip of linen and tied it off.

A flood of pain surged through her, and she dropped so fast back into her body her breath whooshed.

Dimly she heard Altan ask, ~What happened? Please answer me, Marta.~

She knew he'd felt the sharp slice on her wrist.

~I'll be there soon. Please, hold on to yourself. Don't leave me.~

Her hand clenched slightly. She felt his warmth as if he were next to her. She started to drift again, but the pain in her broken hand and slashed wrist and belly brought her back. The stone table, icy against her back, sucked at her body heat.

She watched Pol help Readen to one of the pillars, carefully carrying the brimming bowl in front of him. Dipping his fingers in the blood, Readen began tracing it into the symbols on one side of the pillar, chanting more strange words, "Dalla, Itza Larrak, Alka Ra," again and again. She watched, transfixed through the haze of her pain, as the symbols began to glow dull red.

A dark cloud of motes appeared beside the pillar, and an enormous shape began to coalesce. Readen chanted louder, faster, "Dalla, Itza Larrak, Alka Ra," again and again. The figure leached light from the room, gradually taking form.

The torches along the walls flickered, throwing wild shadows. A giant, winged beast, a grotesque, hulking creature, exuding power, formed out of the dark mist. Its black form absorbed the light around it, creating a halo of darkness.

Ugly, and at the same time oddly beautiful, it settled two clawed feet firmly on the stone floor of the cavern and looked at Marta, cold avidity in its deep-set yellow eyes. Its eerily humanoid appearance terrified her.

Thin, metallic wings furled and unfurled behind it and a delicate ringing sound bounced and echoed through the cavern. Nudging a panting Readen aside, it licked Marta's blood from the pillar.

"Ah, this one is perfect!" Soft, sibilant sounds that Marta could barely hear sent cold fear piercing into her to lodge hard against her heart, to freeze her lungs until she gasped to breathe. "Finally, you have brought me my way back into Adalta."

Altan reached the basement, following the path from Marta's memories. Running on pure adrenaline, he snatched a heavy ring of iron keys from the guardroom wall and started searching the cells. She wasn't there. He found Malyk in one of the cells deep toward the end of a long tunnel. The cell door next to his hung open.

There was no sign of Marta, but he knew she'd been there. He sharpened his Air senses. Her essence was faint, but it was there, just discernible through the prison stench. He swallowed his panic. There, on the grey sheet, lay a small gold circle, her earring.

Malyk sat on his filthy cot, grey head in his hands. He looked up, his eyes blank, when Altan called his name for the second time. "Who are you?"

"Altan Me'Gerron, sir. Where is Marta? What has he...?

"I'm sorry. I had to eat the food. I was getting so weak." Malyk's words slurred. His head threatened to drop to his chest again. He straightened with effort.

Altan took a deep breath. His heart beat faster as he stifled his impatience. "Yes, sir, I understand, sir. But where have they taken her?" Malyk looked around him, dazed, and stood, his eyes focusing toward the empty cell next to him.

"Oh, they took her." His voice was desolate.

"Where?" Altan repeated, clenching his teeth in frustration. His body strained toward the man. Then he remembered the keys. He fumbled with the lock and swung the bars open. He took Malyk carefully by the shoulders and turned the slack face of the old man toward him.

"Can you concentrate? Where did they take her? I didn't find her in any of the cells." He forced the dazed man to look him in the eyes, willing him to focus. He took a deep, shaking breath. Panic could do him no good.

Malyk licked his lips. "Oh, yes, I remember you now." He shook his head. "They took her to the cavern."

"What cavern? Where?"

He turned his head to the end of the hallway.

"There."

Altan looked. "There's nothing there!"

"Yes," he whispered, shivering. "Yes, there is."

Altan turned to leave then looked back around. "Your cell is open. You can make your way back upstairs. Daryl will have the keep secured by now. You'll be safe."

A surge of kindness and pity for the old man he remembered as so strong welled up. "You'll be safe," he repeated, and he turned away from the mixed hope and fear on the old man's face as he stared at the open door of his cell.

Marta screamed again, her throat so torn her cries were scarcely audible. The knife moved slowly, deliberately, cutting another shallow line across her right breast. It burned with fire. Warm blood spread down her ribs.

Pol held the bloody knife up in front of her face and smiled. "Do you want to choose where I cut you next, beautiful lady?" He leaned close over her, his voice soft, his other hand sliding up and down her arm in a terrifying parody of concern.

"Tell us where Daryl is. Tell us what he plans to do." Readen's voice was stronger.

He doesn't know what's happening. I just need to hold out a little longer. Altan will come. Marta ignored the frailness of her hope. She tried to move away from the silver knife.

Her body, naked now, her clothes cut away, burned everywhere from a hundred stinging slices of the little knife, deep ones, shallow ones. The raw bump on the back of her head ached and pulsed with the erratic beats of her heart.

Pol pressed a fat finger hard on her crushed hand. A white flash of pain screamed through her. She squeezed her eyes shut and reached through the pain and confusion for her connection with Adalta. Once again a rush of searing power suffused her, separating her from the pain. She floated in the comforting green. A fringed wingtip brushed her mind.

The dark monster paced around the rectangular limestone table, its form a shimmering, shifting blue-black, its movements sinuous. Its talons clicked on the stone floor. The clicking noise stopped. The soft singing of its metallic wings chimed behind her head.

"Try again now, Readen, my own son," it said. "Forget your worry about your brother. It's this female you must take. I have given you the spells. You must possess her and make her immense channels mine. They reach deep into the heart of Adalta, pure, empty, virgin channels. She is my way back to this world."

"You must try, Pol." Readen pushed a reluctant Pol toward the table. "Take that stone from her."

Marta closed her eyes and focused a searing beam of green and gold light on her opal. Pol reached, his hand shaking, hesitant. His fingers touched the pendant, and another fiery ball of power pulsed through her. Pol fell back and landed hard on the floor, his body crumpled, twisted, his face screwed in pain, anger, and shock.

"Why isn't this working? How can she be stronger than Malyk? She's not even from this world. Why can't we take her power? The stone protects her. How can we get it off?" Readen's tone was high, the voice of an angry, frightened, petulant child.

"It is not her power I need. It is her body. She is my way back. When her body is mine, I can leave this cavern prison and begin again to make this planet Larrak."

The Itza Larrak's voice sent cold terror deep into Marta. She shook, her shivers uncontrolled.

"You don't seem to be any help," Readen snapped.

Talons clicked toward Readen, and the Itza Larrak's shifting

SHERRILL NILSON

image swirled around him. Readen fell to the floor, his hands over
his head, his body jerking.

"You have doubts, little one?" The voice was even softer, its
menace tangible in the flickering light of the chamber.

"No, no. I'm sorry. I'm sorry. I don't mean to doubt you."
Readen's shrill voice echoed. The Itza Larrak moved away from
him, and Readen pushed back to his feet, his movements slow and
careful as if his very skin was on fire.

The clicking sounds resumed as the creature circled Marta's
table again. Unable to look away, her eyes followed it. The Itza
Larrak walked, around and around, yellow eyes never leaving her.

CHAPTER THIRTY-FIVE

Altan moved through the labyrinth of dark passageways leading beyond Marta's cell. He grimaced, and a small ball of light rolled off his fingers and floated in front of him, lighting his way. Concentrating on Marta's memories, he made his way, cursing at every false turn, to a small door with a warded lock hidden in a shallow nook where the passage seemed to dead end.

He touched it gingerly. A sharp tingle jumped to his fingers. He understood Reardon's arcane wards now. He skimmed his fingers across it, concentrated hard. There it was. He wrapped his talent around the strands of alien magic and pulled hard, listened for the snap, pushed the door open, and ducked through.

He sensed a new presence somewhere ahead of him down the long, narrow passage, its malevolence palpable. His anger flared, heating the opal against his chest.

He stopped just inside and leaned against the wall, dizzy, so exhausted his legs shook. His muscles spasmed. His head pounded as spent adrenalin washed out of his body. Pain bloomed from a myriad of small sword cuts and one larger one.

She was ahead of him. Oh, Adalta, such torture. He felt every cut on her body. Even in the midst of fighting, he had felt them—

now, they all but overwhelmed him. Suddenly the opal at his throat flared searing hot against his skin, and coruscating colors blazed through his shirt.

His eyes closed, and breath hissed from his lungs. His legs collapsed, and he slid down the wall to the damp floor. Fighting through Marta's pain and his exhaustion, he reached for his connection with Adalta. He jerked as a fresh wave of terror lanced through him, and the opal flared hot again, burning his chest.

Something was with her besides Readen. He could taste the evil. He had never experienced such corruption, even near the Circles of Disorder. He swallowed against the tightness in his throat and pressed his cheek against the cold wall, his fist tight around the opal pendant.

Altan reached again, pulling strength from the bedrock of Adalta. He could hear soft crooning in his head. Kibrath and Sidhari sang strength into him, into Marta. He drew from them. Tears ran through the dried blood on his face, dripping off his jaw and turning the dried bloody splashes on his tunic red again.

His head swirled until he couldn't tell whose pain stabbed through his body. He rolled to his knees, breathing heavily, muscles burning, but he couldn't push himself to his feet. He had used his body too hard—fighting and sending energy to Marta. It was too much. He reached deeper into the ground beneath the stone floor.

A growing warmth began to burn away the fatigue and the spent adrenaline. Slowly he solidified his link with the heart of Adalta. Strength moved into his legs, his arms. The discomfort from his cuts and bruises intensified, but it was strength he needed. He couldn't afford to heal himself now.

Holding fast to the opal, he channeled as much as he could through his connection to Marta, fighting to keep a balance between his own need for strength and hers, forcing himself not to give her so much it weakened him. *What creature am I going to have to fight?*

Altan rose to his feet, brightened the ball of light glowing in front of him, and started down the passageway, stronger every minute. A hot stab in his right wrist dizzied him for a moment. He breathed great gulps of air, pushing more fatigue away. The sense of evil grew

stronger. He ran, the light ball throwing wild patterns on the stone walls ahead of him.

Marta was weakening. The lacerations all over her body burned. Pol had begun to cut the sensitive skin on the inside of her thighs. Unthinkable thoughts about Readen raping her seeped in despite all she could do to keep them away. How much longer could she keep him away? Every breath was excruciating. Pain flared every time her chest moved. She closed her eyes, listening to the clicking of the Itza Larrak's clawed feet circling her. It stopped, and she opened her eyes.

The creature leaned close over her, its flickering body not solid enough to touch her. Glittering yellow eyes in its too-close-to-human face searched hers. She shivered, beyond terror, hypnotized.

Talon-tipped metallic digits traced intricate patterns as they moved down her body, inches from her bloody skin. Where they passed, her flesh spasmed in a twisting rope of agony.

She shivered and fought to remain conscious. Her eyesight darkened around the edges. She could think of nothing but throbbing hurt and the grotesque monster leaning over her. The sibilant song of its delicate metallic wings, furling and unfurling in slow movements, stirred her terror higher and higher until it rang loud in her ears.

"Something helps her." Its face contorted. "My enemy," it breathed. "I can sense it. Adalta is in her." Its hands hovered over the opal. "And a human being. This is the focus. This jewel links her to the human from whom she draws strength. You must break this link."

Marta heard it move around the head of the table. It spoke again. "If I can take over her body, I can reach deep into Adalta. Her channels are pure and wide, just waiting to be used. I will drain Adalta this time. I waited eons for this, Readen, my own son. Eons to create one like you who could bring me back. Who could free me from this cursed cavern. You must remove her life force from this body, Readen. You must. You have the spell."

It stalked toward one of the pillars. Its voice echoed horribly through the chamber. "More blood," the Itza Larrak hissed at Pol.

Marta turned her head, her eyes, on the big man who cringed and moved as though pulled forward, hands rubbing at his sides, eyes flicking between Marta and Readen, between the Itza Larrak and the cavern entrance.

Pol's hands shook as he held Marta's left arm over the small silver bowl and sliced sharply down her wrist. Her head swirled, and blood flowed into the cup. She longed for oblivion, for surrender to the blackness that surrounded her, but her wracked body refused to let go. He placed a thick pad against the cut and wrapped a bandage tight around it.

Her vision dark around the edges from pain and loss of blood, she watched Pol carry the little bowl carefully to the column where the Itza Larrak waited with Readen. It was brim full.

She was nauseous and weak. She strained at the thongs holding her, breathing as deeply as her injured body would let her. Several of the freshly scabbed cuts broke open. More blood seeped into the stone.

She watched as Readen rubbed her blood into the symbols on the pillar. The opal burned against her skin. It blazed color. Refractions of its light glittered above her on the ceiling of the immense cavern.

The Itza Larrak chanted the same strange syllables Readen had used before in a low, tuneless hiss. "Galal sabitti ata me peta baka." The symbols began to glow red. The monster, more solid now, closed black talons around Readen's wrist. It rubbed and scraped his hand up and down the symbols on the column.

Readen moaned and struggled to pull away. It didn't stop, forced his hand down each long column of symbols, pressing hard, smearing Marta's blood and Readen's into the grooves of the arcane symbols. When it released him, Readen collapsed. He lay on the floor beneath the pillar, the Itza Larrak chanting over him, then he pushed up, his brown hair black with sweat. His exultant face radiated dark power.

Readen's eyes focused on Marta. She shuddered and watched him walk toward her, filled with power stolen with her own blood.

~Marta, I'm nearly there.~

Altan's sudden voice in her head sounded loud, sharp as if he stood next to her. She moved her head side to side on the stone.

~Marta, I'm nearly there.~ The voice was insistent, repeating the words over and over. Her eyes blinked. Tears dripped down the sides of her face into her sweat-soaked hair.

She began to sink through the stone into the bones of Adalta. Deeper and deeper, surrounded by water and rock, the bones and blood of the planet, she sank into the heart of Adalta. Darkness lifted and a pinpoint of light grew in the distance. She felt the rush of giant wings.

The bright, green-gold radiance of newly unfurling leaves bloomed beneath her diaphragm, spreading through her. Bit by bit it seeped into her, and the pain her body suffered faded into it. She floated, feeling the light accumulate, suffusing her.

Clarity burned through Marta's mind. Motes of brilliant light stormed around her, an armor of strength. It threw back the darkness that emanated from the chanting Itza Larrak and the exultant Readen.

Marta saw every detail of her life. Of her childhood, of the death of her father and the barrenness and loneliness that followed. Altan's face shining with love, her connection with Sidhari, with the other Karda, with her Mi'hiru friends, the small sycamore as its essence surged through her.

All of it, every connection she made on Adalta, melded together to forge her resilience. Finally, she remembered with perfect clarity the dream of Adalta when she first arrived on the planet. She experienced anew its force and power.

With a gasp, Marta embraced the surge of power flooding her talent channels from the center of Adalta. She welcomed it, breathing it in. Her reach expanded over the surface of the planet, drawing from the roots of the trees and grasses, the rocks, and the trickles and plunges of water carrying life through them.

She reached up into the wind, the clouds of life-giving rain, feeling the warmth of the huge red-gold sun, the green of the grasses and trees slowly spreading over the barrenness that had nearly destroyed Adalta eons before. Marta reached for it all.

She reached for Altan's love and strength. She reached for Sidhari, for all the Karda she felt gracing the skies of Restal. She drew it in. All of it, all the power of Adalta, she gathered into her. The stone lying on her chest burned and glowed. Her back arched and her body contorted with spasms. Her mind stretched toward breaking with the immensity of it. Time slowed to one long, searing, soaring moment as the power of Adalta pulsed and flooded into her flesh, into her bones, into her being.

Light gathered, and she opened her eyes. It swirled into the enormous spirit Karda of Adalta, radiant, angry, wings mantled, its great, hooked beak opened in a scream that filled the cavern. A crystal in the wall shattered. Adalta faced the Itza Larrak across Marta's form.

"You cannot have my planet," Adalta said. Her powerful raptor's beak pointed toward Readen. "This one is defeated. He has nothing but the empty words of your empty mysteries. However much blood he drenches them with, he cannot hold against Marta. She is a creature forged in love and life." She nodded toward Readen again. "His is but a selfish quest for power bought with the agony and death of others. He fails."

"You are wrong." The Itza Larrak's fury battered against Marta. "This planet will be the Larrak's now. We will feed on its destruction. I will awaken my army. I will call the others of my kind to me. This one,"—it gestured one taloned hand toward Marta—"is useless to you. She cannot hold against my son. Her body will be mine."

Marta reached as far as the loose tether on her arm allowed, grabbed Readen's wrist, and held hard. Power burned through her body, her mind, her soul.

He tried to jerk away.

Her back arched in a savage spasm, but she held fast against his struggles.

Readen collapsed in violent convulsions to the stone floor.

A harsh, grating scream echoed through the cavern, pounding against the walls, and the Itza Larrak disappeared.

The torches flamed out, and the cavern was black.

Cool, green feathery blankness settled over Marta, and she lost herself in it, resting, healing.

Altan stopped at the entrance to the darkened cavern, stunned. His ears rang with echoes of the horrible scream. The malevolent presence was gone. Silence filled the enormous space in front of him, holding him, frozen.

He struggled to brighten his small ball of light. His boots rang harsh on the stone floor as he ran, fear tearing at him. Marta lay still on the limestone block, her body striped with blood, her chest barely moving. Readen lay crumpled and senseless on the floor beside her. Altan shoved him aside and reached for her. Her clothes and the ropes that bound her were ashes.

He shook out of his tunic, wrapped it around her, and picked her up gingerly in his arms. Her body weighed little more than a half- grown youth. Her skin was translucent, not a mark on it despite the blood smeared across her, drenching the stone beneath.

Altan hiccuped a sob. He bent his head and pressed his lips to her sweat and blood soaked hair. She was too pale: dark smudges surrounded her sunken eyes. Her bloody body had no visible wounds, but he wondered what cuts and bruises still bloodied her mind.

He held her for time unending, pouring strength into her with everything his talent could bring. He didn't look up until he heard Daryl enter the cavern.

Three of Daryl's men were behind him, faces pale, eyes wide. Exchanging a long, silent look with Altan, Daryl nodded and walked to Readen, crumpled unconscious on the floor beside the limestone block.

He stared down at him for a long moment, his face hard with emotions Altan couldn't name, then abruptly motioned his men to pick up the unconscious figure. "Lock him in a cell away from everyone." He led the way back down the tunnel, a small ball of light in front of him, Altan carrying Marta behind.

The walk back through the tunnel, past the cells, and up the stairs to the keep above was interminable. Altan carried her as gently as he could, not wanting to hurt her further. He never looked up from Marta's white face, framed by bloody wet snakes of auburn hair.

The halls upstairs were secure. The sentries he had posted smiled as they saw him approach, full of the news of their success. The smiles faded as they saw his pale burden and his tear-streaked face. "She's not dead," he repeated fiercely over and over. "She's not dead."

Daryl stopped at the top of the stairs to the second floor. "There's a room for you just through here." With a glance at the frail figure in Altan's arms, he tightened his lips and led his friend down the hall into a large, light-filled room. "There is a bath through that door to your right with hot running water from the roof cisterns. I'll have one of the helpers bring a night shift for her. I've sent for our packs. They'll be here shortly."

Altan nodded. He barely registered the words. Daryl left quietly.

Altan carried her to the bath, turned on the wall spigots, and unwrapped her. He ran warm water to cover her, removed his filthy clothes, and stepped in, easing himself behind her, cradling her against him, washing her body with a soft cloth. Dried and flaking blood covered her body, but there was not a single wound on her pale, pale skin.

The water ran red, blood from the deep slice on his arm mingling with hers. He turned the spigot to let more hot water flow, letting it run through her hair, rubbing in soap that smelled of chamomile and rosemary, and rinsing it over and over.

She'd hate the horrible mess of her hair, he thought, and felt a smile twitch the corner of his mouth. What a small thing to fret about. He sat holding her against his chest until the water cooled. He heard the door to the other room open and close twice, the maid with towels, someone with a night shift, his pack.

He lifted Marta carefully and carried her to the bed in the big room. Drying her with the soft towels, he pulled the shift over her head. He found a carved wooden comb on a dresser and crawled into the bed with her, bodies damp from the bath. Settling her against his chest, he pulled up the linen sheet and a wool blanket, tucking them around them both, and gently began to work at the tangled mess of her hair, not thinking of anything but the feel of the damp auburn strands on his sword- calloused hands.

He laid her head carefully on the pillow and curled himself around her, his face buried in her wet curls, and gave himself over to tears and sleep and the sweet-sharp smell of herbal soap.

Two days later, Marta smiled at him as Altan helped her up the steep path. Littered with rocks and overgrown with bushes, unused for years, it was barely visible. They stopped on a small ledge and sat together on a rock, leaning against the hillside. He turned her toward him, tracing his fingers down the side of her face. ~We'll rest here. Are you sure you're up to this? I can do it myself, you know.~

~I know. But I have to do this. I just need to rest for a moment. It feels good to be outside.~ She looked up at him. "No one ever needs to be able to get into this cavern again. Daryl collapsed the other end. We need to seal this passage."

She spoke aloud for the first time since the cavern, her voice firm and determined. "I wish I could do it myself. I know I might have the talent now, but without your help, I don't have the knowledge or control."

She felt him watching her face as she looked down the steep hillside to Restal Prime spread out below them, the rambling wings and courtyards of Restal Keep, the square towers with their tall arched windows, the spare dry hills with their patchwork of green fields beyond the walls. Light glinted off the neglected greenhouses.

He was worried, she knew, but she relaxed into the peace inside her. And the strength—not physical, she was still weak—of her talent. It was there—shining inside her. He reached for her hand, cradling her long fingers in his calloused palm, playing with them. She twisted around to smile up at him, and his tension eased.

They moved on up the rough, obscure trail, picking their way carefully through loose rocks, thick roots, and overhanging bushes. They stood together at the top, looking across the wide, deep ravine at the small, dark hole in the cliffside that opened into a tortuous tunnel to the cavern below the mountain.

"I think this will do," she said and moved to the side of the trail to sit on a large flat rock, warm from the sunlight, patting it beside her. He sat with his arm around her, and she rested her head against his shoulder.

She was still short of breath, but the peace she felt inside wouldn't allow any irritation or impatience about it. She stirred before she could get too comfortable. She still tended to get lost in that peace if she wasn't careful. The feeling was lessening—it was part of her healing, she knew. Not the outside body healing, but the inside hurts that cut deeper.

Altan helped. Sidhari helped—her news about the fledglings helped. But mostly, she knew, it was Adalta taking care of her.

She looked up at him. "Are you ready?" He smiled down at her. "Always."

She felt inside her for the Earth talent roiling and pushing at her and reached for him. Her mind curled together with his, followed his experienced lead, felt his steady control bolster her when she faltered.

She felt her way into the cliff above the opening, into the dirt and around the rocks, building and knotting their connections, sending her request deep into the craggy hillside across from where they sat. She marveled at this amazing new Earth talent.

They began to tug, slowly, inexorably. The ground surged as the stones and dirt of the cliff opposite them began to slump. They pulled harder. Sweat shined on Marta's face, dripped through her hair and between her breasts.

Altan's strength wove with hers in unbreakable tendrils, adding the control she didn't yet have, branching wide, pushing their way into the belly of the hill.

The cliffside across from them began to move. Thunder sounded—growling—growing.

Then with a great rush, the cliff fell, rocks scattering and tumbling to the bottom of the ravine. They watched in wonder as clouds of dust surged and boiled.

They sat for a long time while the thick dust settled to the grass around them, Alton's un-bandaged arm firm around her shoulders. She rested one hand on his chest, the other arm tight around his waist, her head on his shoulder.

Rain began to drizzle. He pulled his cloak up over their heads and wrapped it around them. Muddy drops fell on their outstretched legs.

Marta drew up her knees. The drizzle cleared the air 0f dust, and she saw the massive tumble of rocks and dirt that covered the entrance to the cavern.

~It's done now, love. Both entrances sealed behind tons of rock.~

She sat, silent for several long minutes. ~I hope so.~

He dropped his cheek to her hair and pushed the loose drifts of it back behind her ears.

He kissed the top of her head. She drew in the smells of salty sweat, leather, and the woodsy scent of his soap, and she knew she would be all right.

They sat together for a long, long time before they stood to walk, hand in hand, back down the mountainside.

EPILOGUE

R eaden came back to consciousness slowly, head splitting, body aching in every muscle, every joint, unable to move a finger without pain. His eyes searched the dimly lit space around him. His fingers explored the hard surface below him, the rough blanket wadded against his side. Bars formed in his vision. Gradually, he realized he was inside them. Locked, like one of his own prisoners, in a cell.

Rage—the impotent rage he had felt as a child, again and again as Daryl bested him at everything he tried—suffused him. Daryl had bested him again. Altan, Marta—they didn't matter. It was Daryl who won. The always-so-solicitous, always-so-apologetic- about- besting-him Daryl.

"Pol!" he shouted. "Pol!" Again and again, he called out to the jailor who had served him for years, since his childhood. He shook with frustration. He reached his consciousness out toward the cavern and failed, his power depleted, erased. All the knowledge and power he had worked for since he was a small boy was locked away from him. He knew they had destroyed the cavern.

He had only what was in his memory. It would have to be enough. He tried to reach for a Circle of Disorder, but there was no power to aid him. He called out to the Itza Larrak and heard empty silence. He lay on the hard bunk in an eternity of helpless fury.

The echoing sound of boots on stone, flickering light, and a rattle of keys roused him. He watched through slitted eyes as a guard set a lantern on the stone floor. He opened the cell door, pushed a tray of food and a bottle of water through, then closed and locked it again. Readen wanted to lick his lips at the guard's nervousness, his wary looks at what he thought was Readen's unconscious form. A tiny trickle of power from the guard's fear seeped into Readen. He waited until the man had disappeared back up the hall before he got up and retrieved the tray. He ate slowly and thoughtfully, swallowing rage with every bite.

Readen pulled the rough blanket around him against the cold and damp and began to forge that hot rage into a cold, unbreakable weapon of revenge.

ALSO BY SHERRILL NILSON

Hunter Adalta Vol II Available on

Amazon

Falling Adalta Vol III

Amazon

Read on for an excerpt of *Hunter* after

Acknowledgements

ACKNOWLEDGMENTS

I could not have written this book without my sister, Alice V. Brock, author of the prize-winning mid-grade historical novel, *A River of Cattle*. We spend so much time working together we are almost co-authors. I've had support and encouragement from all my talented family, including Phil Vincent (author of the thriller *Varuna*), Jeri, Abbie, BJ, Heather (for the romance), Jim, Keith, Myrna, Brett, Daniel (for the fight scenes), and my friends Monica and Lorrie—all of whose careful reading made the book so much better. Special kudos to Kurt Nilson, whose cover makes the Karda come alive and whose illustrations add so much to these books, and Sven Nilson for his immaculate formatting help.

Special thanks to story editor Nathan Riding, to Reina-Shay Broussard and Eve Church, proof readers. And to so many who supported me when I was disheartened or off track—I hope you know who you are and how much I appreciate you. Thank you to Jody Thomas at the West Texas Writing Academy, to Margie Lawson of the Lawson Writer's Academy. Also the members of Austin's premier fantasy/science fiction critique group, Slugtribe, who helped me early in my process before I moved back to Tulsa.

It takes a village to write a book.

ABOUT THE AUTHOR

Sherrill Nilson used to raise horses. Now she writes about flying horses—with hawk heads and wicked talons. Author of the Adalta Series, she's been a cattle rancher, horse breeder, environmentalist, mother of three, traveler to exotic places—even a tarot card reader. She lived in Santa Fe and Ruidoso, NM, San Francisco, and Austin after leaving the hills of Eastern Oklahoma and her ranch.

She lives, writes, and reads SciFi/fantasy in Tulsa, Oklahoma— back where she started as the oldest of seven kids (don't ask to drive), three of whom are writers.

She doesn't have a dog, a cat, or even a bird, but she does have an old Volvo convertible and loves to drive around with the wind blowing her hair. It's how she gets her vitamin D.

SherrillNilson.com

 facebook.com/SLNilson

 twitter.com/sherrillnilson

 instagram.com/sherrill.nilson_author

SAY HELLO

Sign up for my newsletter at www.sherrillnilson.com.
I sometimes post working-version scenes from the next novel in the series, versions of the next book cover, etc., and I will appreciate your comments.
Join me on my Facebook page, follow me on Twitter @sherrillnilson and @sherrill.nilson_author on Instagram, visit my Amazon Author Page. You can email me at sherrillnilson.com/contact.
And if you liked this book, leave a review on Amazon and/or Goodreads.
I'll appreciate hearing from you. Telling me what you like (or don't like) makes me a better writer and makes me write faster. It's nice to get to know the people who read my books.

Please read on for an excerpt from

Hunter: Adalta Vol II:

HUNTER:ADALTA VOL II

Excerpt from Chapter One:

Tessa Me'Cowyn paced from her window to her bed to the door. She pressed her ear to the varnished oak. She could hear clashes of metal on metal, shouts, screams, running feet echoing up to the corridor, growing closer, louder, ever more threatening.

Or was this finally rescue?

After weeks as a hostage in Readen's keep, the elegance of the furnishings, the thick rug, the private bathing room didn't make Tessa feel any less trapped.

She dropped into a chair at the table and pushed away her cold, half-finished breakfast. If she didn't get out of here soon, she'd smother. She sucked a breath through her tight throat and looked toward the door. Who's winning?

The door smashed open and splintered against the wall. One of Readen's mercenaries stepped through. His unkempt hair waved wildly in his aroused Air talent.

Tessa jumped to her feet, knife in one hand, fork in the other. Her heart slammed into her throat. Her mind a startled *can't think, can't think.* She stared at his bloodied sword. She stared at the slow you're-all-mine-little-girl smile spreading across his hard face.

She backed away. Her breath refused to come.

He followed, sheathed the sword, unbuckled the belt, let it fall to the floor.

She forced her feet to move, to get past him to the door. He stepped closer.

Her breath stuttered. She choked on his rank smell of sweat, blood, and battle.

"Watched you for days. You're the prettiest of all the hostages." His voice was low, harsh, gravelly with lust.

"I'm a protected hostage. If you touch me, the regent will kill you." Her too high voice squeaked in her ears. Tessa recognized him now—Dix Ward. He'd stared at her every time she went to the main hall at dinner. Stopped her in the halls with a too-friendly hand on her arm until she refused to go anywhere without one of the other hostages and started keeping her room locked. She swallowed the tiny bit of moisture left in her mouth and edged closer to the door.

"The regent"—the sneer was audible in his voice—"is too busy right now. Or off in his cellars again. He won't be Regent long. We're losin' the battle. I'm takin' what I can. Then I'm out of here. Maybe you'll wanna come with me. Time to get a little closer so I can show you why." He unbuttoned his tight breeches, moved to block her from the door, and grabbed for her.

Tessa slashed at him with the knife and jumped back. A line of blood beaded across the back of his hand.

He laughed, bringing his hand to his mouth. His tongue licked the blood. He thrust with his hips. "Such a little knife against this big sword."

She ducked to the right. He moved faster. He seized her arm and slung her toward the bed. Tessa stumbled over his belt and fell on top of the sword.

She rolled away and grabbed the hilt with both hands, scrambling to get a knee under her, trying to jerk it from the scabbard.

He grabbed the scabbard. Tessa held on, and the sword pulled free. He laughed harder and tossed the sheath to the side. "Such a big sword for a sweet little bit like you. I've got a better one you can grab."

Tessa braced herself on one knee, both hands tight on the hilt, and shoved the blade straight up in front of her just as he lunged. It cut up into his chest, buried almost to the cross guard. He looked down. His eyes widened in disbelief and filmed over with the opaque veil of death.

He let out a long breath. His knees collapsed. His body fell on her, flattening Tessa on her back. The sword pommel jabbed into her diaphragm. Her breath whooshed out.

Her face mashed into the hollow of his shoulder, and she couldn't breathe. Her lips clamped tight against the welling blood from his dying heart.

She shoved. Hard. Her hands wouldn't let go of the sword. They were trapped.

Tessa shoved harder, fighting for air. He was heavy. Too heavy.

Twisting to the side, she shoved again. Freeing one leg from her tangled skirt, she hooked it around his big thigh, pushed and pulled herself out from under his torso. The scratchy wool of his jacket dug into her cheek. His body rolled to its back. One arm flopped over and slapped loud on the stone floor.

The sword frozen in her hands, she stood, put her foot on his chest and pulled. It slid out of his chest with a horrible sucking sound.

She shook so hard she could barely stand. The clash of swords and yelling men outside her room receded. The room shrank till all she saw was the blood on the sword, on her hands.

Tessa stumbled to the spindly chair beside the table and rested her head on her knees. Her hands gripped the sword hilt like they were glued.

Gradually her breathing slowed, and her head cleared. She forced her fingers away from the sword and dropped it on the table. Blood stained the white cloth, blending with a spill of bright red preserves. Tessa stared at the sword, refusing to look at the body sprawled near the bed. She staggered toward the bathing room and scrubbed at the blood on her hands, her face, her throat. Tessa leaned over the water bowl for a long time trying not to shake, trying not to feel the blood that soaked her blouse, trying not to think.

She'd watched people die. Her mother—

But this time she'd killed.

Urgent need sent her whirling to the commode. She retched until her stomach muscles could force nothing more out and sank to the floor. The cold flagstones pulled the heat out of her face, out of the image of the body lying twisted and still by the bed. Soothed the nausea that welled from the clammy, wet feeling of the dark purple splotches of blood on her fine blue linen shirt.

She tore at her clothes. *Get them off. Get them off.* She stripped, throwing everything in a corner. Holding a towel under the faucet, she soaked it and scrubbed her body everywhere she could reach, trying not to see the blood and the pink-tinged water dripping on the floor.

But he might not be the only mercenary roaming this wing of the keep. She forced herself back into the other room, breath coming in hard gasps. She froze. His body sprawled on the floor, blood seeping between the flagstones.

Biting hard on her lip, Tessa un-froze, grabbed the coverlet from her bed and threw it over the body. It missed his head, and his open eyes stared at her. The man would have raped her. He'd laughed at the sword in her hands, seeing only the beautiful face, the long silver hair.

Shaking, muscles quivering, adrenaline washing out of her, she pulled open her wardrobe, grabbed a tunic and split skirt and pulled them on. She fell into a chair. How did one ever get over killing someone, even in self-defense? *How could I do that? How did I know what to do when my mind couldn't work?*

Minutes passed. The yelling, the sound of battle faded to silence. The long sword lay on her breakfast tray still leaking blood into the splotch of bright red preserves. *I'll never be able to eat cherryapples again.* Tessa forced her legs to support her and moved past the broken door into the hall. She had to get away from the body lying on her floor, get away from the blood, get away from the room that hadn't even been a *safe* prison.

She ran. And smashed into a broad chest. Hands gripped her arms hard. Tessa screamed and fought, kicking, biting, struggling to get loose. Her chest was bursting, her throat tearing with frantic screams.

"Hush, lass. Hush. Do you na know me? Hush, now. It's Cael, Tessa. It's Cael. Hush, now. Tell me what's wrong."

She stilled and looked up at the broad, deeply lined face almost hidden by his leather helmet. "Cael. Cael." She knew him. Cael, who had been her father's armsmaster for years until he disappeared when she was twelve. Her body began to shake so hard she could only stand because he held her arms. "I killed him, Cael. I killed him."

Cael pulled her to his chest, and she felt him jerk when he saw the body on the floor inside the room. "So I see, lass. So I see. I know him. He's a bad one. You did good, Tess. You remembered what I taught you before I— You did good."

He pushed her away from him, rubbing his hands up and down her arms. "Now remember what else I taught you. You do what you have to do, and then you move on to what you have to do next." He held her gaze, matching her breath for breath until she began to calm, then let go.

Tessa staggered then caught her balance. She looked at his leather jerkin and helmet. "You're one of Readen's men. Cael, how could you be one of Readen's men?" She stepped back.

He looked behind her down the hall. "I can't explain now, Tessa. I have to get away before I'm found. Just don't tell anyone you saw me. Except Krager. Tell him. But only him." He touched her shoulder. "I was right, Tessa. And your father was wrong. You are extraordinary." And he left her standing, staring after him, but calmer, oddly calmer.

He left so long ago she'd almost forgotten him. She talked him into giving her sword lessons when she was ten. They kept at it for two years until her father discovered them, and Cael disappeared.

She took a deep, stuttering breath and turned away from the carnage in her room. She had to think about something else, move on to the next thing like Cael said.

Wounded. There would be wounded. *My blocked talents may make me useless as a healer, but I can still do triage and basic nursing.* Tessa skipped over the thought that there would be more blood.

Tessa ran as fast as she could, stopped before she turned each corner and watched for Readen's mercenaries, but she saw only a few dead bodies. Her stomach lurched each time. Four guards stood in the corridor at the bottom of the third stairway. They wore purple and yellow armbands—the colors of the guardian heir— Daryl Me'Vere's colors. Her steps faltered, knees weak with relief. The usurper Readen was defeated.

The lieutenant caught her before she fell. "You're Tessa Me'Cowyn, aren't you?" His voice was so steady, so strong and sure, relief threatened to take her legs from under her. Daryl had won. The rightful heir was back and in control. "Your father is looking all over for you."

"I'll need to get to wherever the wounded are. And someone will need to send for healers."

"They've probably already been sent for, but to be sure—" He nodded at two of the guards who left at a run. "The wounded are brought to the receiving hall. We'll take you there. Not good to be roaming these corridors by yourself. No telling who you might run into.""

Tessa swallowed. One of those no-telling-whos had already run into her. "There's a body in my room. I...I..." Her tongue was thick, her words distant in her ear.

He nodded. A flicker of respect crossed the concern in his face. "I'll take care of it."

The doors to the huge receiving hall stood open. All she could see were wounded and dying. She saw no healers. None of the other girls who'd been held hostage with her were there. A few scattered servants helped the injured, doing their best. But they were overwhelmed and under-trained. She was all there was. And she wasn't enough.

The keep's steward, Lerys, stood, red-faced, arms flying, arguing with another lieutenant. "Guardian Roland won't stand for these people bloodying up the hall. Send them to Healer's Hospice. They'll be taken care of there."

Tessa couldn't believe her ears.

The lieutenant was having the same problem. "You need to bring more linens, sir. And fresh. This pile of cleaning rags won't do." He gestured to the mound of cloth in the arms of the servant behind Lerys. Tessa recognized Elda.

Lerys stepped back half a step, palms out in front of him. "The guardian—"

Tessa stepped in front of him. "Guardian Roland isn't here. No one's seen him for two tendays, and these guards need help now."

"Miss Tessa. You shouldn't be here." He turned to the lieutenant, his tone officious. "Have someone escort the holder's daughter to her room. It's not appropriate for her to be—"

She interrupted him. Fury scoured away any fear, any feeling of inadequacy. "Lerys. Bring everything you have. I'll need pallets, sheets, even tablecloths. Whatever we can tear into bandages. I'll need alcohol and all the herbs, tonics, and antibiotic salves you can find. These people are bleeding and dying."

"All I have left are the good linens. I can't have them all bloody and—"

Tessa turned to the tiny housekeeper standing just out of Lerys's line of sight. "Melayne, you know what we need."

The woman nodded and left in a hurry.

"You can't just override my orders." Lerys sputtered and spittle sprayed. He turned to the two guardsmen behind Tessa. "Take her to her room."

They both shrugged. She was a holder's daughter. She outranked the steward.

Tessa ignored him and turned to the room filling with wounded, cursing her blocked talent. She should be able to heal them. Instead, too many would die before the healers arrived. All she could do was sort out the most severely injured, stabilize them and be grateful that she never stopped studying despite her blocked talent. There was still much she could do, and right now it was triage that was most important. *The healers won't be long. Please, Adalta, let the healers not be long.*

She turned to the servant holding the cloths. "Elda, are these clean?" Elda nodded. "Then start tearing them into strips. Fold some pads." The woman laid her bundle down and started ripping.

A young guard with a slashed abdomen lay on the floor just inside the door of the receiving hall. Tessa grabbed a strip from the servant, folded it into a pad and pressed it firm against his belly. She scanned the man beside him. Blood dripped down his chin from a deep slash across his cheek. "Here," she told him. "Hold this here and press firmly. You're better off than he is."

"What do I do if—?"

"It's not a deep cut. Just keep pressure on it till the healers come."

Tessa smiled her best you'll-be-alright smile to take the sting out of her words. She pressed a pad to his bleeding cheek and wrapped a bandage around his head to hold it. Then she moved to the next guard where Elda was already holding a large pad to a young woman's chest. A bloody froth of bubbles seeped from the sides of her mouth and pooled into her hair.

Tessa swallowed a gasp and dropped to her knees next to the pale woman. She lifted the guardswoman's icy hand, noting the blue fingernails. An awful rasping sounded from the wound in her chest despite the pad Elda pressed against it. The too-young woman wasn't going to make it until the healers came.

Tessa tried desperately to connect with Adalta. She tried forcing her consciousness down through the stones of the floor into the bedrock beneath the keep, into the tiny rivulets and streams that ran through the earth. She searched her mind and body for the faintest hint of connection to Water or Earth.

But she couldn't pull the power up, couldn't see the core of the wound, couldn't feel what was needed to heal it. She should be able to manipulate the vessels, bones, and tissues—to realign, to mend. But the images skittered away as they always did.

Tessa opened her eyes. The woman's eyes were fixed on her face, eyes full of fear and pain and questions. She tried to speak, and the words caught, choked off by the frothy blood that bubbled with every feeble breath. Then the fear and the pain and the questions were gone. Tessa watched bright red blood spill from the woman's mouth, and after a long, long moment, pulled the edge of the sheet over the face no older than her own and fought the familiar upwelling of helpless shame. Shame was an indulgence she couldn't afford right now.

She stood, staring down, clasping her hands together till they cramped. *No use crying over my lost talents. She's gone. And I can't bring her back. Even with talent, I couldn't bring her back now.*

"Renewal," she whispered.

"Renewal," said Elda.

Tessa swiped her forearm across her damp eyes and looked for the next person who needed the little she could give. She went back to doing what she could, thankful she never stopped learning about the ordinary healing of herbs, salves, and wound care from whomever she could talk into teaching her on the Me'Cowyn Hold. Thankful they had dared to do so behind her father's back.

The minutes it took the healers to get from the guild house to the hall seemed hours. Hours-long minutes of tearing sheets, pressing thick pads to bloody wounds. Hours-long minutes of washing and bandaging the less critical cuts and slashes she could treat without talent, of covering too many stilled faces. But the healers finally arrived. She directed them to the critically wounded. And she followed—bandaging and splinting, brewing aspirtea, applying antibiotic salves—until the healers finished the urgent cases and could begin to take care of the simple broken bones and lighter wounds.

There was only endless time bending over wounds, wrapping meters of bandages, emptying buckets of bloody water, and carrying pails of clean water from the kitchens. Endless time until Tessa stood up from the young man whose broken arm she helped healer Evya, the guild house mother, set. She staggered. Evya grabbed her before she fell.

"You need to stop. Get some water and some food. Melayne set some out in the little anteroom. She put several cots and pallets in there for us." She looked at Tessa's face. "Don't object again. You nearly fell before I caught you. If I have to, I'll give you an order."

Tessa wanted to grin, but she was so tired she could only raise one side of her mouth. "I don't know if you can order me. I'm not one of your healers."

"Oh, I can give the order. I just can't make you follow it. So consider it a strong suggestion from your healer to eat and rest. You're exhausted, and your talent is so depleted I can't even sense it."

Tessa turned away. She was too tired to pretend. It wasn't depleted—she had no talent.

Printed in Great Britain
by Amazon